be sweet

diann hunt

THOMAS NELSON
Since 1798

NASHVILLE DALLAS MEXICO CITY RIO DE JANEIRO BEIJING

This book is dedicated to the four little girls in my life who know the true meaning of "Be Sweet." Thank you for the joy you bring to me, Macy Zimmerman, Micah Zimmerman, Zoe Zimmerman, and Abby Hunt! I love you, granddaughters, more than words can say.

And to my two grandchildren on the way, Baby Boy Zimmerman and Baby Hunt, I can't wait to greet you with open arms!!

Love,

Nanny

Published in Nashville, TN, by Thomas Nelson. Thomas Nelson is a trademark of Thomas Nelson, Inc.

Thomas Nelson, Inc. books may be purchased in bulk for educational, business, fund-raising, or sales promotional use. For information, please e-mail SpecialMarkets@ThomasNelson.com.

Library of Congress Cataloging in Publication Data
Hunt, Diann.
Be sweet / Diann Hunt.
p. cm.
ISBN-13: 978-1-59554-194-9 (softcover)
ISBN-10: 1-59554-194-2 (softcover)
1. Middle aged women--Fiction. 2. Single women--Fiction. 3. Michigan--Fiction. I. Title.
PS3608.U573B4 2007
813'.6--dc22

2007015673

Printed in the United States of America
07 08 09 10 11 RRD 6 5 4 3 2 1

one

If I'd worn my ruby slippers today, I'd click those babies together three times and chant, "There's no place like home." Unfortunately, it won't work for me. Number one, my name isn't Dorothy. Number two, I don't own a pair of ruby slippers, and, last but not least, my home is in Maine, not Kansas.

Okay, so I'm not in Maine either. I'm on my way to my sister's house, which happens to be in my hometown of Tappery, Michigan. A couple of miles from her house, I've stopped at Lighthouse Bakery to buy some cookies. My taste buds can no longer abide store-bought sweets, so bakeries are my constant friend.

Back in Maine I own a beautiful oceanfront property, have more money than I need, and I feel confident and in control. Yet when I come back to Tappery and see glimpses of my past—the love I never thought would end, the miscarriage, pain, affair, separation, divorce, and shame—my confidence shatters into a million pieces. Hence, the cookies.

Which brings me to my current dilemma of hiding behind a cardboard cookie display while Gail Campbell, a.k.a. former high school class gossip queen, heads straight toward me.

Standing at five-eight and with honey-blonde hair that brushed my shoulders—and still does—the senior class voted me a Michelle Pfeiffer look-alike—an honor Gail always resented. No doubt she's already noticed my extra twenty pounds.

There's no place like home. There's no place—

"Well, Charlene Kaiser—it is Kaiser, isn't it?—what on earth are you doing in Tappery? Or have you finally come to your senses and moved back home?" She laughs at herself, but I don't join her. Well, not until she snorts anyway.

Dressed in a black leather miniskirt, tight-fitting blouse, and tall spiky heels, she prances toward me lugging a baby on her hip. Perfect round circles of red blush dot each of Gail's cheeks, and her eyelids glitter a bright blue, making me wonder if the bulbs blew on her makeup mirror.

Stepping casually out from behind the fake cookie and almost knocking it over, I flash a wide smile. "Actually, I came home to help with the syrup harvest and to help plan a family gathering."

She hesitates, no doubt hoping I'll tell her more, but I don't.

"Oh, so where do you live now?" she asks, while quickly assessing my hips.

"Seafoam, Maine."

"Are you married, working, both?" She acts all hyper here. "We've got to catch up, girl."

Oh, I'm sure you'd love whatever tidbit of gossip you can get.

"I sell commercial real estate," I say, taking note that her eyes widen enough to satisfy me.

"I don't understand how all that works. Must be hard to move commercial property. I imagine there are some pretty lean times," she says, looking hopeful.

"Actually, it's quite a lucrative job, if you do it well." I'm pretty sure

I hear a harrumph while she studies me. The ball's in my court, and I'm practically rocking on my heels. "Oh, and I've taken my maiden name of Haverford back."

Gail's Barbie eyebrows spike into upside-down *V*s. "Oh? Never remarried?" She leans in for my answer and holds her breath.

"Nope." Before I can stop myself, I look at the little girl on her hip and say, "A baby at *your* age?"

Her eyelids flutter, and she shifts the baby on her hip. "This is my granddaughter, Carrie Matilda." It's hard to miss the emphasis on the middle name. "You may recall my middle name is Matilda."

"How nice for you." A tiny pause. "She's, um, sweet." Poor kid can't help it if she has her grandma's beady eyes, and I'm not even going to mention the pointy nose. That would be rude.

"It's too bad you don't have any grandkids. They're the greatest." Her hand flies to her mouth in mock apology. "Oh, sorry."

She knocks the wind out of my lungs in one blow. We both know there will be no grandchildren, because I have no children. "No problem," I say with a carefree attitude, trying to conceal the searing pain she's caused me. The ball's now in her court.

"I still think it's just dreadful what Eddie did to you."

"That was a long time ago, Gail. It's over." The last thing I want to do is talk about my failed marriage with the town gossip.

"Still, he was such a stinker."

Not quite the name I had in mind for him, but whatever.

A frown pulls her brows together. She looks me over. "I almost didn't recognize you."

Yeah, I've put on twenty pounds since I was here last. Thanks for noticing.

"You look a little"—she glances at my thighs—"um, different somehow."

In a flash, I tuck the hand holding the bag of cookies behind my back. A knowing smirk tugs at the corners of her mouth. She's got the ball and is heading for a slam dunk.

"Don't we all," I say, as in, *honey, there ain't enough cream in Wisconsin to fix those ruts in your face.* A tiny twitch of my lip is all that's standing between my smile and a snarl.

Shame on me. My sister Janni would never think things like that—a fact which my mother loves to point out. It's true that Janni doesn't have to fake sweetness. It flows from her as naturally as sap from a maple tree. Still, ask her to throw out her instant coffee and creamer for a mocha latte, and she'll hurt you. Am I the only one who can see that?

Little Carrie Matilda starts to squirm. Bless her. "Well, I guess I'd better get going. My family is waiting on bagels this morning. Good to have you back in town," Gail says as she edges away. "Hey, if you stop over at the gym, I'm there most every day. Just look me up." Another glance at my body. "I'd be glad to help in any way I can. Ta-ta."

My blood pressure shoots up fifteen notches. *Oh, yeah? With that face you could feed and clothe a plastic surgeon's family for the next five years.*

Mouth pursed, eyebrows furrowed, I clench the cookie bag in a death grip and shove through the front door.

My emotions begin to calm as I drive the familiar winding roads into the rural area of Tappery. Naked maples that now stand frigid, cold, and unyielding will soon release a sugary sap fit for a king and will blossom a thick mane of green.

Gazing over the countryside, I keep in mind that the Scottens are looking for prime property in this area that will support a discount store. They hope to set up chains across the country, so I told them I would look around. I'm almost positive I'll be able to come up with something, and thus secure my promotion to partnership at McDonald Realtors. Reaching over, I turn up the radio and sink back into my leather seat. Though I try not to let my ego get the better of me, it can't hurt to let the community see that I've done all right since my days in Tappery.

A one-lane, wooden bridge groans beneath the weight of my BMW, while the swollen river below bubbles and races over smooth boulders and eroded debris. It seems only yesterday I stood on this same bridge and experienced my first kiss with Eddie. My heart still gives a slight twist with the memory.

Isolated patches of snow remind me that spring has not fully arrived. Yet, obviously enough warmth has caused some snow to melt and fill the riverbeds.

Farmhouses, a weathered grist mill, red wooden barns, and rusty barbed-wire fences color the rolling hillsides. A smattering of cattle meander about. Small forests cluster in the distance. Here and there, monstrous new homes stretch across properties where abandoned farmhouses and log cabins used to stand. Though I have my privacy at my cottage in Maine, it's hard to imagine I once lived in this type of isolation, among cattle, horses, and open meadows. Give me the sounds of water lapping the shore over cattle mooing any day.

As I draw close to Mrs. Walker's homestead, I ease on the brakes and think back a moment to the memories of lazy Sunday afternoons on her wraparound porch—sipping iced lemonade, munching on maple cookies, and swatting flies while listening to the tales of her younger days. Since Mrs. Walker lived just down the road from us, Mom never minded when I went to visit the elderly woman. In fact, this was one of the few things I did of which my mother approved.

Wonder how much land comes with her property? If I remember right, she only had a couple of acres, but out here it's hard to tell where property lines begin and end. I doubt there's enough land here for the Scottens to build their store, though. Crumbled concrete dusts the foundation of her front steps, leaving jagged edges. The wooden porch swing, now faded with age, still hangs from rusty chains. A splintered birdhouse hangs from her front maple tree. From where I sit, it doesn't look like a viable property for any of my clients. How sad to see that the new owners don't keep the property up the way Mrs. Walker did.

As I drive down the gravel lane that leads to our homestead, I roll down my window. The sweet scent of early spring rides on the cold afternoon breeze, reminding me of maple syrup, tulips, and spring break. Memories of sailboat rides cracking through fresh water waves soon follow. A lifetime ago, this was my home.

I shove the shifter into park, grab the bag of groceries from the backseat of my red Beemer, and step out of the car. Glancing around, I see that the farm hasn't changed much since Daniel and Janni moved in, though the chicken coop looks a little rough—as in, one stiff wind and it's history. They'll need to fix that if they ever decide to sell.

The floorboards creak beneath my heels when I step onto the sagging porch. Those extra twenty pounds are mocking me—I can feel it. Warped wood ripples here and there, making my steps unsteady. They need to fix that too.

The late February wind whips past me, and I pull my jacket closer to my neck. After several knocks on the door with no answer, I turn the knob and the door cracks open.

I poke my head through the opening. "Janni?"

"Sure, Carla, I'd be glad to make dinner for them. I'll have the meal to their house by seven."

Saint Janni lives on. Still doing for others while Mom would say I do for myself. One glance around the living room, I see things haven't changed. Same old furniture. One thing about Janni that makes me crazy is she never moves anything. If I moved one thing in this room, she'd notice.

After slipping off my shoes—a custom I started once I bought new carpet for my own house—I follow my sister's voice to the kitchen, feeling the thin, spotted carpet beneath my feet. It's hard to figure out whether my sister and brother-in-law are poor, frugal, or just plain set in their ways. Passing a stand, I reach out and turn a Precious Moments figurine from facing north to slightly southeast.

Rounding the corner, I peek over at my sister. In her red apron, she looks every inch the image of Betty Crocker. Her no-fuss, chin-length bob suits her. Cradling the cordless phone between her shoulder and chin, she washes her hands at the sink. It looks as though I'm not the only one hefting around extra pounds, but then I'm not one to point fingers.

Janni has been a domestic diva from the start. Everything she creates is a success, from her delicious home-cooked meals to her hand-sewn, quilted place mats.

With my cooking phobias, I'm just happy to find a plastic fork for my Chinese takeout.

Right when I open my mouth to say Janni's name, something sharp whacks at my nylons, causing a stinging sensation on the backs of my feet. I turn and see a full-grown brown squirrel that has evidently followed me into the kitchen. It is sitting on its hind legs, little arms extended, taking wild swipes at my heels. A scream starts from my toenails and works its way up and out of my throat with such force that it causes the windows to rattle. The creature's bushy tail thrashes the air with razor-sharp snaps, while his pointed barks shoot at me machine-gun style. My legs flail wildly around the room—carrying the rest of me with them—which only fuels the squirrel's attack.

My sister charges into the room with a large broom. Suddenly, I'm not sure who scares me more, the squirrel or Janni. Her eyes are wild and popped open wide. The veins on her neck are ballooned and purple. She's gonna blow. That squirrel had better hightail it up the nearest tree.

"Get out of here," Janni screams, broom waving madly. She thumps a nearby stand and wallops the sofa—which to her horror shoots dust to the four corners of the room. Fueled by anger, Janni goes after the squirrel, who's going after me, who's making a beeline for the hallway closet. Once I get there, I yank open the door and cram myself inside as fast as I can. Evil squirrel takes one final swipe at me before the door closes completely, and I hear his nails scrape the door. For the blip of a heartbeat, I feel sorry for him. But with the sting in my heels, I get over it.

Standing in the dark, I hold my breath and listen to the sounds of whacking, feet scampering, pictures falling off walls, and loud wails coming from Janni, the squirrel, and the house.

When everything but the hall clock is finally silent, I click the knob on the closet door, shove it slightly open, then carefully stick my lips through the crack. "Janni?"

She doesn't answer. My feet stumble on something beneath me. I'm not sure if it's safer in this closet or out there with the wild animal—the squirrel, that is, not my sister.

With my heart thumping against my chest, I push open the door and peek out. "Janni?"

"In here."

Stepping out of the closet, I glance back at the floor to see an assortment of boots and shoes smushed to smithereens, compliments of my extra twenty pounds.

When I walk into the living room, I find Janni sprawled across the sofa.

"Did you get him outside?" I ask, slumping into the chair across from her.

"I got him in his cage," she says, lifting her index finger as though she barely has the strength and pointing to a large gold cage perched in the corner of the living room.

My mouth sags open.

"Sorry about all that. Wiggles is normally very sweet, but he doesn't like strangers. He'll warm up to you."

"Let me get this straight. That squirrel lives *inside* this house? As your pet?"

Smile back in place. "Last spring, right after you went home, we had a storm. Lightning struck a couple of our trees. Wiggles was only a day or two old when we found the nest. His eyes were still closed. Mama had abandoned him, poor thing."

I glance at my shredded nylons and don't feel sorry for him in the least.

"So I fed him milk with a pinch of maple syrup in it through an eye dropper." She smiles. "He survived."

Please. She even rescues squirrels? I've tried to feed birds in the winter. Even I have my moments of charity. They repay my kindness with droppings on my car. "And you're glad, why?"

She chuckles. "Well, like I said, he's only that way with strangers."

"All that running after the squirrel stoked up my furnace," I say, taking off my sweater.

Janni climbs out of the sofa, which appears to be a struggle for her. "So how are you, sis?" she asks in an animated voice, all excited and happy.

We stand and share a hug.

"I'm good. Though my heels hurt."

She pulls away and looks me in the eyes. "I've missed you."

"You too." Guilt washes over me in that familiar way it does when I come to Tappery, but I have my reasons for staying away. "I have to know one thing before we go any further."

"Yeah."

"Does that squirrel make messes around your house?" Okay, so I just can't get past that wild-animal-staying-in-her-house deal.

Janni laughs. "No. He's paper-trained. When he has to take care of business, he goes back to his cage."

"You're kidding, right?"

"Nope. You think I'd keep him in the house if he wasn't trained? No way."

I toss another glance at the hairy rodent and shake my head.

"Why don't I show you to your room? You can settle in, then we'll come down to the kitchen and get something to eat." My sister's answer to life's problems is food. Proof positive that we're blood relatives.

"Sounds good."

"Wonder who moved this?" Janni asks, turning the Precious Moments figurine back to face north. Do I know my sister or what?

Tossing a quick glance at Wiggles, I heave my luggage up the stairs behind Janni. "Just so you know, if Thumper and Bambi show up, I'm outta here."

"Oh, once you get settled in, you'll see it's not so bad to come home for a visit." Janni's words come out in short puffs of air. "Harvesting syrup, working on the scrapbook, hanging out with family. The fun is just beginning."

Something about the way she says that causes dread to crawl all over me. But that's silly. It's only for a few weeks.

What can happen?

two

"I brought you a treat," I say, as I join Janni in the kitchen. The heady scent of sweet maple hits me the moment I enter. "I'd recognize that smell anywhere." The aroma that fills the kitchen whisks me backwards in time. "Did I ever tell you that Ariel's Bakery in Maine makes an apple-and-maple cheesecake to die for?"

"That's nice." Janni turns away from the oven and stares at what I've brought.

"It's a pizza cookie," I say with pride as I open the box, and we stare at the pizza-sized chocolate chip cookie, sprinkled with M&Ms and a drizzle of chocolate. "Ariel's Bakery." I smile, take it over to the counter, grab a knife from the drawer, and start cutting it.

Janni's eyebrows arch and her chin lifts. "Guess your taste buds aren't used to home-baked goodies anymore, huh?" She gathers a warm batch of maple cookies from the cooling rack and adds them to a plate.

"No offense, Janni, but you know I rarely cook and never bake, so I've just gotten used to the gourmet stuff."

"You won't try my cookies?"

"I'm sure they're delicious, but right now I'm in the mood for chocolate. Maybe later." Grabbing a plate, I place a wedge of cookie on it, grab a napkin, and join her at the table.

Janni's watching me.

"What?"

"Are you always this hyper?" she asks in a slow, deliberate manner.

"If you think this is hyper, you should see me after three shots of espresso." With a chuckle, I slip into my seat.

Janni grabs a mug, throws in a teaspoon of instant coffee and creamer, then shuffles her way to the table. "I don't know what people see in those fancy coffees. They're so expensive."

"It's more than coffee. It's an experience."

She stares at me. "You sound like a Hallmark commercial."

I shrug. After a quick prayer over my cookie, I dig into my treat. Wonder if God will answer the part about making it a blessing to my body.

Janni reaches for a maple cookie.

"Did you make those with last year's maple syrup stash?"

Janni laughs like a hyena. Literally. It scared the pajeebers out of me as a kid. Here I am edging fifty, and to this very day it causes chills to climb up my back.

"Still the same old Charlene. And to answer your question, yes. This is from last year's supply. We're not addicted to sugar like you are, so it lasts awhile around here." Janni takes a bite from her cookie. The fact that my sweet sister looks like a roly-poly doll? Well, it just makes me question the truth of her statement, that's all.

Janni walks over to the refrigerator and grabs a pitcher of milk. Real milk. As in five-hundred-grams-of-fat milk. Okay, I'm starting to understand this roly-poly thing.

"You get your luggage unpacked?" she asks, pouring milk into a glass, then turning to me.

"Yeah, I'm unpacked. No milk for me, thanks. I save my calories for what's important." I wave my slice of cookie.

She returns to her seat at the oak table. "Look at you, pretty as ever."

I roll my eyes. "Yeah, and about twenty pounds over my ideal weight," I say, munching my cookie.

"So you have a little meat on your bones. It makes you look healthy."

"Now you're beginning to sound like Mom."

"Well, it's true. You've always been too skinny. Just like both of our parents."

"Which would explain why I have the chest of Shirley Temple—when she was two."

Janni chuckles. "Wonder where I got my weight problem?"

Since I'm president of Cookie Eaters Anonymous, I won't mention her eating habits.

"You know, I've always marveled that despite the fact that all of Tappery envies your looks, you've never fussed that much over yourself. 'Course, with your kind of beauty, you can get by with a swipe of lipstick and mascara. It takes the rest of us hours to fix ourselves up so we won't scare little children."

We both know Janni doesn't spend over five minutes on her makeup, but I wisely keep silent. "Oh, stop." I pause to give her time to say more. She doesn't. "Besides, you can cook. I can't boil water."

Janni laughs. "You could if you wanted to."

"I want to, believe me. Do you know how hard it is to make spaghetti without boiled water? I love spaghetti."

Janni shakes her head. "Mom and Dad offered to give you cooking classes."

"I didn't want the pressure of having to measure up to you," I say, surprising myself with the confession.

"It's only fair. I couldn't compete with your beauty."

We lock eyes. "Are we having a 'clearing the air' type moment?" I ask.

"I think so. You know, you could watch one of those cooking shows on TV." Janni puts her drink down.

"I tried once. The cook was preparing a seven-minute meal. By the time she finished, I was ready for a nap."

"You're pathetic."

"I know."

"Hey, I ran into Gail Campbell at the store."

Janni looks up at me. "What did she say this time?"

"Nothing much, really." I pluck a chocolate chip from my cookie and eat it. "You know, that woman should carry around a crowbar the way she's always trying to pry information out of people."

Janni laughs.

"Did you know she has a granddaughter? Poor kid looks just like her."

"I feel sorry for her."

"I do, too. Even makeup can't fix those beady eyes."

Janni turns a wry look my way. "I meant Gail."

"Why on earth do you feel sorry for her?"

"Think about it. If she had a life, she wouldn't care so much about what's going on in everybody else's."

"I guess. There's still no excuse for it, though. She just wants to stir up trouble."

"You have to let it go, you know."

"Why should I care if she and Linda talked about me in high school and caused me to have zero friends? There's nothing to let go." I sink my teeth into another bite of cookie. A big one.

She stares at me too long, and I try not to squirm. "She shouldn't have spread gossip, but you have to let it go, Char. It happened a long time ago."

"Exactly. It's a thing of the past. Let's leave it there, okay?" Hello? It's not as though I haven't gotten over it. I have a life, thank you very much.

"Okay," she says with reluctance.

"So how are the boys?" I ask, referring to her two sons—my nephews—whom I love as though they were my own.

Smoothing down her apron she says, "Ethan is in love." Her eyes shine here. "He stays on campus most of the time or goes home with Candy."

"Her name is Candy? She sounds *sweet.*"

Janni groans. "Blake, on the other hand, says he doesn't want to deprive the women of America by settling down with one girl. Can you imagine?" She sighs. "I doubt that he's cracked open a textbook all year."

"Hard to believe those kids are already in college. Will they be here at all to help with the syrup?"

"Only during spring break. You'll meet Ethan's girlfriend then. She's a doll." Janni rises and takes her empty glass and dish over to the sink.

"Sounds like you'll be joining the ranks of grandparenting before you know it."

"Let's get them married first, shall we?" she calls over her shoulder as she rinses her dish and glass with water, then places them in the dishwasher. "I'd sure love a little one around to spoil and then send home." She walks back to the table and reaches for my empty plate.

"You touch that, and I'll have to hurt you," I say, reaching for another sliver off the round cookie.

Surprise lights her eyes, and she blinks.

"Janni, don't ever come between a woman and her cookies," a male voice says behind me.

Swiveling around in my chair, I see Janni's husband, Daniel, step through the back door. He's dressed in brown bib overalls, a brown and white plaid shirt, and thick, manly boots. We're talking serious boots here. With the size of his feet, I'm thinking he could stamp out an entire generation of ants.

Twinkling blue eyes and brown hair with a smidgen of gray peek from beneath his white baseball cap, while a graying goatee frames a smile that says life is good.

"The man is smarter than he looks," I say, jumping from my chair. "How are you doing?"

Daniel laughs and whisks me into a bear hug that makes my feet leave the floor. My nose tickles from his generic version of Polo. The man never changes.

"I'm good. How's my big sister?"

"Hey, be careful about that 'big' stuff, will ya?" I tease. "I'm feeling a tad sensitive."

"Aw, I've picked up bigger twigs than you."

"Have I mentioned you're my favorite brother-in-law? 'Course, I don't have any others, but still."

With a hearty laugh he puts me down and turns to Janni. "How's the love of my life?" He reaches down and gives her a kiss, making my heart squeeze. My sister may not have nice carpet, but she's rich in other ways.

I straighten my Liz Claiborne blouse that Daniel wrinkled with the hug.

"What are you doing home so soon?" Janni asks.

"Not many customers today," he says, pulling up a chair and grabbing several cookies. I scoot the pizza cookie from his direct view. It might hurt Janni's feelings if he doesn't eat her cookies, after all. I'll just take it back to my room when no one is looking.

Janni pours a glass of cold milk and places it in front of him. A shadow flickers in her eyes. "Business sure has been slow lately," she says, searching his face.

"It will give me a chance to fix the doorknob on the bathroom upstairs." He tosses her a wink, then glances around. "Hey, you didn't throw away the paper, did you? There are some good coupons in there."

Janni rolls her eyes. "No. It's on your chair in the living room."

He smiles and pops the last of the cookie into his mouth.

Say what you will about Daniel, he will never waste a penny. Ever. On anything. He's a coupon clipper from the word *go*. He can outclip any woman in the county. Before the ink is dried on the page, he's snipped it, stuffed it in his pocket, made a beeline for the store, and handed it to the cashier. He's the only person I know who can buy a hundred dollars' worth of groceries for a buck and a half.

"How are things at Ort Hardware anyway?" I ask, referring to their store.

He chews a minute. "Maybe Janni's already told you there's a new hardware store in town, so things are a little slow right now since we're sharing the customers. It's newly opened, though, so that may die down some. You know how it is in business."

I nod.

"So what's been going on with you, Zip?" Daniel asks, referring to the nickname of Zipper that my dad gave me back when I was sixteen and thin, which, by the way, no longer applies. Funny how I could eat anything I wanted until about a year ago. Now suddenly the pounds are starting to stack up.

"Oh, same old, same old," I say, polishing off my last bite of cookie in the nick of time, what with that whole "Zip" thing.

"Oh, Janni, did I tell you Tappery General has chocolate chips on sale, two bags for the price of one?" Daniel empties his glass and swipes off his milk mustache with the back of his arm. He's a true manly man—well, except for that coupon thing.

"Okay, I'll pick some up."

"I have a coupon for it that I'll give you." He turns to me again. "So you're back for your syrup, huh?" He grabs two more cookies, and I'm seeing why Janni makes their own food. He'd cost them a fortune at the bakery.

Before I can say anything, Janni jumps in. "It's a drug for her, you know. She's addicted to maple sugar." She picks up the carafe for the coffeemaker and fills it with water. "I need some coffee. Either of you want any?"

"Talk about *my* addictions."

She blinks, looks at the carafe in her hand, and laughs. "I guess we're even." She plugs in the pot. "But at least my coffee doesn't cost four bucks a cup, and it's every bit as good."

My sister lives in her own reality.

Daniel chuckles, stretches out his legs in front of him, and gives in to an enormous yawn. "I'll take a cup."

"Yeah, I'm back for the syrup, but also to help Janni organize Mom and Dad's fiftieth anniversary celebration."

Daniel rubs his goatee. "Oh, that's right. That's just around the corner."

"It will be here before we know it," Janni says, grabbing cups from the cabinet.

"Good thing you women are in charge," he says, reaching for another cookie.

"I can hardly wait to show you what I've gotten done on the scrapbook." Janni places a coffee tray, complete with cream, sugar, cups, and saucers, in the middle of the table.

"Yeah, she's sure worked hard on that. I've hardly seen her." Daniel winks at Janni.

She grunts. "You haven't seen me because your eyes have been glued to either the TV or the coupon page of the paper."

He scratches his jawline. "Just looking out for our retirement."

"Daniel, with the way you save money, you could have retired when you were five." Janni's face doesn't flinch.

My jaw goes slack.

"Just the same, you'll thank me one day."

She ignores him. "As for the scrapbook—"

"Could he really have retired at five?"

"That's what his mother told me."

"Hey, lemonade stands are big business," Daniel cuts in.

"Could I interest you in a seaside vacation home?"

"As I was saying," Janni draws out the words as though we're hard of hearing, and we need to read her lips. "You can help me with the scrapbook. That way we'll get finished sooner."

I lean my chin into the palm of my hand. "Retired at five, really? Then what's with the carpet in the living room?" Well, that came out before I could stop it.

Janni puts her hands on her hips and glares at Daniel.

He holds his hands up. "I know, I know. We're going to replace it." He turns to me and in a staged whisper says, "Thanks a lot, sis."

"Sorry. But what's the use of having money if you never spend it? A woman needs to feel good about her home."

Janni gives a curt nod. "Just what I've been telling him."

"Aw, Janni, you know I'm just waiting to see how business goes."

She nods and says nothing. To my way of thinking, he's carrying that frugal thing way too far.

"Anyway, back to the scrapbooking—"

"Keep in mind that I'm craft challenged. I've never been able to do a thing with Cheerios besides eat them," I remind her.

"You sell millions of dollars' worth of real estate every year, but you can't put together a scrap page? It's mind-boggling, I tell you." Janni shakes her head. "Don't worry about it, though. I'll teach you."

"Thanks, but I have enough to do already."

"Such as?"

"For one thing, I rented the Carpenter Center—"

Janni gasps. "That place is expensive. I've already reserved the church fellowship center."

"It's only money, Janni," I say, sending Daniel into a coughing fit.

"Then I thought we could get Yvonne's Catering to serve the food. I've checked all over town, and they seem to offer the best menu for the money. I have a notebook with sample menus, price quotes, and brochures on everything I've checked into." I've silenced her with my wealth of knowledge, no doubt.

"What kind of food?" Janni asks when she finds her voice. "I was going to prepare something simple." Instead of being impressed with my research, she sounds miffed.

"You? Whatever for? It doesn't have to be that much work. Let me get my notebook." That's sure to wow her. I run upstairs to my room, grab the black three-ring binder, and run back downstairs. "Let's see," I flip through the pages. "They have hors d'oeuvres of basil risotto cake with sun-dried tomato—"

Janni scrunches her nose.

"They also have chicken and scallion skewers with orange sesame soy glaze. They have two more choices of prosciutto, garlic and artichoke puff, and potato apple pancake with smoked salmon and dill crème fraiche." I look up at Janni whose mouth is dangling.

"People actually eat that stuff?" she asks.

I grin and nod. "Isn't it fun?" I look back at the menu. "Then we could offer a sit-down dinner. We'll need to decide which main course we want to go with, though. They have roast beef, roasted Cornish hen, and artichoke cannelloni with mozzarella, lemon béchamel, and fresh thyme—"

"Wait. I wanted this to be a luncheon affair to give everyone more time to visit. Folks that age don't want to be out late—especially if they're driving any distance at all."

"I see your point, Janni, but that's exactly what everyone else does for these things. We want this celebration to be different. A sit-down dinner is elegant."

"I've never heard of half those things on the menu!" Janni's voice is high-pitched and squeaky. "Mom and Dad are picky eaters. Did you know that?"

"They'll be too excited to eat, anyway."

Janni takes a long, deep breath and finally releases it. "We don't need all this expense, Char. It doesn't have to be a citywide bash."

"They've been married fifty years. No small feat in today's world. The Carpenter Center will see to it that tables are covered with ivory linens. They'll provide the eggshell china trimmed in gold—oh, the decorations will be in gold, of course, in keeping with the traditional fiftieth anniversary. For table centerpieces, I was thinking something along the lines of table mirrors with gold candle holders and cream-colored candles. We'll give them the celebration they deserve. Don't be so cheap."

Janni gasps. The look on her face says she wants to hurt me. "Is this about you salving your guilt for rarely coming home?"

"What?" It's a good thing she's at the opposite end of the table, or I might yank her hair out. "That's a mean thing to say, Janni."

"Well, Miss All That, just because I'm more practical doesn't mean I care any less for our parents."

"You're not practical. You're cheap."

"Hey, I forgot to tell you, Janni. Guess who I ran into down at the hardware store?" Daniel interrupts, obviously sensing the tension in the air.

"Who?" I play along, but this anniversary shindig discussion isn't over by a long shot.

"Russ Benson."

Janni tries to pout, but her eyes light up at the mention of the name. "You remember him. He used to have a big crush on you in high school," Janni says, as though she can't imagine why.

"The name sounds familiar, but I can't place him."

"He was in your math class. I think he might have helped you once or twice with geometry."

A fuzzy image comes to mind. "Hmm, a tall, skinny kid who smiled a lot?"

"That's the one."

"Obviously, he wasn't the greatest teacher. I flunked."

"Probably because he was more interested in you than teaching."

"Yeah, whatever."

"He was kind of long and lanky back then. But let me tell you, he's changed."

"Hey, watch yourself," Daniel warns.

Janni smiles, slowly releasing her bad energy—whatever that means.

I read that somewhere, and it seems to fit her right about now. "Oh, you know no one comes close to you, Danny." She walks over and gives him a shoulder rub.

"Short and bald?"

Janni gives me a puzzled look.

"You said he was long and lanky and that he's changed. Good grief, do I have to explain everything?"

Janni just glares. "Anyway . . . Russ was the guy with great teeth—like Donny Osmond. I'll bet he flosses a hundred times a day," she says, suddenly all dreamylike. Over flossing.

Daniel laughs. "Could be because his dad's a dentist." Janni's intense massage causes his words to vibrate.

"He was a sweet guy, if I remember right," I say.

"Yes, he was." Janni's no doubt getting all excited that my brain cells are working for me.

"You girls are talking like he's dead or something," Daniel says.

"So, is he short and bald?" Now I'm dying to know.

Janni leans toward me, her fingers still working their magic on Daniel's shoulders. "Trust me, he's not short, nor is he bald." She feigns a whisper, but I think Daniel's onto her.

"Keep massaging, and I won't care what you say." Daniel is practically starting to purr.

"Did he mention why he wasn't at church last Sunday?" Janni asks.

"Yeah, he had to perform an emergency root canal." Daniel's words are slurring together.

"Talk about anything else?" Janni asks.

"Guy stuff."

Janni playfully slugs him on the shoulder. "Oh, you're no fun." Massage over.

He protests, but she ignores him. "Hey, wouldn't it be fun to have him over while Char's here?" Janni says as though she's just come up with the best idea.

I groan. "Please, don't try to set me up. I'm already dating someone back home."

"Is it serious?" Daniel asks.

"I don't do serious."

"We've noticed," Daniel and Janni say simultaneously. "By the way,"—Daniel treads easy here—"I went into the bank today. Linda Kaiser wanted to know if you were in town. Said she thought she saw you leaving the bakery."

"Gail probably called her the minute she left the bakery." Of course, I would run into Linda and Eddie. Tappery is a small town. Still, I can do this. I'm not the same person I was when I left. They'll see.

"I know we told you that Linda and Eddie had split up, but I'm not sure if you knew it's official now. Their divorce recently went through. And you don't have to worry about running into him in Tappery, because he evidently just took off and married wife number three."

The news causes me a moment of hesitation. "Well, if Linda wants sympathy, she's not going to get it from me." And I wanted to prove to the town I'd changed—show them that now I'm able to hold my tongue and actually be sweet. Who was I kidding?

"I think it's been hard on their daughter, Carissa."

It takes a moment for that to sink in. I forgot about their daughter. The child I should have had. "Let's see, since Eddie and I got divorced just a few months before she was born, that would make her—what—about six now?"

"She appears to be about that."

Daniel gets up and puts his hand on my shoulder. "Sorry if I upset you, sis."

"Upset? Who, me? Why should I care?" I say.

"Glad to hear it. Well, I'd better get going." Daniel heads out of the room, then turns to Janni and winks. "Oh, and throw on an extra potato tonight, honey. Russ is coming to dinner."

three

"*Are you sure you want to walk out here, Char?* It's not exactly summer." A wisp of breath shrouds her words as Janni stuffs the scarf deeper into her coat.

"When I have the time, I like to take a walk before dinner. Besides, I can use the fresh air." No need to tell her they keep their house so hot, it could melt iron.

Tiny snowflakes drift from a gray sky, like feathers from an open pillow, while our feet crunch through brittle twigs and old leaves. The wind dashes through the backyard trees, swirls around us, and then races into the distant forest.

Janni yawns. Her steps are slow and deliberate. I don't mind, though. Walking in the woods is the one time I actually force myself to "stop and smell the maples," so to speak.

"Are you all right?" I ask.

Janni shrugs. "Should probably take some vitamins. It seems no matter what I do, I'm always tired."

"Maybe it's your thyroid. If your levels are low, that could give you low energy."

She stops and turns to me. "How did you get so smart?"

"Finally, someone notices. Hey, let Gail in on it and maybe she'll pass the word around town."

Janni chuckles and picks up a twig, tossing it from our path. "I suppose I need to bite the dogbone"—Janni never gets clichés right—"and go to the doctor."

"You have to keep up on things at our age, Janni. Regular checkups, yearly pap, mammogram, all that."

"You're right. I'll call soon."

"The air seems barely cold enough to snow," I say.

"That's a good thing, or we won't get much sap. Cold nights, mild days, that's what we need." Janni lifts her gaze toward the sky. "Weatherman says it's not supposed to stick."

"That's good." Our feet scuff against the ground, breaking the silence.

Janni glances at me. "Don't you miss this place, Char?"

"I miss the forest." Just then a white-throated sparrow calls from a nearby tree. "My life is very different now."

"In a good way?"

"In a great way. I love my work, the frenzied world in which I live."

"Must be exciting."

"It is. So how many chickens do you have now?" How I can go from exciting to chickens, I'll never know. The rusted hinges screech when I yank open the coop doors.

"We have about fifteen chickens."

When we step inside the coop, the ammonia smell takes my breath away. My lungs protest, making me cough.

"Yeah, I know," Janni says. "It's hard to take when you've been away from it for a while."

"Hard to take? You should provide oxygen masks at the door," my muffled voice calls between my fingers.

Wooden floor boards complain as we shuffle through the pathway littered with straw, feathers, and a strutting chicken or two. Resting on a wooden shelf that runs around the building, chickens plump on their tangled nests like fluffy pillows. Basket in hand, Janni reaches under a squawking hen and pulls out a couple of eggs.

"Since you haven't done this in a while, why don't you check the next one?"

We step over to the next bird. I take a deep breath—well, as much as I dare considering the smell and all—and shove my hand under the irritable chicken. She gives me what for. Can't say that I blame her. "Sorry," I say to the chicken, "I know you don't know me all that well, but we are family, after all." The chicken doesn't look convinced. My fingers grope around the nest and land upon some warm eggs.

Janni laughs and shakes her head while I pull out the eggs, put them in her basket, then look around.

"There's a rag over there," she says, reading my mind.

"Thanks." I wipe my hands on the cloth. "A hand sanitizer might be a good idea out here," I say, glancing down at the soiled eggshells.

"It's farm life, Char. My, how citified you've become."

"I can live with that."

We continue on through the coop, filling the basket with more eggs. Janni stops in front of a hen. "Henrietta here has been coming up empty lately. I think she's tired . . . and old."

"Boy, can I relate."

"Oh my goodness, Char, you're not old. Why, you know as well as I do, maples have to be forty years old before they start to produce sap. So I figure life gets good after forty."

I stop in my tracks and stare at her.

"What?" Janni asks.

"Are you having a brainiac moment?"

Janni shrugs. "It happens now and then."

"Why do you keep her around if she's not producing?" I ask.

Right then Henrietta squawks, and her eyes pop open wide. It could be that whole Janni-sticking-her-hand-into-Henrietta's-nest thing, but I don't think so.

"Bite your tongue! Henrietta is like one of the family. You don't put something out to pasture just because it can't produce anymore."

"Another profound comment? Knock it off, will ya? My brain just can't handle it. I want more cookies."

"*Gourmet* cookies." Sarcasm lines her voice, but she laughs and shakes her head.

When I glance once more at Henrietta, I'm almost positive she is wearing a ha-ha sort of smirk. Can chickens do that?

Janni scuffles toward the door of the coop, and I follow. We step outside, and I take a breath so deep I fear I'll pop a lung.

"Oh, before I forget to tell you," I say between gasps, "don't plan on me for dinner. I'm going to go see Mom and Dad."

"Are you doing that because Russ is coming over? He goes to our church, you know. He and Daniel get together for coffee. They're good friends. Daniel really didn't invite him because of you. He was teasing you." She leads the way to the barn.

"Seeing him will be like a blast from the past, and I'm not—"

"Char, you can't wipe out your past. It's part of who you are. You never come home anymore."

"I have a new life. I don't need to prove myself to anyone anymore." Well, maybe I want to show the town I'm successful, but I don't *have* to prove anything. I merely *want* to.

"Then it shouldn't be a problem for you to come home. You admitted to me that you're a workaholic. Why? Are you sure you're not still trying to prove yourself?"

"Yes. I just enjoy selling real estate. Janni, this isn't my home anymore. My home is in Maine."

Silence hovers between us.

"It must be nice to have purpose in your life."

"You have purpose, Janni. Your family, your friends, your circle of influence ripples all through town. You've never had to prove yourself. You are the town saint. You can do no wrong." I hide the sneer in my voice.

Janni looks down at her hands and whispers. "You're the one who never had to prove yourself. To anyone. You were homecoming queen, for crying out loud—the envy of all your peers."

Right. And all I ever wanted was a *real* friend. "You can't understand."

"Come on, Char. You're beautiful. What have you ever had to prove?"

"Looks aren't everything. I'm the black sheep of the family. See the big *D*?" I point to the middle of my forehead. Town loser, lost her husband to another woman. That's me—that *was* me. Not anymore. I'll show them.

"*D*?"

"Divorcee. Not exactly model material here."

"It happens."

"Yeah, whatever."

"Everyone makes mistakes, Char. I'm just saying it's time to move on."

Yeah, uh-huh. Her mistake? If I think real hard I can probably come up with something—like too much salt in the potatoes?

More silence.

"Did I tell you that Russ moved back to take over his father's dental business? His dad hasn't retired completely yet, but he's working part-time. He could have retired several years ago." She bends over to pick up a tin bucket someone left out. "By the way, did you know Russ served as a dentist in the military?"

I shake my head. I'm not all that interested in hearing about Russ, but at least it gets Janni off her soapbox.

"His wife died last year. Aneurysm, I think it was."

A sad ping skips through me for the skinny kid from high school. "I'm sorry for him, but as I said, I hardly remember him."

Okay, maybe the memory of him is becoming clearer, but I don't need to give her any fuel. My sister is on a mission. I can feel it, and I don't need that right now. I'll admit Russ was a cute and sweet guy in high school. Unfortunately, Eddie already had my heart tied up in a nice, neat little package with a bow.

"He seems to be doing all right now, though I'm sure it's been a hard road. Mom keeps me filled in." Janni chuckles.

A broken tree limb pokes through my path, and I step over it. "Mom?"

"Yeah, she cleans his condo for him. Gives her something to do—and something to talk about."

Suspicion floods to the surface. I narrow my eyes at her. "Is this a conspiracy?"

Her hand flies to her throat. "I don't know what you're talking about." She's not even trying to hide the fact that she's lying. So much for that saint business.

"Shut up."

"What?" She's acting offended.

"You do too know what I'm talking about. You all are trying to set me up with this guy. I'm dating someone back home. I told you that."

"Yes, you did, but you said it wasn't serious. Besides, what's the big deal about eating dinner with an old friend? We know you don't want a serious relationship."

My feet stop in place. "Now, see, why do you say that? If I found the right person, I would consider it."

Janni stands there with her hands on her hips, judgmental eyes staring me down. "Well, you've had countless dates since your divorce, and the fact that you haven't gotten close to anyone in over six years tells me something."

"It tells you I haven't found anyone I care about yet."

Janni backs away, palms up. "Okay, I'm sorry." We take a few steps in silence. "You're over him, right?"

"Who?"

"Eddie Kaiser. Your ex-husband, remember?"

"I was over him the minute I caught him kissing Linda Loose Lips."

Janni turns to me. "I'm sorry, Char."

"I'm over it."

"You sure?"

"I'm sure. When did Russ move back?" I ask, wanting to talk about anything other than Eddie and Linda.

"A couple of months ago."

"Wonder if it was hard for him to come back."

"It's not such a bad place to live, Char."

"I know that, but being in the military, he's probably seen the world. Tappery can hardly compare with all that."

"Yeah, I guess you're right," Janni says, surprising me. She never admits I'm right about anything. She's up to something. I can feel it.

Paint chips dust the ground when Janni slides open the massive opening to the barn. A handful of gray and white kittens shoots out from the door. Janni laughs. "Oh yeah, we've got some barn cats. I'm not sure how many, but I think around five. They keep mice at bay."

I forgot about the mice. Do I really want to go inside?

Janni steps in, and I reluctantly follow. Not exactly Chanel No. 5 hitting me in the face here, but it beats the chicken coop. I'm not a prima donna, mind you, but my cottage by the sea is looking—and smelling—better all the time.

"Click on the light, and I'll get the door," Janni says, lugging the barn door to a close while cold air races around the room.

Excited about the prospect of visitors—or maybe it's the promise of mealtime—the animals poke their heads over the half doors of their stalls. Finding the light switch just before the outside light disappears, I flip it on. A lone bulb dangles from a long, brown extension cord.

"Daniel promises to fix this place up with nice lights one of these days."

Yeah, probably right up there with the carpet. But, hey, it's their house.

"Evening, Elsie." Janni edges over to the black-and-white Jersey's stall, and I follow. Elsie gives the appropriate moo, her bell jingling slightly as she stamps in place. Janni scratches ole Elsie behind the ear. I give her a couple of pats on the head and I'm good.

"You're really not a farm girl anymore, are you, Char?" Janni moves on to Mr. Ed, their horse. Weird, I know, but I didn't name him. He snorts and stomps about for attention.

"Me and farm life? Think *Green Acres,* Zsa Zsa Gabor. That's me. Okay, maybe I'm not a total big-city type. I love seclusion, but I'm not a farm girl either. Just give me a cottage tucked away on a craggy bluff overlooking a breathtaking view. Oh, and throw in a few trees, and I'm good."

"You don't want much, do you?"

I shrug.

Janni gets a faraway look in her eyes. "I can only imagine." Mr. Ed's muzzle nudges against Janni's hand. She pats the white patch between his eyes. "Okay, okay." Walking a few feet to her right, Janni scoops a handful of grain from an open burlap bag and gives it to Mr. Ed.

"I've invited you to stay with me on more than one occasion, you know," I say.

It's really quite disgusting how that horse's lips flap over her hand to get the grain.

"I know." She wipes horse slobber on her coat, and I think I'm going to be sick. Dust and grit grind beneath her feet as she makes her way to the back stall. "It's just so hard to get away."

"Maybe you haven't noticed that your boys' rooms are empty?"

"True, but Daniel can hardly fend for himself, and who would look after the animals?"

"Last time I checked, Daniel was over eighteen. And as far as the animals are concerned, don't you have an animal-friendly neighbor?"

"Yeah, but it's not that easy to get away."

"It's your call. I'm just saying you've been invited. Who's this?" A bleating white goat peers over the rough, wooden door.

My sister brightens. "This is Tipsy, our fainting goat."

My gaze pins Janni in place. "An inside squirrel and a fainting goat? You're scaring me."

She giggles. "If Tipsy is startled, she'll faint. Isn't that right, Tipsy?" Janni coos while scratching the goatee beneath Tipsy's chin. Poor thing must be menopausal, all that hair. "I fell in love with her when we visited a farm in Tennessee, and Daniel bought her for me."

The barn door slides open and we turn. A gust of cold wind follows Daniel inside, stirring hay and dust about the room.

"I see you've met Tipsy," he says, brushing the dust from his hands and stomping clumps of dirt from his feet. "Hey, let's show Char what Tipsy can do."

"Daniel, don't make her do it now. It's cold," Janni says with a pout.

"You know it won't hurt her. Come on."

"Oh, all right." Janni unlatches the door in front of the stall and lets the goat out. It's been too long since I've been around farm animals, so I step back. Besides, I don't want that thing fainting on me.

"Time to eat, Tipsy. Time to eat," Daniel says with far too much enthusiasm while clapping his hands.

Tipsy circles in place once then suddenly keels over onto her back, legs shooting straight up like broomstick straw. Her little tail wiggles lickety-split while she's down, and she's back on her feet in two seconds flat.

Everyone laughs.

"No matter how many times I've seen her do that, I still get a kick out of it," Daniel says with a chuckle, rewarding Tipsy with food.

I'm beginning to wonder just what kind of life Janni and Daniel have here.

"So, is it a trick that she does to get food or what?"

"No, she fell over because she was excited. Food excites her," Janni says.

At that very moment I share a sort of *Freaky Friday* bond with Tipsy.

Daniel grabs a shovel and scoops into the burlap bag, causing a misty spray of grain to shower the air; then he heaves it over to the feeding trough for Mr. Ed.

"We'll have to clean these stalls tomorrow," he says.

"I know." Janni lifts a pitchfork and spreads fresh hay in the stall. I grab another one and spread hay in Tipsy's stall; then Janni leads the fainting goat back inside.

Once the animals are fed, watered, and bedded with hay, we step outside.

"Did you see much sap in the bags, Janni?" Daniel asks, his boots stomping across the hard ground. Good thing the ants are hiding, or they'd be history.

"Yeah, they're filling up."

Daniel pushes his baseball cap further up his forehead. "Sure wish those boys were home to help."

"Can't you get some teens from the church to help?" I ask.

"We might have to. I hate to bother other folks, but we could sure use a few more hands. It works best if we can get a couple of shifts going. Janni needs help in the kitchen to make food for the workers too."

"Char's right. Let's check with the kids at church. Teenagers always want spending money."

"We got some retired guys that might be able to help out too." Daniel's beefy arm reaches over and pulls Janni to his side as we step up to the porch. "Right now I'm getting mighty hungry. Whatever you got in that Crock-Pot is driving me wild, woman." Daniel nuzzles Janni's neck, and she giggles.

Please. First horse slobber, now this? My stomach can only take so much. One glance at my watch tells me I haven't much time before Russ will be here. I'll just grab my handbag and head to Mom and Dad's.

Once we step inside the house, I rush past Daniel and Janni and up to my room. After running the brush through my hair, freshening my lipstick, and grabbing my handbag, I trot down the stairs.

"I'll see you guys later tonight."

"You aren't staying to eat with us?" Daniel's lips form a pout.

"I need to go see Mom and Dad."

"Janni made beef stew."

He knows that's my favorite, doggone him. "I know. She'll have to save me some."

"No promises," Daniel says with an evil grin. Remembering how he chowed down those cookies, I figure I'm out of luck on the beef stew.

"Come on, Daniel, let her go. Mom will give her what for if she doesn't get over there."

"Hey, you're not leaving because Russ is comin', are you?" Daniel asks, fidgeting with the keys in his pocket.

Do you see this, God? They're pressuring me. You promised to help me through this, not give me more than I can bear and all that.

"Danny, we'll talk later." Janni's voice is firmer now, for which I'm grateful.

After tossing her a smile, I edge for the door, reach into my handbag, and dig for my keys. Once I find them, I yank a little too hard on the doorknob, causing it to fly open and my keys to drop to the floor. Bending over, I reach down and pick them up when I hear a deep-throated cough coming from the outside. I shoot upright and make a desperate attempt to smooth my hair.

"I was just getting ready to knock," says the man on the other side, who's dressed in khakis, a blue Polo shirt, brown loafers, and a toothy grin that melts my heart like a clump of chocolate in a warm kettle. "Charley, is that you?" His teasing blue eyes penetrate mine, setting butterflies loose in my stomach.

Charley. It's hard to remember the last time someone called me that. I think I was in high school.

As awkward as this moment is right now, I'm thankful I'm not a fainting goat. Falling on my backside with my legs shootin' straight up isn't quite the look I'm going for.

"Hi, Russ."

four

"How's the geometry coming along?" Russ says.

My mouth clamps shut just short of drooling. The heat in my face cranks up a hundred degrees. *This* is that skinny, gangly kid with the big, perfect teeth? Let's just say he's grown into his teeth. His hair has thinned a little, but it's still a rich mocha brown. The added wrinkles around his sparkling blue eyes give him a rugged, handsome appearance.

Okay, God, maybe I can bear this.

I let out a delicate chuckle. "I'm afraid my geometry days are over." The good news is he recognizes me—extra twenty pounds and all. 'Course, with the way I'm sweating, I just might lose five pounds right here in the doorway—which would be a good thing, because right now I'm struggling to inch my way past him. He takes a side step. We're caught in this face-to-face, trying-to-get-around-each-other thing. It feels as though someone is trying to beat her way out of my chest, and if Russ stands any closer, she'll clobber him. The smell of his woodsy cologne makes me want to set up camp. And I can't stop staring at those rippling biceps. Boy, he must work with some pretty heavy teeth.

"You leaving?" His words are so close, his fresh breath grazes my face. Somebody gulps out loud, and I think it's me.

"I haven't seen Mom and Dad yet." If only I had some gum. It's one of those Dentyne moments where you're caught off guard. Speaking of guard, I sure hope my deodorant is working. A facial blotter would come in handy right about now too. "Just got here a little while ago and thought I'd better head over and see them."

A flicker of disappointment flashes in his eyes and my heart somersaults.

"It's been thirty years, and I only get an 'I'm afraid my geometry days are over'?" Though the sparkle is still in place, his eyes droop.

I just stand there smiling with teeth that are three months overdue for their semiannual cleaning. My feet have deserted me, I'm sure of it. I want to check, but if I look down, my head will thump against his chest, and we could be wedged between the door frame for life. I consider it, but only for a moment.

"Will you be back soon?" he asks, with a definite "I hope so" look on his face.

"Probably not tonight," I say apologetically. My heart is drumming so hard, I could give Ringo a run for his money.

We stand there another second or two, though it seems a millennium. "Um, well, I guess I'd better go." I edge past him.

"Maybe I'll see you around. I live in Tappery now, you know."

"Yeah, I heard that," I call over my shoulder. "See ya." I wave, then dash to my car. By the time I settle into my leather seat, my mutinous heart is beating ten times its normal rhythm. It has to be the thyroid meds. Yeah, that's it. I'll have it checked when I get home.

My fingers fumble with the keys, then I stick them into the ignition and, with a flick of the wrist, start the engine.

"Deep breaths, Char. Deep breaths." Breathe in and out, slow breaths. Inhale, one, two, three, four; exhale, one, two, three—

A tap sounds at my window, and I scream. Once my heart kicks back into its natural beat, I reach for the button and roll down the glass.

"Sorry, didn't mean to scare you. Just wanted to make sure you were okay." Russ's face is too close again. For a fleeting moment I'm tempted to grab him by the neck and drag him into the car, caveman-style.

"I'm fine," I say, sounding like Snow White sucking helium.

"All right. You were just out here awhile, and I wondered if something was wrong."

"Oh, uh, well, I was, uh, looking for something in my purse." *That was the best line I could come up with?* My entire vocabulary leaves me with one glance into his eyes.

He hesitates. "Sure you won't stay?"

My brain screams yes, but Mom's stern face comes into my mind, and I hear myself say, "I'm sorry, I had better not stay tonight."

He nods. "See you later." He gives the top of the car a quick pat.

I smile, roll up my window, and peel rubber, no doubt flipping pebbles and twigs upon Russ's pants legs as I go. Who am I kidding? I could have kicked up a boulder the way I peeled out.

My emotions are out of control. I've probably been watching too many romantic movies lately. It's unnerving, that's what it is. The last thing I need is a romantic complication in my life. Okay, so he's handsome. Those kind of guys are a dime a dozen. I married one, and look where that got me.

Needing time to calm down, I realize going to Mom and Dad's isn't an option right now. With a flip of the car's turn signal, I head for another place. Just like old times.

Lord, please help me while I'm here to keep focused on what I have to do, and please keep the painful memories away.

I'm doing fine sticking to comfortable friendships. That's what I have with—um, well—okay, I'm just stressed right now. His name will come to me as soon as I calm down. I'm sure of it.

Turning my car onto the road, I settle in for the ride when my cell phone rings. Once the earpiece is in place, I flip open my phone. "Hello?"

"Hey, Charlene."

The nameless man. Little neurons reach to the far corners of my brain and finally bring it to me. "Hi, Peter." Peter McDonald. Friend, broker, and owner of McDonald Realtors. The one person who refuses to shorten my name. In fact, if he heard Russ call me Charley, Peter would probably duke it out with him. No, maybe not. A fight would mess up his hair—saying nothing of the grime it would leave on his Cavalli pants. Anyway, he hates nicknames, period. He says names are given to us for a reason and out of respect for our parents, we should use them in their entirety.

Our relationship is like a comfortable pair of shoes. Nothing to get excited about, but at least there's no pain involved. I suppose that's why it works in the office. Slightly more than great friends, we've managed to keep work separate from our personal lives.

Not that he isn't good-looking. Quite the contrary. With a lean body—that he works out daily—stretching to a full six foot two, some would say he borders on perfection. He combs his thick, sandy hair back from his forehead, and, trust me on this, it does not move for the rest of the day. When I first met him, I thought his hair wasn't real because it never moved. One time I feigned a moment of passion just so I could run my fingers through it. When it didn't shake loose, I figured it was real. Passionate moment over.

His stuffy ways have cramped my flair for fun on many a day, but we have real estate in common, and that seems to work for us. In fact, sometimes I wonder if he doesn't "wine and dine" me because I'm the most profitable realtor in the office. Guess he's just like everyone else.

"Good to hear your voice," I say.

"Yeah? Maybe you're missing me?"

"Maybe."

"So how's life on Sunnybrook Farm?"

"Don't get me started."

"Want me to come and rescue you?" he asks.

"Your last name is McDonald. I don't trust you. Farming is in your blood."

"When are you coming home?" Like my mother, he ignores my jokes.

"I just got here, remember?"

"Oh, yeah." Papers stir in the background. No, wait. I'm sure there are tidy little stacks. He would never have papers strewn about his desk. That would be me. "Have you spotted any land for the Scottens yet?"

"Peter, I have been here less than twenty-four hours."

"Sorry. When are you going to give up the syrup and just enjoy the good life?"

"Give up the syrup? Never! Besides, my family is here. I have to come back sometimes."

"I guess."

"Working late?"

"Yeah. I just sold the Sanderses' house."

"That's fabulous, Peter."

"And my best girl isn't here to celebrate."

The fact that he says *best* girl doesn't elude me. There's that safe relationship thing again. Peter made it clear from day one that he was never going to marry, and that was fine with me. I've gotten along by myself for all these years, and I don't need a man telling me what to do at this point in my life. We are free to have other "friends."

"I'm sorry. That's great news, though. Such a beautiful property."

We move on to discuss how things are going at the office, and by the time we hang up, I'm driving through the brick-lined streets of downtown Tappery and soon pull my car up to a beach by the shores of Lake Michigan.

A fresh gust of icy air grazes my cheek when I climb out of the car. Maybe this wasn't such a great idea. Lifting my face toward the dusky skies, I watch the twinkling stars and take a breath, the chill reaching deep down into my lungs. Oh, what I wouldn't give for a maple macchiato with a triple shot of espresso right about now.

Moonlight shimmers across the lake and illuminates my path toward the shoreline. Pulling my coat closer to my neck, I carefully avoid the cascading wall of ice that has formed from the icy winds and breaking freshwater waves near the shoreline. A few diehard beach lovers stroll along and lift a smile as we pass one another in the misty twilight.

The howling of the wind, the somber call of the lake, and the isolation of the moment all cause me to pause and reflect on my life. How many times did I come here when I needed to think and clear my head as a teenager? When life hurt too much, I always met God in the forest or on the beach.

As the smell of lake water mingles with the misty air, my gaze lifts skyward. I love the sense of worship that falls over me when I stand before Lake Michigan or the sea by my cottage—or even when I'm tucked away on my favorite tree limb where no one can see me or hear me but the Father. "Why do things have to change?" A gust of wind circles and carries my words out to the lake, while my feet trudge along the sand and my heart whispers heavenward. With my bad attitudes lately, I'm surprised He's still listening.

By the time I make my way back to the car, I realize it's too late to visit Mom and Dad. It's just as well. I'm not sure I'm up to it tonight.

"*And how long have you been here, young lady?*" Mom barrels through the front door of Janni's house in a huff. That's one thing about my mother that never ceases to amaze me. Upon meeting her, it always seems we're in the middle of a conversation—or confrontation.

"Good morning, Mom. Good to see you too," I say, closing the door behind her.

A blur of white whips past me. Say what you will about my mother, there is no denying she has a great head of hair.

She drops her purse by the sofa. Pulling herself up to her full four-foot-eleven-inch frame she turns and faces me, all twigs and skin. "You didn't answer my question. And why weren't you in church this morning?" Bony fists settle on her hips like a gun belt. I believe Mom was the secret to my father's pastoral success for forty-two years. I've seen her on more than one occasion yank a sinner by the ear and drag him to the altar. Once her pale blue eyes lock on you, there's no use fighting it. She *will* win.

"Well? When did you get here?" Her toe is tapping now.

I sigh. "Yesterday."

Her mouth drops. "And why didn't you call or come over?"

"I was tired, Mom. I knew I could see you today."

"You didn't even come to church, Charlene Haverford. We needed help in the kids department." She makes that last statement as though it's my fault. Her eyebrows take a sharp dip south, and her lips pucker like a bad seam. "We've taught you better than that."

"I'll tell Saint Peter at the pearly gates that it's totally my fault."

"Oh, that's right, make light of the Gospel."

"I'm not trying to do that, Mom—"

"Everything is a joke to you, Charlene. A party."

"Not true. I'm not exactly having fun at this moment."

She stabs a pointed stare straight through me. We both know joking isn't the only thing she has against me.

"Sorry." Why is it that at the age of forty-seven I'm reduced to a five-year-old when my mother's around?

"You know what I always say—"

It takes everything in me to keep my eyeballs from rolling back in my head. I recite the words with her in my mind, but dare not move my lips.

"There's a time to joke and a time to listen."

I could be wrong, but I think I learned to quote that before my first Bible verse. "I'm sorry, Mom," I try to say with an appropriate amount of contrition. "Did Janni tell you I was here?" The little snitch. No wonder Mom favors her.

"No. I ran into Gail Campbell."

"*She* goes to church?"

"Now, don't you get ugly, Charlene Marybelle."

Okay, the fact that she gave me the middle name of Marybelle should tell you something about my mother. Number one, that she's terrible with names. Number two, she flunked all the "which one does not belong here" questions in school.

"You have to admit her tongue drips more than maple trees at sap time," I say, laughing at my clever self as I edge over to the sofa.

Mom sucks in air. "I will admit no such thing, young lady. You know my motto, if you don't have something nice to say—"

"Come sit by me?"

Mom blinks. I'm trying to make her laugh, but it's not happening. "You know, if you don't have something nice to say, come sit by me." I'm laughing, hoping to set the example. Mom's expression is totally snatching my joy. "It's a joke, Mom."

"Well, you can make fun all you want. But it's still true. If you don't have something nice to say about someone, you shouldn't say anything at all. You need to learn to control that tongue of yours."

Now there's the pot calling the kettle black. I'm not sure where I got my sense of humor, but I can tell you right here and right now it was not from my mother. I sink down into the sofa. And I do mean sink—as in, if I slip under the cushion, they may never find me again. Which, at this moment, might be a good thing.

"Hey, everybody, we're home," Janni says, entering through the back door and into the living room. "Hi, Mom." She grins and tosses me a wink.

The least she could do is help me off of this sofa. With a grunt, I try to heave upward, but it's like climbing the Alps. Maybe I should yodel. That would get their attention.

"Why didn't you tell me your sister was in town?" Mom snaps.

"She hasn't been in town long." The sound of hanger wire scraping against a metal pole muffles Janni's words as she hangs their coats in the hall closet. "You and Dad want to join us for lunch, Mom?"

Oh, yoo-hoo. Anybody notice I'm struggling to get off this sofa? Can we say Venus flytrap? Wait. Did someone say "Feed Me"? I'm almost sure I heard that coming from somewhere beneath the cushions. This is Stephen King material, literally, and I want out of here.

"No. We have plans after lunch. The Hillarys are celebrating their fiftieth anniversary. *Their* daughters are throwing a big party for *them.*" She stares pointedly at Janni and then at me.

My arms and legs flail about as I fight for my life from the bowels of the sofa.

"What *are* you doing, Charlene Marybelle?" Mom asks, staring at me for only a fraction of a second before she turns back to Janni.

"How nice for the Hillarys," Janni says to Mom before discreetly tossing a wink my way. "They're your neighbors, right?"

Janni's comment catches Mom off guard. "Well, of course they are."

At last, with one final exertive push, I roll myself out of the sofa and dump onto the floor with a loud thud.

Janni and Mom look at me.

"For goodness' sakes, Charlene Marybelle, what are you doing down there?" Mom asks.

Thanks for caring. "Looking for coins?"

Janni walks over and puts her arm around Mom. "Well, if you want to come over for coffee and dessert later, we'll save you some. It's your favorite, chocolate éclair."

Mom's shoulders relax. She bites her lower lip. "Oh, dear. That is my favorite. Well, we'll see what your dad wants to do." She perks a bit. "I've made maple chicken for lunch, but save me a bite of dessert."

Janni can calm Mom down as fast as I get her stirred up. Mom and I are as different as maple and sludge. 'Course, my opinion of which one of us is sludge would no doubt differ from her point of view. But then we've never agreed on anything.

"Okay, will do." Janni walks Mom toward the door while I heave my stiff self up from the floor and brush myself off. I twist my head from side to side to kick up a little blood flow and oxygen to my starving brain cells.

Mom turns and walks over to Wiggles's cage. "Hi, little fella, how are you?" she coos, poking her fingers through the slits in the cage to scratch Wiggles's belly that is now shamelessly exposed. My jaw practically drops off its hinges, and I'm almost sure Wiggles sneers at me. The little rat.

"Don't forget the dessert, Janni." Mom calls out before turning an expression of reprimand my way. "Char, you behave yourself." She steps through the door and yanks it shut.

I look at Janni. "I told you that you're her favorite."

"I'm stuffed," I say as Janni and I waddle into the living room. "What was that again?"

"Enchilada casserole. I picked up the recipe from a cooking magazine."

Not quite the cuisine I'm used to, but hers is, after all, *homemade.* I nod. "You know, I still can't believe the way you handled Mom, and she totally listened to you. You've always had a way with her." I step over to the oak rocker and sit down. If I try that couch again, they might not dig me out 'til Thanksgiving. "Mom always did like you best."

She looks at me point-blank. "Thank you, Tommy Smothers."

"Well, it's true." Kicking off my shoes, I settle onto the rocking chair and start, well, rocking.

"Yeah, right. You're simply the"—she gestures quotes with her fingers

—"ambitious daughter who's made a lucrative living out East," Janni says with a touch of sarcasm. "Besides, you know as well as I do that sometimes she listens. Sometimes not."

The dark circles beneath Janni's eyes make me wonder if she's resting well at night.

"That's true."

"Mom has been acting a little strange lately," Janni says, settling onto the sofa. She yawns and pulls an afghan over her as though she plans to take a nap. I make a mental note to time her when she tries to escape the cushions.

"How so?"

"Well, I'm not quite sure what it is. Kind of secretive. She never travels the same way twice, almost like she's hiding from someone."

"I knew it. Mom's past is finally catching up with her. She's an AWOL Marine sergeant. I've always known that."

Janni giggles. "You're awful."

"I know. It's what I do best."

"I think she's a little disoriented from the move and everything." Daniel plops down beside Janni and stretches out his arm behind her. His thighs are slowly disappearing into the cushions. I'll have to remember to sit there if Russ comes back for a visit.

"Well, no doubt living in a condo is a little different than being on this farm where they've lived most of their lives," I say, eyes still on the sofa, hand within grabbing distance of the phone in case I need to call 911.

"At least they know they can come here anytime they want."

I nod. "That would help ease the loss." After taking a drink of iced tea, I put my glass on the coaster next to the phone on the stand. "So how did dinner go with Russ?"

"He was real disappointed you didn't stay," Daniel says.

"Danny, behave yourself." My sister turns to me. "We had a nice dinner. He caught us up on how his parents are getting along, shared a little about his travels in the military, that kind of thing."

"Did you guys round up any more help for the syrup?"

"Nothing definite yet. But I think we'll be okay. We have Daniel—"

"In the evenings, after work," I interject.

"Well, we have the boys—"

"Who won't be here until spring break and then only for a week."

Janni frowns, hesitates, and then brightens. "There's always you and me—"

"And we'll be working in the kitchen to take food out to the workers."

"What are you, the voice of doom and gloom?"

"I try."

"So I've noticed."

"Oh, and we have a kid from Tappery's General Store who wants to earn some extra money. Said he might be able to help us—"

"Also over spring break."

"And don't forget Mom and Dad," Daniel says. "When they're up to it."

"Okay, let me see if I have this straight. We've got a part-time man, two part-time teenagers, one possibility, two retirees, and two kitchen helpers with no full-time crew to feed?"

Janni rubs her jaw and makes a face. "I see your point."

"Well, the good news is most of the workers you have lined up know the business, so we'll get the job done." My voice is upbeat and encouraging, but I have to wonder how we're going to pull this off. It's a skeleton crew for sure. Speaking of skeletons, I wonder if there are any lurking between those sofa cushions.

"We can handle it. Fifteen acres, about three hundred fifty taps, we'll get by." Daniel smiles, he and Janni completely lapless as they sink further into the sofa. It could be one of those Narnia things. Instead of a wardrobe, they have the sofa where you sit down and slip into another world. If he disappears, I'm so not doing double duty on the maple trees.

"Okay, let's think this through. We need someone to drive the truck while others empty the bags of syrup into the pan on the back of the truck bed."

"Yeah, then the real work begins down at the Sugar Shack." Janni shakes her head. "Now I'm beginning to wonder how we'll get it done."

"We really need to work in shifts when things start buzzing. Once that syrup is ready, it's ready," Daniel says, heaving himself partially up, thereby bringing his thighs back into the light of day. He brushes some dirt from his boots and leaves debris on the floor. No wonder they have carpet issues.

"We'll figure out something." No need to tell her I have major doubts. "You know what Mom always says, 'Things could be worse.'"

"Mom could write her own book of quotes."

Just then a rap sounds on the door, and Janni gets up. We enjoy a chuckle until Janni opens the door and Mom's standing there as big as you please, suitcase in hand.

Mom takes one look at Janni and says, "Well? You gonna let me in?"

Janni slowly steps out of Mom's way. "You didn't need to bring your suitcase over just to have dessert, Mom." We're both practically holding our breath here.

"I need a room," she says, matter-of-factly, closing the door behind her. She turns back to Janni. "I'm not living with that man another minute."

five

"Which room do you want me in?" Mom asks, already moving toward the stairway. Janni and I lock eyes. Mom doesn't notice.

"Whoa, come and sit down. What's this all about?" Janni helps Mom move over to a nearby chair and get situated before she can unpack her clothes and fill out change-of-address cards.

She looks up at us with eyes as wide and round as pancakes. "I've tried to keep it from you girls, but the truth is, your Dad is—"

We scoot forward to the edge of our seats.

"He's—" She grabs a maple cookie from the plate on the coffee table.

"Yes?" I say, impatient for her to spit it out.

"Well, he's tryin' to kill me." She falls back into her seat with a thump and bites into her cookie.

The silence that follows is deafening. I'm feeling quite proud of myself that I haven't rolled onto the floor in a fit of laughter. "You're kidding, right?"

"One kidder in the family is enough," Mom snaps, then goes after her treat with a vengeance.

"Mom, you know Dad would never hurt you. What happened?" Janni asks.

"Lots of things, but the last straw was after our nap today. He said he was going to make us some coffee. I came into the kitchen, surprising him, and found rat poison on the counter not far from where he was making the coffee." Her eyes are wide. "If that's not proof enough, I don't know what is."

"Well, maybe he was trying to catch a rat."

"Janni, you shouldn't call Mom a rat."

Janni gasps, and Mom looks as though she has murder on *her* mind.

"I'm kidding."

"Char, this is serious." Janni turns to Mom. "Well?"

"The only rat in that house is your father. Now, I don't want to talk about it anymore," she quips, nose upturned, lips pursed. "I'm going to bed." She springs to her feet. "Where is it?"

"Well, since the boys are coming home for spring break, I'd better put you in the study. We have a daybed in there."

Mom finishes her cookie and grabs another one. I get my cookie fetish honestly. "I'll go there now. I'm tired."

"I'll come help you get the bed ready." Janni turns to me and rolls her eyes before climbing the stairs with Mom.

Now, back in Maine they call me a workaholic because I'm at the office every day but Sunday, working long hours. But I have to say here that I'm more worn-out from watching my family for the last twenty-four hours than I have been working in the office for the past six years.

Janni comes down the stairs, shaking her head.

"What's that all about?" I ask.

"Who knows?" She chews nervously on her upper lip. "How am I going to work on that scrapbook with her hovering over me?"

"You might have to work in the barn," I joke. Then I can eat my cookies in peace.

Janni brightens. "That's a great idea. We've got an old portable table we can stick out there," she says excitedly. "Then if Mom walks in on us, we can throw hay over it. You're a genius."

"Wait. Remember, you're on your own with this scrapbook thing. I'll have my hands full gathering table decorations and planning the food."

"I still don't understand why you have to make this such an expensive production. We have nothing to prove."

"I told you, I want it to be very special for Mom and Dad. It has nothing to do with proving anything." What does it hurt to lavish some of my wealth on my family and the town?

"Janni, I'm going to call it a night," Daniel says, when he enters from the back door.

"What have you been doing?"

"Checking on that broken hinge in the chicken coop. I'll get the hardware at the store tomorrow and fix that for you." He climbs two stairs.

"Danny, um, there's something you should know," Janni says.

He turns and looks at her.

"Mom's moved in."

"I've missed you, Char," Dad says, giving me a big hug, then a kiss on the cheek.

"I've missed you, too, Dad. Thanks for meeting us for breakfast." Janni and I scoot into our seats in the booth, causing the vinyl to squeak in protest—and this *before* breakfast.

Dad's slight frame—though he's taller, his build is not much bigger than Mom's, really—slips into place across from us. His lips curve in a smile, but his face looks gaunt and wrinkly, reminding me of a dried apple.

I stretch out my hand and touch his arm. "You okay, Dad?"

"I'm fine, Zip," he says, his gold tooth flashing front and center, compliments of a kick from our long-ago pet mule, Francis. Like the roots of a tree, Dad is the foundation for our family. The patriarch. This whole thing with him and Mom is a bit disconcerting, to say the least.

Just then the waitress steps up to our table, and we order our drinks. Janni and Dad get coffee. It amazes me that people can drink that cheap stuff. I opt for orange juice.

Dad looks at Janni and then me. "It's hard to believe you girls are all grown up." He shakes his head. "Seems only yesterday I hauled you down to the general store for penny candy."

"Boston Baked Beans, Lemon Drops, candy necklaces—"

"Wax lips, candy cigarettes."

Janni gasps. "We weren't supposed to get those."

"They were my favorite. Sorry, Dad."

"Those were the days," he says as though he didn't hear a word we said.

I decide to play along. "Remember how you used to throw us into the hay piles?"

Dad's mouth splits into a wide grin. "I sure do. Your mom would have a fit because she was always afraid there might be something in the hay to hurt you."

"What's going on with Mom?" Janni asks, slipping out of her coat.

Dad shakes his head. "I don't know, girls. She's acting so strange. I'll look up from reading the paper, and she'll be staring at me. When I go into another room, I feel her presence behind me. She peeks at me through cracks in the door, and has even followed me to town."

"What do you think it is, Dad?"

He shakes his head. "I have no idea." No one speaks of the fearful possibilities.

"How long ago did it start?" Janni asks.

"I started noticing a couple of weeks ago," he says.

The waitress brings a pot of coffee and places it on the table. Janni picks it up and starts filling her and Dad's cups. I take a deep whiff. Even the cheap stuff *smells* good.

"Why would she think you're trying to kill her?" I ask.

Dad's head jerks up. "She thinks that?"

"She mentioned something about rat poison," Janni says, as though she hates to bring it up.

It does seem a little odd that he would have rat poison next to the coffeepot, but our family is a little strange, after all.

"I woke up from our nap before she did, so I thought I would surprise her with some coffee. I was trying a little multitasking. You know, take care of our recent mouse situation while fixing her some coffee. She took one look at the coffee, the rat poison, and drew the wrong conclusion. Is that what you're saying?" Dad wraps his hands around the coffee cup and gazes into it. "She has to know I would never hurt her." He looks up. "Maybe she's just worn-out from our move and all."

As we settle in to breakfast, we try to encourage Dad and then talk about the good old days. When it's time to leave, I pick up the tab, and we make our way out to our cars.

"She'll come around. Don't you worry. We'll get to the bottom of this," I say. Janni nods in agreement. "And Dad?"

He turns to look at me.

"Get rid of the rat poison. I don't want you accidentally putting it in your coffee."

"This car is awesome, Char," Janni says, fiddling with the seat controls when we get in my car. "I can't imagine riding in style like this on a regular basis."

"You get used to it." With a flip of the handle, I click the turn signal in place, and we hang a left. "What do you think about Dad and the rat poison?"

"Well, of course I don't think he's trying to kill Mom, but lately, he seems preoccupied, so I could see him putting the poison in her coffee without meaning to, and that scares me."

"Sounds as though they both have issues that we'll have to iron out between now and their anniversary." I sigh. "The stress of the party is enough without adding this."

"No kidding."

"Hey, I'm excited about your new coffee shop," I say, pointing to the new building as we drive by.

"Yeah, I guess. As you know, I enjoy my own coffee."

"I'll have to convert you," I say with a laugh.

"Oh no, you don't. We can't afford it."

"Yes, you can, and you know it. You and Daniel carry that frugal thing too far. Sometimes it does a woman good just to get out of the house once in a while. Especially with all the extra company you have these days."

Janni sighs. "It does sound nice."

"You sure you're all right?"

"Just tired of being pulled in so many directions." She flips down the visor, checks her makeup, then flips it back up. "I know it sounds selfish, but I'm ready to do something for me."

"We all need periods of refreshment. No one can fault you for that."

We drive a little further, and I spot a house for sale. "That looks nice and roomy," I say with a nod toward the house.

"You still spend Sunday afternoons going through open houses?" Janni asks with a chuckle.

"I admit it. I love to walk through homes, get ideas for layouts, all that. Since I've gotten more into the commercial side of things, I don't get to go through homes as much. I keep busy studying the markets, working with commercial buyers and sellers, all that."

"Ever the workaholic," Janni says as we pull up to a stoplight.

"I'm not a workaholic. I simply love what I do, so it doesn't bother me to work overtime."

She shrugs. "Just think you would have more of a social life if you worked less."

"Moving commercial real estate takes hard work and time. It's different than selling residential properties." I'm hoping she'll ask me more about it, but she doesn't. Spotting our high school, it seems a good time to change the subject. "Wow, the old school sure needs a face-lift."

"Yeah, they're starting renovations in the fall."

"That's great," I say, though I have to admit the chipped brick and gaudy graffiti fits my memories of high school. Flashes of homecoming, basketball games, Eddie, Linda . . . "So how are The Evil Friends?"

Janni turns to me. "You still call them that?"

"Doesn't it still apply?"

"Don't know. I don't run in their circles. Actually, I feel sorry for Linda."

"You feel sorry for everybody. How can you feel sorry for her after what she did to me?" I shoot back before I can stop myself.

Janni looks at me. My face heats up ten degrees, and mad tears spring to my eyes.

"You have to let it go, Char."

I turn my attention to the road. Obviously, I've been working too hard. My emotions always tell on me. "Look, I'm not the one who had the affair, okay? They conceived that baby during our marriage. Mine and Eddie's marriage, Janni. I've let it go, but I can't forget. She lured my husband away when I needed him most. And he willingly betrayed me. No one gets over that." The words sting my soul as they leave my lips.

Janni sighs. "Eddie has left a trail of broken hearts. He'll regret it one day."

"I doubt it. Once a jerk, always a jerk."

Janni shakes her head. "An unforgiving heart and bitterness can do more harm to you than he and Linda ever did."

"Look, Janni, don't preach to me. I've heard this business all my life. The truth is, I believe God is good, but people stink. Linda stole my husband. My chance for a family. I'm not bitter. It's just a fact. She took my life and made it her own."

"It was wrong of her, but you have to forgive her."

"Who says I haven't forgiven her?"

"Have you?"

"Hello? It's not as though I've set out for revenge, have I?"

"We all make mistakes, Char." She turns to me. "All of us."

six

"I wonder if this is how Daniel Boone felt blazing a trail," I say, shoving branches out of my way as we walk through the woods the next afternoon.

Janni chuckles. "Maybe. Though I imagine his paths were not as easy to get through as ours." We take a few steps in silence.

"Did you get the menu ordered for the party?"

"Had to. The time will be here before we know it." Now that she's grown used to the idea of a fancy party, there's no use telling her I ordered the menu while I was still in Maine.

"Still getting cards in the mail?" I ask, stepping over pinecones.

"Yep. Almost daily. I think we'll have a good crowd. Still think we could have done it in the church fellowship center. It would have been appropriate what with him being the pastor for so long."

"This isn't a church matter. This is about their lives together as husband and wife. Hey, what happened over there?" I ask, pointing to some trees with severed branches on the ground below them.

"We had a bad storm last fall and haven't been down here to clean up yet. It always amazes me how nature can beat the trees up, but somehow they manage to survive."

We step around the debris. "We'll just finish off these two rows of trees here," she says, pointing. "They were the only ones Daniel and I didn't get to on Saturday."

My fingers trail the rough bark of a tree. "Funny how they dry up during the winter." *Just like me—dried up. Used. At least that's how I feel when I return to Tappery.*

"Yeah, it's pretty amazing."

"Won't be long until we'll be eating pancakes for breakfast, lunch, and dinner," I say.

"Mom probably wouldn't like that any more than she appreciated the turkey dinner last night."

"Oh, you know Mom. She's just a tad opinionated." I laugh. A hole in the ground makes me wobble a moment, and I try not to think about the fact it could be a snake hole. The only thing that sets my mind at ease is in knowing the ground is still frozen, so they're not likely to be slithering around outside. "Besides, she dug into those maple buns this morning like nobody's business."

"And then complained about them after eating four." Janni sighs.

"You know, it amazes me that you and Daniel got so many trees tapped by yourselves."

"Some friends from the church helped. It shouldn't take us long to finish up."

"You sure are blessed with people who love you."

"You know, we really are. Let's start with this one," Janni says, stopping at an old, sturdy maple. She studies the tree a moment, her fingers rubbing across the bark for the scar from last year's drilling.

"It's cool how these trees heal themselves."

"How do you mean?" Janni lifts the gas-powered drill in place and bores a new hole about a half-inch wide.

"You know, we drill a hole, then the following year, the only way we can find it again is by the smooth bark around it because the hole is already filled in." I pull a spile—the metal spigot that's used to tap maple from the trees—from my backpack, plug it into the fresh hole and hammer it into place. Then Janni attaches the metal top of the plastic bag onto the spile. She tugs at it a couple of times to make sure it's secure.

"Yeah, that's true. It's pretty cool, really." She holds the drill against her left shoulder and marches to the next tree. "Don't you miss this, Char?" She positions the drill for the next hole, and we go through the routine again.

The tangy scent of bark and forest mingle with the cold air. A clear blue sky shines above us as we crunch over the hard earth, crusted with the frigid layer of winter.

"I do miss this place. The forest is so peaceful. I especially love to walk through the sugar bush," I say, referring to the grove of maples that are tapped for sweetness. A melancholy mood sweeps over me as I realize there's not an ounce of sweetness left in me these days.

"Now you have quiet walks along the beach." Janni drills the next hole. I plug in the spile, and we finish off another tree for tapping. "I can't imagine having a view of the ocean from my living room the way you do."

"It is wonderful," I say, thankful for my life in Maine, yet wondering why my past life won't let me go—or is it the other way around? "You should bring your friends up sometime."

Janni gives me a sideways glance. "This coming from Miss I-want-to-be-alone?"

"I told you, you're always invited. You know that." We walk a little further. "It might surprise you to know that I entertain on a fairly regular basis."

"Do tell."

"Yep. Peter and I together, really. He's more of the socialite than I am."

"And do you have the meals catered?"

"No. Peter's a frustrated chef. But if he didn't make it, I'd send for a caterer."

Jani shakes her head. "Well, you're doing better than me. I haven't entertained in a couple of months. Just not in the mood for company—outside of family, I mean."

"Look Janni, I'm no doctor, but you seem a little depressed. Is everything all right?"

She turns to me. "That's just it. Everything is fine. I have no idea what's going on with me. My moods are up and down."

"It happens at this stage in our lives. Our hormones get messed up."

"I'm not as old as you, Char. No offense."

Okay, she's in denial. "Well, I'm not exactly aged wood, but whatever."

"I have to say I'm impressed that you're still seeing Peter," she says, quickly changing the subject. "This one's lasted—what?—six months?" We stop at the next tree and run through the routine for tapping. The smells of a hot drill and bark chips permeate the air while bits of wood spray about.

"Ew, that does sound serious, doesn't it?"

"Wealth, a busy dating life, lots of friends—you've got it all, Char."

"Oh, I wouldn't say that. But you can," I tease to cover the shadow over my heart.

"Char, this is just sister-to-sister here."

I brace myself.

"Do you think you'll ever be able to care about anyone again the way you cared about Eddie?"

"Eddie who?"

"Ha-ha."

We stand in front of another tree, and she turns to me. "I'm not going to drill until you answer."

"No one has ever come close." My throat clenches around the words, making them barely audible.

Janni lifts the drill and begins to bore a hole in the next tree, just the way Eddie put a hole in my heart so many years ago . . .

"If you don't mind, as a follow-up, I thought I would check on the trees that we tapped on Saturday," Daniel says, already heading toward the front door. "It will be too dark to see if I don't get out there pretty soon."

"How about we go with you?" Janni finishes tying the loop on her work boots, I pull on my coat, and we join him at the door.

"I'll clean up the kitchen," Mom calls from the next room.

"Thanks," Janni calls over her shoulder as we step outside.

"I'm going to check out the property, so I'd better take the truck. You want to go with me or walk?" Daniel asks.

"We'll walk and meet you there," Janni says.

He nods and heads for his truck while we walk toward the trees.

"You didn't have to come. I just had to get out of the house and away from—" Janni stops herself.

"She's getting to you too?"

"Yes."

"I didn't think anybody got to you."

"Are you kidding? 'You need less flour in your gravy, Janni. It's too lumpy. Too many marshmallows in the sweet potatoes. Did you see that curtain move? Is someone else in this house?' I want to lock her in her room."

This coming from my passive sister makes me laugh out loud. Then she joins me.

When we quiet down she says, "Guess I shouldn't complain. She put up with enough from me in my teenage years."

My sister drips with sweetness. Sometimes I just want to slap her. Okay, I don't mean that, but I haven't had a sweet thought in, well, years. The least she could do is throw a healthy fit once in a while.

"To quote a wise woman, 'You need to let it go.'"

She looks at me and smiles. "Okay, okay."

Daniel pulls up in the truck and gets out. He tugs gently on the spiles to make sure they're secure as we go from tree to tree. "Good job, girls."

Janni smiles and winks at me.

Daniel takes off his cap, runs impatient fingers through his hair, then yanks the cap back on. "The sap's dripping along. We've got to line up some help, and fast."

"I'll call around tomorrow and see if I can get some helpers," Janni says.

Daniel nods. "You girls want a ride back to the house?"

"You can," Janni says to me, her feet barely trudging along. "I need to check on the animals."

"I'll help you." Wow, I'm having a Janni moment. All sweet and helpful. Must be from hanging out with the maples.

"Suit yourself," Daniel calls over his shoulder with a wave.

"Boy, I'm tired," Janni says. "It doesn't look like all that much work, but when you get into it, it takes a lot of effort."

"Sure does," I say.

"After I go into the house and check on Mom and Daniel, I think I'll work a little on the scrapbook. That always calms me down. I'm really glad you came up with the idea to do it out in the barn. Though it's cold, the solitude will be great out there."

"Does that mean you don't want me to help you?"

"Not at all. I just mean it gives me space away from Mom. Bless her heart."

We laugh together.

"I've missed you, Char. No one understands me the way you do." She slides open the barn door.

Her comment surprises me. She shares a deep friendship with her friends. Surely, they know her better than I do. I've always envied that about her. My friends are the surface type. The ones who come over for barbecues and talk about the weather, politics, and work, but their conversation never ventures into, say, why I have never remarried. Not that I could answer. How can I when I don't know myself?

In no time, the barn is alive with Mr. Ed's breath blowing through his nostrils, the scrape of iron against the wooden floor as he paws the ground, and the soft mew of hungry kittens. I bump into the bulb dangling from the extension, then walk over and tighten the cord so it's out of harm's way.

"You okay?"

"Yeah, just startled me." I keep my eye on the swinging bulb.

Janni adjusts herself on the stool near Elsie. Picking up the kittens' food bowl, I walk it over to Janni and hold it low enough for her to position Elsie's, um, spigot directly over the bowl, give it several squirts, then walk it back to where I picked it up, the kittens all the while clamoring around my feet.

"Do you ever wonder if this is it, Char? I mean, our lives are half over."

"Whoa. Hold everything. How did we go from our past to being one step away from having the dirt kicked over us?" I stand and brush debris from my hands while the kittens go after the milk. My back catches a moment, and I do a couple of waist twists.

She chuckles. "I don't know. Just thinking how fast time goes."

"What's with the pondering life thing? Your birthday is still in August, right?"

"Yes. I was just thinking out loud, I guess."

"Well, stop it."

She looks at me a minute, and we both start laughing. The conversation then moves to her boys, and suddenly I feel bad that I've cut her off. Maybe she wanted to talk about something important, and I stopped her with my stupid joking around. Mom's words come back to me: "There is a time to joke and a time to be silent."

Why can't I ever get things right?

"That banty rooster was at it again today," Mom says when we step inside. "I got after him with the broom."

I lock eyes with Wiggles. He creeps back onto his perch and eats sunflower seeds as though he's not the least worried about the broom. But so help me, I'll wallop him good if he ever claws at me like that again. Without thought I kick off my shoes and rub my sore heels.

"Sometimes he needs that," Janni says, pulling off her shoes and sagging onto the other end of the sofa, across from Mom. "Where's Daniel?"

I take a seat in the recliner nearby where I can keep a watchful eye on the sofa.

"He's in your bedroom, watching TV. I don't know why he doesn't stay down here to watch it. He's being antisocial, that's all."

"Mom, this is his house. He's worked hard today."

"Well, just the same. It's rude."

Janni sighs. "Have you heard from Dad?"

Mom lifts her chin. "No, and that's fine by me. The farther he stays away from me, the better."

"Mom, you and Dad have been married for almost fifty years. Don't you think if he wanted to kill you, he would have done it by now?" I ask, trying to get her to see how ridiculous the whole thing is.

She leans in toward me. "You don't know your dad." She turns to Janni. "He's changed. You haven't been around him the way I have. He walks around the house with a hammer in his hand. He's just biding his time, waiting for an opportunity, I know it."

"To hang a picture?"

They turn to me.

"He's waiting for an opportunity to hang a picture? Well, after all, he's carrying a hammer." Mom's staring daggers at me. I'm wondering who wants to murder whom here.

"Why would he need a hammer?" Janni asks.

"Exactly." Mom looks at us to see if there is a trace of belief in our expressions. "He never listens when I talk to him—it's as though his mind is always someplace else."

"That pretty much sums up half the world's male population," I say with a chuckle. They both glare at me. I clear my throat. "We'll keep an eye on him."

Mom nods and leans back into her cushion. It's just what she wanted to hear. "Hey, they opened that Smooth Grounds coffee shop today."

Discussion of coffee always lifts my spirits. "Yeah?" I glance at my watch. "I'll bet it's still open. Want to go?" I ask Mom and Janni.

"No, I want to watch a movie," Mom says. "Got any good ones?"

"You're welcome to look at our pile of DVDs. I'm going back out to the barn," Janni says.

"Whatever for?" Mom wants to know.

"Tipsy's been acting a little odd today. I want to check on her, and maybe clean things a bit."

Janni must be struggling again.

"This late at night? You sick?" Mom asks.

"No."

"How about I grab us a coffee, and then I'll come out and help you?"

"That's nice, but I don't need any coffee. I just want to unwind, really," Janni says.

"Well, you two do your thing. I'm going to watch a movie," Mom says. "Janni, you be careful out in that barn by yourself."

We rise from our seats. Mom digs through the stack of DVDs while I grab my coat from the closet and head for the door. "Char, you watch your speed on the country roads. You might hurt a critter crossing the road. You aren't in the big city now."

"Thanks for the reminder," I say without adding, "and thanks for worrying about *me*." Janni and I slip into our coats and head outside.

"Do you want me to stay and help? I can do coffee later," I offer reluctantly.

"No, go enjoy your coffee. I can use the alone time, no offense," Janni says.

"None taken."

We wave good-bye as I punch my car remote to unlock the doors and climb inside. Since the farm is out in the country a ways, it takes me about fifteen minutes to get to Smooth Grounds. Fortunately, it's still early evening, so they'll be open for a while. My heart flips at the sight of the store. Do I need a life or what?

After placing a couple of business calls on my cell phone, I step inside the shop. Excitement rushes through me with the whir of the cappuccino machine and the quiet conversation of people huddled around wooden tables. Though I love the isolation my cottage provides, the scent of coffee always makes me think of work, people, the hustle-bustle of life, and that energizes me. Janni's house is so laid-back, it's starting to drive me crazy.

After I get my maple macchiato with three shots of espresso, I find a seat. Fortunately, I remembered to grab the latest issue of *Real Estate* magazine from the backseat of my car. Sipping on the hot macchiato, I browse through the pages, catching up on industry news, profiles, and meaty articles. Ignited by the inspirational articles or the three shots of espresso, I'm not sure which, fresh zeal replaces my lethargy, and I'm ready to get back to work. I pull out my Palm Pilot and make a couple of notes on clients I need to contact and land in town I want to check out. Then I pull out my cell phone and call my house to check for any messages. Jotting down the numbers on my Palm, I click off my phone and prepare to return some calls, deciding first to take another sip of my macchiato.

"Hey, Charley, mind if I join you?" The familiar deep voice grabs my attention and makes me choke on my drink. It's like my esophagus has shrunk to the size of hanger wire. Air tries to get through, but the passageway is closed. Consequently, I make this heaving sound that terrifies everyone in the shop, including me. Russ Benson slaps my back a couple of times, then suddenly my windpipe opens like a midnight rose at, well, midnight. Everyone turns away to their own little discussions—most likely about me—and my breathing settles into a normal pattern once again.

"You never answered me," Russ says, still hovering by my table.

"I was kind of preoccupied." My voice sounds like sandpaper scratching wood.

He laughs. "May I join you?"

No. "Yes." I flip my Palm Pilot closed and tuck it back into my handbag. After another sip of my drink, I'm convinced my tastes have turned their allegiance to cold drinks. Russ helps me shrug out of my coat.

"*Real Estate* magazine, huh?" He smiles at me. "I hear that you're a successful Realtor out East."

Janni or Daniel must have told him that. "I do all right." My words have all the warmth of an arctic blast. A shadow crosses his face, making me feel guilty. My mind searches for something to say. "I'm sorry about your wife, Russ."

"Thanks."

"Are you doing okay?"

He stares at his hands. "Yeah. It was hard. We had our rough spots, but Cathy was a good woman. I don't know if it's something you ever really get over, losing someone, I mean."

Tell me about it.

An awkward silence follows.

"Janni told me a little about your life in the military. Sounds interesting." My feeble attempt at thawing the frost from my icy-cold demeanor.

"You were talking about me?"

My gaze shoots to him. "Well, I mean, she brought up the dinner, and I—er, uh, I mean, she mentioned the military thing, and then I—" It occurs to me that I'm babbling like Porky Pig. The smile on his face tells me he's picked up on that too. Oh, he's trying not to, I'll give him that, but he's smiling. Eyes, mouth, the whole shebang are in on it. "You're making fun of me."

"No. I'm sorry. It's just nice to know you were talking about me." His twinkling eyes peer over the rim of his cup as he takes a drink.

Before I can comment or even think about it all, the bell jangles over the door.

"We're having a class reunion, and I didn't know about it?" a voice intrudes.

When I look up, my heart sinks. It's Linda Loose Lips in the flesh. And let me just say it's good to see an extra, oh, I don't know, fifty pounds on her—okay, thirty, but still.

She extends her hand to Russ. "Linda. Linda Appleton-Kaiser." She runs her fingers along the edge of her shoulder-length black hair and smiles. Same old Linda. She turns to me. "Char," she says with forced politeness.

Just then Gail walks inside, arms waving wildly when she sees us. She practically gallops over to our table. For the life of me, all I can see are galloping lips. "Oh, isn't this so fun? I'll grab my frappe and join you."

Russ looks at me. I look at Linda. Linda looks at Gail.

"How about this? The paparazzi all present and accounted for," I say with a fake smile. "Did you bring your notebooks and tape recorders, so you don't miss anything?" I turn to Russ. "Good to see you again, Russ. I have to go."

Hot tears scald my eyes and my breath sticks in my chest as I dash through the coffeehouse door and slip into the night . . .

seven

"Whoa, you're up early," Janni says when she comes down the stairs.

"Yep. Already been to the coffee shop and had my macchiato. Thought I'd go out and feed the animals for you." I've also been poring over my anniversary planning notebook. I need to stop by the store and see if I can find some gold ribbon to serve as napkin rings.

Janni stares at me so long I'm afraid she's mummified. It might be that whole morning look, but I don't think so. "Are you all right?"

"Yes. I want to help. Besides, I need some fresh air."

"Well, the barn isn't exactly the place for fresh air."

"You have a point. But at least I'll get in a couple of gulps before I enter the barn."

"Are you sick?"

"Too many cookies before bed," I confess.

Suspicion fills her eyes. "Uh-oh. What happened?"

"Can't a girl have a cookie binge without a major interrogation?"

"You only eat cookies before bed when you're upset. What gives?"

"I really don't want to talk about it right now. Maybe later. Over coffee, okay?"

She frowns. "Specialty coffee, I presume?"

"You got it." I smile. "It's probably too cold to stay out for long. I'll be back soon." Tucking my scarf into my jacket, I walk through the open door. Frigid air stings my face the minute I step outside. Had I known it was so cold today, I might have reconsidered that helping-out thing.

When I slide the doors into place, another gust of cold air swooshes through the barn. I turn on the light.

The animals peek over their stall doors. "Good morning, guys," I say. A couple of the kittens curl and mew around my feet.

Elsie's unimpressed and keeps chewing something I don't care to think about. Mr. Ed watches me with interest. Tipsy is a little skittish, so I'm trying to move in a nonthreatening way.

After filling their food bins with oats, feeding the kittens, stacking up more hay, and giving everyone water, I make my way to the place that is near and dear to my heart. The hayloft. This place was also one of my favorite hangouts, well, next to walking in the woods and going to the lake.

Climbing the few steps of the ladder, I step onto the floor of the loft and glance around. The perfect thinking place. A wonderful spot to work on floor plan ideas.

Besides an old trunk and some hay, there's nothing much up here. Walking over to the corner, I plop down, causing the woodsy scent of fresh hay to fill the air. My body relaxes in response. All the years and it's come to this. Me. In a hayloft. Alone.

The barn doors creak open, letting in the sound of a car passing down the gravel road. "Char, you in here?"

"Up here, Janni. In the hayloft."

Her footsteps scuff across the floor, then climb the wooden ladder. Her head pokes through the opening.

"What are you doing up here?"

"Being a kid." I vigorously rub my gloves together to keep warm.

Janni hauls herself off the ladder and steps over to me.

"Where's Mom?" I ask.

"She's getting ready to go out to breakfast with her lady friends from church."

"You don't think anyone will tell about the anniversary party, do you?"

"I sure hope not. It's not easy keeping something like this a secret."

"Have you gotten any letters back or responses from former members of the church who have moved away?"

"Yeah, we have," she says with excitement. "I put them in here." She walks over to the trunk and pulls out two packets of letters bound together. "These people are coming." She holds up the stack in her right hand. "And these can't make it." She lifts the packet in her left hand.

We go through a few of the letters together, talking about what those people meant to our lives and how good it will be to see some of them again.

"What's all this other stuff?" The musty smell of age lifts as I sort through old newspapers, bound letters, a baby's blanket, vintage clothes, family pictures, and assorted documents.

"A little bit of everything, I think. Mom had this trunk in the attic, but I had Daniel bring it out here temporarily so we—or I—can work on the scrapbook." Janni turns over some pictures and looks through them.

"You know, I was thinking that while you're working on the scrapbook, maybe you could pick out some pictures of Mom and Dad that we could display in gold frames at the party. Carpenter Center is going to put out a round table with a gold tablecloth where we can display those photos and your scrapbook."

"Do I get any say in this?"

"Well, of course you do. You're not crazy about the idea of photos?"

"It's not that. It just seems you're planning everything, and I get very little part in it."

"That's not true. You're doing the scrapbook."

"Always something to prove, huh, Char?" Before I can respond, she holds up her hand. "I can't talk about it right now." She's going through some mood thing, so I drop the matter. For now.

"Since there's not enough sap to do anything yet, why don't you make whatever calls you need to make for the party, and I'll start sorting through pictures while Mom's at her breakfast." Janni pushes herself up from the floor.

I'm thinking I'd better get on her good side before I tell her my plans about the string quartet I hired for the party.

"So you never told me what happened that made you binge on cookies last night," Janni says after lunch when we meet back in the barn to sort through photos.

"Russ came into the coffee shop." Careful not to ruin my manicure, I lift tiny scraps of paper and toss them in the throw-away pile.

Janni writes something on the paper with scrapbook ink.

"*That* made you binge on cookies?"

"Hey, you have such great handwriting, you could put the names on the place cards at the party."

"We're having place cards?" she asks, disbelief hanging between us.

"Is that all right?"

She sighs. "I guess."

Not wanting to give her time to get stirred up, I return to our discussion. "Russ joined me at the table."

"You're kidding." She plops a stack of pictures down beside her.

"Nope. But it gets better."

I have Janni's full attention now. "What happened next?"

"Linda Kaiser joined us." My words come out in a frosty cloud. I rub my arms back and forth with quick strokes.

"No way!" For a moment I think she's going to do the fainting-goat thing, but she holds her own.

"It still gets better."

"Oh my goodness, I can't stand it!" she says with the enthusiasm of an excited puppy.

"Want me to stop?"

She grabs both my hands and shouts, "No!"

"Gail joined us too."

With a gaping mouth, Janni is totally speechless. It's as though someone stole her favorite recipe and sent a ransom note.

"What did you do?"

"What I do best. Opened my mouth and said the wrong thing." I tell her about my snide remarks and my dramatic exit.

I'm certain Janni is judging me right at this moment, but she doesn't let on. "You manage not to see anyone for thirty years, then wham! You practically see your whole graduating class."

"It's hardly my whole class. It just happens to be two of the people in all the world I would prefer never to see again in this lifetime. At least Eddie didn't show up."

"Is it better or worse now that you've seen them?" Janni holds her gloves next to her face.

"It's all right. I survived. But I hope it's the last time I see them."

"So sad," Janni says, rummaging through the next batch of pictures.

"What's sad about it? It's not as though I did anything wrong."

"No, but it's sad that things turned out the way they did. If Eddie hadn't—well, you would still be here, around family, where you belong."

"I'm happy where I live, Janni. I'm successful in my business. Life is good. Eddie is a jerk, but he did me a favor."

Janni grows quiet. "I'm sorry, Char."

"Let's just forget it."

"I sure miss Aunt Rose," she says.

"Me too."

"I'm glad you got her place. You deserve it."

"She got me through that divorce. I had to get away from Tappery. The memories. The gossip. Gail Campbell. Linda and Eddie. Aunt Rose offered me a safe haven."

"Well, you helped her, too, in her last days when she really needed it."

"It was the least I could do. I never dreamed she would leave me the cottage." I turn to Janni. "Let's just hope I don't have to see any of those guys again while I'm here."

"Tappery is a pretty small community."

"Thank you for pointing that out. I'll visit the coffee shop in the off hours and do my grocery shopping the same way. Surely I can go that long without seeing them."

"Even Russ?"

"Oh, Russ is okay, but I don't want to see him if I can help it. I'm dating Peter, after all. Besides, Russ lives here. Long-distance relationships never work."

"If you just want to stay friends, it should be no big deal if you run into him, right?"

"Well, I don't want him to think—"

"So you tell him where you stand up front. You're dating someone back home. Period. You can only be his friend. 'Course, that's all that you are with Peter too. Am I right?" She's making a point, but I ignore her. "So it shouldn't be a problem to run into"—she uses finger quotes here—"'a friend' in Tappery."

"I see how your mind works. And let me just say, it's scary that I understand it." We both laugh.

"Good. Now that that's settled, I need to tell you something."

"What?"

"Um . . ." she looks down at her gloved fingers. "You know, Daniel was looking for some people to help with the sugaring, and, well, we have a friend who has another job, but he said he could help out here and there."

"That's great," I say, though I don't know what this has to do with me.

"The friend is Russ Benson."

After checking with Carpenter Center, I'm relieved to find they have crystal glasses with gold accents to use with the china. So that's one less worry. I put a checkmark beside the list in my notebook and make a mental note to shop for ribbon today. Just then the front door shoves open, causing me to jump.

"Hey, Aunt Char," Blake says, dropping his bulging duffle bag onto the floor.

"Blake Ort!" I shout, bouncing out of my chair and rushing to the door to give him a squeeze. He hauls his muscular six-foot-something self over to me and pulls me into a bear hug. Like father, like son.

"How are you, kid?" His broad shoulder reduces the sound of my voice to a muffle. He pulls away, and I look up at him. I tousle his hair, which isn't easy to do since he's taller than me. "Still breaking girls' hearts?"

A lopsided grin erupts on his face. "Can I help it if I'm so doggone good-looking?"

"It's your calling."

"Exactly."

It's easy to see why Blake breaks hearts. He's handsome and fun.

"Hey, Aunt Char," Ethan says, stepping through the door. A whoosh of cold night air rushes in, making me shiver. A long-haired brunette follows close behind. Ethan has the blonde hair of the Ort family, but his brown eyes and round face are every inch his mother's—as is his body build. He's shorter and a bit thicker. He kinda reminds me of Barney Rubble. Still, his smile could charm the sap from a maple tree.

"Great to see you, Ethan." I grab him and give him a hard squeeze.

Janni saunters down the stairs, and Daniel comes from the family room to join us. Nothing short of a fire would make them run. I've entered the land of Mayberry.

After everyone finishes hugging, Ethan introduces his friend. "Everybody, this is Candy Walling." Cute dimples peek from the corners of her mouth when she smiles, and love flickers in her gray eyes, I'm sure of it.

"Candy has offered to help with the sap. Isn't that sweet?" Janni's gaze goes from me to the boys who are laughing. "What?"

"You said 'isn't that sweet?' Get it? Sweet, sap? Candy? Notice anything?" I tease.

She rolls her eyes. "Anyway—" She draws the word out like a Slinky. "It will be great to have the extra help." She tosses a smile of thanks to Candy.

"Oh, by the way, I met a girl over at the coffee shop today. She's twenty-four and looking for a temporary job," Daniel says.

"What were you doing at the coffee shop? My coffee not good enough for you now?" Janni says, hands on her hips.

"Just wanted to see what all the fuss was about. You still make the best coffee," my brother-in-law graciously says, though we both know better, and gives her a peck on the cheek. She instantly softens.

Blake jumps in. "Twenty-four? Would I like her?"

"Put your tongue back in your mouth, Big Boy. You may need it for dinner," I say.

He shrugs.

"I thought we could use the extra help, so I told her to be here at nine on Monday morning."

"Would I like her?" Blake presses.

"We can use the help, that's for sure," Janni says. "And you, young man, behave yourself. By the way, you boys need to know that Grandma is staying with us for a while," Janni whispers.

"Why is that?" Blake asks.

"Long story. We'll tell you later."

"Which room are Grandma and Grandpa staying in?" Ethan asks.

"Grandpa's not here," Daniel says.

"Grandma's staying in the study." Seeing the boys' wide eyes, Janni says, "Go upstairs and put your things away. We'll talk later."

We all chat awhile, and then the kids get their things put away in their rooms. Candy will stay in Ethan's room while Ethan bunks out with Blake.

"Boy, it's great to see those kids," I say, joining Janni in the kitchen.

"Isn't it?" She pulls a pizza crust from the fridge, stretches it onto a pizza pan, then spreads homemade sauce on top.

"I considered going to the high school and announcing that we needed help but thought better of it." After washing my hands, I help top the pizza with pepperoni slices.

"Why? You afraid you'll run into—"

"The Evil Friends," I say, clawlike hands in the air, fingers wiggling. "Boo, ha, ha, ha."

Janni laughs. "Get me the cheese from the fridge, will you?"

"Sure." A package of blended mozzarella and cheddar is on the top shelf, so I pull it out. "This what you want?"

"That's it. Thanks." After washing the sauce from her hands, she rips open the package and sprinkles the cheese. "Well, you don't have to be around Russ, you know. We'll all eat together, but you don't have to sit by him."

"Oh, it's no big deal. Besides, it's not like he's shown any interest in me other than being polite. Just because he had a crush on me thirty years ago, doesn't mean anything today. We're both different people than we were then." Trust me on this. He's *way* different. Not that I care one way or the other. "Thirty years changes things, right? I mean, all you have to do is look at my thighs to see that."

"You need to learn to be comfortable in your skin," Janni says, taking a bite from a chocolate chip cookie, caring not one lick that her slender self disappeared years ago. I'm not sure if she's comfortable in her skin or beyond caring anymore. "I think it's really sweet of Russ to offer to help. Though I wonder if he would have offered if you weren't here."

"Oh, please. He's just being nice."

"Well, I saw the way he glowed right after he saw you at our house. There was more than nice in his eyes, let me tell you. So if you're not interested, you'd better let him down gently."

"Oh, yeah, sure. I'll just walk up to him and say, 'Thanks for helping with the syrup, Russ. And by the way, I thought I'd better clear the air. I'm dating someone back home, so we're just going to keep this at the friendship level, okay?' To which he will reply, 'I wasn't wanting to do otherwise.'"

"You underestimate yourself." Janni shoves the pizza pan into the oven and closes the door. She turns to me. "But then you always did."

If I'm all that, why did my husband leave me?

eight

On Monday morning, my eyes refuse to pop open until I've had my morning run to the coffee shop. My maple macchiato is just what the doctor ordered. Once I drain my cup, I wrap myself in so many clothes I could win a part in *The Mummy,* and then I head out the front door with the others. We've been collecting sap for a couple of days, so Janni and I plan to help gather sap then come back early to prepare lunch.

"You guys ready to go?" Janni asks, eyes bright, skin glowing. Early in the morning. Sometimes it boggles my mind that we're blood relatives.

Blake, Ethan, and Candy look worse than the old-timers. Dark circles shadow their eyes. And their hair? Nothing short of hosin' them down can fix that.

"Wait. We can't leave. That new girl isn't here yet," I say.

"I wonder if she's going to show up," Janni says.

"It's possible her enthusiasm waned with the morning light. It happens. After all, if Godzilla hadn't been sleeping in the next room, disguised as my mother, I might have stayed in bed this morning."

Janni gasps. "Char!" The kids laugh, and she's trying very hard not to join them.

Just then we see a lone walker headed our way.

"Must be the new girl," Blake says with a mischievous grin and wiggling of his eyebrows. He walks out to meet her while the rest of us look on. When they get closer, Blake gives me a thumbs-up and throws a "vavoom" look my way.

She's so cute, I half expect her to sprinkle fairy dust. She reminds me of someone. I can't put my finger on it, but I think it's that gal I sold the Williamson house to recently. We quickly introduce ourselves. She tells us her name is Stephanie Sherwood.

"Thanks for coming. We can always use extra help," Janni says.

Stephanie stares at Janni a moment without saying anything. I don't know if she's nervous or if she thinks Janni's weird, because come to think of it, I look at Janni that way too.

Janni must sense Stephanie's nervousness, because she reaches over and gives the young girl a hug. "We really appreciate you showing up."

That's why everyone loves Janni. She has such a way with people. So warm and sweet. Just like a cinnamon roll. It's disgusting. Me? I'm about as cozy as a hedgehog. I am my mother's daughter.

"Thanks for giving me the chance," Stephanie says. She seems a little choked up. Before my morning coffee, I'm exactly the same way.

We fall into step together as we all make our way toward the woods.

"Well, I may just have to call in sick after spring break and stick around," Blake says.

"*Stick* around?" I ask.

"Ha-ha," he says to me, his eyes never leaving Stephanie.

She ignores him. "So what are we going to do right now?"

"We're going to take the bags from the trees, pour the sap into some buckets, dump them in a big tank in the truck, put the bags back, and then Daniel will take the truck down to the Sugar Shack."

"What happens there?"

"We'll run the sap through a pipe from the tank into the Sugar Shack where it will flow into a holding tank. If we have enough sap, we'll start the evaporator and begin the sugaring process."

"Do we have to make the syrup by tonight?"

"We have to run the evaporator as soon as possible, because the sap can spoil, same as milk. But once the water is evaporated from the syrup, we can stop until tomorrow."

Janni jumps in, breath heaving as though she hasn't walked this much in a month of Sundays. "The good news is several of our friends have called and will be coming at various times this morning. We should be able to empty the bags and get to the Sugar Shack fairly quickly. Then there are several who have offered to work second shift throughout the syrup process, so I'm relieved."

"Oh, that's great," I say, pushing away the twitch of envy that springs up every time I see or hear about her throng of friends. Same friends she's always had. Lifelong friends. She's the one with the good life.

"Sounds like a lot of work," Stephanie says.

Blake's shoulders rear back, and he gives a studly smile. "Oh, don't worry, we'll have plenty of help. Plus, Ethan and I know the ropes. We'll be done in time to go out for pizza." He tosses Stephanie a wink. She stares at him as though she's met his kind before.

With great effort I force myself to slow my fast clip and walk at the same pace as the others. After weaving our way through a maze of shagbark hickories, oak, fir, and beech trees, we finally come to our first maple, where we all gather, waiting for Daniel to show up with the truck. How many times did I wander out here with Eddie where we talked and dreamed of our future together?

A hum of chitchat joins with birdsong and the lone cry of a train whistle in the distance.

My cell phone rings. In the heart of the forest, it seems almost sacrilegious. Quiet chatter continues in the background when I answer. "Hello?"

"How's my best girl?"

That little phrase is starting to irritate me. "Hi, Peter."

"Oh, that was enthusiastic."

"Sorry. We're ready to work on the trees."

"Sounds serious."

"You remember the pancakes and maple syrup I made you? It *is* serious."

"Oh yeah. Do you have any of that left around here?"

"Are you at my house?" That idea bugs me a little bit, though I should be happy. He's probably cleaning. Maybe I should tell him about the empty cookie box I stuffed under my bed.

"Yeah, I left my suit coat over here. I came back to get it."

"Oh."

"Is something wrong?"

"No, nothing's wrong." *Just get out of my house, please.*

"Well, I wanted to check in and see how you're doing. The office isn't the same without you. The sales are down." He laughs, but his little comment reminds me once again that someone wants me for what I can do for them.

Before I can work up a good comeback, Daniel pulls up in his black, rusty truck. It's seen a lot of sap seasons. The engine stops. Hard metal crunches against metal as the driver's door opens and Daniel climbs out. But when the passenger door squeaks open, the scene seems to play out in slow motion. Dressed in jeans, slick leather boots, and a thick, black winter jacket, Russ steps out, taking long strides in our direction. Light shines on his hair and glistens in his eyes, while his hands are stuffed deep in the pockets of his jacket.

He's a lean, mean, macho machine.

"Charlene, you still there?"

"What? Oh, yeah. Yeah, I'm here."

Russ moves within earshot. "I miss you, too, Peter," I say as loud as I dare. Russ's eyes meet mine. I smile, wave, then turn around. Doesn't hurt to let Russ know others are interested in me.

"Huh? I miss you too." Peter sounds confused. It's not the first time.

"Well, listen, I need to go. We're getting ready to collect the sap. Make sure you lock my door when you leave." He's a fanatic about leaving things the way he found them, so I know I don't need to say that. It bugs me that he still has my spare key. I gave it to him when I got tied up in a house closing so he could get preparations started for a company gathering we were having. I'd forgotten about it until now.

"I'll take care of it. Talk to you soon."

Taking a deep breath, I stand with my back turned to the group. Russ looks good, too good. I refuse to let my heart get tangled up that way again.

Though Peter is starting to bug me, our current arrangement works. My heart stays out of the mix. And I aim to keep my heart safe from now on, even if it kills me.

"Hi, Charley." Russ's earthy-scented cologne reaches me before he does.

One look into his warm blue eyes, and I figure I'd better get to work on my epitaph.

"Seems we keep bumping into each other." A nervous laugh follows. I think it's mine, but it could have come from Russ. I'm a little disoriented, so I'm not sure.

"How did you manage to get off work today?"

"My patient list is just getting up and running. We're a small office. Dad's covering things today. He knew Janni and Daniel needed help."

It seems everyone comes to their rescue. We follow the others to the tapped trees where we start emptying the bags into a couple of big buckets. The smell of the bark, the woods, the sap, all bring a flood of memories of our family working and laughing together as we made the syrup. Funny how I'd forgotten the good memories.

Russ lifts the bag from a tree and dumps the clear liquid into a big bucket.

When we were kids, Dad used to put metal buckets instead of plastic bags on the trees to collect the sap. Janni and I hated cleaning the sticky sap from those buckets, so Dad would bribe us with maple cookies. Seemed as though those cookies could take the sting out of most anything. Thankfully, these days we only use the buckets for transferring the sap.

I take a deep breath. "Listen, about the coffee shop—"

"Forget it. I understand completely."

"You do?"

"I went to the same high school, remember?"

The fact that he understands, and remembers their loose tongues, melts me in a way I hadn't expected.

"So was that your boyfriend?"

"Who?" I walk over to the next tree and lift the bag to empty.

"On the phone—oh, never mind. It's none of my business."

How can I explain what Peter is to me when I don't know myself? "We're good friends more than anything."

More of Janni's friends soon join us in the woods and start dumping bags of sap into the buckets.

"So, Russ, do you have any children?" Why did I ask that? I need to keep this on a friendship level. Nothing personal.

He shakes his head. "Timing was never right. All the military moves. You know how it is. How about you? Did you and Eddie have any children?"

I shake my head. "We lost one. Never had any after that." We take a few steps. "'Course, you probably know Linda and Eddie have a daughter."

"Yeah, I saw Linda and her little girl at the grocery together when I first moved to town."

While we work our way through the trees, pouring the sap from the bags into gathering pails, we talk a little bit about the military, his parents, and his dental business.

"You don't mind settling down in Tappery?" The air is filled with the hum of people talking, sharp footsteps thumping against the hard ground, liquid pouring into buckets. Lifting a heavy bag of sap from the tree, I bend over to dump it in the bucket.

Russ laughs. A deep, rich laugh, masculine and strong. "You find it hard to believe that anyone would willingly do that?"

With a shrug I say, "Just figured since you traveled with the military, you'd probably want a more exciting place to live, that's all."

He looks around at the trees and takes a deep breath. "Actually, it doesn't get much better than this." Then he turns to me and smiles, making my heart skip a beat. "In fact, I was kind of hoping you could help me come up with a floor plan for a new house."

With curiosity, I look at him. "You're thinking of building?"

"Yeah."

"How fun." Excitement always rushes through me when I think of building a home. Though I sell mostly commercial property now, I've always thought it would be fun to help people build homes. "Well, I'm not an expert, but I'd be happy to give you some ideas."

"Great. Janni told me you like to make sketches of floor plans, so I thought maybe you could come up with some sketches for me, and we can go over them together."

Something about the way he says "together" causes my heart to flutter.

"Sure. You'll need to give me a list of what you want in a home, and we can go from there." I lift a plastic bag off the next tree and prepare to dump it into the bucket.

"Listen, Charley, I wanted to get alone with you this morning because—"

His lips keep moving, but suddenly I can't hear a thing. It's like watching an episode of *Mr. Ed* on TV without sound. I just can't get past the I-wanted-to-get-alone-with-you thing. Russ's big, strong hands move about as he explains whatever it is he's explaining.

"Charley? Look out!"

The sharp tone of his voice brings me back to my senses, and I look down to see that I've missed the bucket and dumped the sap all over my Nikes.

Instead of moving into action, I stand there as though I'm in a dentist's office sucking novocaine. By the time I remember to move my feet, I've formed roots. The sap holds me firmly in place. As in, just stick a spile in my mouth and hang a plastic bag.

People around me smother laughs. The kids say, "Ew," which helps immensely.

"Are you all right?" Russ asks, pulling on my arm to help me move. A schlepping sound akin to the sucking of a plunger ensues, and with each step I attempt to take, Russ has to pluck my foot off the ground to keep me moving. That's one way to slow me down.

Every leaf within a three-mile radius attaches itself to my shoes. I'm a leaf vacuum without the vacuum part. If I ran a few laps through the woods, this place would shine like the picnic area of a state park.

Suddenly the image of how I must look hits me in full force. I'm picturing *Babes in Toyland* with the talking trees. I start laughing—so hard that I can't move. I just wobble. Like Humpty Dumpty—with hair. That thought alone sets me into another fit of laughter. Maybe it's the stress of the visit. Maybe it's seeing Gail, Linda, and Russ. Maybe it's the sap, or just that I'm worried about sprouting leaves, or that if I stick out my arms, birds will build nests. All I know is humiliation and me go together like pancakes and syrup.

And I'm laughing, why?

Blake turns and points to me. He starts laughing and soon Russ and the other kids join in a full-scale heehaw. In no time at all, the whole woods are alive with laughter.

When it finally dies down, Janni says, "I'll go up to the house and bring out some warm water to pour over your feet and pants so you can get them off."

With a fading chuckle, I nod. Then Russ and I walk toward the house in silence. Well, all except for the schlepping sound.

"Listen, this probably isn't the right time, but I may never get you to hold still long enough any other time."

I want to stop and stare at him, but I'm afraid I'll become a habitat for Chip and Dale—I'm talking chipmunks here, just so you know.

"I'm going nowhere fast this time." My voice has a half-tease, half-growl to it. I glance at the trail of footprints I've left behind. With every step my shoes have ripped bits of grass up by the roots.

"Did you hear me?"

I blink. "What? Oh, sorry, no. It's the sap and everything—" I lift a foot for emphasis and sap drips from the edges of my shoe.

Frustration flickers on his face. Who can blame him? "What I was saying, well, I'm sorry about you and Eddie and Linda, all that—"

"Huh? Oh, yeah." Not the most impressive vocabulary lineup, but there it is.

"Okay, the water is out in the tub. Just a few more yards, Char, and you'll make it," Janni says, as though I'm trying to swim the English Channel. She steps to the other side of me and, noticing our silence, says, "Am I interrupting something?"

Russ blows out a sigh and obviously gives up on the meaningful conversation. But I mean, honestly, how deep can we get at a time like this?

He lifts a slight smile. "No, that's all right," he says. Then he turns and whispers to me. "Maybe if I get lucky, you'll be my partner this afternoon."

I'll admit Russ is handsome and charming, but I'm not interested in a relationship. If that's his goal, he's barking up the wrong tree.

With the extra help, we are able to get down to the Sugar Shack in record time.

Russ and the boys chop firewood to keep the heat under the evaporator going. That's the highlight for me. I love the smell of burning wood. To this day the crackle and scent of burning wood makes me want to curl up in a corner with a good book—or eat pancakes.

Janni turns to Stephanie and Candy. "My job is to make sure the sap doesn't scorch or overflow. As you can see, it runs from this preheater pan down through the maze of the evaporator." Together we watch the sap slowly filling the main evaporator. "Once it's hot enough, it will flow into the lower evaporator pan, where it stays until it reaches the proper density."

"That's where I come in," I say. "I then check the thermometer to make sure it reaches seven degrees above boiling and test the density with the hydrometer." I lift the fragile glass tube so they can see what it looks like. "Once it's ready, I open the spigot so it falls into the bucket." I show them the spigot.

"Then Char and I both pour the syrup from the bucket into cone filters that are in this bigger tub where the sugar sand, niter, or calcium deposits—whatever you want to call it—are removed. Then the syrup is pumped into a finishing pan that is fired with propane gas." Janni turns to me. "Hopefully, we'll have some help with this part after today, so we can keep our minds focused on one task."

"Right. Once the syrup is in the finishing pan, you take over," I say to Candy and Stephanie with a smile. "You'll add the filter aid at this point. The syrup will boil a little more. Then it will go through the pump via the filter press for final filtering."

"This is where the filter aid is sifted out," Janni says.

Daniel walks up behind us. "Then the syrup is pumped into the syrup holding tank in the canning room. It drops into the canning tank, where it's heated to 190 degrees for bottling, and pours out of the spigot into a bottle. And that's it." He grins.

"Wow, I had no idea so much went into the syrup process," Stephanie says. "No wonder my dad always bought the imitation stuff. He said it was cheaper."

"Cheaper, but there's no comparison in taste," Janni pipes up.

"It's worth every bit of the effort," I say, smacking my lips together.

"We're not doing all that tonight, though," Daniel says. Once it goes through the evaporator, we'll shut down things and start with the filtering process tomorrow. We have more people coming to help then."

"Great. We'll be done soon, and then we'll go up to the house to start dinner preparations," Janni announces. "You kids want to join us?"

"Candy and I are going to head over for pizza," Ethan says, giving Candy a sideways hug. "You guys can come along, if you want," he says to Blake and Stephanie.

Blake turns to Stephanie, who shakes her head. "You guys go on. I'm going to finish up here."

"You don't need to stay, Stephanie. You've done your part," Janni encourages.

Stephanie looks from Janni and Daniel back to the kids and finally shrugs. "Okay, if that's what you want."

Janni smiles and waves as the kids leave.

"You have to stay, Russ. You've earned it," Daniel says with a playful punch at his friend's arm.

And they keep throwing us together, why? Daniel just doesn't get it.

Russ's gaze flits to me. For some reason, I look at the floor. Yeah, that's me. Miss Confidence comes to Tappery, and she's reduced to staring at the floor.

"Sure, I'd love to stay."

"I've got an idea," Daniel says, causing me to hold my breath. "Why don't we go to the Tappery Grill for dinner?"

Janni claps her hands as though she's just been told by Mr. Dentist that she is cavity-free.

Russ looks at me. A smile starts at his mouth and soon flickers in his eyes, causing my stomach to flutter. The thought of running occurs to me, but even a Prada sale couldn't motivate these weak knees right now.

nine

"I don't know why you get so nervous around Russ."
Janni walks over to her dresser, lifts a comb and starts teasing her hair.

"Who says I'm nervous?"

"Otherwise, why would you be eating those cookies before dinner?"
Janni's hair is now three times its normal size. One stiff wind, and we're liable to find her in Wisconsin.

"Well, if you'll glance at your watch, you will see that it is way past dinner. Besides, there are only a couple of crumbs left."

She sighs, still teasing her hair. "It took longer to do the sap than I thought it would. Oh well, at least the restaurant stays open until eleven o'clock."

She drops her hands, and her hair is sticking straight up in every direction. It's scary, really.

"You're nervous."

"That too," I say, munching through another hunk of sugar.

"For goodness sakes, Char, he's just a friend. Why are you so upset about all this?"

"Could be your hair, but I'm not sure," I warble with a full mouth behind my hand. I have some manners, after all.

"What?"

"I'm not upset. I'm fine." I root through my bag in search of more crumbs.

"I'd love to believe you, but your behavior suggests otherwise."

I stop rooting long enough to look up at her. "So what's your point?" Lifting the bag, I tilt it over my open mouth and let the crumbs fall.

After spraying her hair in place, Janni turns and gives me a hard stare. "How do you stay so thin eating like that?"

"Whoa, sis, unless you want to be enshrined in the Basketball Hall of Fame, you'd better tone that hair down."

Her hands reach up and touch it. "That bad?" She turns back to the mirror.

"Think basketball on steroids."

"Thanks. Aren't you going to get ready?" she asks, clearly wanting me out of her, um, hair.

"I'm going, I'm going. Besides, I'm out of cookies. Need to make another run to the Lighthouse Bakery."

"As I said, pathetic."

I shuffle out of her room, and once I'm out of reach, I holler, "Pathetic, but I have normal hair." A cookie fetish, yes. Bad hair, no.

The restaurant is located east of town in an area that's just starting to build up. A couple more buildings are midway through the construction process, with signs that say a plaza of some sort will be coming soon. Might be a good place for the Scottenses' store. As we make our way to the table, I claw my Palm Pilot out of my bag and scratch out a note to check into the land.

"This is great, thank you," Janni says as the hostess leads us to a large table in a back room where some of Daniel and Janni's friends are already waiting on us.

One glance at the flickering candles on the white linen tablecloths, and I feel as though I'm back in Maine where life is good and little thought is given to the cost of fine dining. I must say I'm surprised Daniel was willing to come here. He must have a coupon or something.

Russ pulls up a chair beside me. "Okay if I join you?"

He seats himself before I can answer, and I smile.

Over stuffed chicken, sautéed vegetables, chocolate mousse, and dark gourmet coffee as soft as velvet, Russ and I discuss our occupations and his life in the military. Not only am I attracted to him, but also by the time the evening is over, it occurs to me that it can't hurt to be seen on the arm of such a fine dentist while I'm in town. He's highly respected, after all, and it might give me a little leverage if I find the right land to dicker over. When I get ready to go home, there's no harm done. Just two old friends going their separate ways.

"Do you remember the time I helped you with your homework, and Eddie thought I was moving in on his territory?" Russ asks the question in total innocence, not realizing he's stirring loose the dust of old memories better left forgotten.

"Uh, I'm not sure I do."

"Oh, now that I think of it, maybe you didn't know." He takes a small bite of roll, chews, and swallows. Then he snaps his finger. "That's right. He approached me after school one day and told me to stay away from you."

I gasp. "He did? What did you do?"

"I told him it would take somebody bigger than him to keep me away from you." Russ grins, and my heart lodges smack-dab in the middle of my esophagus, allowing no air to pass whatsoever.

"Eddie was a pretty big guy. He could throw his weight around." I'm stunned that Russ would take him on. He could take him now, no doubt about it, but back then he wasn't all that meaty.

Russ laughs. "He'd have killed me, sure as I'm sitting here. But I wasn't going to let him bully me into staying away from you." Here he turns to me and looks me square in the eyes. "I liked you too much for that."

His words make my face hot. Eddie's face flashes before me. Russ's smile torments my peace of mind. The room suddenly feels small, stifling. I can't breathe.

"You okay?" Russ asks, concern in his eyes.

I claw at my jacket, and he helps me pull it off.

"You're burning up. You all right?" Now panic lines his face.

Grabbing my glass of ice water, I gulp it down. The meal is over, why torture myself? I turn to Janni, "If you'll pay for my meal, I'll pay you when you get home," I say.

"Are you all right? Your face is red." Janni looks worried.

"I'll be fine. I just want to go back to your place."

She nods.

I turn to Russ. "I'm sorry, Russ. I don't feel so well. I'm going back to Janni's. It was nice to see you again."

"Can I drive you home?"

I muster a smile. "I'm thinking Seafoam, Maine, is a little too far of a drive. See you later."

What has gotten into me? Sure, coming here brings back painful memories, but for crying out loud, I've been divorced forever. I'm not in love with Eddie anymore, so what's with me?

Shoving the car gear into park, I haul myself out and see lights on in the house. Mom's already there. I'm not in the mood to face her right now, so I grab the sketch pad from my seat and head for the barn.

The night air is cold, which is a good thing. I'm so hot my body could generate enough heat to bake cookies. Once I'm in the hayloft, I pull off my scarf and unbutton my coat.

Settling into the straw, I try to figure this out. A kitten finds her way up to me and curls around my feet, meowing here and there. Wonder if she's hungry? Before I can get up, she climbs on my lap and falls into a heap. I smile in spite of my mood.

"Oh, to have your uncomplicated life."

My head leans back against the wall. If only I hadn't agreed to come. But I wanted to show them that I've changed. Unfortunately, so far I've only managed to make matters worse and prove what an idiot I am. I'll see the syrup season and the party through, but once I get back home, I'm staying there.

I want to talk to the Lord about it, but I don't know what to say anymore. My face begins to cool, and I start feeling better. Reaching for my sketch pad, I bend my legs so I can prop it up against my knees and not bother the kitten. After grabbing a pencil from my handbag, I turn to a blank page and set to work.

Let's see, the Parnell family from my church in Maine is looking for a Cape Cod home. I'm not their Realtor, but it doesn't hurt to sketch something out for them. They're a family of four, so four bedrooms allow for a guestroom. Working my pencil feverishly against the paper, I sketch out upstairs bedrooms and baths, dormer windows, a living/dining area combo on the main level, and a kitchen. I decide a guestroom might be nice tucked into a corner on the main level to give guests easy access in and out and still give the family privacy. To me, finding the right home is as important as picking a spouse—for those who are looking for one, anyway. After all, it's where people spend the majority of their time outside of work. It should be a happy place.

"Are you all right?"

Janni's voice startles me, and I jump, causing the kitten to saunter off of my lap in search of a more restful place.

"I'm sorry, I thought you heard me come up." She climbs off the ladder. "Seeing that pad in your hand, I guess I should have known better. Always working." Boots scuffing against the floor, she walks over to me. Her bones creak as she kneels down.

"I've told you before, I don't sell residential property anymore."

"Then what are you doing?"

"Just sketching."

"So, what happened back there?"

"I'm not really sure, but I had to get out of there." A front porch would be nice on this house, a small one, but big enough for the family to sit out and visit with the neighbors.

Her hand stops my pencil in place.

"What?"

"You need to deal with things, Char. You're not the only one with a past, you know."

This from Miss Perfect. She knows nothing of my pain.

She stares at me. "I know they hurt you. It was awful what they did. But you've let them stop you from living. You don't come home because of something that happened over six years ago."

I don't say anything. I can't say anything. She doesn't understand. No one does.

"I don't mean to minimize your pain, Char. I know Eddie hurt you, but he didn't deserve you." Janni takes my hand, causing my pencil to fall and my sketch pad to teeter on my lap.

"Who says it had anything to do with them?"

"Russ is worried it's all his fault because he was talking about Eddie."

My gaze is fixed on a hay bale. "I tried to play by the book, do everything right. It doesn't work." My voice sounds hard and it startles me. Hadn't I worked through all this?

"There are no guarantees in this life, Char."

"Then what's the point of it all?"

"We do the best we can, leave the rest to God."

"That's easy for you to say."

"I won't bother you any longer. See you in the house," Janni says, edging down the stairs.

I know she's trying to help, but she only makes me feel worse. There's no way she can help me.

Someone like Janni could never understand.

Before leaving the hayloft, I decide to place a call to the Scottenses. It's better to do it in private so I don't have to hear my sister harping about me being a workaholic. After several rings, I get the Scottenses' answering machine and leave them a message about the possible property out east of town and how I will look into it unless they tell me otherwise. Just as I flip my phone closed, someone's scream brings all of us out into the cold night air. Mom's kicking and fighting, while Dad's trying to hold on to her.

"Dad, Mom, what's going on?" Janni asks.

"You see there? He's trying to kill me." Mom yanks herself free from Dad's grasp and points at him. "Milton, now what are you going to do? They caught you red-handed."

Dad lets out a tired sigh. "Forevermore, Viney, I wasn't trying to kill you. I was trying to hold you still long enough to talk some sense into you. And to see why you were peeking through the windows of our home this afternoon. You've got a key. Why didn't you just come on in?"

Mom hikes her nose. "I wasn't peeking."

"You were too."

"I thought I spotted something on the window blinds. Wanted to check it out." A rush of sharp air whips past us, and Mom shivers.

"You tried to run over me this afternoon. Admit it!" She jabs the air with her wild finger.

"You had me so flustered I put the car in reverse instead of drive. I didn't mean to do it."

"You see there?" Mom says to us. "He tried to kill me." Mom gives him one of those "mom looks" that has always struck fear in my heart. "Don't you get me started, Milton."

"Well, why don't we all go in and have some hot coffee, talk this out a little bit?" Janni suggests.

If Dad doesn't kill Mom, Janni's coffee will. No, that's not true. It's too weak to kill someone. Torture, yes. Kill, no.

"Don't you leave me in the room alone with him," Mom says in no uncertain terms. It does seem a little odd, the rat poison and the "accidentally almost running her over" thing. Still, I know my dad, and it makes no sense.

By the time we all settle at the kitchen table, everyone's calmed down a little. Though I have to say, Mom is keeping her distance. She's at the farthest point away from Dad. In all my life, I have never seen my mom afraid of anything.

"Why did you come over here?" Mom's boxing mitts are back on before the start bell can ring.

"My daughters and grandsons are here."

Mom folds her arms across her chest. "Hmmph!"

"How are the boys, Janni? I haven't seen them yet."

"They're good, Dad. They're looking forward to seeing you." Janni pours Dad a cup of coffee, adds two scoops of cream and one package of sweetener. She then fills cups around the table.

"Stop coddling him, Janni. He's trying to kill your mother." It's kind of creepy that Mom's talking about herself in third person.

"If you don't have something nice to say—" I begin, but Mom cuts off my air supply with one glance.

Okay, I see how it is. Do as I say, not as I do.

"Tell them how you stalked me today at the grocery store." Mom's lips are drawn together so tightly they're turning white.

"I wasn't stalking you, Viney. You were in the produce department. I needed tomatoes. I wanted to make that spaghetti sauce you used to make when the kids were little."

At this I let out a chuckle, and let me say, if looks could kill—well, I'm thinking there's someone walking on the wrong side of the law at this table, and just for the record, it ain't Dad.

Janni puts down the pot of coffee. "Okay, this has gone on long enough." She turns to Mom. "What possible reason could Dad have for wanting to kill you?"

"Two words. Gertrude Irene Becker."

Dad rolls his eyes.

"That's three words," I point out with a chuckle before taking a drink from my mug.

Janni gives me a dirty look. "What does Mrs. Becker have to do with this, Mom?"

"He wants to get rid of me so he can have her, that's what."

At this, I cough.

"My goodness, Viney, what has gotten into you?" Dad shakes his head.

Okay, now I have to say that even after I get my voice back, Mom's comment renders me speechless. Mrs. Becker is four times the size of my dad. She's a sweet lady, but that woman could swallow him whole. Why, if she was in the same room with him and she sneezed? She'd blow him into eternity. My head hurts just trying to wrap around the idea of these two together.

"Mom, please!" Janni says. "Mrs. Becker is a nice lady, and she would never—"

"She could charm the feathers off a chicken, that one." Mom sits ramrod straight in her chair, face pinched, sassy attitude in place.

"If you don't have something nice to say—"

Mom scoots her chair toward me, looking every inch the Terminator, and I lean back, palms up. "Okay, okay." By the time this evening is through, she will never use that phrase on me again—either that or *I'll* be dead.

"I saw the way she gave you that 'come hither' look last Sunday at church. I've seen you whispering too."

"Mom!" Janni's doing everything she can to keep from cracking a smile. "Everyone knows Mrs. Becker always has spots on her glasses. She never takes time to clean them, so she's always trying to look around the smudges. There is no way she would even know how to give a come-hither look." Janni and I both giggle together.

Mom's nose points heavenward, mouth pursed, white eyebrows arched in proper form, giving her the appearance of high society. Give her tea and crumpets, and she could pass for royalty. "Well, I know what I saw." She shifts on her chair. "Besides, your father always favored her peanut-butter pie over mine."

Dad's mouth sags open. "I never said any such thing."

"You didn't have to. I saw you take an extra piece of her pie at the church gathering a couple of weeks ago."

"Well, I eat more than that of your pies! Remember that pie you made—"

"Not the way you ate that one. You went after it as if there was no tomorrow. He's trying to get rid of me to get to her, girls. You mark my words." Her knobby finger wags at us.

"It's those doggone books you're reading, Viney. I told you that."

"What books?" I ask.

"Don't you try and change the subject, Milton Haverford," Mom snaps, all the while shoving something behind her back.

"What books? What's behind your back, Mom?" I know she's going to be so mad at me when this is all over that she'll no doubt try to put me up for adoption, but I'm not exactly in her good graces anyway. "Come on, hand it over."

"I will not. It's a romance book, and it's none of your concern," she snaps. "You mark my words, he's after Gertie Becker."

"All I know is since you started reading those books, you've been acting strange." Dad runs his hand through his balding head of hair.

"Well, now, that's real funny." Mom leans toward Dad across the table. "Tell me this, did you come up with the rat-poison idea or did Gertie?"

"Viney, that woman is *your* friend. She doesn't mean a thing to me."

The way Mom is pointing, her finger looks lethal. "You're in cahoots. I just know it, Milton Haverford. You old goat."

"Aw, talk some sense into her. I'm going home." Dad rises from his chair. His pants bag, shoulders stoop. "Tell the boys I'll be back to see them later." He shuffles into the next room where he mumbles something to Daniel then steps through the front door.

"Mom, you're wearing him out with all this nonsense," Janni says.

"I'm going to bed." Mom marches over to the sink, rinses out her cup and saucer, stacks them in the dishwasher, then stomps out of the room.

I turn to Janni. "Well, that went rather well, wouldn't you say?"

ten

"Now there's the Char we all know and love," Janni says as I slug my way into the kitchen the next morning, complete with tattered robe and Garfield slippers. "Want some coffee?" She must think I'm desperate.

I am, so I nod. At least it will get me through until I can go to the coffee shop. "Thank you," I say, sagging into my seat at the table. "What day is this?"

"Tuesday."

"I can't believe I've been here over a week already."

"Time flies when you're having fun," Janni says.

"Yeah, whatever."

"With all the money you make, Charlene Marybelle, why don't you buy yourself a decent robe?" Mom asks, joining us in the kitchen. "Hmm, that smells good, Janni."

"She spends all her money on specialty coffees," Janni says in a hoity-toity voice while lifting her pinkie.

"Bring the coffeepot over here, Janni," I say, trying to mask the growl in my voice. There is no way I can handle my mother or Miss Perfect this early in the morning without coffee. Even bad coffee will do.

Completely clueless, Mom spreads jam on her toast as though she's just having the best time.

"I like this robe," I say with upturned nose. Taking a sip from my cup, I try not to wince. "I bought it ten years ago. It's comfy, warm, and lived-in."

"Anyone can see that it's lived in," Mom says. "Wouldn't hurt to clean it once in a while."

Drink your coffee, don't say a word.

"You remind me of someone." Mom stares at me a moment then snaps her fingers. "Got it. That Maxine cartoon. You know, the one who always wears a tattered housecoat." She laughs.

Oh sure, she can joke, but I can't. I would point it out, but I'm just too tired to squabble this morning.

"Did you tell her about Russ?" Mom asks Janni.

My nerves come to life despite the small swallows of caffeine. "What about Russ?"

"Nothing really. He just called last night after you went to bed."

"Stop twinkling, Mom."

"What?" She acts all aghast. "I can't help it if I twinkle."

"Trust me, I know you can't help it." It's nothing short of a miracle if my mother twinkles. She'll sputter, spurt, and shock, but never twinkle.

"Well, it's nice, just the same. I don't know what's the matter with you, Char, passing up a perfectly good man like Russ Benson."

"I'm not passing up anybody, Mom. There's nothing there. I'm dating someone back home. I told you that."

"Dating, schmating." She tears off a hunk of toast and brings it to her mouth. "You haven't had a decent date since—"

Janni gives a slight gasp.

Mom stops herself—another miracle—and holds the toast at her mouth as though someone has clicked the remote, and we're on pause. I stare at her.

"Well, no one is forcing you to date Russ, Char. But there is no denying he is a good man," Janni says, bringing motion, and air, back into the room.

"I know." Lifting my cup, I take another drink of coffee, which, by the way, reminds me of car oil—weak car oil, mind you—though I've never actually tasted it before, I'm almost positive this is how it would taste.

"Did you look outside?" Mom asks, pulling back the kitchen curtain so we can see. "Bet we won't get much sap today."

Beyond the window, snowflakes swirl and flutter about the air before piling on the ground.

"Aw, it's supposed to be gone by afternoon," Daniel says, his boots scraping across the kitchen floor when he enters the room. "I'm covered at the store, so I'll be collecting sap today. The boys will be down in a minute. They're helping. You coming?" he asks Janni, point-blank.

"Yeah, we're coming. I've already taken care of the animals."

Excuse me, people, but is it too much to ask to start my day with a cup of coffee, albeit bad coffee, and a moment of silence? I may have to change my Bible reading to morning so I'll have the strength to face all this.

Just a few more weeks and my life will be back to normal in Maine—hopefully, my mind will be too.

By the time we've finished bottling the last bit of syrup for the day, my joints are screaming like a woman in labor. Okay, I don't know anything about that, but I've heard stories.

Everyone else has left the Sugar Shack. I told Janni I'd lock up as soon as I put away the last crate of bottles. Once I'm done, I pull on my coat and step outside into the cold air. We didn't get a lot of sap today. Hopefully, the days will grow milder soon.

Just outside the door, I roll my head from side to side to ease my aching muscles, then I lock the door.

"Tough day, huh?"

My hand flies to my throat, and I swing around. "Russ, you startled me."

"I'm sorry. I was sure you heard me crunching through the snow. I'm not exactly graceful."

That makes me laugh. We fall into step with one another. We hit a rough patch of ground and Russ tenderly reaches for my arm, guiding me forward, causing my throat to constrict.

"I came down here to see if I could help, but Janni told me everything was done for today, and you were finishing up."

I stop to look at him.

"What?"

"Why are you doing this? You work all day then come here. It's exhausting work." We walk again.

"Isn't it obvious?" The way he says it makes my heart catch. "Janni and Daniel are my good friends."

A flicker of disappointment shadows my heart and heat climbs my face. "Oh sure, I know, um, well, right." I stumble over my tongue and trip over a littered branch all at the same time. Russ grabs my arm once again to steady me, causing my face to warm.

"You okay?"

"Yeah." I brush away the comment. "I'm fine." I'm a fine—idiot. This is Janni's fault. She's filled my mind with ideas about Russ. Ideas that obviously aren't true. He isn't here for me, he's here for them. He's just nice to me. I was stupid to think it was any more than that.

Russ gazes up at the sky. "It's great being outdoors. Doesn't matter if it's cold or hot. Since I'm stuck in a stuffy building all day, I can hardly wait to do something outside."

We talk along the way about the party plans and the string quartet I hired for the elaborate affair.

Large, fluffy snowflakes drift among the trees, muffling our footsteps to soft patters. As we edge closer to the house, a thump wallops my backside and I swing around.

"You've been hit," Russ says with a throaty laugh. He points to my coat where a snowball has obviously splattered and fallen away, leaving a dusty, white powder behind.

We glance around us. Quiet giggles fringe the air.

"There!" Russ scoops a chunk of snow between his gloves, packs it into a ball and wallops Blake in the arm as he runs for cover. Soon Ethan, Candy, and Stephanie shoot out from behind trees, laughing, darting through the snow, torpedoing us with more snowballs. I haven't had a workout like this in days. Okay, months. Years?

"Hey, let's build a snowman," Blake says when we reach the backyard.

"You go in the house and get a scarf, hat, and buttons for his face," Stephanie says. For being the new kid on the block, she's a little bossy. Reminds me of someone—oh yeah, me.

"How about while you're doing that, we'll go in and get some hot chocolate started?" I smile at the kids. They agree and set to work. As Russ and I head for the porch, he grabs my arm and turns me to him.

"Hang on a second." Pulling off his glove, he reaches up and brushes snow from my face. The warmth of his fingers flames my skin. "I thought you might get cold." His words are thick as his eyes search mine, taking my breath away. He smiles, and we once again make our way to the porch.

With the way my heart is racing, I hope I can handle the stairs.

It's hard to imagine Janni and I came from the same womb. Once I stepped into the kitchen, I would have scooped some hot chocolate mix in heated water and called it a day. Better still, I'd have gone to the local coffee shop and ordered a steaming cup. Not

Janni. She has milk heating on the stove with a homemade chocolate sauce that could make Ben and Jerry sit up and take notice. Not only that, but also she's prepared a batch of homemade maple bars. She's a Martha Stewart wannabe.

In the front room, the kids clamor through the door. Boots come off. Coats, scarves, and hats are dumped to dry.

While Janni stirs the chocolate mixture on the stove and I gather some mugs, Blake comes into the kitchen, walks up behind Janni, and gives her a full-fledged hug. "Smells great, Mom."

Must be wonderful to be a mom.

She shivers. "Thanks, but you're getting snow on me and on my clean floor."

He laughs and backs away. "Okay, okay."

"It's about ready, so if you want to gather the others, that would be great."

He nods, starts to leave then turns back to Janni. "You know, sometimes we think things are going to be worse than they really are," he says.

Janni and I stare at him.

"You having a deep moment, Blake?" I ask.

"Well, it's just that I thought this week was going to be a bust, what with Ethan having Candy here and all. I know that's selfish. But I'm having a great time—with everyone." He flashes a blinding grin—Russ must have worked on his teeth—and goes back outside.

"Wonder if a certain young woman is why he's changed his mind about this week," Janni says with a wink.

"Stephanie is cute." We lift ladles of the velvety drink from the kettle and pour it into mugs.

"Yeah, she is. I'm glad Daniel brought her here. She's a hard worker."

Just then Stephanie walks into the room. "Can I help with anything?" She turns to Blake. "You'd better get those clothes off. You're dripping all over your mom's floor."

Blake grins. "You women are all alike."

It tickles me to no end that she's so bossy with Blake when she hasn't known him long. She'll fit right in with the rest of us—well, me anyway.

Janni smiles and puts a dollop of marshmallow creme on the last mug. "We were just talking about what a hard worker you are. If you want to help us set the mugs on the table, that would be great."

"Sure." Stephanie walks over to the counter, grabs a couple of filled mugs, and carries them to the table while I grab napkins and plates. She puts the maple bars on a serving plate.

Once the kids are served, we take a tray of mugs of hot chocolate and a plate of maple bars in to Daniel and Russ in the family room and place the tray on the coffee table.

The kids' laughter wafts from the other room, the fire crackles in the hearth, and the hot chocolate and sweet bars soothe while we enjoy each other's company. Why don't I do this more often? Though Peter and I have friends over occasionally, I don't really stop to savor the moments. I fuss about how the house looks, whether the food will get cold before we eat—all things that don't really matter if we're having a good time.

"This is so nice," Janni says with a sigh as she eases into her chair.

Daniel stretches his legs onto the ottoman in front of him. "I'm worn-out." He looks at Janni. "I didn't tell you, but Ralph Knight, the guy who retired last year? He's working for me while I stay here to do the sugaring. He wanted a few hours, and I could use the help so I don't have to go back and forth."

"Sounds like a good idea," Janni says.

I take my place beside Russ on the sofa and bite into a maple bar. They're pretty good. Not bakery-good, but good. "Ariel's Bakery in Maine that I told you about makes this fabulous double-fudge chocolate chip cookie. I should have some sent here so you can try them."

"I prefer homemade cookies, myself," Janni says with a lift of her chin. "Specifically, oatmeal."

"That just goes against the laws of nature."

"What?"

"Throwing something healthy like oatmeal in with a decent batch of sugar. It's wrong, Janni. Don't you ever do that."

She blinks but refuses to be deterred. "Homemade cookies may take more time than running out and buying goodies, but my family is worth it."

Is she rubbing it in my face—that I have no family? "I wasn't putting down your cookies, Janni, I was merely stating that—"

"I know what you were stating, Char. Money is too hard to come by in this family to go traipsing off to the coffee shop or bakery at our every whim."

"Money is hard to come by? I don't think so. You said yourself that Daniel could retire if he wanted to."

"Hey, we're going to play a round of Aggravation. Anyone want to join us?" Ethan asks.

"A game of Sorry might be fun," Daniel jumps in.

We all get the subliminal message. There's already enough tension in this room to choke a horse. Ethan gives us a strange look.

"You kids go on without us," Daniel says.

"I'm not saying there's anything wrong with homemade stuff, Janni. But since I don't cook or bake, buying from the bakery works for me." Before she can rant about her Martha Stewart ways, I turn to Russ. "So, Russ, how are your parents getting along?"

He blinks, obviously feeling caught in a familial war zone. "They're doing great, really. Dad's glad to finally slow down a little from the office. I think he might be driving Mom crazy, though." He chuckles.

"We know all about that, don't we, Janni?" Daniel says, attempting to ease the tension.

"What's up?" Russ asks.

"You don't want to know," Daniel says with a laugh. "Viney works for you. That should answer your question."

Russ's right eyebrow shoots toward his hairline. "Oh," he says with a nod.

It's obvious we don't have to say another word.

"She thinks Dad is trying to kill her," I say, as my blood pressure calms down a bit.

"Good thing she's not here, or you'd be in trouble," Janni says, slowly getting over her snit.

"Have you seen our dad?" I ask Russ. "He's as scrawny as some of Janni's chickens."

"Hey!" Janni says.

I'm not sure if she's offended over the chickens or Dad. Most likely anything I say from here on out will rub her wrong.

"You mean she's staying here?" Russ asks.

"You didn't know?" I take another sip of chocolate.

He shakes his head.

"I thought she would have told you by now," Janni says. "Maybe that's a good sign. Means she might go back home."

"Soon, I hope," Daniel says, and Janni hits him on the arm.

"It's not fit for man nor beast out there." We hear Mom's voice calling from the front room.

"Speak of the devil."

"Char! She's still our mother."

"Could have gotten switched by mistake at the hospital. I'm holding out for that one," I mumble.

Daniel laughs, then stops when Mom enters the room. We exchange pleasantries as Mom settles into her seat on the sofa. I'm just thankful we're not in the living room. That sofa scares me.

"You're keeping my place nice and tidy, Viney. Thanks for doing such a good job," Russ says.

Mom brightens as though she's been handed a bouquet of roses. "You have a nice place. Large condo with a small yard so you don't have to mess with it." She turns to me. "You need a place like that, Char."

"I have a place, Mom. Aunt Rose's cottage is perfect for me."

"It's too small. You have the money to get something nicer."

"It's a cottage—not exactly a dump." Shall we talk about Janni's carpet?

"Still, in your line of work you should be entertaining more, getting your name out there."

She's such an expert. At everything. I sigh.

"I love Char's house," Janni defends. "She lives alone, Mom. It's not as though she needs tons of room."

Thank you for pointing that out. In front of Russ, no less.

We discuss real estate, gas prices, and world economics. Just when I think my brain will explode, my cell phone rings. It's a client.

"I'd better take this. Good night everyone." I smile at Russ.

As I stand to leave, he catches my hand and gives it a quick squeeze. "'Night, Charley."

The brush of his hand causes emotions to tangle inside of me like an unruly vine. I can't get to my room fast enough.

Once I'm ready for bed and sink between my sheets, I think over the evening and Mom's comments about my house. Seems no matter what I do, I can't please her.

Funny how after all these years, as a forty-seven-year-old woman, I'm still looking for my mother's approval. Then there's Janni with her constant reminder that I need to "let go." I have let things go, haven't I, Lord? I'm sure I have. It's just that coming back here stirs up old memories. A pain so tangible, it haunts every breath I take. I can't help that. It doesn't mean I haven't forgiven Linda and Eddie. It's just hard to forget. That's all it is. I reach for my Bible.

Forgiving is a process.

Forgetting is impossible.

eleven

After picking up gold ribbon at the store, I stop at the bakery to pick up some more cookies. Just when I open the door, I see the unthinkable. Dad and Gertie sitting at a table together. They don't see me, so I race back to my car. I suppose I should approach them, but I have no clue what to say. I need time to sort this out. Maybe Mom's right after all.

I head back to Janni's house, step inside, and see Janni sprawled out on the sofa. "What's wrong with you?"

"Totally zapped of energy," she says. "Sometimes I wonder if it's worth all the work."

With the threat of my maple syrup supply dwindling, my senses sharpen. "How can you say that, Janni? Why, maple sugaring is much more than the work. It's tradition. It's family. It's—"

"Tomorrow's breakfast," she says dryly.

"Well, that too." I pull off my gloves and jacket and put them in the closet, then turn to her. "Besides, we didn't even make syrup today. Doesn't it help when we get a day or two in between?" I make myself comfy on the rocker.

"I guess."

"Maybe you're staying up too late to work on that scrapbook. All that cutting and pasting. If you ask me, you're a frustrated second grader."

"Oh, that's cute." She sits up and plumps her pillow, holding it tightly in front of her belly. She's got that hair thing going on. It's not Betty Bouffant, though, I'll give her that. It puts me more in mind of a used Brillo pad. Funny how I notice those things. Must be a gift. "I'm pleased with what I'm getting done on the scrapbook. Some of those letters that people have sent are priceless."

"Which reminds me. Do you think Mom and Dad still have the topper from their wedding cake?" The gentle rocking in this rocker makes me think I could do the grandma thing—if I had any grandkids.

"Yeah, they do. Mom showed it to me one day when we were going through some things at the condo."

"I thought it would be nice to use it on the cake for the party."

Janni nods with little enthusiasm.

"Also, I wanted to ask you to choose some people who could share some favorite memories they have of Mom and Dad. You know the folks better than I do." Flipping open my notebook, I make some notes. When I close it, I realize she hasn't said anything, and I look up. "Is that all right?"

"Whatever you want. Since this seems to be your party."

It's just best to leave that alone. "Listen, Janni, I just saw something disturbing."

She stiffens. "What is it?"

I explain about seeing Dad and Gertie at the bakery. "Is that weird?"

"That is strange. If they were working on a project for church, wouldn't he tell Mom?"

"If you were him, would you tell Mom?"

"Good point. Well, we'd better keep an eye on things."

I nod. "Still getting cards in the mail?"

"Every day. Folks sure love them."

I stop a moment and scratch the heel of my right foot, which, by the way, is still recovering from Wiggles's attack. I glance at the caged squirrel. Satisfied that he's not going to bother me, I turn back to Janni. "Where is everybody?"

"The boys took the girls to a movie, I think. Daniel's over at the store. Mom's at the library."

"Hope she doesn't spot Dad and Gertie together or it's hard to tell who will hurt whom."

"There has to be an explanation." Janni yawns and stretches rather unenthusiastically, then slumps back into the sofa. *The* sofa, by the way. My fingers are mere inches from punching 911 on the cordless.

"Are you sure you're all right, Janni?"

"It's like my ambition is gone. I don't care about much of anything."

"Are you pregnant?"

"Ha-ha."

"It's been known to happen to women your age, you know."

"It would take a small miracle at this point."

Oh, how I would have loved such a miracle a few years ago.

Janni runs her fingers through her hair, and they get stuck in a curl, so her fingers work through it. She turns to me. "Besides, that kind of excitement never happens around here. I told you before, I have a boring life."

"How can you possibly say that? You're one of the busiest people I know, always taking care of other people, seeing to their needs, watching over your boys, your household."

"You see, that's just it. I'm tired of taking care of everyone else."

This is so not Janni.

"I know that sounds selfish, but it's true." She stands up. "I'm sick of this stupid farm, the store, everything." She throws the pillow onto the sofa, and I'm wondering if I should back out of the room and re-enter.

"Why did you buy this place last year if you didn't want to be here?"

"You couldn't understand."

"What's to understand? I thought you loved this place and didn't want the family to lose it."

"That's exactly it. Mom and Dad love this place and didn't want the family to lose it. For once in my life, I wanted to do the responsible thing."

"What do you mean, for once in your life? You've always been the responsible one, Janni." This conversation has definitely taken a turn south, a direction in which I hadn't planned to travel.

Just then the front door shoves open. "Anybody home?" Mom calls out.

"I need to go check on the animals," Janni says.

"I'll do it. You just rest."

Janni's comments surprise me. She must be going through some midlife crisis, perimenopause or something. Daniel would be well-advised to hibernate for a year or two.

Mr. Ed whinnies as I step inside the barn. I think he favors me because he gets his food and water quickly when I'm in charge.

"Well, hello, Mr. Ed." His ears perk forward, and he edges toward me. I give him some oats and check his water supply. Grabbing the pitchfork I poke at some hay in the bale Janni threw down earlier this morning. He nudges me. I want to think it's his way of saying thanks, but the truth of the matter is he's checking my coat pockets for sugar.

We're alike, Mr. Ed and I.

I move forward to check on Elsie and Tipsy when I hear a noise. My heart freezes in my chest. I stop and listen. Nothing but Mr. Ed shifting in his stall and flapping his lips.

When I'm about to move on, I notice hay drifting from the hayloft. Someone is up there. My breath sticks in my chest.

"Who's there?" I call out. Yeah, right, like anyone's going to answer.

Clearing of throat. "Um, Aunt Char?"

My body teeters. Taking a moment to steady myself, I then look up to see Blake leaning over the hayloft with Stephanie right behind him.

My eyes grow wide. I know this, because I now see in a panoramic view.

"Aunt Char, this is not what you think," he begins.

Yeah, whatever. "I thought you went to a movie."

"We didn't go."

Okay, do I look stupid? "You shouldn't be out here like this, Blake." I'm irritated, and my voice shows it.

They climb down the ladder. "We were talking."

"Let me handle this," Stephanie insists. "I'm going to tell her, Blake."

"That's not necessary, Steph," he says.

"Excuse me, let me be the judge of that."

"Don't tell Mom, okay, Aunt Char?"

"Tell her what?"

"I'm going to talk to your mom too," Stephanie says matter-of-factly, brushing hay from her shoulders.

"About what? Blake, we trusted you." Though he's not my son, I've always loved these boys like they were my own.

"I didn't do anything, Aunt Char." He holds up his hands as though I'm Marshal Dillon, and he's on the other side of the law.

"See, Blake. I'm going to tell her," Miss Take Charge says, causing my blood pressure to rise.

"Would you please stop talking about it and just tell me?" My toe is tapping here, and it's not a happy tap.

"We were talking," Blake says.

"That's the best you can do?"

"It's the truth."

"Why not talk in the house?"

"We wanted some privacy," he defends.

"You could have gone into the living room or the kitchen."

"It's not the same."

"It's like this," Stephanie begins.

"Don't tell her."

"Tell me what?"

They're going back and forth again. I'm tired, and they're getting on my last nerve. I lift the pitchfork in attack position, feeling every inch the bad cowboy caught up in an episode of *Bonanza.* "Tell me, doggone you."

Blake looks worried—as well he should be.

"You have to promise not to tell Mom."

"Excuse me, is there something in the way I'm holding this pitchfork that gives you the idea you have bargaining power?"

His Adam's apple bobs with a loud gulp. "Then we're not telling you," Blake says, giving Stephanie a warning glance. The firm set of his jaw shows me he means it. I've never seen Blake like this. I have half a mind to prick his boot.

"He was going to let me stay here tonight," Stephanie says.

"Oh, man, Steph, why'd you go and tell her?"

My jaw slackens, and I stare at her. "Stay here? In the barn? All night?"

"She needs a place," Blake jumps in.

"Why? Did it not work out with your new friend?" Referring to the place where she was staying with another girl she'd met only a few weeks ago.

"No. Her boyfriend moved in last night. Things got a little crazy."

My heart squeezes. I turn to my nephew. "That still doesn't explain what you're doing out here."

"She needed some blankets and stuff." He stares at his boot.

"What's the big deal? You know your mom would want to help you. Why didn't you just ask her, Blake?"

"I know. But she's going through something right now. She's acting,

I don't know, kind of weird. I didn't think she could handle it. She's all stressed out or something."

"Your mom is a little tired, but that wouldn't stop her from helping Stephanie for a night or two."

"Blake, are you out there?" Janni's voice calls from the porch.

"She must have spotted my car. Be right back." He pokes his head through the door. "Yeah, I'll be right there, Mom." He walks over to Stephanie and gives her hand a quick squeeze. "Let me know if you need anything else."

When Blake leaves the barn, I look back to Stephanie. "I'm sure Janni would have no problem with you staying inside. You can't stay out here all night or you'll freeze."

"I've stayed in worse than this."

Something in the way she says that makes me believe her.

"I'm not sure where to begin, but I need to talk to you," Steph says, as she gears up to tell me something. What's to begin? Is she planning to take up residence or something? An overnight stay does not merit a "serious discussion." Hopefully, she and Blake aren't getting serious already. They've only known each other a few days, after all.

Before Stephanie can say anything further, a police siren screams in the distance, growing in volume. Tires squeal, gravel crunches, and all finally come to a stop just short of ramming into the barn—or so it sounds.

"What is going on, Officer?" I ask Toby Millington as we rush out of the barn. There he stands, by the squad car, red and blue lights swirling around us.

"Ask her," he says, pointing to Mom as she steps sheepishly out of her car.

"Viney Haverford, I don't know what you think you were doing, trying to outrun the law like that. If your husband hadn't been my pastor all my life, I'd lock you up."

Toby is plenty steamed, but Mom was his Sunday-school teacher years ago. I know good and well she put the fear of God in him. He won't mess with her. Though I'm thinking a night in jail could do her a world of good.

"Mom! What happened?" Janni asks, stepping out the front door. "You all right?" She climbs down the steps to stand by Mom.

"She's all right. You might want to check with Officer Millington here on how he's doing, though." I chuckle.

"This is serious business, Char. Someone could have been killed," he says.

"That's what I always tell her," Mom joins in. "She thinks everything is a joke. I taught her better than that."

"Wait. This is not about me." Maybe I'll go back in the barn and get that pitchfork.

"All I know is some man was stalking me." There's that gnarly finger again looking like it's going to poke out an eyeball. She strikes fear in my heart every time she does that. That's the very same finger she used to wag under my nose when I did something wrong as a kid. "I think your father put him up to it."

"Oh, Mom, you can't be serious," Janni says.

"I am too," Mom snaps.

"She ran a red light—"

Janni and I gasp simultaneously.

"—almost hit another car and then when I came after her, she hit the gas and didn't stop till we got here."

Janni turns to Mom. "What were you thinking? You could have been killed."

Mom makes a face and stares at her shoe as she scuffs it into the dirt.

"I hate to do it, but I gotta give you a ticket, Viney."

Mom's head shoots up. "You'll do no such thing, young man. I'll march you right over to your parents."

"Mom." Janni grabs Mom's arm. "Toby is no longer in your Sunday-school class. He represents the law in this town, and you can't talk to him that way."

"I can and I will."

This adds fuel to the flames. Toby's eyes turn a livid blaze of brown. He gets out his ticket holder and starts scribbling like there's no tomorrow.

I edge over beside Mom. When she sees him writing furiously on the ticket, she gets that look on her face that spells trouble and opens her mouth to speak, but Janni and I both clamp our hands over her mouth in the nick of time. She kicks up gravel with her feet, but we won't let her make nary a peep.

"I'm sorry to give you this, Viney, but I have to do my job." Since we have her arms held down, he extends the ticket to Janni. Mom contorts and twists her body and her feet paw at the ground while she tries to break free from our grasp. Picture a snorting bull in front of a waving red cape. If Toby knows what's good for him, he'll skip the lecture and get out of Dodge.

"See you later, ladies. Give my best to Pastor Haverford." He tips his hat, climbs back into his car, and leaves.

Smart man.

Once he's out of earshot, we drop our hands. I rub my aching arms and shoulders, noting that I haven't exercised this much in months.

"Why did you cover my mouth?" Mom's eyes are shooting fire. Her arms are waving. "I aimed to give that young man a piece of my mind."

"Come on, Grandma," Blake says, putting his arm around her, "let's go in the house and get some ice cream."

Janni rolls her eyes, and we all turn to go inside.

Before following the others, I take a quick glance behind me and get a glimpse of the back of Mom's car. The license plate stops me in my tracks. Instead of the usual numbers found on the plate, black letters tiptoe across it, spelling out the words BE SWEET.

It could be me, but I'm thinking that's just wrong.

twelve

"Hey, Aunt Char, you'd better hurry up and get in here before Blake eats all the ice cream," Ethan calls out when Stephanie and I enter the house. Ethan and Candy share a laugh, and he gives her a hug. I remember being young and in love once . . .

Spoons clack against bowls, spirits are high. Emotions tangle inside me.

"You'd better leave me some," I say, giving Blake a playful punch in the arm.

"I saved you some. In fact," he says, reaching into the cupboard for a bowl, "I will make you a special creation of my own."

Janni turns and stares at him. "You're serving her?" She walks over and puts her palm on his forehead. "When is the last time you've had a checkup?"

"Hey, I have my moments of charity," he says. "Especially where Aunt Char is concerned. She's my favorite aunt."

"I'm your only aunt, but I'm okay with that."

Blake shrugs, and the others laugh. Once he finishes his creation, he hands the bowl to me, and then we join the others at the table.

"Would you look at that," Mom says in wonder when she sees my bowl piled high with ice cream, banana slices, maple syrup, and whipped cream.

"This boy has missed his calling," I say, patting Blake on the back.

"For this we spend big bucks to send him to a university?" Daniel works the scissors around an ice cream coupon in the paper. "Can't you learn that at the community college?"

Blake drops his spoon and stares at his dad. "Their creative department is lacking, Dad."

"What made you think someone was following you, Grandma?" Ethan asks abruptly.

We are now entering a war zone.

"Because he was," she snaps, while using her spoon to chase the last slurp of ice cream around her bowl.

"How do you know he was following you and not just going in the same direction?" Blake asks with a grin and a wink.

Oh sure, stir up a hornets' nest, then go back to school.

"All I know is when I turned right, he turned right. When I went left, he did too. That's just beyond coincidence in my book," she says with attitude.

"Mom, this is a small town. There aren't a whole lot of different ways to get somewhere," I say dryly.

She stares at me so long, I'm afraid if the light catches in her glasses just right, she'll burn a hole in my face.

"He was following me." Mom says this in such a way as to stop all further conversation right here and right now.

Janni and I exchange a glance. We have to get Mom help. The question is: how do we get Mom to do anything she doesn't want to do?

"I hope it warms up soon. Those taps aren't flowing as good as last year." Daniel stomps his boots against the floor of the doorframe.

"It will work out. It always does," Janni says. She slugs over to the coffeepot and pours him a cup.

He eyes Janni a moment. "You doin' okay, honey?"

"I'm fine." Her body language says otherwise. She sits in a chair at the table and takes a drink from her coffee cup. That could be the problem right there.

Daniel turns to me. "How are you today, Char?"

"Can't complain." If I did complain, it would be about the coffee, but in one of my rare moments of restraint, I keep my mouth shut.

"Since you get a reprieve from the sap, you ought to take time for a fun girls' day," he says to Janni, surprising me.

"Hey, that's a great idea," I say, turning to Janni. "You up for it?"

"What's there to do around here?"

"Oh, I don't know. I thought because you live in a historic town with quaint shops and cozy cafés that are mere miles from beautiful scenes of Lake Michigan that we might be able to come up with something."

"It's too cold to enjoy the lake."

"Oh come on, Janni. There's plenty to do around here. We could even go for a massage, if you want."

"The boys are home. I don't want to leave them."

"You don't need to worry about us," Blake says as he shuffles into the kitchen, bed-head and all. "We can find plenty to do." He flashes an ornery grin and wiggles his eyebrows.

My thoughts flit to Stephanie, and I'm wondering if she stayed warm enough last night.

"I know, but I want to spend time with you while you're here."

"We thought we might go bowling later," Ethan says, sauntering into the kitchen with Candy right behind him. He grabs a box of cereal. "You can go with us."

Janni doesn't look interested. "I'm not in the mood to bowl."

"Well, you can think about it," Ethan says, sitting down at the table with his cereal in tow.

"Okay," she says, as in, "whatever."

"We'll take care of the animals this morning, Mom," Ethan says. "Candy wants to see how we feed them."

Blake gives me a glance and a nod as if to say they know about Stephanie being in the barn.

"Thanks," Janni says.

We talk to the kids while they eat their cereal, then Janni fills her cup with another round of coffee and suggests we go into the living room. I'm wishing I had some of Ariel's cinnamon rolls here. Maybe I'll call her later and order some goodies to get me through this visit. Needing caffeine, I grab my cup of motor oil—er, uh, coffee—and follow Janni into the living room.

"You know, we had better call Stephanie and let her know she doesn't need to come to work today." Janni settles into the sofa that kidnaps people. Still, when I glance at her disappearing thighs, I'm thinking the sofa could become my friend.

My brain scrambles for a response. "Uh, yeah." Am I not great with words?

Janni reaches for the phone.

"You know, maybe we should have Blake call her so you can enjoy your coffee while it's still hot."

She smiles. "He does seem drawn to her, doesn't he?"

"Blake," I yell before she can change her mind.

He pokes his head into the living room. "What's up?"

"Your mom thought someone should call Stephanie and let her know not to come to work today since we're not sugaring." Blake throws me a knowing glance.

"Oh, okay, I'll get ahold of her," he says.

"Can you believe we're edging fifty, Char? We'll be senior citizens in the blink of an eye." Janni stares glumly into her coffee cup.

I laugh. "What in the world brought that on?"

She looks up at me. "Oh, I don't know. Maybe going through the old pictures of Mom and Dad and seeing how fast the time has gone. Only yesterday, Mom was fifty."

"Thanks for the reminder. Now you're starting to sound like Dad." Her depression is sucking me in like a vacuum, but I'm resisting every step of the way.

"See what I mean? We're old."

"Speak for yourself. I'm middle-aged, thank you very much."

"Only if you plan to live until you're ninety-four."

I blink. "Huh?"

"Forty-seven times two equals ninety-four. That would make forty-seven middle age for you. Frankly, I doubt if you'll live that long with the way you eat cookies."

Reality hits me between the eyeballs. "I'm *past* middle age?" The words strangle me. A moment of desperation zips through me, but I roll up my sleeves and bulldoze it away. "I am not past middle age," I hiss.

"You're in denial."

Right now I'm ready to hurt her. "Before you go any further, I feel it's only safe to warn you that your Christmas present is on the line."

"Fair enough. But it's still true."

"Janni, what has gotten into you? Up until now, you've been one of the most upbeat people I have ever known. Is this your dark side?"

"Yes, I guess that's what you could call it." She swirls her spoon around her coffee.

"Well, snap out of it," I say with no compassion whatsoever. "Reminds me of Mom. You need some fun in your life."

"That's just it. As I told you, I'm tired of all this." Her hand sweeps the air.

"Is there something else you'd rather be doing with your life?" I take a sip from my mug and try to pretend it's a macchiato. It's not working for me.

"I don't know." More peering into her coffee. Maybe she's noticing that car oil thing. "Bungee jumping?"

That little comment almost makes me spurt coffee from my nose.

She glares. "What? You don't think I'm adventurous enough?"

"I'm thinking a wild night of scrapbooking is more your cup of tea." Maybe I should buy her a Hula Hoop. Excitement and exercise all in one package, saying nothing of the safety factor compared to bungee jumping. "It's hard for me to understand this, Janni. You have a perfect life. A Walton kind of life, you know? A family that loves you, lots of friends, security, all that."

"That's easy for you to say. Miss I-own-a-cottage-on-the-beach-and-a-BMW-with-plump-leather-seats."

Somebody is bitter.

"Material things, Janni. They can't love you when you're lonely or help you when you're sick. But you—you have family." Even as the words come out of my mouth, they startle me. The reality of the comment sinks in. That's me. I'm alone. Emotions lurk behind my eyeballs, and I'm thinking Janni's mood is affecting me big-time.

"It's not enough anymore," she says in a whisper.

"Where are you in that whole perimenopause thing?" I ask.

Her head darts up. "I have no idea what you're talking about. I've got a long ways to go before I get into all that."

"You are forty-five, Janni. Some women start as early as forty."

"Well, I don't." Her bark has a Doberman Pinscher quality to it.

"It's not a bad thing. It's a fact of life. Happens to all of us. Though I have to say, it's never bothered me much."

"I'm too young."

"Okay, whatever. One of the side effects is depression."

"Who's depressed?"

"And attitude. Definitely attitude."

"Who has an attitude?" she snaps.

"Come on, Janni, if I extended my hand to you, you'd bite it off."

"I would not. Well, not the whole hand anyway." She cracks a weak smile.

"Have you had any hot flashes?"

"What's that?"

"They say your body can shoot into flames out of nowhere. A total meltdown threatens you and anything within a fifty-mile radius."

She stares at me, mouth gaping. "And you've experienced this?"

I shake my head. "I've just heard stories. The good news is, if you're lost in the woods, you can rub your hands together real fast and start a fire." I laugh. She doesn't. But I'm on a roll, so I continue. "I have one friend who says her age spots are really singed skin brought on by hot flashes."

"Why would I be in perimenopause if you're not? You're older than I am."

I shrug. "Just lucky, I guess. Some people experience symptoms, some don't." I try not to appear smug, but I have to say I'm quite pleased with this little twist of fate. From what I hear, attitude is a big thing with perimenopause, so maybe Janni will be stripped of sainthood and start acting like me.

Just then my cell phone rings. It's probably just as well that we end this conversation. Give her time to think about our discussion.

"Hello?"

Janni gets up and walks over to the window and peers out. "Stephanie's coming out of the barn. Wonder what she was doing in there?"

Adrenaline shoots through me as Janni walks over to put her shoes on.

"Is this Charlene Haverford, Realtor at McDonald Realtors?" the man on the phone asks.

"Yes, it is."

"I'm Jeremiah Bell, and I am moving into your town. Lydia Harrington recommended that I contact you about a commercial property we're interested in just outside of town."

Janni's tying the last knot in her shoe, and I'm worried she'll catch Stephanie with blankets.

"Yes, well, I'm out of town, and will be for several weeks. If you need immediate assistance, you could contact Peter McDonald, or I would be happy to help you when I return in a few weeks." I give him the number.

"Well, we are in a bit of a hurry. Thanks for the number. It's a shame you can't help us. You came highly recommended."

He then rambles off my attributes, which I'm tempted to linger on, but right now I don't have the time. Stephanie and Janni are about to collide. Janni's just not in the mood for this.

"Thank you so much for considering me, but I assure you that Peter can handle your real estate needs. As I said, he is the owner, and he has an eye for a good purchase."

"That's good to know. I'll give him a call. Thank you for giving me your time."

We hang up. Most likely, I've just lost the chance to make a lot of money, but there's more at stake here. Janni is mere inches from the door.

Stephanie will have some explaining to do.

thirteen

Just as I flip my cell phone closed and head toward Janni, someone knocks hard on the upstairs bathroom door. My gaze darts from the front door where Janni's headed to the pounding upstairs.

"Who's up there?" I ask, hoping to divert Janni's attention from Stephanie.

She whips around. "I don't know. It must be Mom."

We both run up the stairs.

"What's wrong, Mom?" I ask.

"Well, what do you think is wrong?" she snaps. "I'm locked in the bathroom, and I don't have a book."

My mind just refuses to dwell on that.

"Okay, we'll get you out in a jiff," Janni says, scrambling toward her bedroom and motioning for me to follow. She closes the door behind us once we're in her room. "Last night Daniel installed a new doorknob on the bathroom door," she whispers. "I need to call him to see what to do."

"You think he'll know what to do? After all, he put it on in the first place and it's not opening," I point out.

She gives me a dirty look and picks up the phone. "He'll know. Probably something simple."

Mom pounds again on the bathroom door, and I open Janni's bedroom door to shout down the hall. "We're working on it, Mom. Just a second."

"At my age, I don't have a second," she yells back.

Mom's never been big on patience. If memory serves me—and it does—she always had a migraine on the Sundays when Dad would cover that fruit of the Spirit. Now that I think about it, that explains a lot.

With a swivel, I turn to face Janni. "She's not happy."

Janni sighs. "I know. I'm on hold. They went to get Danny."

More pounding. Janni and I roll our eyes and giggle.

"Might as well enjoy it now. Once she gets out, we're in for it."

Janni nods. "Hi, Danny. Listen, you know that doorknob you replaced on the bathroom door last night? Well, it's not working. Mom's trapped inside the bathroom." Janni frowns. "Daniel, it's not funny." Pause. "She has no book." Now her face reflects that Daniel gets the seriousness of the situation. "Uh-huh?" Janni listens, nods, and finally says good-bye.

"I guess there's some kind of tool that I need in a drawer downstairs." She sighs. "You can either go with me or stay and talk to Mom."

"Well, that's a no-brainer. I'll go with you." It's not that I'm scared of my mom or anything, but well, I could use the exercise of going up and down the stairs.

Janni throws a smile that says she totally understands, and we sneak past the bathroom in hopes that Mom won't hear us. A floorboard creaks beneath my feet.

"I'm growing mold in here! Somebody get me out." More pounding.

Mom's petite fists pack a mean wallop. I wouldn't be surprised to see her bony self come poking through the splintered door.

"Be right back, Mom. We're getting some tools."

"Oh, for heaven's sake," she says before collapsing into silence.

I clap my hand over my mouth to keep from laughing and hurry down the stairs.

"You know, we need to find a way to get her in for some help," Janni whispers. "Since she cancelled the last appointment, we'll have to think of something creative. She just can't stay here. Dad is worried sick about her. His constant calling and her paranoia are making me crazy."

"I know. We'll have to put our heads together to come up with something. Two brains are better than one—especially in our case."

"Ha-ha."

When we reach the cabinet, Janni opens two drawers. "You look through this one, and I'll look in here," she says, already burrowing into the metal debris.

"What are we looking for?" My fingers shuffle through the tools, but I have no clue what I'm doing.

She grabs a handful of metal thingamajigs and scatters them onto the countertop. "I'm not sure. Some long, skinny thingy that we can stick into that little hole in the knob."

My fingers sort and riffle through the mess while I repeat "some long, skinny thingy," over and over.

Janni doesn't see it in her pile, then starts clawing her way through mine. "I don't see it."

"Must be nice to know what you're looking for."

She moves to another drawer. "You know, that long, skinny thingy that opens doors."

"Yep, that pretty much nails it down for me."

We continue our search around the kitchen and on into the garage where Janni finally finds the tool she needs in a cardboard box tucked behind a big, unopened package of sunflower seeds. "Here it is." She waves the tool victoriously and it flies out of her hand and under the car.

Our gazes collide. "Let's lay some newspaper down so we don't get all dirty." We grab a stack from the pile of saved papers and lay them on the floor. My body sinks onto the cool cement floor, taking my temperature down twenty degrees. The heat in their house has my internal thermometer all messed up. I think I'll stay here.

"I see it," Janni says again. Her arm stretches so hard to reach it, I'm thinking she'll pop it out of her shoulder socket, but still she's about a half inch short of her goal.

"Rats. I can't reach it. 'Member how I used to call you Olive Oyl because of your long arms? Why don't you try it?"

"Flattery will get you nowhere." With a heave, I scoot myself in until I'm under the car. Stretching toward the object, my fingers grope for it, making it roll toward Janni.

"Got it." She says that as though she's just won the gold cup. The realization of my predicament washes over me. Now Mom's not the only one who's stuck. "Hey, could you bring my coffee to the garage? I'll need the caffeine to haul myself out."

"Oh come on, you can do it. I have faith in you. Besides, you can't hide from Mom forever."

Shoot. I hate it that she knows me so well. I wiggle out from underneath the car and reluctantly leave the cool cement.

"Sounds like she's settled down some. At least she's not pounding anymore," Janni whispers as we climb the stairs.

"We've got it, Mom. We'll have you out in no time," I say as Janni works the tool into the door.

Mom doesn't respond. She's plenty mad by now, I'm sure. I'm thinking once that door is open, I'm standing way back. She'll come at us like a killer bee.

"There we go," Janni says, swinging open the door while I step behind her. She gasps.

I peek over her shoulder and look with disbelief inside the bathroom. The wind is blowing cold air through the open window, the cotton curtain lifting in the breeze. Cookie crumbs dust the floor.

I've always thought Mom had a superhero mentality, but I never thought she'd actually try that flying thing.

We both scramble toward the window and look out. Mom must have stuck her feet in the ridges of the brick. Her footprints dot the snow toward the back door. We suck in air at the same time.

"What did you expect?" Mom's voice makes us jump, and we whip around.

She's standing behind us, arms folded under her chest. "Well? I told you the clock is ticking. When you're my age, you don't have time to wait in a bathroom. I've got a book to read." She waves her book and stomps down the hall and into her room, slamming the door behind her.

"When's Mom supposed to get back from cleaning Russ's condo?" I turn the fried chicken in the skillet while Janni finishes whipping the mashed potatoes. Dad is in the living room talking to Daniel and the kids about how society pushes old people into retirement whether they feel like it or not.

Janni glances at the clock on the wall. "Should be any minute." She licks the potatoes from one of the beaters. "Want one?" She stretches out the other one to me.

"No thanks. I'd rather have cookies." Of the bakery kind, mind you.

"Thanks for the reminder." Bending over, she pulls the maple cookies from the oven, then straightens herself, the look on her face telling me that her back protested. "Well, just remember to save your cookies for after dinner."

"Yeah, whatever." Since when does she tell me what to do? When I wash up for dinner, one of those chocolate chip cookies in my bag upstairs is history.

My cell phone rings. Janni rolls her eyes and leaves the room. Once I answer it the Realtor on the other end lets me know there is no more property available east of town in that area of new construction that Janni had showed me. It's too bad, because it would have been a good place for the Scottenses' store, and it's already zoned for commercial use. I thank him then click my phone closed. I'm back to square one.

Janni returns to the kitchen. "You are such a workaholic."

The front door shoves open, feet stomp on the rug and Janni looks at me.

"Mom," we say simultaneously.

"What are *you* doing here?" Her sharp voice reaches to the kitchen, and we scramble out to the living room to calm her down.

Before Dad can respond, Blake cuts in. "Now, Grandma, if you don't behave yourself, I'll have to put you in a smelly nursing home." He tosses a cheesy grin. For a moment, no one in the room breathes. A chill runs down my spine and perspiration pops over my brow.

If there's anything I've learned over the years, it's that Blake can get by saying things to Mom that no one else would ever dare say. If they did, they wouldn't live to tell about it. Still, I'm wondering at this moment if his life hangs in the balance.

She blinks. Twice. Hard. I think I hear a gulp in there too.

A chuckle sounds in the corner of the room—actually it's located around the vicinity of Wiggles's cage, but that can't be it. Pretty soon, another chuckle, until everyone is laughing and the tension is easing.

Except for Mom. Her nose tips north, and she marches herself right into the kitchen. "Janni, Char, in here. I need to talk with you." She snaps her fingers and points toward the kitchen like Barney Fife on a mission.

We reluctantly follow.

Once in the kitchen, she whips around to us. "What's the meaning of this, you two? You know that man is trying to kill me," she says, waving her finger under Janni's nose. I'm smarter than that. I stand two feet away.

Janni doesn't appear ruffled in the least. "First of all, he is not *that man.* He is my father." With deliberate, calm steps, Janni walks over to the cabinet, pulls out glasses for dinner and immediately fills them with ice. "Second, he is your husband. I will not allow this to go on another minute. We are going to talk things out. Tonight."

The frightening thing here is that Janni sounds suspiciously like our mother. If what they say is true, that we become our mothers, heaven help us all.

Mom crumples a little. For a moment I see a flicker of regret flash across her eyes. Whether the regret is over her behavior or the fact that she has to stay and talk things out, I'm not sure.

"Just don't leave me alone with him." She turns and walks out.

fourteen

Halfway through the meal, Dad speaks up. "How ya been, Viney?" He passes the potatoes the second time around the table.

Mom glances at him a moment. "I've been okay." Her shaky hands reach for her glass of water, and she takes a drink.

"You cook just like your mother, Janni," Dad says. "Your mom used to make family meals as though she was cooking for an army." Dad laughs and scratches his neck. "Used to invite over half the church so we wouldn't be eatin' leftovers for the next month."

We all laugh, and Mom visibly softens.

Dad's right. Janni is a good cook, but I just want to point out that she's still making the same meals that she's made for the past twenty years. Wonder if she ever tries any new recipes? I'm thinking no.

"You been taking your medicine?" Mom asks Dad.

"Yeah."

She nods and stares at her plate. My heart breaks for them both.

Whatever has prompted Mom's fears of Dad, her head believes it, but it appears her heart is refusing to go along.

Amid the clanging silverware and the jostle of ice cubes against glass, Dad puts down his fork and stares straight at Mom. "I miss you, Viney, and wish you were back home."

The surrounding noises come to a halt. We hold a collective breath and wait on Mom's response. To our surprise she looks up with tear-filled eyes and says, "I miss you, too, Milton."

Janni glances at me, her eyes flickering with hope.

"Well, it's about time you two saw the light," Blake teases.

Everyone smiles. Dad reaches across the table and pats Mom's hand, and suddenly her wrinkled cheeks flame red.

No need to question Dad about his meeting with Gertie. Things will blow over, and I'm sure it was nothing. My heart melts at the sight, and I try to imagine them years ago in their courting days. Their love has always been the strength of our family. That's part of my problem. I've never found anything in a relationship that comes close to what I've seen in my parents. Dad loves Mom with every inch of his heart. That's why this whole thing with Mom has been disturbing to us all. For her to doubt him shakes the foundation of our family. Maybe we're through the worst of the storm now, though.

"Hey, let's play some checkers," Ethan says, shoving his chair away from the table. He walks to Janni and stoops over her, planting a kiss on her cheek. "Great meal, Mom."

The kids all agree to play. The guys head for the living room while Janni, Mom, and I start cleanup duty.

"Mom, you go in there with Dad. We can take care of things here," Janni says. I want to bop her. Three pairs of hands are better than two, after all.

"I've always done my part, Janni, you know that," Mom says, rolling up the sleeves of her blouse and checking the water temperature at the faucet.

Janni and I walk over to the table while Mom gets the dishes going.

"Maybe she'll go home tonight," Janni whispers with unabashed glee.

"Don't hold your breath," I say.

Janni frowns at me. "If there's a bubble of joy in the room, you have a way of popping it," she whispers.

"I'm a realist, Janni. History tells me things are never this easy where Mom is concerned."

A dull shadow replaces the shimmer in her eyes. Just call me the joy snatcher. Why can't I let her live in her own reality, a place where everything is rose-colored and happy? She needs that. Especially now, when the walls of her world are turning gray. I catch up to her before she's too close to Mom.

"You're probably right. Maybe we should pack her clothes for her before she changes her mind."

Janni's smile lifts back in place, eyes mischievous and conspiring. Eyebrows arched. "Yeah."

By the time the kitchen sparkles and we've discussed the basics of house decorating, the kids have finished two games of checkers and the guys are almost finished with their movie.

"Where's Mom?" I ask when we enter the family room, chocolate chip cookie in hand.

"She went to her room for a minute," Daniel says.

"You got any apples, Janni?" Dad asks with a grin. If that old adage about an apple a day keeps the doctor away is true, my dad should live to be a hundred and fifty-two. He loves apples.

"Yeah, there's a bowl of apples on the counter," she says. "I'll get you one."

"No, you sit yourself down. You've been working all evening. I'll get it myself." Dad pushes himself off out the chair and heads for the kitchen.

"Boy, things are going great," Daniel says, rubbing his hands together. "I wouldn't be surprised if your mom was upstairs packing to go home now."

Janni practically salivates. "Really?"

Daniel gives a vigorous nod.

Janni turns to me. "What do you think now, Miss Realist?"

I smile, wanting desperately to say, "Don't hold your breath," but I keep still. Time will tell. Mom's walking down the stairs right now. With the third bite of my cookie, a twinge of discomfort calls from a back molar.

"Where's your dad?" she asks.

"He's in the kitchen, getting an apple."

Mom flashes a smile and heads for the kitchen.

"Did you see that grin? I'll bet she's going to tell him she'll go home with him tonight," Janni says.

"Let's go see," I whisper.

Daniel shakes his head, grins, and picks up the coupon section of the newspaper.

Janni muffles a giggle behind her hand and follows close behind me as we skulk toward the kitchen.

"Milton, I wanted to talk to you a minute," Mom says.

We hear him turn around. Mom screams, and her brittle bones clatter into a heap on the floor.

Janni rushes to Mom, kneels beside her to make sure she's still breathing. She is.

I dart forward to see if Dad's all right. One glimpse at him, my jaw goes slack and my vision blurs. Time seems to stand still while Dad stands before us, rigid posture, eyes glazed. He doesn't move an inch, but it's what I see in his hand that causes my breath to catch in my chest.

It's a machete. And it's pointed straight at us.

Okay, so I'm exaggerating a little. It's not exactly a machete, but Dad is holding a kitchen knife. A big one. He blinks, then throws the knife into the sink and runs to Mom. "You okay, Viney?"

"Don't you touch me," she hisses, jerking her arm away. Mom scrambles to her feet and points the bony finger that makes grown men tremble. "We caught you red-handed." She pokes him in the chest with a thump that makes *my* chest hurt.

"Caught me what?" he asks, completely clueless. He's backing away while she continues to stab him with her index finger. Finally, the lights come on. His eyes grow wide. "Why, Viney, you don't think—"

"Yes, I do think, Milton Haverford. You and Gertie are in cahoots, that's what." She turns to us. "I told you he was trying to kill me."

Dad sighs as though he's been through all this before. "I was not trying to kill you, Viney. I was peeling an apple. You called to me, and I turned around." He steps over to the skinless fruit, picks it up, then walks to Mom. "I was hungry, Viney. That's all." He bites so hard into the apple, it shakes his top dentures loose. With dignity, he snaps them back into place and walks out with an attitude that causes Mom's age spots to turn fire engine red.

"Don't you dare walk out on me, Milton Haverford," Mom shouts after him.

"I've had enough, thank you," Dad says, heading toward the door. He stops and whips around to face Mom. Striking the air with his pointed finger, he says, "And furthermore, Viney, you're not welcome home until you come to your senses."

"Well, that was a bust," Janni says in the family room after Dad leaves, the kids go to a movie, and Mom goes to bed for the night.

"No kiddin'." Daniel lifts his legs onto the ottoman. "I sure hope we're not putting all this money into a party that's not going to happen," Daniel says, picking up the scissors and the coupon page of the newspaper.

"We still have a little time. They'll surely get things patched up," I say, my toothache growing a tad more intense. It's been a while since my last checkup, so I make a mental note to set an appointment when I get back to Maine.

"One can only hope." Janni's chin slumps into her palm.

"Hey, what if we make her miserable while she's here?" Daniel says.

"Daniel, she's our mother. We don't want to do that," Janni says.

"Why not?" I chime in.

"Char!"

"Well, she doesn't belong here. She belongs with Dad. They're both miserable." Digging an emery board from my purse, I start whacking away at my nails. My sister and Mom have beautiful nails. They don't ever get them professionally done, yet they have perfectly strong, manicured nails. I pay big bucks to get mine worked on, and they are paper-thin, chipped, and expensive. The manicurist probably puts stuff on them that makes me have to come back.

"I know." We think some more. "Maybe the boys could play loud music."

"They're scared of her. They won't do it," I say.

"Blake will." Daniel's face brightens with hope.

"No, Daniel. I won't have you making Mom think we want to get rid of her," Janni says.

"But we do," I remind her. Janni gives me a look of reprimand. Just like Mom.

"Oh, all right." Daniel pushes himself out of his chair. "I'm going to bed."

"What an awful night," Janni says, stress making her look five years older.

"Yeah. Let's go eat some cookies."

Janni gapes at me.

"What?"

"Doesn't any of this bother you?"

"Yes. Want to try one of my cookies?" I call over my shoulder.

"They're not your cookies. The bakery prepared them." Janni follows me into the kitchen.

"Yes, and I bought them." We plunk ourselves down at the table, a plate of the bakery chocolate chip cookies between us, cold milk in wide-mouthed mugs for easy dunking.

"Now, this is much better," I say, dipping my cookie into the chilled skim milk—hey, I watch my calories—then taking a bite.

Janni stares at me. "You don't let much get to you, do you?"

"Things get to me, but I don't let them linger there."

Janni takes a bite of the cookie, and her eyes widen. "These aren't bad."

Her words are a sort of truce between us. "Maybe I should try one of yours."

She smiles, walks over and grabs one, then gives it to me.

I take a bite and have to say I'm pleasantly surprised. "These are good, too, sis."

"Are we having a bonding moment?" Janni wants to know.

"Um-hum, over cookies."

"If I could eat like you do without gaining weight, I'd drown my sorrows in cookies too."

"Well, there is that little matter of the extra twenty pounds. Still, if I didn't walk on the beach every morning, I'd really be in trouble."

"Don't you ever worry about walking by yourself?"

"Not where I live. A bunch of retired folks out there. No one has the energy to hurt me."

She chuckles.

"So are you enjoying having the kids home?"

"Yeah. I miss those boys. You know, though, after Ethan and Candy started dating, it really hit me that soon someone else will take first place in my boys' lives, and I will no longer be needed."

"You'll always be needed, Janni. You're their mother."

"Yeah, but you know what I mean. Things will be different when they have their own homes."

"I guess. But you'll find plenty to keep you busy."

She smirks. "To use your phrase—whatever."

"Say, what do you think about Stephanie?" Given Janni's current mood, I probably shouldn't ask about Stephanie sleeping on the couch, but I promised Blake I would try, and they'll be back soon.

"She's a sweet girl."

I hesitate. "Listen, Janni, I know you have a lot on your plate right now, but you need to know that I found Blake and Stephanie in the hayloft last night."

Janni gasps and starts coughing.

That didn't come out exactly like I had hoped. "I didn't mean to imply—"

Janni struggles for breath. "What exactly did you mean, Char?" she asks in a raspy voice.

"She was staying up there. Blake had just gotten her some blankets and a pillow. It seems she was kicked out of the other place."

Janni's cough finally settles down. "You mean the person she was staying with kicked her out?"

"Yeah, a boyfriend moved in, and Stephanie moved out."

"When did this happen?"

"Just yesterday."

"And she has no other place to stay?"

"Right. I'd be happy to give her my room—"

"Well, of course she can stay here. You know I would never turn anyone down who needed a place to stay. Why would you even hesitate to ask me, Char? I don't want that child sleeping out in the cold barn."

"It's just that you haven't been quite yourself lately, and I wasn't sure you would be up for more company—especially nonfamily company. Still, I only let her stay out there last night. I wanted to offer her my room, but didn't know how you would handle it if you saw her there."

"Well, she won't be staying out there tonight if I have anything to say about it," Janni says, rising. "I'll grab some blankets and pillows. She can sleep in the family room on the sofa sleeper."

By the time the kids return, Janni and I have Stephanie's place on the family room sofa bed ready for her.

"Is Dad in the doghouse?" Ethan asks, looking at the sofa bed.

"No, he's not in the doghouse. This is for Stephanie," Janni says.

We all turn to a surprised Stephanie. She looks at me.

"Yes, I told her. And she's happy to have you join us."

"Absolutely," Janni says, pulling Stephanie into a hug. "For however long you need, honey, you're welcome to stay here," Janni says.

Tears fill her eyes. "Thank you. I'll earn my keep while I'm here, I promise." Makes me wonder if she's planning to move in.

"Sheesh, it's only a sofa bed, Stephanie. And a lumpy one at that," Blake says. "You want to stay in my bed?"

A collective intake of air here. From the looks of Janni, we may need to make a mad dash for the smelling salts.

"I meant you could stay in my bed, and Ethan and I can come down here."

"Sure," Ethan joins in.

Blake looks at us and rolls his eyes. "Get your minds out of the gutter, Mom and Aunt Char."

"No, I'm staying right here." Stephanie says. "It's great."

"Well, now that we've got that settled," Ethan says, "I'm hungry."

"You just ate a whole bag of popcorn and Twizzlers," Candy says.

"And your point is?" Blake asks as they make their way to the kitchen.

"You miss this?" I ask Janni.

She chuckles. "Crazy, I know, but I do."

I'm tired and want to go to bed, but they have their heat so high I keep waking up in the middle of the night, sweating like a pig on a spit. Still, no one else says anything. Tappery has a discount store that stays open all night. I'll head over there and see if they have a small fan. "I think I'm going to run to the store," I say.

"At this hour?" Janni thinks her entire family should be safely tucked in bed by nine o'clock.

"Yeah, I feel like going out a little while."

Janni shakes her head. "Well, you have more energy than I do. I'm going to bed. Danny gave you a key to let yourself in, right?"

"Yeah."

"Okay. Don't stay out too late."

"Yes, Mom." Though my coat is gaping open, I step outside into the cold night air and feel better instantly. No wonder Janni is lethargic all the time. All that heat would zap anyone of their strength.

fifteen

"Since we have other helpers, we'll be back to bottle the syrup in a few minutes. Stephanie and I are going to run into town and get a coffee," Blake says the next afternoon. "She wants to check on her possible job status too."

"What about Ethan and Candy?" Janni says, watching the sap sift through the cone filters. Sweat is beading on her face. "Are they going?"

The temperature from the fire makes the room warm, but Janni's having a hot flash if ever I've seen one.

"They're sticking around." He laughs at his pun. "Get it? Sticking?" Stephanie gives him a playful punch in the arm.

"Don't quit your day job," I call out.

"They'll be back down in a few minutes," Blake says.

"Okay." Janni's forehead creases. "But don't be too long. The syrup will be ready to bottle soon, and we can use all the help we can get." She swipes her face with her arm.

"Yeah, we'll grab the coffee and come right back. Anybody else want anything?"

"Absolutely. Maple macchiato with three shots over ice," I say, not wanting anything hot. At least my mood is better today. It helped to buy that small fan last night. With it blowing on my face all night, I didn't wake up once.

"Get me something cold. Anything, I don't care." Desperation lines Janni's voice. Maybe with her surge in temperature, they'll turn down the heat in the house, and I won't need my fan after all.

"There's money in my purse up at the house," I say to Blake.

"These are on me." He flashes his heart-melting grin.

"See ya." Stephanie smiles and waves.

"Can you believe that girl runs five miles every morning?" Janni says.

"She does?"

"Yep. She told me so when I caught her coming in the house this morning before I even had the coffee made. She was dressed in sweats, her face all aglow with healthy vitality."

"Well, tell her to stop it. She'll make the rest of us look bad."

Janni chuckles. "That's what I thought too."

"Do you think it's possible that you keep your house too warm, Janni?" I tread easily here.

She gives me a dry stare. "Daniel keeps the temperature at sixty-four."

"Oh." Not quite low enough to cause hypothermia, but close. Suddenly it dawns on me how hot I've been. I think I'll keep that little fact to myself until I can figure out what's going on. Hopefully, this toothache that's back in full force isn't the culprit. I decide to change the subject. "You know, the sap is down a little this year, but what are you going to do in the years when the sap production is high?"

"What do you mean?"

"Well, you can't do this by yourself, and the boys won't be around to help forever."

"I know." We leave our position at the finishing pan. Janni goes back to watching the sap in the evaporator, and I watch the temperature gauge.

"'Course, knowing you, you'll always have friends ready to lend a helping hand."

"We do have great friends." She glances at her watch. "Hey, we'll need to go start dinner soon."

Just then the door swings open, and Russ walks in, causing my heart to flutter like a fallen leaf in the wind.

"Hi, everybody." He looks straight at me, and we exchange smiles.

"So how's Peter?" Janni whispers with a smirk.

"Peter?" As in, Pan? Cottontail? Who? It takes me a minute to realize who *Janni* is, why she's talking to me, and what country I live in.

Janni laughs.

"Pe—Peter is fine," I stammer.

Her little bit of teasing irritates me. I'm not sure why. Maybe I don't like people assuming things. Such as assuming there is a relationship developing between Russ and me. Just because my stomach flips when he walks into a room doesn't mean anything. It does the same thing when I eat burritos. Russ is nice to me, and I think he enjoys my company, but he's more concerned about being a friend to Daniel and Janni. For all I know, he's showing me attention to gain their favor.

That little thought rocks my world for a moment.

Pulling off his leather jacket, he places it on a chair in the corner. A guy from the church switches places with him, and Russ starts shoving wood into the fire, his muscles flexing with the effort. I try not to stare, I really do, but let me just say he could put Popeye to shame. I'll bet he snacks on spinach.

I'm picturing the two of us enjoying a quaint picnic in a spinach field. Is there such a thing?

"You ready to go?" Janni interrupts my little daydream.

A girl can't have a single private thought in this place.

"Chili and cornbread, does it get any better than this?" Blake says while chewing on his corn bread.

Janni laughs. "It does my heart good to cook for you boys."

"What? It's not like I don't eat," Daniel says, patting his well-padded, round belly.

"I know, but it's hard to get excited about cooking for two people."

"I'm excited when you cook for two people," Daniel says. "Especially when one of them is me."

Janni's chin hikes. "I'm a woman of the millennium, thank you."

Blake stops chewing and stares at her.

"Well, I am. I've worked hard all these years, I deserve to go out and eat once in a while."

"Yes, you do," I agree wholeheartedly.

Everyone's attention is now fixed on me. "Well, she does. There comes a time in a woman's life when you have to stop living for everyone else and enjoy life a little."

Daniel blinks.

Russ stares at me so long, I'm afraid there's corn bread on my face.

"It's not as though I'm a women's libber or anything," I blubber, "It's just that—"

Russ holds his hand up. "We get it. And we agree." He winks, and his mouth splits into a wide grin.

I'm not sure, but I think my toes are curling.

"We do?" Daniel asks, mouth gaping.

"Sure. Janni's served others all these years. There's nothing wrong with her being served once in a while."

Janni settles back into her chair, looking completely content at this turn in the conversation.

"So you're not going to cook for us anymore?" Daniel looks as though Janni snatched his favorite flannel shirt from his drawer and took it to Goodwill.

"Most of the time I am. But once in a while I want you to take me to a candlelight dinner prepared by someone else."

"But I love your cooking."

"And you'll get it—now and then. But sometimes I need to be served."

This is a liberated Janni that I have never seen before. Daniel stares at her a moment and goes back to his chili. "As long as I eat, I guess it doesn't matter where we eat."

"Exactly," Janni says with a snap of her head. "Besides, I love to cook. I'll still be doing plenty of it. I'm just saying once in a while, I would appreciate the option of going out. I might even sign up for cooking classes at the community college."

"I think it's great that you want to do some things for yourself. There's nothing worse than a mom with too much time on her hands, living only for her kids," Stephanie says.

"Aren't you going to eat any corn bread?" I ask her, pushing the plate of corn bread her way.

"I try to keep my carbs to a minimum."

Just then all forks come to a standstill, and we stare at her as though she's a museum exhibit.

"Where are you from, Stephanie?" I venture. *Mars?*

"Illinois."

"Did you go to college there?" Just want to make sure she's dating material for my nephew—though I can't imagine anyone who doesn't like carbs fitting in with this family.

She laughs. "Yeah. Went to a community college for a couple of years, then transferred to a university. Graduated with a teaching degree."

"What will you teach?" Janni asks.

"Physical education," she says with a smile. "Hence, the backpack adventure."

"That would also explain the five-mile runs and lack of carbs," I say. *The girl has issues.*

She smiles.

"Any siblings?" Daniel asks.

"No. Dad died of cancer three years ago. I love my mom, but ever since Dad died, she's been suffocating me. Things finally came to a head about a month ago, and I left. I've called her to let her know I'm okay, but I just can't go back. Not yet."

"I'm sorry, Stephanie," Janni says. "It's a mom thing. She's afraid of losing you, too, and yet it sounds like her fear has pushed you to the point of leaving. I'm sorry for both of you."

Stephanie studies Janni a moment, as though she's considering the comment.

"I didn't mean to be a downer. Mom and I get along. I'm just on a quest, and she doesn't like it because she's afraid it will take me away from her."

"It's hard when our kids grow up," Janni says, eyes glazed.

"Could she feel threatened in other ways?" I ask.

"How do you mean?" Stephanie asks.

"Oh, I don't know. Maybe she's afraid you won't come back. You'll find a life apart from her, since you're traveling." I'm sure that's Janni's problem, the boys going off to college, empty nest. It's as though mothers have to find a new identity when their kids leave home.

"That could be some of it." Stephanie twists the cloth napkin in her lap, and I figure it's time to move the discussion in a different direction.

"So, Daniel, how did we do on the syrup today?"

Daniel drops his spoon into the empty bowl in front of him and leans back in his chair. "We got about fifteen gallons."

"That's pretty good. Too bad it takes forty gallons of sap for every gallon of syrup," Ethan says.

"It's the nature of the beast." Daniel tips his chair back on its hind legs.

"Just keep praying that we have nights that are cold enough and days that are mild. We're hoping to get enough to give some to the shut-ins at our church." Janni's head whips around to me. "Without touching your stash, of course."

I smirk. "Do you honestly think I could deprive little old ladies of their maple syrup?"

Janni gives me a pointed stare.

"Well, all right, maybe I could." Everyone laughs, but I don't think it's funny. What kind of person denies little old ladies their syrup?

Exactly. I need professional help.

"So where did Blake and Stephanie go?" I ask when I come down the stairs after dinner cleanup to join Janni in the family room where she's filling out place cards for the anniversary party. "I heard his car pull out of the driveway."

"They went to check on Dad," Janni says. "Mom is out with her Red Hat ladies."

I settle onto the rocker. "My penmanship isn't that great, but I can help with those."

"No, that's all right. I actually enjoy it," Janni says.

"Suit yourself." I reach for my sketch pad and pencil.

"Did you ever ask Dad about his meeting with Gertie?" Janni's brows have slipped to their concentration position.

"No. The night I was going to bring it up, he and Mom were doing great until he pulled the knife on her."

Janni chuckles in spite of herself and shakes her head. "Well, I'm sure it's nothing. Dad doesn't seem to be happy about retirement. Now that he's got all this extra time on his hands, he seems to be dwelling on the past."

"Yeah, I've noticed that. 'Course, Mom's weirdness isn't helping."

She nods.

While my pencil moves across the pad, I ask, "Do you think it's wise to encourage Blake to go out with Stephanie?" I'm probably out of line, but he is my nephew, after all.

"Oh, I don't think it hurts anything. They're just good friends."

My mouth dangles a moment, then I snap it shut. "Have you not noticed that she's gorgeous, and he slobbers every time she walks in the room?"

Here she goes with that hyena laugh again. "Char, you are such a drama queen."

"Janni, she doesn't eat carbs."

"Oh, good grief, Char, you're acting as though she belongs to some kind of weird cult," Janni says with a laugh.

"I'm telling you, today it's carbs, tomorrow tofu. You mark my words."

"Listen, Char, Blake is a normal young man, yes, but he's not stupid. He acts the same way with other girls. He's just interested in girls, period."

"Precisely my point." The front elevation of a coastal home with lots of long windows takes shape as my pencil sketches along the page.

Janni walks over to pick up some stray socks and empty cups that the boys obviously left on the floor. She stops and looks over my shoulder. "Oh, I like that. What is it?"

"Just an idea for another home."

"I love vaulted ceilings," Janni says with a sigh before moving on to her seat. She scoots a pillow out of her way and sits down. "Anyway, don't worry about Blake. He'll be all right."

"It's just that you know nothing about this girl."

"I know nothing about the girls at school, either. But I do know my son, and I trust him."

"He has hormones."

"Yeah, so?"

"Hormones can't be trusted."

"I know all about raging hormones. But Blake has a good head on his shoulders. You have to let it go and trust somewhere along the line."

There she goes, hitting me with a life lesson again. "Okay, but just remember, hormones can affect good judgment, that's all I'm saying."

"Thanks for the warning."

"Well, I'm home." Mom shoves the door closed behind her and yanks off her winter wraps to reveal a purple blouse and black pants. The sting from the night air remains on her cheeks, causing her face to match her red hat. Speaking of hats, that hat is so big the wind could have carried her to Canada.

"Well, you look chipper," I say.

"I am. Despite the fact that my husband is trying to kill me."

"Mom, you're not telling people that, are you? Dad's a pillar in this community, and you could really hurt his reputation," Janni says.

"Well, if he kills me, everyone will sure know about it."

Now I see where I get that drama-queen stuff.

"Mom, have you told anyone?"

She averts her gaze. "Not yet." Her eyes dart to Janni. "But I will if this keeps up."

"Does anyone know you're staying here?"

"Yes, my friends know. They think I'm here so I can spend time with you," she says to me.

Right. As though she would put herself out like that to spend time with me. Miss Divorcee.

"You and Dad need to go to counseling, Mom. You have to know that." Janni is either my hero or she's stupid. The jury's still out on that one.

"I'm not going to any counseling. We've mentored half the people in this town. We won't be airing our dirty laundry to some snot-nosed kid who used to be in my Sunday-school class."

"If you don't have something nice to say . . ."

Mom's head cuts toward me, and I see murder in her eyes.

"Well, I think I'll go to my room now." I just couldn't live with myself if Mom went to prison because of me.

"Smart move," she says.

Sometimes her comments make me so mad I want to steal her Depends. That would teach her to hold her tongue. 'Course, she'd have to hold something else too.

"Behave, you two," Janni says with a yawn. "I just don't have the strength to referee."

"It's the menopause."

We both turn around with a start.

"What?" Janni asks, poised and armed for battle.

"You're starting menopause. I've been watching you. You're depressed. You're having hot flashes. You're irritable. You have all the signs."

"Char says snappy things all the time, is she in menopause?"

"Hey, don't bring me into this."

"She was born that way," Mom says.

My gaze zips to her. "Thanks a lot, Mom."

"Well, you're irritable, too, Mom," Janni snaps.

"See what I mean?" Mom says with a victorious grin. "It's the menopause."

We just can't win with our mother.

sixteen

The next evening, after a dinner of lasagna, garlic bread, salad, and a light chocolate mousse, I rub the bump—okay, bulge—on my tummy and realize I may need to do a forty-years-in-the-wilderness journey just to get back to my previsit size.

My eyelids droop from another day of sugaring, but the thought of falling asleep after dinner would make me a prime candidate for AARP, so I tell Janni I'm going to take a walk and I'll be back.

Before I know it, I've tramped to the edge of the forest. Spotting my favorite gnarled maple, I walk over to it and run my fingers along the rough bark. I've always loved this tree. Its low, thick branches made for easy climbing when I was a kid. How many times did I hide out here when I wanted to be surrounded by nature and away from Gail and Linda's gossiping tongues?

In front of the maple, I glance at my Nike-clad feet and my short jacket, and my mind suggests the unthinkable. Well, it's unthinkable for a forty-seven-year-old. That thought alone challenges me to do it. With a sharp glance in all directions, I make sure no one is around. The last thing I need is an amateur photographer snapping a picture and plastering it on the Internet with a joke about middle-aged women—or should I say post–middle age? No, I think I'll stick with middle age.

I wedge my foot between the crook of the sturdy limb and the tree trunk. Taking a deep breath, I hold tightly to the limb and hoist myself up onto the branch with a grunt. Let me just say it was much easier when I tried this the last time—which was about, oh, I don't know, thirty-two years ago?

Scooting along the rough bark, I finally settle into a fairly comfortable spot and look around. The air exhilarates my tired lungs. It encourages me to try the next branch up. Bracing myself just right, my arms hug tightly around the tree while my foot gropes for the next branch and lops over the side. My fingers scrape across the jagged trunk until I'm finally able to plop my derriere up on the higher branch.

My ego threatens to get the better of me. You know, that whole nearly-fifty-and-climbing-a-tree deal. A whistle calls through the night air as a freight train rumbles in the distance. Bare branches allow me a distant view of the forest. One glance at all the trees, and it's easy to see why we're tired with the syrup process. It's no easy job.

A gust of cold air whips past me and makes me cough. I've barely settled onto my branch when the snap of a twig below catches my attention.

"Char?"

The voice startles me and nearly takes my breath away. "Stephanie. What are you doing out here?" I ask, trying to hide my irritation. It took all the strength I could muster just to get up here, and I have no intention of coming down anytime soon.

She wrings her gloved hands together. "Um, they told me you were out here. I was trying to find you. Then I heard you cough."

The bark is rough and cold beneath my hands. I should have brought my gloves. "Yeah, well, here I am."

"Listen, I need to talk to you about something." Her voice cracks as though she's on the verge of tears, though I can't imagine why.

"Now?"

"Well, remember, I wanted to tell you something in the barn?"

"Do I need to come down?" If I go down now, I'll never get back up here.

"Well, you can stay up there if you want. In fact, it might be easier on me if you do."

I'm beginning to understand Janni's need for solitude. "Okay, I'm listening."

She goes into a little more detail about her life back home, her father's death, her backpacking adventure, and her quest. The cold from the limb is starting to seep through my pants, and I'm wondering why she couldn't have told me all this back at the house. My mind wanders off while she's talking, until she starts crying.

"So when Daniel brought me here, it was too good to be true," I hear her say. "Still, I don't know how I'm going to tell Janni." She's definitely crying here, and I'm wondering what I've missed.

"Tell her what?"

"Were you listening to me? I said that Janni is my biological mother."

"What?" Stephanie's words hit me like a hard rock against my back, causing me to fling forward. My flailing arms grope for the branch, and my right leg hangs on as though it's hooked and looped at the ends.

"Char? Char! Hang on! I'll help you!" Stephanie runs toward the tree.

"My grip is slipping. I'm not going to make it," I cry out. If she were bigger than a minute, she might be able to catch me, but with her elfin body and my extra twenty pounds, I'd crush her to death.

The rough bark scrapes my palms as my hands peel loose. The wind rips past my ears, and my scream pierces the air, no doubt being heard three counties over. The ground rushes up to meet me, but I squeeze my eyes closed so I can't see. Next thing I know, my body slams into the earth with all the force of a rhino dropping from the sky.

Twigs and rocks embed themselves in my jeans as I attempt to push myself up. Pain sears through my ankle. *Perfect Janni? Not possible. How?—When?—I would have known.*

"Char, are you all right?" Stephanie kneels down beside me and puts her hand on my arm. Worry lines her face.

"I'm fine." Damaged pride, but I'll survive. My fingers reach for my ankle. "I think I might have hurt my ankle, though." *Janni wouldn't keep something like this from me.*

"I'll run to the house for help. Don't move—er, uh, I'll be right back."

"Charlene Haverford, what were you doing sitting up on a tree branch? What were you thinking?" Janni wants to know.

"I was bird-watching, Janni, what do you think?"

"Well, the good news is I don't think it's sprained, but you beat it up pretty good. We'll get you up to the house, wrap it in a bandage and tight tape, give you a couple of pain relievers, and you'll be good to go."

"Found them," Daniel says, lifting crutches in the air as he jogs down to join us.

"Do you guys run a medical clinic or what?"

"When you have two boys, you have your share of sprains and broken bones," Janni says. "Help me out here, Danny."

"Luckily, we have these from when Blake was in junior high, and they're adjustable, so you won't have any problems using them." Daniel gives the crutches to Stephanie, then he and Janni scoop me up beneath my arms and pull me to a standing position. They stuff the crutches underneath my arms and stand close beside me as I hobble back to the house over the rough terrain.

"I still can't believe you climbed that tree." Janni shakes her head. "You might have broken the branch."

"Your compassion is touching."

Janni chuckles before sliding into her seat in the living room. "Okay, I'm teasing." She takes a sip from her coffee mug.

They have me situated on the monster sofa, and I'm still worried about falling into the cushions, but since I'm lying down, I figure I won't go down without a fight. With a glance over at Wiggles, I see him studying me carefully. If I have to stay down here through the night, I'm afraid he'll call in his buddies, and they'll carry me off.

"It was a stupid thing to do. I admit it."

"Oh well, it isn't the first time and won't be the last."

"Thanks, Janni. So nice of you to point that out." I'd like to point out to her that she would have fallen from the tree, too, if she had heard what I heard. There's no way it could be true. Not from Saint Janni. On the other hand, if it is true, and she didn't tell me, she'd better run.

Stephanie does resemble Janni—or am I letting my imagination run away with me? What am I thinking? She couldn't possibly be related to our family. She doesn't eat carbs. She is bossy, though, I'll give her that. Well, if somehow Mom and I are her blood relatives, she doesn't stand a chance. I need some time to think about how we're going to deal with this. It doesn't seem right to blurt out, "Oh, by the way, did you know that Stephanie thinks she is your daughter?" Instead I say, "Without me, will you have enough help with the syrup?" I just go from one panic to another.

"We'll get along just fine."

"No, you won't. You need me."

"Don't worry about it, Char. We'll make do. We have enough friends helping. Besides, by the look of that foot, you won't be down long. In the meantime, you can work on the party stuff."

"Boy, what some people won't do to get out of work," Daniel says, entering the room with a laugh.

"Danny, don't you start," Janni warns. "She feels bad enough as it is."

Hello? It's not like she's been all that easy on me.

"Aw, I'm just kiddin' ya."

Somehow I manage a weak smile. I'm not about to mention the fact that not only is my ankle throbbing, but also my toothache is no longer on the fringes.

"Hey," Janni's eyes sparkle, and her face lights up like Mrs. Claus at Christmas, "I know what will perk you up."

Just hearing those words strikes fear in my heart. "What?"

"Sudoku!" Janni claps her hands together and heads for a stack of magazines.

"Puzzles? You think puzzles will perk me up? Hello? Anyone notice I'm a people person, not a puzzle person?"

"Good luck," Daniel whispers on his way back out of the room.

"Coward," I call after him, low enough so that Janni can't hear me.

"Oh come on, these are fun." She throws a magazine to me, then walks over to put on the easy listening radio station.

We work feverishly on those puzzles. My brain is tired before I get started, but I don't want to be a party pooper, so I play along. Unfortunately, within the first five minutes, I slip into a coma and don't come out until my toothache screams for attention. The pulse in my ankle keeps pace with the soft beat of the music. My head has joined the kettle-drum section. I sink further into the sofa, praying all the while I will disappear, never to be found again.

"Are you doing all right, Char?" Stephanie walks toward me with a cup in her hand. "Macchiato, three shots," she announces with a smile. She hands it to me.

"Thank you, Stephanie. That's so sweet." It's a guilt offering, but still, it's nice. "Did you get some coffee for yourself?"

"Never touch the stuff," she says.

There is positively no way this kid can be Janni's daughter.

"We need to talk," Stephanie says.

Janni puts her magazine down and comes over to look at me. "Oh dear, Char, your color doesn't look so good. You ready for those painkillers yet?"

Try as I might, I have an aversion to pills. Don't like them. Doesn't matter if they're vitamins or medicine, I hate to take them. They always make me choke. But with the way my head, tooth, and ankle are throbbing, what does it matter? I nod.

"Uh-oh, I know she's hurting when she agrees to medicine. Be right back." Janni heads to the bathroom.

"Listen, Char, I'm sorry to spring that on you the way I did, about Janni and me," she whispers.

"Stephanie, would you grab Char a glass of water so she can take her pills?" Janni calls out from the bathroom.

"Sure."

I hate to break it to her that she's mistaken, but she needs to know she has the wrong gal. "We'll talk later, Stephanie. Maybe when everyone goes to bed?"

She nods and heads for the kitchen.

Why didn't I stay in Maine where I belong?

By the time everyone goes to bed and the steps creak beneath Stephanie's feet as she heads my way, my toothache has elevated my pain level to the point of snapping. The sheets are in a tangle from my thrashing about on the sofa.

"Char, is it your ankle? You look awful." Stephanie tucks the sheet in around me and plumps the pillow, trying to make me more comfortable.

Left palm against my cheek, I say, "My tooth. I have to get help." At this point, I'm sure it couldn't hurt any worse if I sawed off my jawbone.

"What's wrong?" Janni calls from the stairway. The pounding in my head must have drowned out her footsteps. "Char? Do we need to call the doctor for your ankle? Maybe you've broken something."

She comes around the sofa, takes one look at me, and gasps. Okay, so I don't look wonderful without makeup, but I hardly feel it should provoke a gasp.

"She has a bad toothache," Stephanie tells her.

"Toothache? I'm calling Russ." Janni steps over and picks up her cordless.

"No!" I yell as best I can with my hand clamped against the left side of my jaw. "You can't call him. Anyone but him."

"Char, it's the weekend and it's midnight. I don't know another dentist in town who would work on you at midnight, over the weekend, when you're not his patient—without charging an arm and a leg."

"I'll throw in an arm and a leg, if that will help." My jaw is tight, and I'm pretty sure my head has swollen to the size of a beach ball.

"No, you don't. Russ is our dentist, and he's our friend. Why, he'd be offended if we didn't call him."

The intense pain shoots through my jaw once again. "Okay, fine. Call him," I snarl.

Janni starts punching in the numbers, no doubt happy that she got her way. I just want to slap her.

"Hello, Russ? I'm sorry to bother you so late, but it's Char. She hurt her ankle falling from a tree—"

I roll my eyes. Did she have to tell him that?

"No, no, she's fine." She looks at me and talks away from the mouthpiece. "Well, you did."

I'm so gonna hurt her.

"And on top of that she has a horrible toothache." *Can we say whiner?* "I was wondering if we could get her in first thing in the morning, and thought you could tell us what we might do for her in the meantime?"

The pain is excruciating, making me want to bang my head against the wall. Yet I doubt even that would improve things.

"Okay, we'll be there." Janni hangs up and turns to Stephanie. "Help me get her dressed. She's going into his office now."

"Now?" I cry. *It's the cookies. I know it's the cookies. If only I had stayed away from them.*

"Now." Janni's snap-to-it movements take over, and if I didn't know Mom was sleeping peacefully upstairs, I would swear that she had morphed into Janni's body. At this moment, there is no way I can imagine the world with two of my mother. That would pretty much send me over the edge.

seventeen

Let me just say, the trip to Russ's office was humiliating beyond measure. I had to wear a bib and keep my drool to a minimum while he prodded around in my mouth as though excavating for diamonds. The good news is my toothache is gone—or at least I think it is. One side of my head is numb, so it's hard to tell. The other good thing is, instead of paying for the filling, I get a free meal out of the deal, as in a dinner date with Russ to Sok's Restaurant.

Once I return to bed in the wee hours of the morning, my dreams take me to a quiet café located on a brick-lined street bustling with quaint shops and happy tourists. Caramel-colored walls, white trim, and white café round tables and chairs adorn the inside. The espresso machine whirs in the background, and the sweet smell of sticky buns and bagels perfumes the air. Russ sits across from me dressed in a crisp navy oxford, open at the collar, muscles bulging against the sleeves. Nice jeans and sneakers give him a casual appearance, but he's still classy all the way in my book.

A dozen yellow roses—my favorite—burst from a crystal vase in the middle of the table, compliments of Russ. He's holding my hand, gazing deep into my eyes. Without a word, he leans toward me, closer, closer, and just as our lips are about to meet, Mom's voice comes crashing through.

"Land sakes, Charlene Marybelle, what are you doing sleeping on that couch? It's time for church." My mother's sharp voice still causes prickles on the back of my neck, and I break out in a cold sweat. Considering my aversion to heat lately, that should say something. To point out that this is a rude awakening is an understatement. But nothing compares to having Russ's face within reach, then blinking my eyes open and seeing my mother's skinny jowls hanging inches from my face. Took five years off my life, I'm sure of it.

"Hi, Mom." I rub my eyes, and she straightens.

"Don't 'Hi, Mom' me. You should be dressed and ready to go." She adjusts her purse on her shoulder.

"Be nice to her, Mom. She bruised her ankle and had to have a tooth filled in the middle of the night," Janni says, grabbing her coat from the closet.

"She what?" Mom looks at me as though she can't believe she gave birth to me.

Janni explains everything. I haven't the strength. To my surprise, Mom's face turns soft.

"I'm sorry, dear," she says, tucking the blanket in around me. "Do you need me to stay home with you?"

The music to *Psycho* screeches through my mind, and my body gives an involuntary shudder.

"I'm staying with her," Stephanie says in no uncertain terms.

Mom looks from her to me. "Well, if you're okay with that, Char?"

"Yes, Mom, that's fine." It's kind of nice to have Mom's attention like this, though I wouldn't go so far as to say I want her to stay here with me.

"Well, all right then." Mom turns to Janni. "Ready to go?"

"Yeah. The boys and Candy went with Daniel. He had to be there early to work the sound system. They wanted to go over to the coffee shop and grab something before church."

Mom nods. "Char, behave yourself." She waves and shoots out the door before I can reply.

Janni looks at me, and we both laugh. "How much trouble does she think I can get into when I can't walk?" I ask.

"You have a reputation." Janni chuckles.

"Don't remind me."

"The chicken and noodles are in the Crock-Pot. The oven timer is set for the broccoli casserole. The salad is in the fridge, and I'll prepare the rolls when I get home," Janni says.

"What, no dessert?" I tease.

"Blueberry pies."

My mouth dangles open. She laughs.

"You are a saint." One glance at Stephanie makes me want to ask, "Or are you?"

"Planning a meal hardly qualifies me for sainthood." She shrugs. "You do what you've got to do," she says. "See you later."

As soon as the door pulls closed behind Janni, I turn to Steph. "All right, let's get down to business." No way I can wait another minute. We need to resolve this now.

She takes a deep breath. "I've been searching for quite some time for my biological mom. She went to college in Illinois, got pregnant, gave me up for adoption. With the help of an Internet agency, I began my search to find my mom and ultimately that led me here to Tappery."

My tongue won't move, and this time it has nothing to do with the shot Russ gave me.

Another deep breath. "It was sheer luck that day at the coffee shop when Daniel talked to the barista about needing help. In the course of their conversation, he mentioned that his father-in-law was Pastor

Haverford and his wife's name was Janni. That's when I knew I had to come and check it out. My mother's name was Janet Elise Haverford."

My breath lingers between my chest and mouth. My tongue still won't move. I try to take it all in. She has to be telling the truth because she knows Janni's full name. Still, this world is full of sly people who try to deceive others. Maybe she wants money from Janni and figures if she's one of the kids . . . Wonder if she's seen the carpet or noticed Daniel's coupon fetish?

"I don't want anything from her," she says, as though she's read my thoughts. "I've just always wanted to know my real mother."

"But you don't eat carbs," I say in utter amazement.

"Huh?"

"Never mind. Listen, I don't mean to be rude, Stephanie, but it's highly unlikely that Janni had a baby without the rest of us knowing about it. Saying nothing of the fact that it would be totally out of character for her. The woman is a saint." My fingers work the cover around me, tucking it in for warmth.

"People mess up."

"Yeah, but not Janni. Trust me on this, I know. After you get to know her, you'll see. There's got to be some mistake."

"No mistake, Char."

No use arguing with her about it. She'll see. "And your mother in Illinois, what's her name?"

"Carol Sherwood."

"Does she mind that you're seeking out your mother?"

"No. Said she always knew I would someday."

"Does she know you're staying at Janni's house?"

"Yeah. Char, just so you know, I tried to tell you about this that night in the barn, remember?"

For a minute, I think back. "Yes, I remember. So what now?"

She looks down at her hands. "I don't know. Guess I just wanted to get to know her a little."

Just what Janni needs right now. Someone to come along and stir up trouble. Talk about an emotional upheaval. "Are you planning to tell her?"

"I don't know."

"I'm not sure she can take it right now," I say. "As you know, she's had a lot of pressure on her lately, and she's going through—well, she's kind of going through some things."

Steph's head jerks up. "She's not sick, is she?"

"No, nothing like that. I think she's going through the changes that women go through in midlife. It affects your emotions and all that. It's a difficult time to handle big things."

Steph looks down again. "Maybe I should just leave."

Part of me wishes she would leave to spare Janni the headache of it all, but I can see the hope fringing on despair in Stephanie's eyes. She won't rest until she finds her biological mother. She deserves to know it's not Janni.

"Do you still want to work at the coffee shop and stay in town?"

"For a little while. At least, that was my goal."

My heart aches for her other mother, since she will have to share her only daughter—once Stephanie finds her biological mother. "What about Carol?"

"No one can ever take her place in my heart. She did the hard work of raising me. She will always be my true mother."

I nod.

"Who all knows about me?"

"I think I can safely say no one." My mind drifts back to those blurry days when Janni was in college. I had already left home by then, but I'd see her at all the school breaks. Surely I would have known if she had been pregnant. There was one Christmas break when she wore a lot of oversized sweatshirts. I shake the memory. It's ludicrous to even consider. "Listen, Stephanie, I know how badly you want Janni to be your mom, but just don't get your hopes up, okay?"

"You'll see that I'm right, Char. You'll see."

Something about the confident way she says that causes a chill to shimmy up my spine. Maybe I should go home while there's still time.

"How ya feeling, Zip?" Daniel asks when everyone stumbles into the house from church, shoving coats and hats into the hall closet.

"Stephanie has taken good care of me." I smile, praying the storm that's soon to erupt won't leave a lot of debris behind. With a curious glance, Janni looks at Steph, then back to me. "The smell of chicken and noodles has been driving me wild," I say.

Daniel goes up behind Janni, grabs her around the middle, then squeezes. "Nobody can cook like my Janni," he says. She lifts her gaze to him. "But I'm still gonna take her to restaurants when she wants to go."

We all laugh together. Does Janni have any clue how lucky she is to have a guy like Daniel? There just aren't many around. I should know. I've made a professional career of dating.

"I'm impressed you got your bedding put away. You could have stayed there all day, you know," Janni says, stepping away from Daniel.

"What do you take me for, a slug?"

Janni chuckles. "Well, you just stay put until lunchtime. I don't need you and your crutches getting in my way in the kitchen."

"Why don't you tell me how you really feel?"

"I'll help you, Janni." Stephanie steps up to the plate. She tosses me a quick glance before trailing behind Janni into the kitchen.

I grab my sketch pad and pencil, and start drawing more ideas on the coastal home. As I work on the outside elevation, I pencil in an ocean setting which makes me a tad homesick for Maine.

Before I have time to think on that, Dad shoves through the front door. "Hey, Dad. I'm so glad you're joining us." Just then Mom harrumphs loud enough for us to hear on her way to the kitchen.

"Don't mind her," I whisper. "She'll come around." I pat the seat beside me. Wiggles barks from his cage, whips his tail, and scampers about. "I wonder what's the matter with him?"

"It's spring. As a wise old owl once said, 'He's twitterpated.'"

That little comment from my Dad renders me totally speechless. Never in all my born days could I have imagined hearing my dad say the word *twitterpated.* Quoting King Solomon is one thing, but quoting the owl on *Bambi*? Well, it's just a little frightening, that's all.

"How's my girl?" Dad gives me a sideways squeeze. "I heard you had a rough night."

"I've had better, that's for sure."

"I remember when you skinned your knee on your tricycle . . ." Dad goes into another story about the past, and I wonder who's struggling more with letting things go, him or me.

"You doing okay, Dad? I mean, really?"

"Yeah, I'm fine." He pats his stomach. "Probably gained five pounds since your mom's been gone 'cause I'm eating a lot of junk food that she won't let me eat." He lifts an ornery grin.

This makes me laugh. "Just make sure you eat some good stuff too. No cake for breakfast."

He winks. "Okay, Zipper."

"I'm flattered that you all are still calling me that, but it obviously doesn't apply any longer."

Dad brushes the air with his hand. "Aw, you're as pretty as the day you were born, Charlene." His eyes take on a glazed look. "I'll never forget that day. You had the most perfect little round head, and such hair! Looked like your mom from the start—well, except you got my family's body type."

I lean into him. "I thank you for that."

"Your mom is small, but her family isn't." He chuckles. "Yeah, it makes you wonder how anyone can give away a precious little one."

His comment causes me to choke.

"What's wrong?"

"A tickle," I explain with a raspy voice. Taking a moment to regain my composure, I look up to him. "What made you think that?"

"Oh, a family at our church dedicated their adopted baby this morning. Just got me to thinking, that's all."

"Well, sometimes circumstances call for the mother to give up the child."

"I suppose they have their reasons. I just knew your mother and I never could."

"And I'm glad." Another hug.

The front door creaks open, and a gust of wind rushes into the living room, causing a chill on my arms. At least I think it's the wind that's causing it.

"Hi, Russ." Dad stands to greet him. "Didn't know you were coming." He shakes Russ's hand.

"House calls, you know. I had to come and check on my patient." He winks and tosses me a grin.

Daddy rubs his jaw. "I didn't know doctors still made house calls." He smiles at me. "I'll let you sit over there by your patient, and I'm going to go into the family room to see what's going on in there. That is, after I snitch something good from the kitchen."

We smile after him. Russ peels off his coat, hangs it up in the closet and comes over to sit beside me. "So, how you doing?"

"Doing well, thanks to my fine dentist." I smile, thankful that I finally have full control of my facial muscles.

"I do what I can. Looks like the swelling went down in your leg." He points to my ankle that's resting on the coffee table.

"Yeah. Another day on the crutches, and I should be fine to walk on it."

"What are you working on?" He points to my sketch pad.

"Some people knit. I sketch house plans." I smile.

"That's a nice house. I like the layout."

"Thanks."

"Maybe you should consider the building business instead of commercial real estate. With the way you love to sketch, I'm thinking that's your passion."

"Say, are you trying to psychoanalyze me?"

He throws back his head and laughs—a rich, warm kind of laugh that makes me feel as though I've been wrapped in cashmere.

"Say, speaking of house drawings, we haven't done much with your house plans."

"Yeah, I know. Maybe we can work on them after lunch."

I nod.

"Listen, Charley, I've been feeling guilty all morning about something."

"Church can do that."

"It wasn't church. I let my mouth get in the way again."

"How do you mean?"

"When I had you in the chair, working on your tooth, I pretty much forced you into saying you would go out with me." Uncertainty clouds his dreamy blue eyes. "It's not like you could easily say no at that point."

"Oh I see how it is. You're trying to back out gracefully," I tease, praying it isn't so.

He covers my hand with his and pins me with his gaze. "That's not it, and you know it."

I try to swallow here, but it's just not happening. My Adam's apple is stuck dead center. Russ's right hand intertwines with my own, and to my amazement, I don't shrink back. His eyes hold me perfectly still.

"How's the numbness?" Lifting his other hand, he outlines my lips with his finger, causing tingles to shoot from my lips to my toes.

I'm glad the novocaine wore off.

"Fine," I squeak.

The liquid blue in his eyes makes my heart threaten to stop. My stomach is up where my Adam's apple is supposed to be. No wonder it won't move.

"I'm glad." His warm, whispery breath fans my cheek as he leans his head toward me, his penetrating gaze looking straight into my soul.

Warning flags should be waving and snapping about now, the same way they always do when someone gets too close to me. But I don't see the warnings this time, or maybe I refuse to see them. For reasons beyond my understanding, I want Russ to see me, to know me, the real me, beneath the wounded layers.

The murmuring throughout the house dulls, and the room around me fades as my eyelids drift lazily to a close and the warmth of his lips meets mine with all the magic of a first kiss. The hint of peppermint mingles with warmth, and we bask in the moment. Tender, gentle, moist, and oh-so-amazing.

"Well, you two about ready to eat?" Mom's sharp voice explodes through the air like shards of glass, ripping through the silence, shattering the ecstasy of the moment. We break apart like the cracked shell of an egg.

Thanks, Mom.

I lick my lips and fumble with my hands. "We'll be right there," I say, without looking up. The sound of Mom's shoes retreating to the kitchen calms me. I look over at Russ, and we chuckle.

He extends his hand to me and lifts me up. "Come on, let's go eat."

eighteen

"Your mom has taught you well, Janni. That was a mighty fine meal," Dad says, causing Mom to blush and adjust the napkin in her lap. "Except I ate too much." He pats his belly that barely makes a blip over his belt.

"Thanks, Dad."

They say the way to a man's heart is through his stomach. No wonder I can't keep a man.

Compliments over the meal lift around the table. We soon clear the soiled plates and load the dishwasher.

Everyone spills into adjoining rooms while Janni and I linger behind to finish cleaning things up. I notice Mom and Dad talking in the living room together. Maybe there's hope for those two yet—if we can keep Dad away from the knives.

"I'll make the coffee," I say, hobbling around the kitchen on my crutches, not because of the bruised ankle, but rather because that kiss has reduced my legs to the consistency of licorice whips.

"Why don't you go sit down, Char? You look a little flushed." Janni sprays the faucet hose over another plate and cleans it.

I lean into her. "Well, it's not from my ankle."

She stops rinsing and looks at me. Her eyes grow wide. "What? What is it? Did I miss something?" She looks excited and ready to throw a party.

My left eyebrow arches. "Wouldn't you like to know?" I walk back toward the coffeepot and set to work.

"Okay, that's just mean," she whispers into my ear. "It's something to do with Russ, isn't it? He brought you bakery cookies?"

I turn to her. "He's a dentist, Janni. I hardly think he would promote cookies. Hippocratic oath and all that." Which, by the way, makes me rethink where I want this relationship to go.

She hits me with a dish towel. "Oh, you. Spill your guts. What happened?"

Looking around, I make positively sure no one is within earshot, then I turn to Janni. "He kissed me."

She gasps, and her eyes get so big, I'm afraid they'll pop out. "You don't mean it," she says like a junior higher on the verge of squealing.

I grab her arm. "Shh, I don't want him to hear us."

"So you like him?"

"He's nice." I limp over to grab some mugs from the cabinet, knowing all the while I'm driving Janni crazy.

"Nice? That's it?"

"Well, what do you want me to say?" I pull the final mug off the shelf and line them up for when the coffee is ready.

"What about Peter?"

I grope to find the words to explain. "As I told you before, Peter and I have a comfortable relationship, but we're each free to see others. We're good friends."

"I see." She studies me.

"What?"

"Oh, nothing. It will be interesting to see how it all shakes out, that's all." She smiles, lifts the carafe of coffee, and starts pouring.

She has a point, but I'm not going to worry about it. After all, I live hours away. It's not like this can go anywhere. Russ is safe. Peter is safe.

I'm safe.

While Russ and I work on a sketch for his possible new home, Dad pieces together a puzzle on a cardboard table, Mom reads her book, Janni works on a puzzle in her Sudoku magazine, and Daniel snoozes quietly beside her. The kids are laughing together over something in the kitchen.

"Milton, are you all right?" Mom's question causes all of us to look up at Dad. Every hint of color has drained from his face. He's holding his stomach as though it might fall out.

"Not sure, Viney." He rushes up from his chair and dashes off to the bathroom.

We all exchange glances. Mom looks worried and darts after him. We follow suit. Nothing like having an audience outside your bathroom door.

By the time we arrive outside the closed door, there are sounds coming from inside there that I don't even want to think about.

"Milton, are you all right, honey?" Mom asks.

"I'm sick, Viney. Terrible sick." He finally opens the door, looking as though he's seen a ghost—or is one, I'm not sure which. "Just like that time I ate too many green apples."

"I'll fix you a place on the sofa where Char stayed. Do you mind, Char?" Janni asks.

"Of course not." Poor Dad is so sick, and I'm whining over a pulsating ankle. Which reminds me, I could use another painkiller.

Janni and I spread clean bedding out for Dad, then the guys help him back to the sofa.

"Probably got a touch of the flu." Mom puts her hand on his forehead. "A lot of that going around."

Dad groans.

"What's wrong, Milton?" Mom scrunches down beside him.

"I got a bad pain under my ribs, Viney. Bad pain."

Russ looks at Mom. "Could be gallbladder."

"We'd better get him to the hospital," Janni says, already grabbing her coat. "Your stuff in here, Daddy?"

"Yeah," he says, between groans.

"Sorry you're feeling poorly, Grandpa," Ethan says, when the kids join us.

"Yeah, me too," Blake says.

"Oh, don't you boys worry. I'll be fine." Dad's raspy breath and pain-filled words do little to assure us.

"I'm going with you," Mom says, clutching her purse in her hand, coat and gloves already on. She's armed and ready.

"You hold the fort down here," Janni says to me.

"I want to go." I'm not sure how I can do it with my ankle throbbing the way it is, but I'm worried about Dad too.

"Listen, Char, no offense, but with the crutches and all, you'll just be in the way. I promise we'll let you know what's going on as soon as we know something."

As much as I hate to admit it, she's right. "Well, let me know the minute you hear."

"Will do," Janni says, grabbing her purse.

"Want us to go?" Blake asks, brows creased together.

"No, you kids stay here. We'll keep you posted," Janni says, giving the boys a quick kiss.

"Okay, we'll start packing, but we won't leave until we know what's going on." Blake, Ethan, and the girls get up and walk out of the room.

We say good-bye to Dad, Mom, Daniel, and Janni, then they close the door behind them. Stephanie glances at me and smiles before leaving the room. Something in her smile reminds me . . .

I get up.

"You don't have to leave on my account," Russ says, looking disappointed.

"I'm not leaving. I just need to talk to Stephanie a moment." When I reach her, I lean in to whisper, "I think Blake has a crush on you and—"

"No problem. It's not going anywhere. I'll make sure of that."

It seems silly to even mention it. Yet, when she smiles again, doubt crowds my heart, and I wonder just how well I know my sister.

I nod and hobble back to the living room and sit on the sofa. "I sure hope Dad is okay."

"I'll bet you anything it's his gallbladder. He still has one, right?"

"As far as I know. Is that something a daughter should know? I mean, am I slime that I don't know if my dad's gallbladder is still intact?"

"No, you're not slime. You could never be slime." Russ walks over to me. "I need to check on my parents, but I can stay for a few minutes," he says, easing in beside me on the sofa, his arm extended behind me, resting on the sofa's top. The light blue oxford shirt he's wearing makes the color in his eyes pop and my stomach lurch. He turns to me. "Your dad will be fine. Janni will see to it."

He doesn't realize how his comment hits me like a two-by-four. "Janni handles everything." Guilt threatens to choke off my words. "No wonder she's burned-out."

"You can't blame yourself for that, Charley."

"I know. But I hate putting all the responsibility on her."

"Why, just because you don't live here? She's chosen to stay. If your parents needed you, you would help them, right?"

"Right."

"Janni knows she can count on you if she needs you."

My thoughts take me where I don't want to go with my parents growing older and more feeble.

Russ grabs my hand again, but this time more in a comforting way. "Everything will be all right. You'll see."

Tears trail down my cheeks.

"Hey, it's okay," he says, pulling me into a hug.

"I don't know what's wrong with me." His arms feel good. Too good. Warm, comforting, strong, safe, sweet. Very sweet.

"You're going through a lot with the way your mom is acting. You're away from home, coming back to a painful place. And you're on painkillers."

"How do you know all that, anyway?" I pull away, grab a tissue from the stand, and dab at my eyes.

He fumbles a moment. "Well, I gave you the pain medicine samples, and you lived here with Eddie for many years. It has to be hard."

More tears. "It is."

"Just don't write us all off because he was a jerk."

"When did you find out about Linda and Eddie, anyway?"

"When I moved back into town."

"Was that when you saw Linda and their little girl—isn't her name Carissa?—at the store?"

"No. Gail Campbell told me first, then I saw Linda and Carissa a couple of weeks later."

"The town crier. Figures." I blot my tears once more.

He laughs. "You know, I've been thinking about our date on Friday night. I don't want to force you into it just because I worked on your tooth, but if guilt works, maybe I'm okay with that."

His comment now causes me to laugh.

"Now that you've had time to think it over, are we still on?"

"We're still on." I smile. He tucks my tissue-free hand into his, weaving his fingers through mine again. I could get used to this.

"You know, I used to daydream about this—when I was in high school, I mean. You, me, like this."

"You're kidding."

"Nope. I'd see you and Eddie at the ball games and wish it was me in his place."

Boy, was I stupid.

Just then my cell phone rings. "Oh, I'm sorry, I'd better get that." Reaching over for my phone, I answer. "Hello? Oh, hi, Peter. Um, good to hear your voice too." Okay, this is awkward, talking to Peter with Russ beside me.

Russ leans over to me, his breath tickling my free ear. "Just so you know, I don't give up as easily as I did in high school." With a wink and a grin, he grabs his coat and walks out the door.

nineteen

"Did you hear what I said, Charlene?" Peter's voice is clearly irritated.

"What? Oh, sorry, Peter. Someone just left, and I was distracted."

"Oh, do I have some competition there?" His words trap me like a prisoner in a house not my own.

"Competition? How can you have competition when we have no arrangement?"

"Uh—oh—uh, yeah, right. Right." The way he stumbles over his words, I'm wondering if he's forgotten that part. Though I doubt he's forgotten it where he's concerned. Men prefer to keep their options open, but it's funny how they want their women to be tied only to them.

"So I guess I do have competition, huh?"

"I didn't say that."

"You didn't say that it wasn't true, either."

"Look, Peter, I'm upset. My dad is in the emergency room right now."

"Oh, I'm sorry, Charlene. I didn't know."

My ankle looks a bit swollen, so I lift my leg on the coffee table again. "We think it might be his gallbladder, but no word from the doctor yet."

"Well, you do what you've got to do there. I'm holding the fort down at the office."

"Oh yeah, that reminds me. A guy by the name of Jeremiah Bell contacted me about buying a property. He sounds like a good, solid client. I told him to contact you."

"That's good to know. He's listed on my callbacks, so I'll get right on it. Why did he call you?"

"Lydia Harrington referred me."

"You have quite a reputation in this town. You do a good job, Charlene. I'm glad you're taking a much-deserved vacation. You've earned it after closing on those three big deals last month, but don't get used to it."

"Used to what?"

"Staying away. We need you back here to keep business afloat."

My back bristles when he says that. That's why he wants me back. So I can bring in the money.

"Uh-oh, you're quiet. I know we've agreed to you cutting back, but I'm just saying don't leave me, okay?"

Like a noose, his words wrap around my neck and cut off my air supply. I can't seem to shake it. It's not as though I'm planning my future around him. We're friends. He comes over, and we entertain friends. We give each other something to do on a Friday night. Period. Besides, we both know the main reason he wants a personal relationship with me has to do with real estate sales.

"You always say to follow your dreams."

"Yeah, but that's only if they keep you here," he says with a forced chuckle. "Listen, Charlene, you're not—"

My heart softens. "No plans to leave right now, Peter. Relax."

"Okay. Are you getting lots of syrup?"

"We're doing okay. I won't be able to help for a couple of days."

"Why not?"

I explain what happened with my ankle, leaving out the parts about Stephanie and Janni.

"Leave it to you to climb a tree. I never realized you had such tomboy tendencies."

He's probably grimacing over the thought of me mingling with tree dirt. "Yes, Peter, it's true. I get dirty. I've even been known to have holes in my jeans."

I think he gasps here. "Well, I forgive you," he tries to sound as though he's joking, but I know better.

"I can't tell you how relieved I am." A cell phone rings on a nearby table. It appears in all the excitement, Dad left his phone behind. "Listen, Peter, I've got to go. Dad's phone is ringing."

One glance at the Caller ID tells me it's Gertie. "Hello?"

She hangs up. Guess she doesn't know he has Caller ID.

Before I have time to worry about it, Janni's phone rings. "Hello?"

"Char, it's Janni. Looks like Dad's got a bad gallbladder. They're going to keep him sedated tonight so his pain is minimal. Then they're going to do laparoscopic surgery tomorrow. They think everything will be fine."

"Oh, poor Dad. How's Mom holding up?"

"She's doing fine. Hasn't said any more about him trying to kill her, so that's good." Janni stretches.

"Are you coming back soon?"

"Yeah. Dad needs to sleep, and I think Mom does too."

"So does their daughter, meaning you."

Janni chuckles. "Guess I do at that. Everything okay there?"

"Yeah, it's fine. The kids are still packing. Must be all that clean laundry. They just don't know how to handle it."

Janni lets out a laugh. "I think you're right. Give them the scoop on Dad, will ya?"

"Sure thing."

"We'll hurry home to tell them good-bye."

"Sounds good. See you in a few."

We hang up, and I let the kids know what's going on. By the time they finish packing, Daniel, Janni, and Mom all burst through the front door.

We gather in the family room and talk a little longer about Dad. The kids decide to stop by the hospital on their way out of town. Soon hugs and kisses are flying around, and we're waving good-bye.

Janni closes the door after them and turns to Stephanie. "Now, don't think just because they're gone that you have to leave. You're welcome to stay here as long as you need. You've been a tremendous help around here. Besides, I'd enjoy the company."

"Even if I got the job at the coffeehouse, you'd let me stay here awhile?"

"Absolutely." Janni starts to walk around, then turns back to her. "Why? Did you get it?"

Steph grins from ear to ear. "Yeah."

"Well, congratulations!" Janni pulls her into a hug, and Steph looks at me over Janni's shoulder.

I wink at her.

"In fact, I need to go there right now. We're going to talk about schedules and all that. They just called me a little bit ago on my cell phone."

"That's great. You go on over. I think we're all going to rest awhile." Janni looks so tired. I want to help her, but here I sit with my bruised ankle propped on a table. I'm thankful Stephanie is such a helpful person. Could Janni really be her mother?

"Boy, it worked out nice that we didn't have to work on the sap today, didn't it?"

"You'd better get that leg back up. It still looks beat-up." Janni stuffs a pillow under my ankle on the coffee table. "Yes, I'm glad we didn't have enough sap, what with Dad's situation and all. Luckily, spring break for our high school starts tomorrow, so some of the teens from church are coming to help out."

"That's great. I was worried about how we were going to do this.

The good news is the weather is cooperating. The bad news is we're not getting as much sap."

"All we can do is what we can do." Janni picks up a newspaper and starts fanning her red face.

"Hot flash?"

She sighs. "I don't know what it is, but I'm sick of it." She fans harder. "It's like I can't get any relief, and it's driving me crazy."

Something tells me things are just beginning to heat up.

The next morning Stephanie takes care of the farm animals. Janni gets the church kids and a couple of adult friends collecting more sap, and I prepare a lunch of sloppy joes in the Crock-Pot for the syrup workers. Then we head over to the hospital with a half hour to spare before Dad's surgery.

"Now, Milton, you be careful, you hear me?" Mom says, loud enough for the entire hospital to hear.

He pats her hand. "I hear ya, Viney. Now, don't you worry. I'll be fine."

A tear slips down her cheek, and my heart turns to liquid. Mom has a hard crust around her heart, but underneath it all, she's very tender.

"Does this mean you're not mad at me anymore?" Dad dares to ask.

"It means I forgive you for trying to hurt me, Milton." She whips out a hankie that was tucked under the neck yoke of her dress and wipes her nose.

"Okay, Mr. Haverford, guess it's your turn," a nurse says as she walks into the room with a couple of orderlies. They get to work on gathering up the essentials while Mom, Janni, and I step into the hallway.

"You can go down to the waiting room and help yourselves to coffee and tea," the nurse says. "He'll be back before you know it." She pats Mom's arm and gives her a warm smile. We all kiss Dad good-bye, then watch as they wheel his gurney down the hallway and finally disappear into the elevator.

The three of us shuffle into the waiting room. Though we know this isn't a serious operation, it's never fun to see someone you care about go through something uncomfortable. Especially at Dad's age.

The sights and smells of hospitals have always made me queasy. No idea why. I can't even stand to watch hospital movies on TV. They all upset me. 'Course, I can get upset over a hangnail.

After I skim through twenty-some magazines and down about ten cups of horrible coffee, the doctor comes in and tells us Daddy is going to be fine. The surgery was a great success. Mom seems to hold her breath until she hears that "Dad's all right" part, then she falls slightly against me as though the weight of the day has finally bowled her over.

We thank the doctor. I turn to Mom and give her a squeeze.

She wipes away her tears. "I've never seen your dad sick in his life—well, other than that time he got sick from eating too many green apples."

Gathering our things, we head for the elevator to grab some lunch in the cafeteria. We'll stay long enough to eat and peek in on Daddy.

"I just can't tell you how relieved I am," Mom says between bites of her sandwich. "Though he was in no real danger, you never know when you get our age."

"That's why you shouldn't spend your time fighting, Mom," Janni says, matter-of-factly.

"We weren't fighting. He was trying—"

Janni holds up her hand. "I don't want to go there right now," she says in no uncertain terms.

It's starting to scare me how much she's becoming like our mother. But let the Heavens rejoice, her firm words stop Mom in her tracks. She says no more and goes back to her sandwich.

"We'll keep Dad at our house for a few days to help care for him, then we'll move you both back home." Janni's words leave no room for discussion.

Mom says nothing, but she's tearing into her sandwich like nobody's business.

Once lunch is over, we visit with Daddy a few minutes. He's so groggy from the whole ordeal, we decide to leave for now and come back later. After pushing the button for the elevator, we chat a moment or two and wait for the doors to open. When the doors part, lo and behold, off steps Gertrude Becker.

My heart freezes in my throat. One look at Mom's face, and I want to scream for the paramedics.

Mom forces a rigid fist on her hip and stares the woman down. "Gertie Becker, what are you doing here?"

Gertie pats her pink hair and smiles. "I came over as soon as I heard, Viney. Is he all right?"

Mom looks as though she could spit nails. We have to do something, and we have to do it fast.

"So kind of you to visit, Mrs. Becker," I say, pulling on her arm, to get her back into the elevator with us. "Daddy's sleeping and not accepting visitors just now."

"Oh dear, I didn't mean to bother anyone. Just wanted to make sure you all were doing okay."

"We're doing just fine," Mom says, nose pointed toward the ceiling.

A few tense moments follow as we ride the elevator, then step out when it reaches the first floor—all of us except for Mom.

"I've changed my mind, girls. I'm going to stay with your father. I'll see you when you come back tonight." Mom waves good-bye until the elevator doors close.

Mrs. Becker blinks, then smiles at us. "Well, you girls have a wonderful day," she says, already making her way outside to her car, no doubt none the wiser.

Once we're inside Janni's car, we lean our heads back and sigh. "Boy, that was a close one," Janni says.

"I know."

Janni pulls out into the traffic. "I just hope Dad doesn't pay for it."

twenty

"Well, I'll bet if Gertie fixed you something to eat, you'd eat it." Mom's fists are locked on her hips, and she's staring Dad down. Dad's barely been home an hour and Mom's already on him like butter on waffles.

"I've had two bowls of soup and a small piece of blueberry pie, Viney. Any normal person would be full by now." Dad sighs and leans back into his pillow on the sofa, his makeshift bed for now. Mom wouldn't hear of him climbing the stairs.

"Come on, Mom," Janni says, pulling on her arm, "I could use some help in the kitchen." Daniel's busy with the workers down at the Sugar Shack.

Though I'm no longer hobbling, I'm slower these days, whether from my ankle injury or my visit here in Mayberry, I don't know. I follow Mom and Janni into the kitchen.

"You've got to stop hounding him, Mom. You're driving him crazy."

Janni pulls clean plates from the dishwasher and stacks them back in the cabinet. We help her put the other things away.

"Well, I'm just trying to take care of him. And doing a much better job than what he was doing for me, I can tell you." Mom throws the silverware into the drawer.

"Hey, go easy on those," Janni says.

"Besides, Mom, you'd better be good to him. Men don't like to be bossed, and you don't want Gertie smooth-talking him."

A giggle escapes me, but the moment I lock eyes with my mom, I wish I hadn't teased her. I'm beginning to understand how that whole mothers-eat-their-young thing happens.

"Listen, Mom, why don't you take a nap? Char and I can finish up here." Janni saves my life once again.

"I'm too keyed up to sleep. I'll go down and help with the syrup."

Once she leaves the room, Janni looks at me and chuckles softly. "You're gonna get us both killed."

After I manage to sneak a couple of cookies, Janni and I head over to the Sugar Shack to help out with the sap process. Smoke curls from the chimney, misting sweet scents into the air and evoking childhood memories. I'd forgotten this part of being home. The sights and smells from the sap. The family working together to accomplish a sweet goal.

With my first step inside, my shoes stick to the floor where sap has spilled. Making the most of it, I tell myself I'm a star at Hollywood's Walk of Fame before slogging over to the evaporator. I relieve the kid on duty watching the temperature. I'm the official temperature-watcher-person in our family. Daddy says I have a knack with the hydrometer, knowing when the syrup is just the right consistency.

I haven't talked to Russ since Sunday night. He must be really busy at work. At least, I hope that's it.

Janni relieves the kid in the canning room and starts bottling the syrup. Two kids still work beside me, watching the filtering and finishing pans. Mom decided she was tired after all, so she's gone back to the house to rest. Janni gets a little reprieve. She's struggling with all this family togetherness in her house, I think.

The steady rhythm of shoving wood into the fire, the crackling sound of snapping wood, the smell of smoke, the hum of voices talking here and there, I love it all. It's hard work, to be sure, but there's something soothing about it.

Just then my cell phone rings, jarring me from my comfort zone.

"Hello?"

"It's Peter. Just wanted to let you know that the Jacobs's business sold."

"Oh, that's fabulous!" I squeal, causing everyone to stop and look at me. "Did you sell it? That's a great commission!"

"Yeah, I did. It's pending financing, of course, but these folks will have no problem swinging the deal."

"You're on a roll since I left. Maybe I should go away more often," I tease.

"I don't think so." His voice takes a serious turn, and I'm not sure I like the sound of it. "Listen, Charlene, we need to talk."

"Is something wrong?" The temperature level is almost where it needs to be, seven degrees above boiling, or 219 degrees, so I keep my eyes fixed on the thermometer.

"No, nothing's wrong. Things are going along well. I'm making decent money. You being gone so much has made me do a lot of thinking."

I gulp here. Something in the tone of his voice makes me very nervous. Peter isn't one to get serious about anything. That's one thing that makes me comfortable with him. I don't have to worry about a heavy relationship or talking deep. We keep things on a surface level and have fun, never allowing the big stuff to crowd us.

"Maybe now is not the time to talk about it?"

Well, actually, no. I'm kind of busy.

"Char!"

Janni's voice slices through the air, and I whip around with a start. The sap is overboiling and the stench of scorching syrup starts to fill the air.

"Oh, Peter, I'm sorry. I have to go. I'll call you later." Hurriedly, I click off my cell phone. All of us scurry about the Sugar Shack, trying to get the temperature down and get things back to normal.

By the time we finish, we're all exhausted, and the day's a total waste. I ruined all that sap, and forever lost the title of being the best gauge-watcher-person.

"Don't give it another thought, Char. Those things happen. We've done it before." Janni lifts the spaghetti from the strainer and puts it in the serving bowl with a bit of olive oil.

"Yeah, but I knew better than that. I've always prided myself on doing a good job where that's concerned." Pouring the thick homemade spaghetti sauce with chunks of meat and mushrooms into the serving bowl, I take a deep whiff. It eases my sour mood somewhat.

"We'll survive. Though we may have to cut down your supply." Janni pulls the crisp garlic bread from the oven, brushes butter over the top, and slices it into pieces before placing it in a basket with a towel to keep in the warmth.

"That's fair." I glance around the table to make sure there are enough settings.

"I'm only kidding. We all share in the work and in the bounty. You'll get the same as everyone else." Janni carefully places the silverware around each setting, and I pour iced tea in the glasses.

"What happened anyway? Important phone call?"

I explain about the call and how Peter's voice and comments made me nervous.

"I knew this would happen."

"What?"

"That Peter would either move on because he can't make a commitment, or that he would confront you and you would be faced with a decision."

"I like Peter, but we're just friends."

"I could be wrong, but it looks to me as though he sees it as more than that."

"Maybe."

"Time to eat," Janni calls out from the kitchen entrance.

Mom, Dad, Daniel, and Stephanie come and join us. The front door clicks open.

"Am I too late?" The tip of Russ's boots appear before he does. I'd know those boots anywhere. My heart somersaults.

"You're right on time," Janni says. She whispers to me on her way to the sink, "I forgot to tell you Daniel invited him for dinner."

"Thanks for the heads-up." I primp my hair, but realize it's too late. Now I'll have to wash my hands again.

Daniel and Russ help Dad get situated, while everyone else settles into their seats. Before Dad prays for our meal, I dash up the stairs, brush on some blush, and spruce up my hair. Not wanting to blatantly announce that I spruced up for Russ, I dab on a slight trace of lipstick then head downstairs.

Amid the clatter of silverware, jostling ice against glass, and chairs scooting against the hardwood floor, everyone laughs about how I ruined the syrup today. For an instant I consider going back upstairs. Until Russ's gaze meets mine. An empty chair waits beside him. He winks and motions for me to come over. He doesn't have to tell me twice.

With a stiff upper lip, I try to take the bantering good-naturedly, but if they're not careful, I could turn on them.

After the hubbub dies down, Dad looks across the table at me and says, "Well, I still say you're the best at the gauge, Zip."

I love my Dad. They've obviously already prayed for the meal, so I bow my head and say a quick prayer.

"You always were a softy where those girls are concerned," Mom says before biting into her garlic bread.

"Hey, remember that time you tried to bake a cake for Mom years ago when she passed her real-estate exam?" Dad says with a chuckle.

Janni laughs. "Yeah, you put too much baking powder in the cake or something and it overflowed. Almost burned the house down. Set off the fire alarms. It was hilarious."

"We had to open every window in the house," Mom says with a chuckle. "But it was sweet that you went to the trouble for me." Mom's little burst of tenderness catches me off-guard and takes the edge off my humiliation.

"That's right. It's the thought that counts, and Zip here went through a lot of trouble for her mom that day," Dad says.

"Yeah, and I never did a thing with that real estate license. But look at you, selling big homes," Mom says.

"Well, I'm not actually selling homes. Remember? I work in commercial real estate these days."

Mom waves her hand. "Oh, I don't understand all that stuff now. It's been too long."

The conversation moves on, and Russ talks to me in hushed tones. "Work has been crazy for the past couple of days."

"A surge of cavities, huh?" I tease.

He laughs. "Don't know if Daniel told you I called, but I did check on your dad."

"Thank you for that," I say, wondering why he didn't talk to me about it.

"I had a good talk with myself about moving too fast with you, so that's why I didn't call you about it."

His comment causes me to choke. Seems I do that a lot—especially when Russ is around.

"You okay?" He asks while he whaps me between the shoulder blades.

"Yeah." I reach for my iced tea and take a drink.

"Anyway, I'll try to be patient." He reaches for a piece of garlic bread and flashes a wide grin. "We need to work on my house plans some more." He looks me in the eyes. "Well, when you have time."

Oh, I have time for you, baby. Wait! Did I say that out loud?

A gasp lodges in my throat.

"Still choked?" he asks, raising his hand to whap my back again.

"No, no, I'm fine." It's true. I am fine. And looking at his blue eyes right now, I decide I've never been more fine. Really fine.

twenty-one

"Okay if I put on some old records?" Janni asks after dinner while Russ and I work side by side on the sofa, sketching out his dream home. Daniel and Stephanie step into the room and join us.

"Sure," I say, feathering my pencil across the paper as I draw up the space for the master bedroom.

"I'm glad you're here, Charley," Russ whispers into my hair, stopping my pulse.

Thoughts of Peter flash through my mind—though I must say his face is a little blurry—and I realize I have to deal with all of this, but for now I just want to enjoy my time with my family and, well, Russ Benson.

"So you say you want a balcony off the master bedroom?"

He grins and nods.

"I take it you have a lot with a view?"

He nods again. "Near the lakeshore."

My eyebrows shoot up. "Wow, that's nice."

"Yeah, I've been keeping my eye on that lot. Dad knew the guy was thinking of selling, so I asked him to let me know when he decided to do it. He did, and I bought it the day it became available. Never even made it to a Realtor. Sorry."

"Hey, whatever works." I smile. "So you're definitely building." Okay, my ego deflates a tad here. I thought he was using this whole building thing as a means to spend time with me.

He gives me a "well, duh" look and says, "That would explain the drawing."

"Oh, yeah, the drawing."

His eyes crinkle with amusement, and now my ego surfaces with the idea that he trusts me with so great a project. Time to get serious about the sketching.

"I'll take you over to the see the lot sometime."

"I'd like that." Clearing my throat, I break free from his gaze. "Okay, so, a balcony off your master bedroom overlooking the lake?"

"Probably sounds crazy because most people want to see the lake from the front of their house, but when I'm in the front of the house, I'm usually busy and wouldn't notice the lake anyway. When I'm in the bedroom, I have time to relax and enjoy."

His words melt over me like syrup on hotcakes, and I give an involuntary shiver. "Sounds like a plan."

"I thought a patio out back with a view of the lake would be good too."

"Good idea." My pencil sweeps across the page as he explains his ideas, and I try to get them in tangible form. "So you like the open floor plan, right?"

"Yeah." He rubs his chin. "How about a small porch on the front?"

"Sounds good." More pencil strokes. "With pillars and white picket-type rails."

"I'll leave that stuff to you. All I know is I want spacious and a balcony with a view."

"This will be great, Russ." I'd forgotten how much I enjoyed drawing up house plans and working on general real estate.

"Thanks." He squeezes my arm, I suppose, from the sheer excitement of getting a new place.

"How about you and Russ pick out some songs you like," Janni says, handing us the stack of records. She pulls out her Sudoku puzzle magazine.

Placing my sketchbook aside, Russ and I finger through the records, picking a variety from Chicago, Jackson 5, Donny Osmond, Carpenters, and other oldies-but-goodies.

Seeing Janni engrossed in her Sudoku, I start to get up.

"Let me put those on for you." Russ walks over and starts the first record.

The minute the music to "Sugar, Sugar" starts playing, my mind zips back to the school rec room where a bunch of us girls met before the school bell rang the start of a new day. We'd play records from the jukebox and sing along. This was one of the songs we played over and over. Even worked out a few choreographic steps, if I remember right. A sliver of bravery comes over me, so I get up and sway with the music. Reverting to my junior-high days, I throw in some arm thrusts, twirls, and leg kicks, causing Janni to look up in surprise. Russ joins the fun and soon punches the air with his fists in awkward movements that make me laugh so hard I'm afraid I'll join Janni with the hyena thing.

When we finish, everyone claps. Then Daniel gets up and pulls out the Three Dog Night song "Joy to the World." Okay, Russ may not be Fred Astaire, but Daniel's movements remind me of Baloo in *Jungle Book*.

Next, Stephanie picks out a song and plays it. The opening line of Helen Reddy singing "You and Me Against the World" squeezes my heart. Tears fill Steph's eyes, but she smiles, so I doubt anyone even notices but me. Tears sting the backs of my own eyes and threaten to spill over.

Stephanie wants a relationship with Janni so desperately. I can only imagine how it would feel to have a child love me that way. She's afraid telling Janni will change everything, and she won't get a chance to truly get to know her biological mother. But Stephanie needs to know the truth so she can move on in her search.

After the record fun, Janni points out that Wiggles hasn't been out of his cage all day.

"Oh no, I'm outta here." I make a beeline for the living room.

"Don't be such a wimp, Char. Sit down. Wiggles needs to get to know you. He won't hurt you if you're sitting in a chair. Just don't move."

"Oh, fun."

"Come on, Charley," Russ says, flashing his infamous grin. "Wiggles doesn't know me either. Sit by me, I'll protect you."

Okay, I'm liking the sound of that.

Daniel laughs, walks over to Wiggles's cage and opens the door. The curious squirrel hops off his perch onto the door of his cage, then takes the next step to freedom.

With skittish movements, he ambles over to Daniel and jumps up on the ottoman in front of him. "We know what you want." Daniel reaches down beside his chair and pulls out a sack full of sunflower seeds. Pouring some into his hand, Daniel feeds Wiggles one seed at a time. Sitting on his hind legs, the squirrel splits the shells off, then nibbles away at the meat of the seed.

"Well, will you look at that," Russ says. "It's amazing to me that he doesn't try to get away. You know, with the call of nature in his blood, you'd think his natural instinct would be to escape outside."

"Why should he? He has everything he needs right here, and he's protected," Janni says.

"Still, it's not his true home."

Russ's words zing me. All this talk about home makes me want to watch *The Wizard of Oz.*

Over the next half hour, Wiggles entertains us with his little antics, but I'm relieved when Janni finally puts him back in his cage.

"I'm surprised he goes so willingly," I say, watching the squirrel run back to his cage at Janni's insistence, hop on his perch, and crack open another sunflower seed.

"As I said, it's his safe place."

Which would explain why I want to stay in Maine.

Russ turns to me. "Hey, want to run with me to the coffee shop?"

"Is it still open?"

"It's only ten o'clock. They're open for another hour."

"You don't have to ask me twice." I grab my coat and drape it over my arm as we head for the door.

"That was fun. I haven't exercised that much in years," Russ says, sliding into the leather driver's seat in his Lexus. One look at his firm self makes me question the truth of his statement.

"Yeah, it was fun." Flipping the visor down, I turn on the makeup mirror light and adjust my makeup. I'm surprised I have the nerve, but one look at my face tells me I've done the right thing.

"You don't need that stuff. You look beautiful just the way you are," he says.

"Please don't tell me your last eye exam was in 1982." My ego is hanging by a thread.

"Nope. Just had an eye exam six months ago."

"Works for me." I brush on a dab of lipstick and flip the visor back in place. Russ's laugh warms me clear through.

"It's great to be back home. The military was good to my wife and me, and we loved the travel, but my heart was always here. Guess I'm a small-town kind of guy."

I give him a hard appraisal. He doesn't at all look the small-town type, but there it is.

"Funny, I would picture you more at home in the hub of a big, noisy city."

"Then you've got me pegged all wrong." He turns off the classical music on the radio as though this is a serious discussion. "Not that I don't enjoy the big city, I do. It's just not where I want to live. Give me quiet evenings on a porch swing among the sounds of crickets and locusts. A lazy afternoon fishing down at the stream." He turns to me, eyes twinkling. "I love the simple things in life."

"And teeth. Don't forget teeth."

"Right. I love teeth." He laughs. "You're still doing okay with that job I did on you the other night?"

"Good as new."

"Great." He pulls his car into the parking lot and kills the engine.

Before I can sneak on more lipstick, he dashes around to my side of the car, opens the door, and takes my hand to help me out.

"Okay, I could get spoiled if you keep this up."

He pulls me up until my face is right next to his. "That's the idea," he says with a husky voice that rattles my constitution.

His fingers reach up and brush a strand of hair from my forehead. My skin tingles beneath his touch as his head dips toward me, lips touching mine so briefly I wonder if I imagined it. Then with another tug, he pulls me a little closer and this time kisses me with enough force to give me a glimpse of the passion that burns within him, but easing up to show that he promises to keep things in line.

Leaving me dazed, he pulls away slowly, gives me a grin, and puts his arm at my back as we head for the door of the coffee shop. It's a good thing he's guiding me, or I'd pull the Tipsy thing and faint straight up.

Once we get our drinks, we find a table and settle in.

"So, tell me about this Peter guy."

"Whoa, you don't waste any time, do you?" I laugh at his boldness.

Russ grins. "It never hurts to know the competition."

There's that word again. I attempt to lift my eyebrow in a seductive, Betty Grable sort of way. "Oh, really?"

"Really," he says, slurping the whipped cream off his frappuccino, and thus confirming that I should leave the Betty Grable look to, well, Betty Grable.

"Peter is a great friend. He owns the real estate company where I work. We've been seeing each other for six months." I take a drink of my maple macchiato, but my eyes never leave his face. "But like I said, we're just friends."

"I see." He swirls the straw around in his cup, stirring the remaining whipped cream into the mixture.

Why is it men can eat real whipped cream without gaining an ounce? In my book that mystery is right up there with the eight wonders of the world.

"Friends or not, six months is a long time," he says, staring glumly into his frappuccino.

"It is?"

"Isn't it?"

"I—I don't know."

"No serious plans on the horizon?"

"No."

"And how do you feel about that?"

"Did you minor in psychology? Am I on *20-20*? Related to Barbara Walters?"

He laughs. "Listen, I know it's none of my business. You don't owe me any explanations." He leans over the table toward me, and his hand covers mine. "But I care about you and guess I wanted to know if you feel the same way."

Oh, believe me, babe, I'm feeling it.

Why is it my tongue refuses to move at times like these? It just flat out will not move. Not even the slightest twitch. It's like an obese snail on sedatives.

A wounded shadow flickers in Russ's eyes. "Oh, I get it." He takes his hand from mine and leans back in his chair. "I've let my assumptions get away from me."

"No, no, it's not that." I reach for him now. "I'm just not sure about anything since I've been back here, Russ. I mean, I like you. I really do. Peter is a great friend, but we've never been really serious in that way. Just comfortable with one another more than anything. Does that make sense?"

He nods. "And he's okay with that? To leave it there, I mean?"

Remembering my earlier conversation with Peter, now I'm not so sure. "He has been." *Up to now.* "It's just that, well, you live here, and I live in Maine. It's hard to have a long-distance relationship."

"Hard, but not impossible."

I smile at his determination.

We carry on with surface conversation after that, and Russ takes me home. Once there, he opens my car door and walks me to the front porch.

"Glad to know I'm still in the running," he says, his lips mere inches from mine. His arms wrap around me and pull me to him as though I'm something fragile that could easily break. Guess he's figured me out. He leans forward and tenderly kisses me again. Then again. Then once more. My teenage years come back in a flurry—my first kiss with Eddie, the thrill of his touch, the wonderment of knowing I was the one he had chosen to share this moment with. Only this isn't Eddie. This is Russ. And the excitement is more intense, even painful—because those feelings are supposed to be dead and buried. Stamped out. Never to return. But they're not dead. They're back. In full force. And to make matters worse? They're all grown up.

I pull away. "Good night, Russ."

His eyes are glazed, his breath shallow. "See you, Charley." His thumb traces the side of my face, causing my cheeks to burn.

As I watch him walk away, my heart twists and my stomach churns. Okay, I knew coming home would be complicated, helping with the syrup and party planning while trying to maintain my life back in Maine. But it was also an opportunity to show my family how I've changed. "Charlene Haverford moves beyond her past to face the future."

Yeah, right.

"Char, get up! The condo next to Mom and Dad's place is burning!" My eyelids blink open, and I find Janni staring over me in my room. Seems my family enjoys startling people first thing in the morning.

"What?" I rub my eyes, wondering if I heard her right.

"The condo next to Mom and Dad's is burning."

Whipping off the covers, I jump out of bed and slip on my robe. "How do you know?"

"Someone from the fire department just called."

"How bad is it?"

"The fireman said they were able to contain it, and it didn't do much damage to Mom and Dad's place. It started in the building next to theirs and they were able to put it out before it did substantial damage to Mom and Dad's building. There is some minor smoke damage that needs to be fixed, though, and he said they wouldn't be able to move back in for a week or two." Janni heads for the door. "Daniel's working with the others on the sap, but I'm going over to Mom and Dad's place to check on things for them."

"Let me get dressed, and I'll go with you," I say, already pulling off my robe and heading toward the dresser.

"Okay, I'll wait. Come downstairs when you're ready." With that Janni turns, and I hear her feet dash across the hardwood and down the stairs.

I get dressed in record time and meet Janni in the living room.

Mom's face is lined with new wrinkles. She wrings her hands together and looks up when I come downstairs. "We want to go with you."

"Mom, let us check things out first, then we'll take you over. It's hard to say what we'll find right now," I say.

"Milton, tell them we're going."

Dad walks over and puts his hand on Mom's shoulder. "It's all right, Viney. They might be right. The more people that congregate there, the more confusion there will be. We'll just get in the way of the workers."

Mom's shoulders slump, and her eyes droop.

"It will be okay, Mom," I say, giving her a hug. "We'll be back shortly and let you know what's going on there."

She says nothing, merely nods.

Dad still looks weak from the surgery, but he's holding his own. "Thanks for checking on things for us, girls."

It breaks my heart to see them looking so—so vulnerable. I haven't realized until this moment just how old they are getting. It's as though I've been looking through a shadowy glass and now I'm seeing clearly. I don't want to face the truth that I might one day lose them. Mom and I have our differences, but I love her fiercely.

"Wish I could go with you," Daniel says, before giving Janni a kiss good-bye. "Call me and let me know how everything is."

Janni agrees.

"It will be all right. You'll see," I say to Mom and Dad, giving them a hug. Janni and I head out the front door, and I pray that I'm right.

"Now, let's see, Mom wanted some pajamas, right?" I rummage through the top drawer of her oak dresser, expecting a couple of cotton housedresses.

"Right."

A gasp lodges in my throat.

Janni turns to me with a start. "What's wrong?"

With disbelief I lift a slinky black negligee from Mom's drawer. "Never in a million years would I have pictured Mom as the Victoria's Secret type." The silky unmentionable dangles from a tiny strap that's hooked on my index finger.

"Eeew." Janni scrunches her face.

"It boggles the mind, doesn't it?" I shake my head. "Don't think about it any longer. It could warp us."

Janni obediently shakes her head. We don't say another word. It's like we're carrying around this deep, dark secret that we don't want anyone to know. And truly, we are. It just wouldn't do for church members to think of Mother in that light. It's not healthy. For anyone.

"Listen, I talked to Greg Boyle at church." Janni lifts one of the suitcases we brought with us onto their bed and starts filling it with Dad's clothes and shaving things.

"The psychologist?"

"Yeah. He says with the trauma of her move, Mom could have retreated into her books and made them her new reality. Maybe that's what's bothering her. She might be reading about a love affair where 'the other woman' is trying to bump off the heroine."

"Could be."

"Maybe we need to hide her books." Janni heads for the closet.

"Getting Mom away from her books? Okay, that should be easy. Right up there with ripping a bear cub from her mama."

Janni chuckles, then disappears into the closet.

"Here's their old cake topper." She reappears, holding the plastic piece with the reverence an actress would give a Golden Globe.

"Oh, perfect!" She brings it over to me. "The traditional wedding couple," I say, inspecting it. "Retro clothes." The wire arch over the couple is covered with garlands of fabric flowers and leaves and an off-white satin bow. Two wedding bells complete the decoration. I set it aside to take with us when we leave. "You know, I'm surprised we haven't seen any of Mom's books here," I say, filling Mom's suitcase with the things from her list.

"Probably brought them all to my house. You don't suppose she's reading smutty romances, do you?" Janni says with pure horror in her voice.

I laugh. "Mom? Smutty romances? Never in a million years."

Janni walks over and lifts the black negligee, dangling it from her finger and setting my stomach to full tilt.

"That does it. I'm looking for books."

Janni nods and joins me in the search.

Turning to the bed stand, I pull open the drawers and rummage through the contents. "Thinking back to all the times I was livid at her for messing around in my room when I was a teenager makes me feel a tad guilty about this."

"You can remedy that by thinking about those times when she had no problem whatsoever reading through your journal."

I whip around to face Janni. "She read my journal?" My breath hovers somewhere between my lungs and my esophagus.

She looks at me. "You didn't know?"

"No." At this bit of news, every smidgen of guilt vanishes.

"Every day she went into your room to read your entries. I spied on her. She never knew that I knew. That's why I never kept a journal."

"Why didn't you tell me?" Ruthlessly, I rip through the sheets and check for a book.

"Thought you knew." Janni flips up the bedspread, gets on the floor, and looks underneath the bed.

"No wonder she thinks I'm a failure. We write things at that age that we don't mean." I check behind lamps and in hidden nooks.

"What? She doesn't think you're a failure. Why would you say that?" Janni pushes herself back up and brushes the dust from her hands. "I'm sure it's not true. You're too hard on yourself. You're not to blame for what happened between you and Eddie."

Pulling a light suitcase from under the bed, I unzip it. "Things are never one-sided, Janni. There are always two sides to every story." Nothing in the luggage, so I zip it back and return it to its place under the bed.

"You can't blame yourself for the miscarriage. Those things happen."

"Because I was exercising."

"You don't know that."

"Yes, I do."

"You have always been fit. Your body was used to it."

"Obviously not."

"Who's to say you wouldn't have lost the baby anyway?"

Once I finish rummaging through the books in the bookcase, I look at her. "I don't know."

"Exactly. You need to let it go. It happened, but it wasn't your fault. It's life. Losing a child is no reason to leave your wife and have an affair." With her hands on her hips, Janni surveys the area. "She must have her books with her."

"I guess. You know how much he wanted children."

"Nothing makes it right. He needs to own up to it. Stop blaming yourself."

We edge our way out of their condo, and just as we pass the hall closet, I take a last-minute look inside. "Bingo," I say, pulling a book from the top shelf.

"What is it?"

"It's a suspense book. I've read this author before, and she could make anybody paranoid. Edge-of-the-seat stuff."

"I thought Mom said she was reading romances."

"There usually is a thread of romance in these books, so she was telling the truth—in a vague sort of way." I laugh. Flipping through the pages, Janni and I read sentences here and there and shake our heads in wonder.

"Do you think this is what's causing her paranoia?"

"Anything's possible with Mom," I say. "But in her defense, I have to say some of what Dad's been doing does seem a tad suspicious."

Janni gasps. "You don't think for a minute that Dad—"

"No, of course not. There has to be some explanation. We just have to find out what it is. In the meantime, keep Mom away from these books." Noting that it's a library book, I tuck it under my arm to return to the library. "Oh, I just thought of something. I'd better get their checkbook in case they need it while at your house." Stepping back into the bedroom, I walk over to the antique cherry desk that has been in our family for years—compliments of our great-great-grandmother on

Dad's side—and reach into the drawer where he's kept his checkbook for as long as I can remember. Sure enough, there it is.

Behind the checkbook is a key with a tag. Pulling it out, I examine it. The tag has the word Harley on it.

"Janni, come look at this," I call out.

She returns to the bedroom, walks over, and lifts the key from my hand. "Hmm. Wonder what that's about?"

"Do you think Dad owns a Harley without Mom knowing?"

Janni's eyes grow wide. "It's hard to imagine. I've never seen him ride one."

"Well, did you see Mom as a Victoria's Secret model?"

Janni winces. "Good point." She hands me back the key. "You know what this means, don't you?"

"No."

"We're going to need some serious counseling."

"Don't I know it."

The phone rings, causing us to jump. "Probably Dad," I say, answering it. "Hello?"

"Viney?"

"No, this is her daughter, Char."

"Oh, uh, this is Gertie. Just needed to talk to your dad a minute."

"He's not here right now, Gertie," I say, loud enough for Janni to turn around and look at me in surprise. I explain about the fire and that they'll be staying at Janni's house. "Could I give him a message?"

"No, no, nothing urgent. Just needed to talk to him. Thank you, honey. I'll see him at church." Click.

"There are far too many secrets floating around here," Janni pulls her keys from her purse.

"Well, I aim to find out what's going on." Clutching my purse, the suitcases, and the key to the Harley, we leave the condo, locking up behind us.

twenty-two

"*It's hard to believe that building is gone,*" *I say,* looking at the charred shell of the building to the right of our parents' place.

"I know. It's scary. I'm so thankful no one was hurt."

The smell of smoke and scorched wood lingers in the air, reminding me of the burned sap.

"Yeah, I'm glad too." I walk over to the charred remains and a somber mood moves in. What if someone had been hurt? What if they left unfinished business behind? Regrets. Life is so full of uncertainties that it makes my head hurt to think about it.

"You coming?" Janni's standing by the trunk of her navy SUV, the suitcases beside her.

"Yeah." Stepping back over to her, I help her put the luggage in the trunk.

No sooner do we have the suitcases loaded in Janni's car than Mom and Dad's neighbor, Mr. Green, hobbles over to us. Bless his heart. He and his wife go to church with Mom and Dad. We'll probably be here for another hour now.

"Well, hello, girls," he says with a tired smile. I don't know about Janni, but I haven't been called a girl by anyone but Dad since elementary school. Feels pretty good.

"How are you, Mr. Green?" Janni says, patting his arm.

Despite the cold weather, the short, bald man with a paunchy middle pulls a handkerchief from his pocket and wipes sweat from his brow. They must keep the heat up in their house too. "We've been working hard to get our place back in order."

He proceeds to give us the lowdown on what he thinks happened, how the Dentons most likely caused the fire, what with the way they leave their lights on all the time. In fact, he decides they're probably the reason for the high cost of electricity these days.

"Oh, that reminds me. We're leaving for a few days while they work on our condo, and I think you'd better move the Harley."

Janni and I exchange a glance.

"Oh, maybe you don't know about it. Gertie asked if I would keep the cycle for your dad. Said it was a surprise of some sort, I don't know."

Shock rips through my veins as my gaze locks on Janni. First Victoria's Secret, now this?

He takes one look at us and scratches his head. "Or maybe your husband could take it over to Gertie's house if you don't want it at your place."

Do I even know my family anymore? Maybe there's something to Mom's suspicions after all.

"Uh, sure, we can take it," Janni pipes up.

We talk a little longer about the price of gas, Mrs. Green's arthritis, and Mr. Green's knee replacement, then he gets us the two helmets and the Harley.

Pulling the key from my pocket, I stick it into the ignition. I turn to Janni. "Houston, we have a fit."

She laughs. We say our good-byes to Mr. Green, then another neighbor helps us walk the Harley over to our car.

"What do you think the surprise is?" Janni asks, running her hand across the seat.

"Who knows? They have an anniversary coming up. Maybe he's going to pull up and take her to the party on a Harley."

She shrugs. "You know, I've driven one of these a few times."

"That's nice," I say, having no idea where she's going with this, so I simply nod. Then it hits me. My gaze collides with hers, and I see excitement staring back at me.

"You can't be serious," I say.

"Why not take it for a quick ride? Just for fun. We can come back and get the car. I need to do something fun, Char," she says as though I owe it to her.

"For one thing, we have on thin jackets and no gloves."

"My hot flashes will get me through. Your grit will help you."

Okay, that strokes my ego for a millisecond, then I move on to argument number two. "How long has it been since you've driven one? Or even ridden on one? You could hurt yourself. Worse, you could hurt me."

"One of my college friends owned one, and we used to ride together," she says.

"You haven't ridden one since college?" My voice is bordering on a shriek. "And you expect me to get on board?"

"Aw, they say it's like riding a bicycle. It will come back to me."

"And if it doesn't?"

"Come on, it will be fun."

It doesn't escape me that she didn't answer my question.

"You've been on one before, right?" she asks.

"Sure. Many times. With an experienced, up-to-date driver. I don't have a death wish."

"Where is my adventurous sister?"

"She died, and I intend to keep this one alive." She's right. She is going through some kind of mood thing—or a midlife crisis. Why, I haven't seen her this excited since her homemade jam won first place at the county fair. I'm putting my life in her hands, for what, a little mood shift? Where is the wisdom in that?

"Please?" While I hesitate a little longer, she digs deep to the root of my sisterly devotion. "You love me, don't you?"

"Not that much," I say, causing her to blink and stumble backwards. "Okay, I'm kidding. But still." I stare at the Harley and then back to her. Upon seeing the eager look on her face, my heart melts. "I know I will regret this," I say.

She claps her hands and quickly straps on her helmet before I can change my mind. Reluctantly, I put mine on. I wouldn't mind full body armor right about now, but I guess this will have to do. Just call me David. But even he had a sling. I have, well, a helmet.

My heart zips to my throat as we climb on the motorcycle. Janni starts the engine, kicks back the stand, and we lurch forward, as does my stomach.

Let me just say here that though I've ridden a motorcycle before, I've never experienced anything quite like this. As we ride slowly through the quiet streets of a neighborhood inhabited mostly by retired people, we jerk as though we're riding a bronco. The idea of going out into real traffic scares the pajeebers out of me. My ankle is starting to hurt again.

Janni calls out something about haste, her waist, or toothpaste, but I can't hear her. "What about toothpaste?" I shoot back.

"My waist. It hurts."

Looking down at my white-knuckled fingers that are clutching five inches of skin on either side of her jacket—has she never seen that Special K commercial?—I see her point. Most likely, I've stopped the blood flow. With any luck, her skin will fall off. She should thank me.

We come to the stop sign at the entrance of the subdivision. "Here we go," Janni shouts with wild abandon, her words evaporating into thin air as she burns rubber behind us. "Yeeeeeeeehaw." She peels into traffic like she belongs to Hells Angels. The roar of the cycle—or is that Janni's voice?—causes trees to quiver when we pass, which is a little frightening, to say the least.

The wind whips against my chin—thankfully, the only exposed part of my face. The ends of my woolen scarf stream behind me like a banner. A long scream pierces the air.

Mine.

This is a Janni I have never seen before. A wild, carefree, motorcycle mama. Before I can blink, we turn down a country road, and Janni leans into her bike like Evel Knievel. My tongue sticks to the roof of my mouth. Fear bumps race up my arms. My hands grip her waist so hard, she'll be down to a size 2 before the trip's over.

"Hang on, Char!" Janni shouts.

Yeah, like she needed to tell me that.

If she leans any deeper into the machine, her head won't show over the handlebars. The engine roars and gains momentum as she shifts gears. I don't know how fast we're going, but the speed of light comes to mind.

Words escape me—one of the few times in my life. With the roar of the wind and the speed at which we're flying down the road, abject terror is snuffing out any possible thought that might enter my brain anyway.

In an instant my life flashes before my eyes—and I do mean flashes. In fact, everything is flashing before my eyes right about now.

"Janni, we need to go home," I yell.

"What?"

"We need to go home."

"Why? This is fun." She squeals. At least I think it's her. I hope it wasn't the brakes.

"Janni, I want to go home." There is definite grit in my voice, and I'm okay with that.

"Spoilsport," she calls back. "All right."

By the time we get back to the condo to pick up the car, my body is frozen to the motorcycle. As in, I need a crane to pry me off.

"Oh, come on. Don't be such a wimp." Janni yanks me off. If I had the strength, I'd bop her one. Instead, I remind myself to be sweet. I'm beginning to think June Cleaver is the only woman alive who has that one down.

"What has gotten into you?" I say when my jaws thaw out.

"That was so exhilarating! It's been forever since I've ridden one."

Excitement colors her cheeks red, while my cheeks probably have all the color of muslin.

"Sorry if I got carried away. You drive the car home, and I'll take the motorcycle."

"Don't you have to have a special license to drive these things?"

"Yeah."

"Do you?"

"Um, no."

"I'm seeing Officer Toby Millington in our future."

"I'm taking it straight home. No big deal."

"What are you going to do once we get it to your house?"

"I'll hide it in the barn. Mom never goes out there."

"Okay."

As I hobble—and I do mean hobble—to Janni's car, I remember how the Israelites would build monuments to the Lord for special events. If I had the strength, I would stop right now and build a monument in thanks for my feet touching the ground.

But something about this whole Harley thing unsettles me. I have a feeling there's much more going on with my sister than meets the eye.

After the excitement of the fire, the motorcycle ride, and working with the sap, I'm exhausted by the time we get back to the house for the evening. Thankfully, everyone was down in the woods when we got home, so we were able to hide the motorcycle in the barn without revealing Dad's surprise—whatever that is.

"Well, it's about time you girls got back. I was starting to worry about you," Mom says when we step inside the house. She's holding a book in her hands. When she sees me looking at it, she puts it behind her back. "You've had a full day."

"Your condo is in pretty good shape, really, considering the building beside you burned down." Janni hangs her coat in the closet, then reaches for mine.

Dad walks slowly up beside Mom, who is chewing on her lower lip, something I rarely see her do.

"It could be worse, Viney," Dad says, patting her shoulder.

She nods.

Dad takes short steps over to the sofa. He's still not feeling quite up to par, but it's amazing what they can do these days. I want to talk to him about Gertie's phone call, but seeing him hobble makes me decide to wait a little while. He's not going anywhere soon.

"Did you and Dad already eat?" Janni asks.

"Yeah, we grabbed a couple of turkey sandwiches."

"Sorry I didn't have time to fix anything for dinner."

"Don't you give it a thought," Mom says. "You girls have had a busy day."

She has no idea.

"Well, I'm starving," Daniel says, throwing open the front door and stepping inside.

After a quick dinner of sandwiches and veggies, Janni takes orders for pumpkin pie and coffee.

"Hey, Sweet Girl." Daniel reaches out and grabs Janni's hand when she walks past him. "Your cheeks look a little red. Are you all right?"

If he only knew.

"I'll tell you later," she says with a giggle and a conspiratorial wink my way.

I want no part of it, thank you.

Once Janni serves the pie, she and I go back into the kitchen to get coffee for everyone.

"Where's Stephanie?" I ask.

Janni starts the coffee. "Mom said she got called into work." I'm thinking she's putting in extra hours to give me time to digest everything she told me.

"You know, Char, that reminded me of the fun we used to have as teenagers. Remember when you took me out for a soda the day you got your license?"

The memory makes me smile as I pull mugs from the cabinet.

"The only difference is that *I* trusted *you.*" Janni's smiling, but her eyebrow is quirked with a reprimand.

"You're right. But back then, we were too young to know fear. Now we can smell it a mile away."

Once the coffee is finished, Janni gets the carafe, and we start filling the mugs.

"At least I didn't scare you like you did me that night I was in the pantry."

I stare at her a moment.

"Don't you remember? Dad went through that phase where he cut back on lightbulb wattage—"

"Oh, yeah! We walked around in shadows at night. Very eerie."

"Right. I was browsing through the pantry one night, and you saw it as an opportunity to scare the daylights out of me."

I laugh. "I crept near the doorway and scraped my fingers on the wall."

Janni shivers with the memory. "And made some spooky noise. I lifted out a weak 'Mom?' Then in a burst of courage, I raced through the door, startling both of us."

"Your scream slashed into the next county." I double over in laughter, and when I finally catch my breath, I see her glaring at me.

"It wasn't funny. It was mean. I had nightmares for a month." Janni puts the mugs on a serving tray.

"Well, before you get your nose twisted out of joint, I might point out the time you put Tabasco sauce in the oatmeal cookies. Not exactly angelic in nature, wouldn't you agree?"

Now she laughs. "I didn't mean to do that, and you know it. The bottle fell from the cupboard, and the lid wasn't screwed on tight. Only a few drops spilled, so I figured the cookie dough was salvageable. Besides, how was I to know you would eat the first cookie?"

I stare at her. "I always eat the first cookie."

"Well, then that's what you get for being greedy."

"And you wonder why I switched to gourmet cookies."

She makes a face.

I'm surprised I forgot the fatal cookie night. I had been convinced that my sister was trying to kill me. Something tells me this is Mom's fault. We're a weird lot.

No wonder I stay away from Tappery.

twenty-three

"Hey, Char, have you seen Janni?" Daniel straps on his boots and looks up at me from the sofa.

"Not since I grabbed my coffee before breakfast."

He rubs his jaw thoughtfully. "Maybe she's out in the barn. Well, if you see her, ask her to bring me some coffee in the thermos. I can't find it, and I need to get down to the sugar bush and help the others."

"And we need our coffee."

He grins. "Exactly." He turns to leave, then swivels back around. "One more thing. Tell her we're out of dill pickles. There's a two-for-one coupon in the kitchen drawer."

It's beyond comprehension that he has the same enthusiasm in his voice over dill pickle coupons that I have for cookies. "I'll tell her. We'll be down there shortly."

He waves and heads out the door. Dad's not up to working in the woods yet, so he's parked on the sofa in the family room, reading his Bible and drinking coffee. I poke my head into the room.

"Have you seen Janni, Dad?"

He looks up from his Bible. "No, Zip, haven't seen her. Did you check the bathtub? Remember how she used to hide there when she was little?" Dad's eyes take on a wistful look. "Might want to look there." He smiles.

I had forgotten that. Since bathtubs had been designated as a safe place in a storm, as a child Janni carried that thought over and went there anytime she needed to be alone or to feel safe. If we couldn't find her, she almost always was in a dry bathtub, reading a book or holding her favorite doll.

"You need some more coffee?"

A grin breaks out on his face. "That would be great." He lifts his mug to me.

"Mom out with her lady friends for breakfast?"

"No, she's upstairs reading."

Uh-oh, could be another interesting day. After filling Dad's cup, I take it to him. "Dad, when we were at your condo, you got a phone call."

He looks up with interest. "Yes?" He reaches for his coffee and knocks his Bible from his lap. A paper slips out. I reach down to give it to him and see Gertie's name and number on the slip. He grabs it and stuffs it back into his Bible.

"Um, it was Gertie. She didn't leave a message, just said she'd talk to you at church."

"Okay, thanks. This is good coffee, Char."

"Listen, Dad—"

"Yeah?"

One look in his eyes and I decide one crisis at a time is all I can handle. "Never mind."

I roam the house in search of Janni. Bathtub is clear. I have to admit that relieves me. The thought of a woman over forty retreating to a dry bathtub bothers me a little. 'Course, with the way she's been acting lately, who knows?

Frustrated, I pass the stand and turn the Precious Moments figurine southward.

She's nowhere in sight, so after putting on my jacket and gloves, I head out the door and over to the barn. Sliding open the massive door, I'm immediately greeted by the kittens. They circle and mew at my feet, and I'm thinking if they had the strength, they'd gnaw through my boots. How odd. Janni normally feeds them by now.

Edging over to their food and water bowls, I see that they're empty.

"Janni," I call out. Nothing. Could be she's in the chicken coop. Quickly, I put food and water out for the animals. Once I'm sure that everyone has what they need, I tromp over to the chicken coop. Taking a deep breath before I step inside, I open the door and brave the smell.

The chickens squawk and strut about, loose hay flutters with the cold air, and the charming scent lingers. But no Janni. Anywhere.

Since I'm already in here, I decide to collect the eggs, though I can't deny that I'm starting to worry about Janni. Before my fears get away from me, I tell myself she's probably already joined the others in the woods.

Rather than make her come back up to the house for the coffee, I return to the kitchen. After I wash my hands, I stack the two dirty cups from the sink into the dishwasher and spot the thermos. Retrieving it, I wash the container and fill it with coffee, then head to the woods to join the others.

Upon seeing Daniel, I march it over to him. He seems surprised to see me.

"So where's Janni?"

"You mean she's not here?" Now my adrenaline kicks in. Mom's paranoia must be contagious. Let's just hope Mom doesn't get wind of this. She'll have posters of Janni covering every available pole in the county before lunch.

"No. Remember, I told you to have her—"

"Yeah." I cut him off. "When I didn't find her in the barn, I figured she was with you."

He looks as worried as I feel.

"Don't worry about it, Daniel. I'll go up and check again, look for clues. She probably just ran to the store."

"Maybe."

"Hey, Daniel, come and see this," one of the high-school kids calls out.

"Well, tell her to come see me when you find her," he says to me.

"Will do."

My heart beats hard when I rush back to the house. It's not like Janni to disappear without letting someone know what she's doing or where she's going. Something has to be wrong.

I comb through the house once more, from top to bottom, and still no Janni.

"Say, Dad, did you ever hear from Janni?"

"You never found her?"

"No. None of us has seen her in a while."

"That's odd." He rubs his forehead while he thinks, and right then I hear the faint sound of an approaching engine.

"Wait. That might be her. I think I hear an engine." I turn around and dash through the front door and screen in time to see Janni, complete with helmet, gloves, and black leather jacket, riding up on the Harley.

She flips up the clear visor on her helmet. "Morning," she says with such enthusiasm I consider hiding her Folgers.

"I have half a mind to flip your screen back down. Where have you been? We've been looking for you."

"Well, you found me." Her cheeks sparkle red, her eyes flash, a wide grin splits on her face. Suddenly, she no doubt sees the smoke puffing from my nostrils. "I needed to get some air."

"That's my line. Hey, where did you get the leather jacket?"

She looks down as if she's forgotten. "Oh, this? I've had it forever.

Never really saw myself as the leather type, but I thought it fit this morning." Looking up at me, she grins. "Shoot, I might get matching leather pants."

"Okay, now you're truly scaring me."

She laughs, just on the fringes of the hyena hoot, and I hold my breath, but it fizzles out. So help me, I want to be mad at her, but this is a side of Janni I've never seen before, and I like it.

"Well, you'd better put it away. Everyone is worried about you," I say, flicking some leafy debris off her shoulder.

"Why?"

"Because no one knew where you were, that's why." I follow behind her to the barn. *I'm* mothering *her*? First Tipsy, and now I'm having a Freaky Friday moment with my sister?

After I open the barn door—and let me just say here, I'm developing muscles that could rival Sylvester Stallone's—Janni lets the engine putter and guides it into the barn with her feet. I walk along beside her in case she falls—which isn't really smart, now that I think about it. After all, she would fall on me.

"I'm sorry if I worried anyone. I took it for an early morning spin and thought I would be back before now. I told Danny where I was going."

"He's the one who sent me looking for you."

She rolls her eyes. "He was in the bathroom when I told him. Guess he didn't hear me." With the bulk of her leather boot, she shoves the kickstand in place. When she pulls her helmet off, her hair bounces lightly against her shoulders. "Do they have enough workers down there?"

"Plenty. Word has caught on at church. I think half the congregation is in your woods."

Janni laughs.

"Luckily we have friends with flexible work hours. I'm surprised the kittens aren't clamoring to eat," she says.

"I already fed the animals."

"Oh, dear. I'm slacking off on my duties." Concern shadows her face.

"It's not as though they would starve from waiting an extra hour." But yes, you are slacking off on your duties.

"Thanks, Char."

"Janni Haverford Ort, what are you doing with that contraption?" Mom wants to know when she sees the motorcycle. The look on her face says she isn't pleased.

Janni and I lock eyes. What can we tell her when we don't know ourselves?

"Did you talk her into this thing, Charlene Marybelle?" Mom's tapping her foot.

"Uh, we're keeping it for someone," Janni blurts, before Mom and I can come to blows.

"Well, don't you get on that thing. They're dangerous. You couldn't pay me enough to get on one of those," she mutters on her way out. Then she swings back around and looks at me, "And if you have any sense, you'll stay off of it too." With that, Mom turns on her heels and marches back to the house.

"Guess it's time to talk to Dad about it," Janni says, looking glum.

"Maybe he wants to buy it for himself." I'm afraid the thought of Dad in leathers and chains could scar me for life.

"Guess we won't be keeping it here anymore." Janni runs her fingers along the seat.

"Janni Ort, have you not approached Dad about this because you wanted to keep it here a little longer for yourself?" Words escape me.

She hesitates. "Oh, don't be silly."

I'm not convinced.

"Tell Daniel to get one for you both to ride. He might surprise you."

"Yeah, right. If it doesn't come with a coupon, forget it."

Daniel is nearly the perfect husband—all except for that coupon fetish of his. "What's he saving all that money for, Janni—an all-expenses-paid trip to the nursing home?"

Janni chuckles, then stops and gives me a deadpan stare. "That's not so funny." She sighs. "Want to help me get the cake ready?"

I'm struggling to read her expression, so I decide to let it drop. "Sure. You'd better go down and let Daniel know you're here, first. I'll get everything ready in the kitchen."

"Yeah, you're right." She takes two steps, then turns back around. "You know where the recipe box is?"

"Yeah."

"Okay, back in a minute."

I wave as she heads toward the woods, and I step onto the porch. Dad soon joins me in the kitchen where I'm going over the recipe for the cake.

"Did you find Janni?"

"Yeah."

It's just better that I not bring up Janni and the motorcycle. Besides, my mind is still trying to grasp that whole deal with Daniel and his coupons. Makes me wonder if he's one of those millionaire types who stuffs money under the mattress. I make a mental note to check under my mattress tonight, just in case.

After Dad and I talk a little longer, Janni comes in the kitchen, her cheeks all rosy, eyes sparkly. She places the thermos on the counter.

"Hey, Janni, after we get this cake finished for lunch, do you think you could run over and see a house with me? You have all that help with the syrup. They won't even miss us."

"Why do you need to see a house?" She eyes me suspiciously. "You planning to move?" Excitement touches her face.

"Me back in Tappery? I don't think so." I laugh. "You know how I love to look at homes for sale. I don't know who lives there now, but it used to belong to the Tuckers. You know, that cute little cottage on some acreage a couple of miles down the road."

"Oh, that's still the Tuckers'. They entered an assisted-living place about eight weeks ago, and they're trying to sell their home. From what

I hear, they've got stipulations on the sale. They want just the right fit for their home." Janni laughs and shakes her head. "It will take someone special to want that small of a home with all that acreage. They want a farmer. We're afraid it will become commercial, and that's the last thing we want in this area."

My ears perk. "How much acreage comes with it?"

Janni frowns. "I'm not sure, a hundred fifty, maybe? Why?"

"Just wondered." It might be a good place for the Scottenses' new store. No need to tell Janni and get her all stirred up before I check it out.

"They've completely redone the inside. Spent a lot of money on it, from what I hear." Janni measures out the sugar and pours it into a mixing bowl.

It would be a shame to tear it down if they've remodeled, but sometimes sacrifices are made in the name of business. "Remember how we used to help them pick apples in their orchard?"

Janni chuckles. "Are you kidding? I still count apples when I can't get to sleep."

"Yeah, but could Mrs. Tucker ever make apple pies."

"That's true. To be honest, I think that's where my love for cooking started."

"You mean when she had us help her out with the pies?"

Janni nods.

"How come it never affected me that way? I just wanted to eat them. Don't tell Mom it wasn't her cooking that did it for you."

"She'd never believe it anyway," Janni says.

I laugh. "They were nice people. I should try to visit them while I'm here."

"They would love to see you, I'm sure."

"So you'll go with me?"

"As long as there are enough workers helping Daniel, why not? Oh, that reminds me. He wanted me to bring down some more coffee." Janni makes a face.

"Don't worry, I can take over on the cake. The recipe's not that hard. Even I can handle it," I assure her.

"Just don't burn down my house while I'm gone, okay?"

She laughs and leaves the room before I can find a rubber band to fling at her.

One glance at the recipe, though, and my cooking phobias return tenfold . . .

"Oh, this is so cute." I step onto the Tuckers' wooden porch that has colored rails and scalloped windows. "This resembles a Mary Engelbreit drawing."

"It does, doesn't it?" Janni cups her hands around her eyes and peers into the window. "Too bad the Tuckers aren't here to show you around."

"I know, doggone it. I'd really like to see it." I glance down at the listing in my hand. "The price is reasonable." 'Course, it's not zoned commercial, so I'd have to check into that for the Scottenses.

Janni glances at the paper. "Wow. With all the redecorating they supposedly did, I wonder why they're asking so little for this and the acreage."

Glancing around, I wave my hands at the barren cornfields across the street. "In case you haven't noticed, this isn't exactly a thriving metropolis. Unless they have a farmer interested, they're out of luck." Or unless I can convince the community that this is an ideal place for the discount store. Though the population is small in Tappery, there are enough people close to this section of town that I think the business could work here. They could throw in some farming necessities, and they'd be good to go.

"Yeah, I guess." Janni chuckles.

"Oh, come look around here, Janni," I say, pointing to the huge maple tree that's at the side of the house with branches that spread to the second-floor window. "Remember how we used to climb that thing?"

Janni chuckles. "You climbed. I watched."

"That's true. Let's go look at the backyard."

We walk around to the back that's lined with dwarf apple trees. "How quaint," I say.

"It surprises me to hear *you* say that, of all people. Since you don't cook, all these apples would go to waste."

"Well, not with Dad around. He eats apples the way I eat cookies."

"Bakery cookies, mind you," Janni corrects. "You know something, you're a cookie snob."

Her comment halts me for a second, but then I decide it fits. "I'm good with that."

Janni makes a face and shakes her head. I walk over to the back door and yank on the knob just to make sure it's not open.

"Be careful, you might get in there and find a dead body," Janni teases.

"Thanks for the warning, *Mom.*"

Janni gives me a pointed stare. "Don't you ever call me that again in this lifetime."

That makes me laugh. We talk about the apple trees as we walk back around the side again.

"That would be the first thing to go if I lived here," Janni says, pointing to the maple tree.

I gasp. "Why?"

"I wouldn't want someone climbing the branches and looking inside my house."

Her comment causes a lightbulb to come on in my head. She must see it because our eyes collide in a millisecond.

"Oh, no." Janni's already shaking her head. "You're not thinking what I think you're thinking."

"Come on, Janni, why not? It just might be open."

"You can't be serious? You just got over a bruised ankle, and now you're ready to risk it again? That ankle might be weak, Char."

"Weak, schmeak, I can handle it."

"I want no part of this, Charlene Haverford." She folds her arms across her chest and turns her back to me. "It's time to own up to the fact that you're too old for this kind of stuff."

"You were too old for anything daring by the time you were five, Janni." Carefully, I pull myself up to the first branch.

"At least I recognize my limitations."

The rough bark gouges my hands, and a branch jabs my leg, but I'm not about to turn back now. "Approaching fifty doesn't mean you're dead," I say, struggling for every breath.

"I can't believe you're doing this. Be careful!"

I knew she would watch. Her motherly instincts would never allow her to look away. In fact, right now she's staring at me as though I'm about to jump off the Brooklyn Bridge.

My foot slips on the bark, and I almost lose my grip. Okay, that scared me a little, but the color on Janni's face scares me even more. It has faded to a dingy white.

"I'm okay."

Her hand is on her throat. "Char, get down from there." I think she's suddenly developed laryngitis because she's talking funny. "I'm going to call Mom."

Another step up the branch. "Okay, that's a low blow."

"I mean it. Get down from there."

"I'm almost there, Janni. Don't panic." Once I reach the window, I anchor myself on the limb and give the window a nudge. It opens. "Bingo," I call down to my sister, before raising the window all the way.

She gasps. "You can't go in there." She steps closer. "That's called breaking in." She's whispering, but her words are on the verge of hysteria.

"Oh, come on, Janni. You said yourself you've been bored." I'm proud of myself for not pointing out that she was born bored. "Let's spice things up a little." I climb inside the room, turn, and poke my head through the window. "I'll meet you downstairs and unlock the front door."

Before she can object, I scurry away from the window. I'm evidently in a guest bedroom. Antique furniture abounds in the home in stark contrast to the updated flooring and colorful painted walls.

"It's really cute," I say to Janni when I open the door. She looks as though she's swallowed sour persimmons. "Hurry up and get out of here, will ya?" Her eyes dart about the room. With skittish movements she scurries from room to room in an effort to hurry me along.

"Calm down. This is no big deal. We'll be out in no time. Come look at this kitchen, Janni. You won't believe it." I take her into the kitchen that boasts cream-colored cabinets and tiled flooring.

She takes a deep breath and seems to relax a little. "Oh my. This is nice." She pulls open the cabinets one by one, and we browse through the walk-in pantry.

"I'm honestly surprised this place hasn't been snatched. No doubt it's all the acreage. Most folks don't need it." But I think I have the remedy to that problem—if only I can get the Tuckers to agree. Still, I have to admit it would be a shame to tear down this lovely place.

"That's true. And if you're not a farmer—well, what's that phrase they always use in real estate?" Janni asks.

"Location, location, location."

"That's it. You said yourself it's not exactly a thriving metropolis."

The sarcasm in Janni's voice surprises me. "I thought you loved it here."

She runs her fingers along a coffee table, leaving a streak behind. "It's all right. But it's not as though we're on the Maine coastline."

There's a hint of resentment in her comment, and I can't imagine why. She's the one with the good life, not me.

"Hey, what's that sound?" Janni stops pawing through the books on the shelf and listens.

"What? I didn't hear anything." My fingers run along the book spines. "Look at this." I lift a copy of *Pride & Prejudice* from the bookshelf.

"Wonder why they left all this furniture? It seems like they'd need it," Janni says.

"They probably left as much as they could to help sell the house. Homes always sell better if you show them when they're furnished."

"Shhh, there it is again."

"What?" Suddenly a scraping sound breaks the silence. "Wait. That sounds familiar." For the life of me, I can't put my finger on where I've heard it.

Janni chews on her lower lip. "What could it be?"

Creeping toward the noise, we edge up the stairway, boards creaking beneath our feet, toward the guest bedroom where I came in. Janni is following so closely behind me that her shoes keep scraping the backs of my heels.

"Ouch," I whisper when we stop a few feet to the right of the bedroom door. I turn a frown to her.

"Sorry."

Just then I peek my head into the bedroom. The hair on my neck bristles as I lock eyes with—a brown squirrel. Panic slices through me, and I scream, which causes Janni to scream, which causes the squirrel to dash through the room, underneath my legs, past Janni, and down the hall at the speed of light.

"He'll tear up the place," Janni screams, her arms flailing about as she runs after the squirrel.

"I'll get the broom out of the kitchen closet," I yell, running after Janni.

A huge commotion follows as we chase the squirrel around the house, waving the broom, screaming, yelling, and barking—well, we're screaming, and the squirrel is barking—thwacking here and there until he finally runs for his life through the front door and heads for freedom and refuge in a nearby tree.

We hobble over and fall onto the sofa.

"Okay, that was exciting," I say, trying to lighten the storm that's sure to come once Janni catches her breath.

"Or not."

"Lucky for us you left the front door open," I say with a laugh.

Janni's gaze rams into mine.

"You didn't leave it open?"

She shakes her head.

"Hold it right there." The deep voice causes my blood flow to stall. "Get up and turn around slowly, ladies."

Janni and I exchange a glance, then turn around to see a uniformed Toby Millington standing before us, badge flashing, gun in position.

With one look at us, his eyes grow wide and his shoulders sag. "First your mom and now you?" He sighs and shakes his head. "You have the right to remain silent. Anything you say can be used against you in a court of law . . ."

twenty-four

"Boy, what is it with you and squirrels?" I say to Janni once we're placed in a holding cell.

"Shut up. We're in enough trouble," she snaps.

"Good grief. You said you wanted adventure. I give you some and you get all mad."

"Riding a motorcycle is adventurous, Charlene. This is"—she looks around at what appear to be angry inmates and lowers her voice—"not." She scoots closer to me. "Wonder what neighbor called the police?" she whispers.

"Gail Campbell."

"How do you know?"

"Lucky guess."

"She doesn't live near there."

"No, but she always seems to be at the right place at the right time."

Janni shoves her chin into her palm. "What a mess."

"At least Toby knew us."

"Poor Toby. Probably figures our family is going down the tubes fast, what with all of us breaking the law."

I laugh. "Oh, well, look at it this way, we can tell our grandkids about this one day." What am I saying? As Gail so graciously pointed out, I won't be having grandchildren.

She looks at me. "We're supposed to tell our grandkids things that will build them up, give them lessons on the road of life. Breaking and entering does not qualify."

I shrug.

Janni glances around the cell and bites her lip. "I sure hope we're not in here long." She inches toward me some more.

"If you move any closer, people will talk."

"Daniel will come," she says, ignoring my comment.

"He's so busy with the syrup. He's not going to be happy about this."

"That's not what's bothering me."

"What is?"

"How I let you talk me into getting sucked into another of your harebrained ideas. When are you going to start acting your age?"

"What? You've got your nerve, Motorcycle Mama. You've got issues of your own to sort out without getting into mine."

"Thank you, Dr. Phil." Nose hiked, Janni inches away from me, looks around, then inches back.

She's miffed, but I don't have time to worry about it. Once we get out of here, I need to call the Scottenses. I have a promotion hinging on it.

The Tuckers come down to the jail and vouch for us. It is so good to see them, and I hope to spend more time with them before I head back to Maine. When we're freed from lockup, we run some errands, mostly in an effort to avoid Mom. When we get back, everyone has gone to their rooms for the evening. Janni is carrying scrapbook stuff into the kitchen and dumping it on the table. I offer to help her. I figure it's the least I can do since I landed her in jail and all.

"I'm so glad we've brought this stuff inside. I'm sure you're still thawing out from working in the barn." I help Janni carry two boxes of pictures from her bedroom into the kitchen.

"Yeah, this is better, as long as we can keep Mom and Dad away. You'll have to help me keep watch for them so they don't spoil the surprise." Janni drops her box on the table with a grunt, then settles into a chair. "I still can't believe we were in jail today."

"At least we didn't have to wear the orange suits. It's totally out of my color scheme. Washes me out something fierce."

Janni stares at me like she wants to hurt me.

"I'm kidding." Why is it I always say the wrong things?

Together we dump a batch of pictures on the table, then place our boxes on the floor.

"How we've managed to steer clear of Mom is beyond me," she says.

My fingers rummage through the pictures. "Well, we'd better get our stories together because we'll most definitely be dealing with her tomorrow."

"Yeah." Janni picks up a picture of the two of us. "Remember this one? We were baking pumpkin cookies. I think you were around nine or ten here, and I was probably five or six."

Leaning over, I look at the picture and laugh. "That's the day Mom got us our first aprons."

Janni's eyes light up. Over aprons. She snaps her fingers. "That's right." She gets up, goes over to a cabinet drawer, and opens it. "I still have mine," she says, whipping out a tattered and spotted pink apron the size of a potholder.

My jaw drops. I'm not about to point out that it would barely fit around her neck, let alone her midsection. "You kept the apron all these years, why?"

"Because it was my first one. You didn't keep yours?"

"It wasn't fashionable until Martha Stewart came along. Why would I?"

Janni shakes her head and stuffs the apron back into the drawer.

"You know, the good thing about that jail deal is it will keep Mom's thoughts off of her paranoia about Dad."

"Yeah, maybe. At least those two are civil to one another now. It's a start."

"By the way, did you talk to Dad about the motorcycle yet?" My fingers continue to sort through the pictures.

"Yeah. Guess he wanted to surprise Mom with a motorcycle ride on their anniversary, as we suspected."

"Did you tell him she wants no part of it?"

"Yeah. He said it belongs to Gertie's son, and he's out of the country, so he asked if we could keep it here until they return. Gertie doesn't have room for it."

"Oh, that's probably why they met at the bakery, and why she was calling him. Well, if you're going to ride that Harley again, you'd better get a license. All we need is for Toby to pull you over."

"You're such a worrywart."

"Did I tell you that I found another of Mom's books in the laundry basket?"

Janni shakes her head. "Suspense author again?"

"One and the same."

"She's hiding them because she's afraid we'll take them away from her." Janni laughs.

"She's right." Picking up a couple of pictures of Mom and Dad with their siblings, I glance up. "We're forkin' out too much money for her to be so suspicious."

Janni agrees, then yawns. A look of complacency has settled over her. She thumbs through the pictures with all the excitement of a slug. She catches me watching her. "What?"

"I really think you need to see someone about your energy level. Like I said, you could have some thyroid issues."

"You're kidding, right? You had me breaking and entering somebody else's house. We were hauled off to jail. From there we went on errands, which included grocery shopping for the week, we're now working on the scrapbook, and you say I have energy issues? Maybe the better question is, are you snacking on coffee beans?"

I chuckle. "No. Though it's not a bad idea for either one of us."

Just then Stephanie bursts through the front door and hangs up her coat. "Hey, whatcha doing?" Her smile brightens the room when she enters the kitchen where we have pictures sprawled across the table.

We explain the events of our day to her and have a good laugh.

"Mom and Dad are in bed, so we thought we would work on the scrapbook. Would you like a turkey sandwich? I can make you one." Janni starts to get up.

Stephanie motions for her to stay put. "I'm a big girl. I can get it myself."

"There's pumpkin pie in the fridge, too, if you decide to indulge," I say.

Stephanie stares at me.

"Alfalfa sprouts?"

She laughs. "Okay if I join you two?"

"That would be great," Janni says, her face brightening.

Stephanie walks over to the fridge while we continue to sort through the pictures. I'm wondering if I shouldn't have discouraged Stephanie from talking to Janni about this whole matter. It's better than allowing her hopes to get too high. When Stephanie realizes she's mistaken, it will likely devastate her.

"Oh my goodness, is that you?" Stephanie asks, pulling a picture of Janni from the pile. Sandwich in hand, she settles into her seat.

My sister laughs. "Guilty as charged." Leaning over, I see the picture in question and suddenly realize how much Janni and Stephanie resemble one another.

"Hey, we sort of look like each other here," Janni says off the cuff.

"Yeah, funny, isn't it?" Stephanie's eyes meet Janni's.

In that instant, it seems as though the dust in the room stops circulating. No one moves. Janni swallows, then looks from Stephanie to me, then back to Steph.

"Am I missing a joke or something?"

"No joke." Stephanie's eyes are still pinned on Janni.

Janni appears confused. "It seems I've missed something, but okay," she says, brushing the air with her hand.

"No, wait." Stephanie grabs Janni's hand. "There is something."

Stephanie looks over to me for support, and I give a short nod. I pray Janni is up for this, what with the jail thing and all. And that Stephanie can handle the truth.

"There is a reason we resemble one another."

Uh-oh, here it comes. *Somebody* is going to be disappointed.

Janni gives a tiny gasp. "What are you saying?"

Stephanie cups Janni's hand between both of hers. "I'm not here to stir up trouble, Janni. I just wanted to get to know you."

Janni's eyes grow wide. "Are you saying what I think you're saying?"

Stephanie swallows hard, then looks at her. "I believe I'm your daughter."

All color drains from Janni's face, and for a minute I ponder where it has gone.

Silence engulfs the room. Janni must be trying to come up with a way to tell this poor girl she's mistaken.

"I know this has to be hard for you," Stephanie says.

Just as I'm about to jump in and help Janni out, she speaks. "You're my dau—daughter?"

Stephanie manages a hesitant nod. Why isn't Janni telling her it can't be? I'm confused.

Janni bursts into tears, and when she regains her composure, looks at us both. "Looks as though I have some explaining to do." I'm shocked to the core. Her lips start moving and I hear the words, but it takes a moment for them to sink in. A college love, bad choices, pregnancy, adoption.

To say she burst my bubble and has now been stripped of her sainthood is an understatement. I visually see myself ripping the saintly crown off her head.

"Char, say something."

"All these years, you let me think you were Miss Perfect?"

"No one is perfect, Char. Least of all me. I told you that over and over. You thought up that perfect business all by yourself."

I feel betrayed somehow. I resented her for being perfect, and now I resent her for not being perfect. "Am I the last one to know?"

Janni looks down at her fingers. "No," she whispers. "No one knows." She turns to Stephanie. "Will you please keep this to yourself for a few more days while I sort through all this, Stephanie? I'll have to ease the news on the rest of the family. It obviously won't be easy, but—I'm so glad you're here."

They both embrace for the longest time, crying together. They're having a memorable moment, and I realize that I'm just mad. How could Janni keep this from us? I'm her sister. All this time she let me think . . .

"What happened to my dad?" Stephanie asks.

Janni bites her lip. "Alex Winters. We were not together after I found out I was pregnant, and then he died in a car accident three weeks before you were born. I'm sorry, honey."

Janni. The perfect one—who lived a double life.

Seeing Janni's reunion with her daughter—a daughter no one knew anything about—and wondering how this news will affect the family, has robbed me of sleep tonight. I think I've worked through most of my anger and decided Janni's going to need me to get through this. She was there for me during my divorce; it's the least I can do for her. Even though she never told me, her own sister, about Stephanie. Like I said, I've worked through *most* of my anger.

My covers feel hot, and I whip them off, leaving only the sheet over me. The small fan that's on the stand next to my bed keeps my face cool but doesn't always help the rest of me. If Daniel keeps the house so cold, why am I hot? The thought that it might be hot flashes hits me, but I'm not buying it. I'm just not the hot flash type. I need only to get back to my own house. It agrees with me.

After wrestling with the covers and heat for a while, I finally give up. Putting on my light robe and socks, I slip down the stairs, careful not to wake anyone.

The boards creak beneath my feet more than usual—or maybe it just seems that way because of all the pie I've been eating. My foot eases off the offending board. They really need to get some things fixed around here.

The sweet scent of blueberries fills the air and something tells me someone has already beat me to the kitchen. When I walk into the room, Janni is bent over the stove, checking on a tin of muffins.

"Have I ever told you about the blueberry muffins I get at the Bagel Station back in Seafoam?" I reluctantly grab the coffeepot and help myself to a cup. "They totally melt in your mouth." Reaching into the cupboard, I retrieve a saucer which my cup settles onto with a slight tinkle.

"Well, my muffins aren't from the Bagel Station, but they're Daniel's favorite. I haven't made them in a while." Janni walks over to me. "Listen, Char, I'm sorry about everything."

"Forget it. I'm the least of your problems." The shadows beneath her eyes tell me she feels the same way. I touch her arm. "It will be all right, Janni. You'll see." Walking over to the table, I settle into a chair. "So, are you making these for Daniel to soften the blow?" I take a sip from my mug. The scary thing is, Janni's coffee is starting to grow on me.

"Something like that," she says, pulling off her oven mitts and joining me at the table. "Like it?" Janni's eyes are twinkling as she watches me. "I bought a new brand—from the coffee shop."

"You bought ground coffee from the coffee shop?"

She nods.

My heart warms that she went to the trouble for me. "It's good, Janni. Really."

"I'm glad." After a long sigh, she says, "You know, you've been asking me if I'm depressed, and I can tell you now that though I believe much of it is hormonal, since the boys have left home, I've had more time to think about the daughter I never knew. I tried to bury my past, and it worked for a while, but having so much time these days to spend alone with my thoughts has brought the guilt back in full force."

I don't know what to say.

"What am I gonna do, Char?"

"It will work out. Things always do."

Janni shakes her head. "I'm not so sure. Daniel is big on honesty, and while I wasn't trying to be dishonest, I just wanted to put the past behind me and not talk about it with anyone, ever." She looks up at me. "As though it never happened, I guess. I should have known it would catch up with me." With her fingers, she twirls a strand of hair.

"Daniel loves you. He'll get over it."

"Mom and Dad don't know. My kids—Blake! He's been flirting with her—" Her hand covers her mouth.

"Nothing happened. Stephanie made sure of it."

"How do you know?"

"She told me that night she told me about you being her mother, and I fell out of the tree."

Janni's eyes widen to the size of muffins. "That's what made you fall out of the tree?"

I nod.

She looks as though she's not sure whether to laugh or cry. Suddenly, a chuckle bubbles out, then another, and another, until she's erupted into a full fit of laughter. I soon join her in side-splitting guffaws. Tension rising up and out with every chuckle. By the time we've finished, the weight of the world has lifted from my shoulders.

"Oh my goodness, I'm so sorry, Char, but it's just that I can picture it all."

"It's all right. It's good to see you laugh."

She squeezes my hand. "Thank you, sis, for being here."

Before I can respond, Daniel steps into the room.

"Umm, something smells good," he says, fidgeting with his belt buckle.

"Do you have help at the store today, or do you have to go in?" Janni asks.

He rubs the back of his neck. "I'm free to work here all day."

"Before you get started, would you mind if we talked a little bit?"

One glance at Janni's face, and Daniel doesn't hesitate. "Sure, Sweet Girl. Whatever you want." He looks at me, then back to Janni. "What's up?"

"Let's eat some blueberry muffins first. Then we'll take a walk."

"Did you see them?" I ask Stephanie when she joins us in the woods. I pull the bag from a maple tree and dump it into the bucket.

Stephanie shakes her head. "I sure hope everything is okay. How long have they been gone, do you know?"

"About an hour or two by now," I say.

"Well, I just came down to let you know I got called into the coffee shop. I'll check back in later."

"Okay." She turns to walk away. "Stephanie?"

She looks at me.

"Don't worry. Things will be fine."

"Thanks."

It's hard to say how long we work before Daniel comes over to me. "You might want to go to the house, Char. Janni could use your help getting ready for lunch." His eyes look red-rimmed and distant.

My stomach dips, and I swallow hard.

The trees offer a calm presence as I make my way to the house. They've sheltered us from the storms of life, provided sustenance, kept us together as a family. Janni's right. We can't let this farm go. We need the trees. We need each other. We'll get through this.

"Janni?" I call out when I step inside the house.

"I'm in the kitchen." Her voice is shaky, as though she's crying.

Quickly, I go to her. "Are you all right?"

She turns away from the sink and lifts puffy, red eyes my way. "I've hurt him terribly." She dabs at her nose with a handkerchief.

"Give him some time. He'll get used to the idea."

She shakes her head. "I never meant to hurt anyone. And what will this do to Mom and Dad?" She looks at me. "How will the boys take it? I've made such a mess of things." She pulls her hands to her face and sobs.

I put my hand on her shoulder. "Janni, take it one step at a time."

She takes a deep breath.

"So tell me what happened." We find our places at the table.

"We took a walk, and I told him everything. He listened intently, hardly ever interrupted me. When I finally finished, I was afraid to look at him, afraid of what I would see."

"And?"

"He stopped walking, put his hand on my arm, and turned me to him so that I had to look square into his eyes. Then he said, 'I just wish you had trusted me enough to tell me. How can I know there aren't other things you've been keeping from me?' What could I say? He went on to tell me that he had a past he wasn't proud of, but I knew about his, and I should have trusted him enough to be honest up front. He believes a good marriage demands honesty."

Right then my ears perk, and I want to know what's in his past that I don't know about, but now doesn't seem the time to ask.

"He told me he loved me, but it will take some time for him to digest everything."

"You see? He'll come around."

Janni wipes her nose again and nods. "Now I have to tell the others. It's hard. Part of me feels sad that I have hurt Daniel, and I'm afraid of hurting the boys, Mom, and Dad. Yet another part of me is so happy and relieved. As I said, thoughts of my daughter have been a big part of my restlessness lately. "

I give her a hug.

"Guess we should get the bread ready; the group will join us soon." We both get up from our chairs and head over to the cupboards. "Enough about me. When's Russ coming over again?"

"Didn't I tell you we're going out tonight?"

"No, that's great." Janni pulls the French bread from the refrigerator and slices off the top.

"Two friends going out to dinner. It's not time to order the invitations."

She blows her nose, then chuckles, washes her hands, and starts buttering the bread while I set the table. Her back is to me, and I watch how she moves around the kitchen. She'll get past this and be just fine. Better even. She has a wonderful husband who adores her, two great sons, and now a beautiful daughter.

I have a house on the beach, a noncommittal boyfriend, and a date with a dentist.

twenty-five

By evening, we've managed to stave off any major confrontations with Mom over the whole breaking-and-entering thing. Mostly because no one told her last night, and she's spent her day cleaning Russ's condo and then shopping with her friends while we worked the syrup, which is starting to slow down. Unfortunately, she has just arrived home. Now, call me psychic, but I think we're about to face the music.

Mom bulldozes her way into the family room where Janni, Daniel, Dad, and I have gathered. Fists planted firmly on her hips, she frowns at us as though we're Gertie's offspring.

"I turn my back for a minute and you two manage to get yourselves in jail?" Her voice is high-pitched and nasally.

I decide to face the family matriarch head-on. "I would call it a misunderstanding."

She stares at me hard. "Let's call it what it is, Charlene Marybelle. Sin, pure and simple. You broke into the Tuckers's home."

Can we talk about the sin of a loose tongue?

Janni slinks in her chair and tries to hide behind her hand. Amusement lights Daniel's face, the first genuine smile I've seen all day.

Dad peers over his newspaper. "The damage is done, Viney. The girls learned their lessons. Let it go."

"Don't you take up for them, Milton Haverford." One glance at Mom's face, and I'd say she's about to become syrup, because she's definitely reached seven degrees above boiling.

"What's done is done." The firmness of Dad's voice makes us all turn to him. "I'm tired of the squabbling, and I don't want to hear another word about it." He awkwardly folds the newspaper and slaps it down on the ottoman in front of him.

Okay, this is tense. I'm almost sure Mom is smoldering. She could combust at any moment. Just when I think one poof will take her to Jesus, she stomps off toward the stairs.

That's probably a good thing, because I really didn't want to face the twenty questions that were sure to come when Russ picks me up for our date.

Before we can figure out how to get out of this uncomfortable situation, someone knocks on the front door.

"Oh, that's Russ. I'll get it," I say, rising from my chair. With a crank of the knob, I open the door. "Oh, hello."

"Yes, um, my name is Carol Sherwood, and I believe my daughter, Stephanie, is staying with you?"

There is a definite audible gulp here. Mine.

Before me stands a tall, stately woman in an expensive black wool coat. Her creamy complexion, aged only slightly with a couple of faint lines, is framed by short, stylish auburn hair—I'm guessing bottled.

"I'm sorry. I know I've caught you off guard. I plan to stay at a hotel in town, but Stephanie called and asked me to come."

"Well, don't just stand there, Char, invite her in."

General Sherman's back.

"I was going to, Mom." I step out of the way. "Please, come in."

By now everyone else has come to see who's at the door. I make the introductions and notice that the few freckles sprinkled over Janni's nose completely disappear.

"Won't you sit down?" Janni's voice hovers somewhere between a squeak and a croak.

"So, you're here to see Stephanie?" Mom wants to know.

Carol's eyes brighten. "Yes."

"She's working down at the coffee shop tonight," Janni offers.

"Oh, do you think it would be all right if I went over there to see her?" Carol fidgets with the gloves in her lap, then looks up.

"It would be all right, but they're pretty busy this time of night. She wouldn't be able to talk much," Janni says.

"Do you know when she gets done?"

"She closes tonight, I'm afraid. Won't be home until around midnight." Janni glances at the Precious Moments figurine on the stand and swivels it to its northern position.

"Well, I'll just find a hotel and call her in the morning." Carol stands. "If you'll please let her know I stopped by?"

"You'll do no such thing," Mom says. "We have plenty of room right here."

Sure, why not? The more, the merrier.

"Oh, I couldn't do that."

"Yes, you can," Mom says, leaving no room for argument, as though this is *her* house. Guess she's forgotten Janni and Daniel took over the payments. There are no words to express the look on Janni's face right about now, but if looks could kill, Mom would be setting up camp in heaven at this very moment.

Just a few more days, and I can get out of this madhouse, head back to Maine, and leave this all behind me.

"I don't want to be any trouble," Carol says.

"You'll be no trouble at all," Janni assures her.

I hate to point this out, but my sister is lying through her teeth.

"Let's see, Stephanie has moved to Blake's room, and you can take Ethan's room, since they're both at school," Janni says.

"So tell us about Stephanie," Mom says, settling in for a good chat.

"Well, I'm sure you already know most everything," Carol says.

My sister and I lock eyes.

"Carol, could I get you something to drink? Coffee, iced tea, water?" Janni cuts in before Carol can tell everyone in the room the truth about Stephanie.

Carol blinks. "Well, uh, yes, iced tea would be lovely. Thank you."

"Would you care to join me? I can show you our kitchen."

Not exactly Parade of Homes, but it will have to do.

The confusion on Mom's face says she's not sure what just happened.

"Well, sure." Carol stands to join Janni.

"Char, maybe you can take orders from everyone else and come help us?"

Hello? Why do I have to be involved in this? Wait. There are still some bakery cookies in the kitchen. "Okay, I'm right behind you." I take drink orders, then follow them into the kitchen.

"Carol, did Stephanie tell you that she told me?" Janni asks while grabbing mugs from the cupboard and filling them with coffee, one for her and the other for Mom.

"Yes."

"Did she call you here?"

Carol nods. "Evidently, she overheard you and your husband talking about her. It upset her, so she called me and told me she needed me. I'm here for her, the same way I've always been."

Okay, that was harsh. I should take the tray of drinks out, but things are starting to get interesting.

Janni measures her words. "I'm not trying to take her from you,

Carol. I'm still adjusting to the news myself. And I need to make you aware that not all my family knows yet."

Carol looks confused.

Yeah, she'll fit in fine with our family.

"But your mom asked about her, so she obviously knows who Stephanie is."

"Oh, yes, they've all met her, but they don't know she's my daughter."

Carol shakes her head. "She's *my* daughter."

This has all the drama of a daytime soap opera. I try to busy myself filling a glass with iced tea for Carol, but I'm afraid Gail Campbell is rubbing off on me.

"Please don't make this a competition. There's no reason we both can't—"

"She only needs one mother."

Janni takes a deep breath. "I was going to say, there's no reason we both can't be there for her. I'm not trying to take your place."

Carol softens a little and rubs the back of her neck. "I'm sorry. This whole thing has me a bit on edge."

Janni places her hand on Carol's arm. "There's room in her life for both of us, you know."

"Is there?" Carol asks, worry lining her face.

"You are her true mother. You did all the work. I will not take that away from you."

"Your iced tea, Carol." I hand her a filled glass.

The sound of the front door scraping against the door frame interrupts the moment.

"We'd better see who that is," Janni says, leading the way back into the living room.

While the two of them join the others, I pour myself a glass of iced tea and turn my attention to my date with Russ that's only minutes away.

Janni comes back into the kitchen.

"Do I look all right, sis? Is this pantsuit nice enough for Sok's Restaurant?"

"You look great." She hesitates here, making me wonder if she's telling the truth. "But—"

Nerves clamor in my stomach, making me uneasy. "What is it? Is something wrong? Is Russ here?"

"Uh, no."

Her answer causes me to release the breath I was holding. "Oh, good, you scared me." Her fixed expression lets me know there's a problem.

"Janni, what is it? Carol? Don't worry, we'll figure it out. Wait 'til Russ and I get back, and we'll help you."

"Char, listen to me. You have someone here to see you. It's not Russ."

Something in the way she says that causes me a moment of panic. I grab her arm. "It's not Officer Millington, is it? Gold or jewels missing from the Tuckers's house, and he's come back with a warrant or something?"

She rolls her eyes. "It's not Toby."

I relax. "Well, if it's not the police, we're good." Lifting my glass of tea from the counter, I follow her into the next room. My visitor is standing in the doorway, hiding behind a dozen yellow roses. Once I place my glass on a stand coaster, I look up to greet the person behind the bouquet.

One glance at him, and I decide jail might be the better option.

"There's my best girl." Peter pulls me close to him and kisses me right in front of God and everybody. Though I try to resist, he doesn't let me go until—

"Guess I should have called first." Russ's tone is even, controlled. It shakes Peter loose and makes my heart flip.

I take a side step. "Russ, hello." Without thought, I wipe off Peter's kiss. "Please, come on in."

He steps inside the house, and I make the introductions.

After a few awkward seconds, Russ says, "Listen, Charley, Peter's come a long way to see you. I'll take a rain check on that dinner." Before

I can respond he looks to Peter. "Nice to meet you," he says, then turns and walks out the door.

"I'll be right back, Peter." I rush outside after Russ. "Hey, wait up."

He doesn't.

By the time I reach his car, he's starting the engine.

"Russ, let me explain."

"You don't owe me an explanation. What I just witnessed pretty much tells me what I need to know. Sorry, Charley."

His foot hits the gas, causing dust and gravel to spit from his tires and car fumes to fill the air as he races out of the driveway. What happened to him not giving up so easily? Ignoring the biting chill, I watch him go, wondering what I'm going to do now.

How could I have gotten myself into such a mess? First off, Peter wasn't supposed to show up. We're friends. Period. And flirting with a dentist from another town should be harmless fun, not complicated. This isn't turning out at all the way I wanted.

The screen door slams closed, grabbing my attention.

"What was that all about?" Peter steps up beside me. "Was that my competition?" His eyes sparkle as though he's just won round one.

For the life of me, I can't find my voice. I know it's there somewhere, hiding away in some dark corner of my voice box. It's probably better this way. I'm angry at Peter for showing up unannounced. At the same time, he's traveled a long way, and he did bring yellow roses, after all. I'm angry at myself for allowing Peter to kiss me, and I'm not thrilled that Russ happened to witness it.

Still, for the record, no one owns me. Not Peter. Not Russ.

No one.

"Are you sure you're all right?" Janni asks when she slips into my bedroom and sits beside me on the bed.

"I'm fine."

"And you're okay with going to the coffeehouse? Don't you and Peter have some things to talk out?"

"I'm just not in the mood tonight, Janni. Being with everyone will provide a diversion, and we can just have a good time. I don't want to think about anything."

"I'm sorry about how things turned out, Char."

"It's no big deal, really. Besides, you've got enough to worry about without thinking about me."

Janni doesn't say anything. She simply pats my hand.

"Did you and Daniel get things worked out yet?"

"We're getting there. Everything will be all right, I think. At least I don't have to worry about telling the boys just yet. One thing at a time, right?"

I smile and nod.

"Let's go downstairs," I say. No sooner do we gather downstairs than someone knocks at the door again.

"Hey, Mom." Blake greets Janni with open arms, followed by Ethan.

And the hits just keep on comin'.

"What are you boys doing home this weekend?" Janni's voice is just a squeak as she steps out of the way while they clamber inside with their duffle bags.

"We live here, remember?" Blake says. He glances around the room, "Hi." He nods his head in greeting to everyone.

Janni makes the introductions between the boys, Carol, and Peter.

"We actually had a fairly light week at school, so we thought we'd come back and see if Dad needed more help with the syrup," Ethan says, tossing a wink at Janni. "Candy couldn't make it."

It's probably just as well, or we would have had to put her in the attic.

Daniel walks over and gives Ethan a hug, then Blake. "I don't care what anybody else says, you two are all right." He leans in and whispers, "Just remember, you have to come back in a week for the anniversary party."

They nod and wink.

"We're heading to the coffeehouse. Want to go?" Janni asks.

The boys don't hesitate. "Sure."

"Let's see, Carol can join Stephanie in Blake's room, and how about you boys stay in Ethan's room?" Janni says.

"No problem," Blake says, heaving his duffle bag over his shoulder.

"Yeah, you go ahead and go over. We'll catch up with you after we dump everything," Ethan adds.

If we keep adding guests, we'll have to provide room keys.

Stephanie steps around the counter and pulls Carol into a big hug. "Hi, Mom." They share a couple of whispers, and then Stephanie waves to the boys and the rest of us. Afterward, she dashes behind the counter and whips around making drinks, blotting countertops, and shining the cappuccino machines. She's Janni's daughter, all right.

I glance at our little mix—Janni's entire family, complete with long-lost adopted daughter, her mother, and now Peter. If I have any doubt that things are about to turn interesting, it flees with one glance at the couple in the corner.

"Now, Char, don't you jump to conclusions. After all, you're here with someone else," Janni says, trying to get my attention off Russ and the woman in the corner.

"Who is she?"

"I can't see. It would help if she turned around. Maybe it's a cousin or something."

"Yeah, right."

Just then the woman gets up and heads for the ladies' room. When she turns so we can see her, fresh pain waves over me, and I think I'm going to be sick.

"Oh, hello, Char," the woman says as she walks past.

"Hi, Linda."

twenty-six

As the woman who stole my husband—and now my date, apparently—walks away, an old familiar ache threatens to cut off my air supply. I'm thankful that I'm sitting down or I'd probably fall. Nausea rolls in my stomach. "I want to go home, Peter."

"What? We just got here. Don't you want your macchiato?"

The whir of the cappuccino machine, the hum of voices, the sharp smell of coffee that usually lift my spirits and put me instantly in a good mood, now heighten my nausea. So help me, if Russ has ruined my love for coffee, I will hide his dental floss.

"Well, as soon as they make our coffee, let's leave, okay?"

Peter looks at my face and no doubt sees the tears pooling in my eyes. "Okay, whatever you want." His gaze travels over to Russ's table and concern flickers in his eyes. "Listen, Charlene," his hand covers mine, and all I can think of is how his nails look better than mine—minus the polish. "I should have told you a long time ago—"

"Maple macchiato with three shots for Char," Stephanie calls out.

"Oh, there's my drink. I'll be right back." I start to get up from my chair.

"You stay put. I'll get it for you." Peter rises and walks over to the counter.

I don't have any idea what Peter was about to say, but he looks far too serious, and I just can't do serious right now. It takes everything in me not to look back at Russ and Linda's table, but I refuse to put myself through that.

"Okay, shall we go?" Still standing, Peter hands me my drink.

"Thank you." I scoot my chair back and stand.

"You're not leaving, are you?" Janni asks.

I lean over to her and whisper, "We'll talk later."

Quickly, we say our good-byes to everyone and head out. The cold air clears my head a little, and my stomach calms slightly.

We climb into Peter's silver Mercedes that smells of clean leather and ocean breeze from a deodorizer hanging under his mirror. The leather protests beneath us—okay, screams—as we settle into our seats. Peter turns to me. "Now what? Back to your sister's house?"

What I really want to do is walk in the woods by myself, but since he's come so far to spend time with me, that would be rude. "Yeah, back to the house, I guess."

Both of us are quiet on the trip to Janni's house. Once we get there, we grab glasses of iced tea, and Peter leads the way to the sofa in the living room. I want to warn him, but don't feel like explaining it all. We slide into the soft cushions and immediately start sinking. Peter straightens the crease in his pants—it makes him wild when the line is curvy—and then he turns to me.

"Charlene, I feel I need to apologize. You've obviously had a difficult evening, and I think my presence here has brought it all on."

We start out at eye level, but Peter is sinking faster than I am. We're having a serious moment, but I have to swallow hard to keep the giggles from surfacing. Peter doesn't seem to notice, as he is having struggles of his own. His hips are out of view, and he's now three inches shorter than when we first sat down. He pulls himself ramrod straight, trying to appear in control, but we both know the monster sofa is calling the shots. He has no idea how ridiculous he looks trying to act as though everything is fine, while he slips into oblivion.

Frustration replaces the concern on his face. A strand of hair dangles across his forehead, which irritates him to no end. The sharp crease in his pants is waning, his cheeks are red, and he's panting.

As his pretentiousness is magnified tenfold, I have to ask myself what I'm doing dating someone I could never love. It's not fair to him or me.

I feel embarrassed for Peter as he wrestles with the sofa, so I stare at my lap. "Things going well at the office?" I ask, trying to change the subject.

Peter sighs. "Things are fine. Cindy sold the Weatherton house."

"Boy, I didn't think that one would sell. Good for her."

He rattles off a couple of other sales—while straightening the pillows around us—but my mind flits back to Russ and Linda. She wins all the way around. Again. Visions of Russ's house drawing surface. No doubt Linda will love the balcony overlooking the lake.

"Listen, I'm tired. I'm going to head over to the hotel."

"I'd invite you to stay at the house, but we're out of rooms."

"That's all right. There's enough going on here, and I think you can use some time to think." He cups my chin in his hand. "I care a lot about you. Now I can see I should have told you that sooner. The question is, am I too late?"

We both know the answer to that question, but I'm just too weary to get into it. I simply stare at him and say nothing.

"Never mind. That was unfair of me to ask tonight. Just give me fair consideration, okay?" He kisses my forehead, brushes something off my shoulder, and grabs his things. "I'll call you in the morning."

"You sure you don't mind driving to the beach, Peter? I mean, it's not exactly summer," I say with a forced chuckle.

"I'm sure. I'd like to see how a Michigan beach compares to Maine's coastline."

Straining, I look up at the clouds. "I'm not sure we picked the best day to do this." A water droplet on the windshield underlines my concerns.

"Oh, well. We have lunch with us," he says, pointing over his shoulder to the well-filled picnic basket in the backseat. "We can sit in the car if need be." He flashes a smile, but it soon gives way to someone else's. Russ. I can't get him out of my mind. But I have to. Linda obviously has her sights set on him. I'd fight for him, but I already lost to her once. Why get knocked down again?

"A penny for your thoughts."

Another droplet of water, followed by more. Soon the sound of wipers sloshing the rain from the windshield fills the car.

"I hope they get the sap collected before it pours."

"It was nice of them to let you off today," Peter says.

"They've had so many friends from church helping that they haven't needed me all that much."

"I thought maybe you could show me around town while I'm here, see if we can find a place for the Scottenses to build their store," Peter says, pulling the car into the empty beach parking lot.

So that's the real reason he came to Tappery. Peter never does anything without keeping his business in mind. I should have known.

"Don't you trust me to find something?"

"Sure, I do. It just seemed the perfect excuse to come and see you."

"Uh-huh." I haul myself out of the car and glance at the sky. It looks as though things are going to get worse before they get better. Just like my life. Hopefully, things will get better, though I don't see how. I'll soon head back to my miserable existence in Maine.

What made me think that? Miserable existence? Hello? My whole plan was to come here, help with Mom and Dad's anniversary, grab my stash of syrup, and hightail it back to Maine, I mean *home.*

"Earth to Charlene? You still with me?"

"What? Er, uh, yeah. I'm sorry, Peter." The weather sure doesn't help with my gloomy mood. "Hey, you want to run in the rain?" I say, in hopes to shake off my gloom. Strains of Neil Sedaka's "Laughter in the Rain" run through my mind.

He looks at me as though I'm crazy. What was I thinking? He'd never mess up his hair.

"Sorry. Not my thing."

Music over. "Can't blame a girl for trying."

"Something tells me this hasn't been such a restful trip for you."

"No, definitely not restful. But I knew it wouldn't be. Maple season is always a busy time for our family."

"Yes, but I think there's more to it than that." Peter glances in the mirror and smoothes the hair at his temples. Then his lips part as he checks his teeth. Do I need to witness this? No. Beyond him rain blurs against the windows, and I wonder what I'm doing here. With him. Peter is handsome, charming, wealthy—and I feel nothing more for him than friendship. Could be that checking-his-teeth deal.

"Peter. It's no use. I need to go home."

He brightens. "Seafoam? Now you're talking."

I blink. "Uh, no, I'm sorry." I take a deep breath and look at him. "Listen, Peter, I care about you. I really do, but—"

He holds up his palm and sighs. "You don't have to say another word. It was written all over your face when he came to the door last night."

His comment makes me blink.

He glances at his watch. "There's still plenty of daylight for me to get on the road." Settling back into his seat, he starts the engine. "To tell you the truth, I already checked out of the hotel. I had a feeling it would go like this today."

"I'm so sorry."

"There's nothing to be sorry about. I came down to scope out some land, see a good friend, and now I'm going home."

We smile at one another, and he turns on the radio, cutting off further conversation. With my face toward the passenger window, I struggle to keep the tears in check. I've lost a friend in Peter, and I've lost Russ.

Peter soon pulls us up to Janni's house, puts the transmission in park, and turns to me. "Look, you scope out the possibilities for the Scottenses. You know the area better than I do anyway. If something opens up, let me know, and I'll get the paperwork in order."

I nod.

He grabs my hands. "Listen, Charlene, we can still be friends, right? There's no reason this has to affect our professional relationship, is there?"

He's worried more about the business than the romance. "No reason."

"Great. See you back at the office." He releases my hands. I say goodbye, close the car door behind me with a wave, and watch him drive off.

"Russ has been trying to reach you. Said your cell phone must be turned off." Janni wipes her hands with a dish towel and turns to me.

"I'm surprised he called." My hand digs into a box of store-bought cookies, and I take a bite of one.

"No way. You're eating store-bought cookies?" Janni's eyes could match that of any Hollywood star caught in a horror movie.

"Peter bought them. I'm desperate."

Janni slides into the chair across from me. "What's wrong, sis?"

"Peter went home."

"Oh, I'm sorry, Char." She takes a cookie from the box.

"It's all right. It's better this way. If you don't mind, I really can't talk about it right now." Reaching into the basket, I start to empty it.

Janni nods. "You guys didn't eat lunch?"

"We didn't get that far." I put the wrapped turkey sandwich into the refrigerator while Janni pours us both a glass of iced tea.

We sit back in our chairs. "How's the syrup coming?"

"They're busy as little bees down there."

"Do they need me?"

Janni shakes her head. "There's no room even if you wanted to go down there."

While Linda and Gail huddled in bathrooms with other high-school girls to talk about me and Eddie, Janni was surrounded by friends who remain loyal to her to this very day.

"I went to the doctor today."

I stop chomping on my cookie and look up. "How did it go?"

"They're checking into that hormone thing."

"And?"

"We talked over the different options, and he's starting me on some things that should help with the thyroid and mood swings."

"You'll be good as new in no time."

"I hope so. I want to feel like my old self again." Janni twirls the ice in her glass with a straw. There's no question all this stuff with Stephanie has taken its toll on her. "Stephanie, Carol, and I are going shopping tonight. Do you want to go?"

"As tempting as that sounds, I think I'll pass. You three need time to see how you all fit together. Plus, I could use the time to think through some things of my own." Janni's family just keeps expanding while mine, well, doesn't.

"Suit yourself. But you're welcome to come along."

"Thanks. Have you told the guys or Mom and Dad yet?"

"No. There's been no opportunity. I have to do it before the boys leave, though."

We talk awhile about the boys, Carol, and Stephanie, and then I stand. "Well, if you don't need me, I think I'll go rest for a little while in my room. I didn't sleep all that well last night." After emptying the contents from the picnic basket, I put it back in its place on the shelf. "Thanks for letting me borrow this, by the way."

"No problem. Sorry it didn't work out."

That seems to be my life's mantra.

"Psst." Someone calls to me when I step out of my bedroom after my nap. "Char, over here."

Daniel pulls me just inside Blake's room.

"Your dad told me Gertie called and said her son is considering selling his motorcycle. Since Janni seems to be enjoying it, I asked Dad to check with Gertie to see if her son would sell it to us."

"Are you kidding?" I'm shocked to the core that Daniel is actually considering it. I'm also worried that Mom will find out Dad talked privately to Gertie.

"Well, Janni just lights up at the mention of that bike. I want to get it for her." He tucks his thumbs through his belt loops. "It just seems, oh, I don't know, with everything that's been going on around here, I figured she could use a little pick-me-up."

All this—after Janni's big secret—and without a coupon. Now that's love. "She will adore it, Daniel." I give him a hug. "You're the greatest."

"This should buy me a few more years, don't you think?" He chuckles.

"I sure do." Clanging noises from the kitchen waft up the stairway. "I'd better get downstairs and see if they need help with anything."

"Okay, don't tell Janni."

"Mum's the word." I smile and edge down the stairs, thinking once again how blessed Janni is to have such a husband and family.

"Well, there's the slacker," Blake teases, giving me a sideways hug. "How's my favorite aunt?"

"Tired." I yawn. "What time is it?"

"You missed dinner, but Mom saved you some. Turkey stew in a bread bowl. My favorite." He rubs his belly.

"Everything's your favorite."

He flashes the ornery grin that curls around this aunt's heart every time. "Yeah, I guess so."

"How'd the syrup go today?"

"We had to pass up about twenty gallons of sap that smelled bad." He makes a face.

"Why don't you just tell me the Dow Jones took a major plunge in the world today? Same difference."

Blake gives me a deadpan stare. "Boy, you do take this syrup thing seriously, don't you?"

Janni enters the room. "Don't get her started."

"Where are Mom and Dad?" I ask.

"They went to the grocery, I think. Mom's on her potato-salad kick."

"Well, keep her away from the syrup."

Janni grins, then thinks a moment. "You know, she hasn't had many sweets lately. She must be getting tired of the sugar."

"That clinches it. I'm adopted. I never get tired of sugar."

Janni laughs and shakes her head.

"So when are you going shopping?" I ask, sitting down in a chair.

"We're not. Stephanie got called in to work. I offered to take Carol, but she wanted to wait until Stephanie could join us. Says she has some knitting she wants to get done, a scarf or something she's knitting for Stephanie, so she's up in her room working on that."

"We're going bowling, me and Ethan. Want to go, Aunt Char?"

"No, thanks. I've seen how you two play. I don't need that kind of pressure. I might go to the coffee shop awhile. Want to go?"

Janni plops in a chair, allowing her legs to hang over the side like a teenager, and smiles up at me. "I can't. Daniel ran to the store, but he'll be right back; then we're going to a movie. You're welcome to go with us."

Loneliness creeps over me. "That's all right. I'll leave you lovebirds alone." I laugh so she won't pick up on my mood. "Besides, to quote Blake, there's nothing worse than old-people love."

"That's right," Blake chimes in.

Janni laughs out loud and waves me away.

"Do I look too stupid in this ponytail?" My fingers reach up and tuck in a few stray hairs.

"No, you look cute in your boot-cut jeans, white top, ponytail, all of it." She shakes her head. "You're forty-seven, and you can still pull it off." She sighs. "And you have a cottage overlooking the sea. Life just isn't fair."

"What*ever*. You have a family that adores you and friends who stand by you through thick and thin. Money can't buy that." My voice sounds a little too serious, and she looks my way. "But I'll take what I can get," I say with a laugh and a swish of my ponytail. I stand. "I think I'll go on over there."

Alone.

twenty-seven

"Hey, Char," Stephanie calls out with a wide grin when she sees me step into the coffee shop.

"How's my favorite barista?" I whisper, careful not to let the other girl hear me.

Stephanie smiles. "It's always better when you're here."

"Okay, you are definitely my favorite niece."

She laughs. "Safe answer."

I lean into the counter. "Everything going all right?"

She smiles. "I think everything will be fine."

Wish I could be that confident with my own problems.

"We'll see how Grandma, Grandpa, and the boys react," she says.

When the other barista moves within earshot, we change the conversation to business at the coffee shop, and soon Stephanie has my macchiato ready.

"Thanks." I head over to an empty table, wondering how long Stephanie will stay with Janni and Daniel. They are enjoying their new-found relationship. All this time, I thought it would be too much for Janni to find out about Stephanie, but instead, this little revelation seems to have given Janni new enthusiasm for life.

After placing a couple of calls to clients, I pull the *Real Estate* magazine from my bag and settle in to relax. The tension melts away with my first drink and flip of the page.

I'm halfway through my magazine when the bell jangles over the door, and I glance up to see Linda Kaiser stepping inside. Major mood dive here. I tuck my head further into my chest and keep my eyes glued to the magazine, though I don't know why. It's not as though she'll want to talk to me or anything.

"Charlene, do you have a moment?"

Then again, I could be wrong. When I look up, Linda is standing by my table.

"Uh, yeah. Sit down." I'm asking her to sit at my table, why? The woman who stole *my* husband, had the baby that should have been *mine*? Saying nothing of the fact that she was with Russ last night.

"Thanks. So how have you been?"

"Fine, thanks." Can we get this over with, please? She probably wants to gloat about her and Russ. Of course the difference here is that Russ does not belong to me. Another twinge. These little twinges are making me mad.

"Listen, I'm not sure where to begin."

I cut her off. "How's Carissa?" How about we just stick with the weather, kids, that kind of thing, and get on with our lives?

She stops and looks at me. "Huh? Oh, she's fine. How did you know her name?"

"Word gets around." For a fraction of an instant, I enjoy watching her squirm with the realization that people in this town talk. She knows all about that. She and Gail could win the "Rona Barrett Gossip Award" for as much as they talked. About me. All the time. She was so jealous of me and Eddie, she couldn't see straight.

Just then Stephanie brings over Linda's drink, and Linda thanks her before turning back to me. She fiddles with the jacket on her cup. "Listen, Char, I know that Gail and I stirred up plenty of trouble in high school, but those days are behind me." When she sees I'm not so easily convinced, she says, "You may not believe it, but this whole thing with Eddie has changed me. Unfortunately, I have a past I'm not proud of."

Well, duh.

"I know this is a little late, but I want to apologize to you. I've been a total idiot." A gentle vulnerability seeps through her comment.

What she says startles me to the core, but I'm not feeling soft right now. Steel wool comes to mind. With absolutely no effort on my part whatsoever to make it easy on her, I simply stare.

"I took your husband away from you and that was wrong."

Oh, now there's a newsflash. "It wasn't you, Linda." Why should I give her the satisfaction of thinking she won him away from me? "He was primed and ready for *anyone*"—definite emphasis on the "anyone" part—"who would give him the time of day." Uh-oh, fangs showing. Still, I don't want her to think she is all that. Eddie was waiting for any woman who would take the bait.

"Yeah, I can see that now." She looks back into her cup.

Well, that wasn't exactly the catfight I was expecting. A pang of remorse hits me, but only for the flash of a millisecond.

"He was vulnerable, I bumped into him one night. We started talking about old times, and one thing led to another."

Eyes boring into her, I say, "Spare me the details."

Linda sighs. "You're not making this very easy."

"Easy? You want me to make this easy, Linda? He was my husband. *My* husband. We lost a child together. We were both hurting—and we handled it . . . differently. I retreated into myself. He had an affair. With you."

"I had some challenges of my own at the time."

"Oh, and so that makes it all right to steal another woman's husband?" What is wrong with me? I thought I had worked through all this, that I had forgiven both of them. Poison is dripping from me like spoiled sap from a tree.

A filmy haze shadows her eyes. "What do you want from me, Char? Blood?"

No, I get queasy at the sight of blood. But I might settle for broken bones.

She sighs and turns the ring on her finger. "I know I can't undo what's been done, but, well, I just wanted to say I'm sorry for the pain I caused you."

The way she says it takes the fight right out of me. I want to be angry—to free all the words that have festered in my heart, but when I look at her at that very moment, I feel pity. She made a bad choice that hurt a lot of people, but it takes two to tango, as Mom always says. And now Linda is hurting the way I did, because another woman stole Eddie from her.

"I'm sorry I bothered you." She starts to get up.

Suddenly, revenge doesn't seem so sweet. I grab her hand. "Wait."

She looks at me and sits back down.

"Look, this isn't easy for either of us. We won't get through it without lots of prayer, but I'm willing to try. It's in the past. Let's leave it there."

"Have you?" There is no accusation in her voice. She asks the question as though she really wants to make sure she's forgiven.

"I've tried to."

"I'm not sure if anyone has told you, but I've moved back, and Eddie is remarried."

"Yeah, I heard. You're better off without him." Eddie's left his mark on both of us.

"Will I get there one day, with the forgiveness, I mean?"

When I look into her eyes, I realize I'm seeing myself not so very long ago. Wounded and bleeding. Who am I kidding? That's still me. "You'll get there."

She nods. "How long did it take you?"

A knot swells in my throat. I merely shrug.

"Thank you, Char. Thank you for giving me closure. For bringing peace."

This is so not the way I saw this play out in my mind over the years. Doesn't she need to know the pain she has caused me? The endless nights when I cried myself to sleep? Yet somehow when I look at her and see the shadows in her eyes, the dark circles, I realize . . . she does know.

Linda takes a drink from her cup. "This has been awful hard on Carissa."

"I'm sorry." And the thing is, I really am. I'm thankful I never had to put a child through that. Funny. That's something I hadn't thought of before now. I've been so caught up in the pain of being childless that I never saw it as a blessing. Still, the idea of it causes my heart to stumble. "I'm sorry, too, for how I acted when we bumped into each other."

She lifts a weak smile. "We deserved it. By the way, I was going to talk to you last night when I saw you, but you were with that guy, and I didn't want to interrupt."

"That's all right. He's just a friend."

"I'm sure Russ will be glad to hear that. He's crazy about you, but then I guess you know that. I ran into him here last night too. Did you see him? He was upset about something, but wouldn't say what."

My heart leaps here. It makes me feel better to know Russ just bumped into Linda out here last night and that he didn't tell her what he was upset about.

Maybe I will call him back.

Though it's late and cold, I walk to the woods to clear my head. The thing that keeps me from weighing five hundred pounds from all the cookies I eat? Walking. Though I don't do it for the exercise benefit, that's just a bonus. It clears my head and settles my nerves. And right now, my nerves pretty much resemble porcupine needles.

The calm wind makes the cold air bearable. A flutter of bird wings in a nearby tree startles me as I wind my way through the trees. Having grown up here, I have no fear of getting lost. I know this forest as well as I know myself. Although right now, I'm not doing so great on that part.

All these years I've been satisfied with my spiritual journey. I survived that whole affair thing, after all. Who wouldn't be a little bitter? It didn't seem out of line; it seemed *human*—or so I told myself. Still, the seedling of bitterness took root in my heart and began to grow, while I tended to other things and hardly noticed.

I step over a fallen branch. Who am I kidding? The only "thing" I tend to is work. It's not as though I help out anyone, really. Oh, I might offer a token lunch now and then to a friend, but when is the last time I took dinner to someone who was sick, picked up groceries for someone homebound or watched children for a tired mom?

Twigs snap beneath my feet as I stop at trees here and there to check the bags of sap. Darkness has settled over Tappery, and I suppose I should make my way back to the house, but I need this. Oh, how I need this time alone. To reflect. To rethink some things. To pray.

It's time to call it as I see it. Bitterness has stripped me of valuable family time and memories. It's held me captive in Maine, kept me locked far away from Tappery.

I love my family. And although my mom and I don't see eye to eye on hardly anything, I love her too. She's ornery, so we've got that much in common. Her expectations make her a bit bristly as far as I'm concerned, but I know deep down she loves me. She has to. I'm her daughter. Besides that, it's a commandment.

Stopping beside a maple, my fingers rub across the bark, and I think again about how the tapped tree heals itself through the year before the next tapping season. Though the hole is gone, the scar is still there.

That's me. I've been fooling myself into thinking the wound was gone, but it wasn't. Layers of denial, bitterness, and anger simply grew over it. Funny, I didn't see that until this visit back home. How could I have been so blind?

A sweet, woodsy scent stirs with the night air, calming my spirit as I talk with God about my wasted years.

Wiping my blurry eyes after prayer, I notice a shadow moving in the distance. Another wipe and glance confirm I'm not imagining things. Breath clogs in my throat. I'm not one given to paranoia or fear, but my nerves are on edge, and the shadow causes my feet to freeze in place.

Branches snap as the shadow moves once again. My eyes strain in the darkness to make out the figure. No one should be out here this time of night. I don't remember seeing Janni and Daniel's car when I got home, so I figure they're still at the movie. That means the shadow is probably a wild animal—and with my luck, most likely a squirrel. Probably a rabid one. I'm not completely out of shape, so I could make a beeline for the house, but curiosity—or stupidity—holds me in place.

The shadow moves again, and this time moonlight glints on a face. Janni's. The breath I was holding comes out with a burst. "Janni Ort, what are you doing here?"

"Hello? I could ask the same of you." She steps over to me, laughing. "Just like the closet days, huh?"

"Except that now I'm a breath away from a pacemaker."

"What are you doing out here?" she asks as we walk along.

"Let's go down by the oaks so we can sit on the bench," I say, leading the way.

"Well? You didn't answer my question. What are you doing out here?"

"Excuse me, but I asked you first."

"How come you always get your way?"

"It's the one perk that comes with age. I thought you and Daniel were going to the movies."

"Someone got hurt at the store, and he went over to the hospital. I don't think it's anything serious, but he always has to check those things out. Don't know the details yet."

"Oh, I'm sorry, Janni."

"Yeah, when it rains, it pours. Speaking of which, that rain earlier today made it a little muddy out here," she says, revealing the mud caked on the bottoms of her shoes.

"So why are you walking around in the woods?"

"To tell you the truth, I'm worried about how to tell Mom and Dad about Stephanie."

I can see her point. Mom won't take this lying down.

"Mom may throw a fit at first, but she'll come around. You know how she is. She'll adore having a granddaughter. Just stand back when you first break the news."

"Yeah, watch out for the belching volcano." Janni chuckles, then sighs. "I sure hope you're right."

When we sit down, the cold steel of the bench seeps through my pant legs and causes me to shiver.

"It's your turn," she says.

I tell her about running into Linda and our discussion.

"Wow, that's tough, Char. I'm sorry. But I'm glad you two talked about it."

"You know, I am too. I think it's the first step toward true healing for me." I turn a dried leaf in my hand.

Janni smiles and pats my hand. Something catches her attention. "What's that?"

"What?" My gaze shoots up, and I squint through the darkness to where Janni is pointing.

"I saw something through the trees, right over there," she whispers.

"Good grief. I've been in this woods a thousand times and never met up with shadows—until tonight."

"There it is again."

My eyes refocus toward the area of the shadow, and thanks to an almost-full moon I see something that puts me in mind of Gollum from Lord of the Rings. A gasp escapes me. "What do you think it is?" I ask, my heart kicking into a jogging pace.

"I have no idea. Can't be Daniel, since he's at the hospital."

"The forest is our friend," I say, trying to convince myself. "Friendly shadows."

"Well, if it's all the same to you, I'd just as soon leave the *friendly* shadows behind and head for the house. Come on." Janni creeps from the bench to a nearby tree. I hate to point this out, but, well, it's not hiding her all that well. She's spilling out the sides like pancake batter in too small a griddle.

Normally, I never experience fear in the woods, but with the current state of my nerves, things are starting to get to me, that's all.

"Where did the shadow go? I lost sight of it," Janni whispers to me over her shoulder. She's shaking so badly, I'm thankful we're not standing under a coconut tree.

"I don't know, but I don't think it's following us." I'm hearing *Pink Panther* music in the background as we tiptoe from tree to tree. "One tree can't shield both of us at the same time. We need to separate. I'll head up to the house that way, and you go over there," I say, pointing.

Janni turns to me and gasps. "You want to separate?" In that instant the whites of her eyes light up the forest.

"Come on, you can do it." Before she can argue, I dart off to the nearest tree.

Night has thickened around us like maple syrup, making it difficult to see anything. If I could get to a clearing, the moonlight would help me, but a cluster of trees is cutting off the light.

A rustle of leaves. The hoot of an owl causes panic to slice through me. This is crazy. What has gotten into me? More rustling. A scream rockets up my throat, but I clamp my jaw tight and make a mad dash for a nearby clearing, running for all I'm worth. Picture Olympic runner, arms in motion, legs moving at such speed my feet barely touch the ground, and I'm blowing out short, cloudy breaths like a chimney with hiccups. At last I thump against a wide tree and bend over, taking in huge gulps of air.

"What are you doing here?" I whip around just as moonlight lands upon my mother's face in a ghoulish glow. For the first time in my life, I'm understanding that whole need-for-Depends thing.

twenty-eight

"*For crying out loud, Mom, what are you doing* walking in the woods at night?" My tight throat attempts to hold the words captive, but they seep through. A tinge of anger traces my voice, and I'm good with that.

"Yeah, Mom, what are you doing?" Janni's shoes crunch fallen twigs as she stomps over to us.

With lips pursed tightly, Mom takes a Superman stance. "I could ask the same of you two."

Just like that? That's her explanation? If ever I wanted to pile Mom's suspense books in a burning heap, it's now.

"We were taking a walk," I say.

Janni looks at me, blows out a sigh, and the three of us walk back toward the house.

"Wait. This isn't about us. It's about you." More steps. "And what's that in your hands?" My eyes narrow to slits when I see the suspense book.

Mom shifts the book to her other hand, and her nose points so high it makes me wonder if she's having a nosebleed.

"She was retrieving her hidden book from the woods," Janni says dryly, stepping over a large rock in the path.

My feet stop in their tracks, and my jaw dangles. "What? You hid a book in the woods? That's just pathetic, Mom."

"Charlene Marybelle, you watch your tongue. I'm still your mother."

Walking again, I sigh. "Mom, we're only trying to keep you from reading those books to help you through this paranoia thing."

Mom stops, stiffens, stretches from four feet eleven to a full five feet before our very eyes, and points that frightening finger just under my nose. "I am not paranoid. Your father was trying to kill me."

"Then why isn't he trying now?"

"He and Gertie probably split up."

Oh, please. I roll my eyes at Janni. She stifles a giggle. "Mom, Janni needs to talk to you."

Janni shakes her head fervently at me. When Mom turns to her, she stops midshake and smiles.

"Well, what is it?"

Janni looks around.

"Why don't you sit over there," I say, pointing to fallen log. "I'll just go back to the house and leave you two alone."

When I turn to leave, Janni clutches the hem of my blouse with all the charm of a pit bull. "Oh no, you don't," she growls between clenched teeth. "You're staying for this one."

"Well, hurry up. I'm cold." Mom frowns when she sits on the tree bark.

"This will shock you, Mom, and probably hurt you, but please hear me out. First off, I want to apologize for any pain this will cause you. I never should have allowed myself to get caught up in the peer pressure. You and Dad did a wonderful job of raising Char and me and—"

"Well, for goodness' sakes, spit it out. My bones are so cold, they could break off right now," Mom says, pulling her coat tighter to her.

She has such a way with words.

Janni blinks, looks at me, then back to Mom. Deep breath. "Okay. It's like this. When I was in college, I fell in love, made bad choices, ended up pregnant, and found out the guy didn't love me after all. He died three weeks before the birth of our baby girl. I put the baby up for adoption, and now I just found out my daughter wants to have a relationship with me."

With all the courage she can muster, Janni spits out her words in rapid-fire succession. A gasp comes from Mom's direction, and I watch in sheer wonder as her eyelids flutter like a paper fan during a hot flash.

Her eyelids finally come to a halt, but her body is so rigid that I'm sure if I blow on her, she'll fall over and break into a bazillion pieces. For the span of a heartbeat, I'm wondering if Janni's confession has carried Mom to her eternal reward.

"Mom, are you okay?" Janni asks.

Finally, she swallows. "Why didn't you tell us?" Her words are vibrating. I can only hope it's not the precursor to an erupting storm.

"I was afraid," Janni states simply, staring at her hands, tears spilling on her coat.

"Did you go through this alone? Did anyone help you?" Mom's soft response causes both of us to blink.

Janni looks at her. "Only my roommate knew."

"You told a stranger but not your mother?" Soft moment over.

"She wasn't exactly a stranger. Besides, I wanted to spare you and Dad the embarrassment in the church and all that."

"What's more important than our daughters' well-being?" Mom stands up here. "When it comes to you and Char, we don't care what the church people think. We love you. I'm not condoning what you did, mind you, but nothing will stop us from loving you. We love and accept you, warts and all."

She looks at me when she says the "warts and all" part.

"We pray daily that you will grow stronger in your walk with the Lord. If He can forgive you, why did you think *we* wouldn't?"

We're stunned to silence. In fact, it's as though the whole earth blinks at this surprising revelation.

Janni and Mom soon become a tangle of arms and hugs, while a chunk the size of a hundred-year-old maple lodges in my throat.

Mom finally pulls away from Janni and extends her arms to me to pull me into a hug with the two of them. Mom's bony arms never felt so good.

With emotions spent, Janni pulls a tissue from her pocket, wipes her nose, and turns to Mom. "I never dreamed you'd be so understanding. I've carried this around all these years, so fearful of hurting you, Dad, and Daniel."

We discuss Stephanie's father, the accident, the adoption, how Daniel's handling everything, and how Janni is going to break the news to the boys.

"You said your daughter wants a relationship. Has she contacted you?" Mom wants to know as we head back to the house.

"Um, I'm glad you asked." Janni turns to Mom. "She has contacted me. Mom, my daughter is Stephanie."

By the time we make it back to the house, Dad is in bed. The light in Carol's room is out, so we assume she's in bed, and Stephanie still isn't home. Mom's determined to wait up for her and be properly introduced to her only granddaughter.

We settle in around the kitchen table with mugs of decaf coffee in hand.

"So what's going on with you, Char, besides the fact you're working yourself to death and you're not giving me grandchildren?"

Okay, that was harsh. But Mom's been so good with Janni's news that I can't help but smile. "Same old, same old," I say.

"Are you serious about this guy who came to visit you—what's his name?"

"Peter."

Mom takes a drink from her cup. "Are you serious about him?"

"Peter is a friend." Though after his visit, I'm wondering if we'll still have that.

Mom stares at me. "He came all the way from Maine to Tappery to visit a friend?"

"And to look over some property." *Do I want to discuss this? No.* "He's been burned before. Doesn't want to marry again."

"I see." Mom continues to peer at me over the rim of her cup.

"What?"

"In other words, he's safe."

"I guess you could say that." Probably very safe now. As in, merely an acquaintance. A boss.

Mom puts her cup down. "Char, you're too pretty a woman to give up on life."

A few days ago, I would have argued that I hadn't given up on life, but now I see some truth to what she's saying.

"What about Russ?" Mom's eyes continue to bore into my soul. I hate it when she does that.

"What about him?"

"You know what I mean. Anything there?" Her thumb runs along the handle of her coffee cup while she keeps her eyes fixed on me.

Mom knows how to cut to the heart of the matter. I shrug.

"You know good and well there's something there, Charlene Marybelle. It's written all over your face."

Her words hit me like a two-by-four. "That's news to me," I say.

"Well, wake up and read the paper," Mom says, causing Janni to laugh, but I'm still stunned to silence.

We all know Mom has a keen intuition about these sorts of things, so when she makes a comment such as this, I sit up and take notice. I mean, it doesn't take a rocket scientist to figure out that I care about Russ, but I haven't allowed myself to evaluate that too much. The truth is I'm afraid to explore those feelings for fear of where they might lead me.

"I don't want to go there again," I say, wishing I hadn't, because Mom's up for this argument, and I'm not.

"One bad apple don't spoil the whole bunch, girl. Remember that song, Char?" Janni pipes up. "By the Osmonds?"

Suddenly, the tune plays in my head, and I smile. "Yeah, I remember."

"Russ is way different from Eddie. No comparison," Mom says. "Eddie always worried me."

"How so?"

"The way he flirted." Mom holds up her hand. "Oh, I know, you always said he was just outgoing, but I saw it as more than that. He had a wild streak, that one."

"Does this mean you don't hold the divorce against me?"

Mom gives me an incredulous stare and reaches out her hand to me in a rare moment of tenderness. "Is that what you thought? I never held that divorce against you, Charlene Marybelle. He left you for another woman. There wasn't much you could do to fight it. His mind was made up. I just never quite knew what to say. Remember, when Eddie left, it felt like we lost a son too. It devastated the whole family."

Being self-absorbed in my own pain, I had failed to see theirs. "I thought I had let you down." Tears surface, and I try everything to hold them back.

"You could never let us down. We love you girls more than anything." She squeezes my hand, then lets go. "I'm not good with words. Never have been. I speak my mind, and that's gotten us into trouble at the church on more than one occasion, I can tell you."

I can only imagine.

"We're a lot alike, Char," Mom continues. "We both speak our minds, and we're both independent." Mom fingers the handle of her mug a moment, then looks up at me. "I suppose that's why I've always been a little harder on you, telling you to be sweet and mind your mouth, all that. I was hoping to spare you the same mistakes I've made over the years."

Mom's little speech has left me, um, speechless. I've always seen her and Janni as being like-minded, both devoted to family and into the domestic side of life. Okay, I've seen them as the family saints—well, all except for Mom's tongue thing. Oh, yeah, and now Janni's college indiscretions. But Mom and I alike? It's kind of nice and scary all at the same time.

"You're an instigator, too. When there was a problem, I pretty much knew you were behind it." Mom chuckles and shakes her head. "You'd get yourself into more trouble when you were growing up." She turns to Janni. "Now, me and Janni, we're both a little manipulative."

I didn't even know Mom knew what that meant.

Janni's eyes widen, and Mom smiles. "Admit it. We both see ourselves as the glue that holds the family together. We do what it takes to keep things in balance—or so we tell ourselves."

Mom's comments smack of Dr. Phil, and I'm almost sure she's recording his shows.

"Guess I should follow my own advice to be sweet, huh?" Mom gives a chuckle, then goes back to her coffee.

Okay, I didn't see that one coming.

"That's an interesting way of looking at it," Janni says, "and I think you're right." She turns to me. "I'm ashamed to admit it, but in a way I was trying to make you more like me."

"Yeah, like *that's* gonna happen," I say with a laugh. Mom and Janni laugh too.

"It's not going to happen because you're wired differently," Mom says. "And it's okay to be different."

"It's not that I thought I was better or anything, but, well, you have to admit I didn't get into as much trouble as you." Janni grins.

Mom winks at me, then turns to Janni. "You both have so much to offer. Janni, people know they can always count on you if they need you.

You're dependable, and you have a servant's heart." Mom puts her hand on Janni's arm. "You're always there for your dad and me, and we're grateful for you." Mom looks at me. "And you, Char, are strong and independent. We know if there's a problem, you will find the solution." This time she touches my arm. "We also know if we need you, you'll be here for us."

"Okay, who are you, and what have you done with our mother?" Another loose-tongue moment, but I just can't help myself. This whole discussion has rocked my world.

"Now, don't think just because I've had a vulnerable moment, that I'm going to stop giving you advice. We all should strive to do and be better. But I just want you to know we never blamed you for the divorce."

All this time I thought they judged me, that I had disappointed them. I stayed away not wanting to face the pain . . .

"Well, that's behind her and she can move on from here, right, Char?" Janni smiles, but she's not fooling me. She's trying to get my mind off things.

"Yeah. Now it's my turn," I say. "You see yourselves as manipulative, but I know that stems from caring about others. If you didn't care, you wouldn't be so protective. I'm sorry for the times I resented that. Mom, I've needed you to be outspoken at times"—I hope she gets it that I don't need it *all* the time—"you're straightforward, and I appreciate that in a person. I always know right where I stand with you. And Janni, you always challenge me to care more about others. Your friends are testimony of your faithfulness to others."

We're all misty eyed as we get up from our chairs and share hugs. Afterwards, we dab the corners of our eyes with napkins, and the front door shoves open. Stephanie steps inside.

"Hey, what are you all doing up?" she asks when she walks into the kitchen.

"We were waiting on you," Janni says. "Mom wants to meet her one and only granddaughter."

Stephanie gasps and turns to Mom, who rises from her chair. They meet in the middle of the kitchen.

"Welcome to the family, sweetheart," Mom says before pulling her into a big hug—well, as big a hug as Mom's skinny arms can give her.

Stephanie's eyes tear up. "Thank you—can I call you Grandma?"

"Well, you'd better," Mom says.

She laughs. "Thanks, Grandma."

We talk excitedly for a little bit, catching up on Stephanie's life, some of the things we've missed, her first day of school, her first date, getting her driver's license, and those types of things.

"Well, now that you're my granddaughter, I don't mind telling you, I just don't think it's right for a girl to strike out on her own, backpacking halfway across the country."

Janni looks at Stephanie and smiles. "You're part of the family now."

The pastor quotes a verse, telling us to forget what is behind and strain toward what is ahead. While he prays, my tears flow. I'm not sure whether they are for me, because I want to hang on to my anger, or for the years wasted in bitterness. The memories I anguished over without seeing the new bitter memories I was creating.

How could I have been so fooled? Everyone else could see right through me. Janni knew. That's why she kept telling me to let it go. Still, I had convinced myself that I had surrendered it all to the Lord, that my "feelings" were completely human. In part, they were. There's a grieving process we go through, but the thing is not to hang on to the bitterness.

Easier said than done, but thankfully, God did not give up on me. I hadn't meant to harbor resentment and unforgiveness. It just lurked in the shadowed corners of my heart and festered. The frightening thing is I'm not sure I know how to forgive and make it final. It's not anything I can do on my own, I know that much. After more tears and praying through the matter, I maneuver myself through the throng of people and make my way to my car, all the while hoping no one sees me or talks to me.

"Charley, wait up!"

My stomach flips. Okay, Russ might be the exception. Though I can only imagine how I look now that my makeup is cried off, I turn around. If he screams, I'm running.

"Hi, Russ." One look in his eyes, and I can finally admit what my heart has been telling me all along. I've fallen in love with Russ Benson.

"I've been trying to reach you." He falls into step with me as we head for the parking lot. The cool breeze sends his musky scent my way, and I breathe deeply. His hand touches my elbow. "Hey, you okay?"

Boulder in my throat here. "Yeah, I'll be fine."

"Want to talk about it?"

"Not right now."

"Okay." We move forward. "Is there a reason you didn't return my calls?"

"I'm sorry. I've been trying to sort through . . . things."

"I understand. I've been doing a little of that myself. So I take it Peter went back home?"

I nod but say nothing. We walk a little ways in silence.

"You know, maybe this isn't a good time, but we never got to eat at Sok's Restaurant, and it's not all that far from the plot of ground I purchased. I could take you to lunch, show you my land, and we could stroll the beach together." His eyes twinkle with hope, and I smile.

My heart flips at the thought of a second chance. "How could I turn that down?"

"Really? That's great."

"I need to let somebody know, though, so they won't worry about me. Plus, I'd rather wear pants to stroll on the beach than a dress, so how about if I go back to Janni's house to change?"

"Okay, I'll go home and change too. Sok's is a nice restaurant, but you can definitely dress comfortably. I'll swing by and pick you up, if that's all right with you."

"That works." I smile. "And Russ"—I look him in the eyes—"just so you know, I did not initiate or expect that kiss you walked in on. We really were just good friends."

Russ tips my chin with his fingers. "I'm glad. Now, hurry up and get ready. I'm looking forward to this, Charley." After giving me a quick kiss on my forehead, he heads for his car.

twenty-nine

"Well, how cute you look," Janni says when they step into the house. "The temperature is warming up out there." She hangs up their coats. "It might even convince me spring is really here." She finally turns around. "So I take it you're leaving?"

"Yeah. Russ is taking me to Sok's for lunch."

Daniel whistles.

I grin.

"You must be excited. Your face is red," Janni says.

I wait for Daniel to step out of the room, and I lean in to Janni. "I hate to admit it even to myself, but I think I'm having hot flashes."

Janni's eyes grow wide, and her hand muffles the erupting giggle.

"Oh, sure, make fun of me."

She flaps her hand. "No, no, it's just that I've suspected you were having them, but you never wanted to admit it. From one hot-flash sister to another, welcome." She extends her hand, but I just look at her.

"Oh, come on, it's no big deal. You said so yourself."

"I guess. I'll just make a doctor appointment when I get back to Seafoam." I walk over to the window and slip back the curtain. "Well, no Russ yet," I say when I turn back to Janni.

"You're going out with Russ?" Stephanie's eyebrows wiggle up and down, and Carol laughs beside her.

"Yep. He's going to show me the lot he purchased too."

Janni's eyebrow shoots up here.

"What?"

"Nothing."

"Well, I hope you don't mind that I'm not staying for lunch."

"It's just that much more for us," Blake says, bounding down the stairs with Ethan right behind him.

"Don't you listen to him, Aunt Char. We'll save you some for later," Ethan says.

"Glad *somebody* loves me around here," I say, giving Ethan a hug.

"Aw, I was just teasing."

"I know." I laugh and give Blake a squeeze.

Upon hearing Russ's car pull up outside, I yank on my jacket and turn to the boys. "See you kids later."

It takes everything in me not to bounce down the porch steps to meet Russ, who is already walking toward me.

Extending his hand to me, he says, "You look great."

"Thank you." The warmth of his hand and the compliment send a shock of emotion through me.

"I hope you're hungry." He pulls open the car door, and I step inside.

"I could eat a horse," I say, sliding into my seat.

Russ gives a hearty laugh, then leans down and plants a quick, unexpected kiss on my lips. His lips are moist, soft. "That's what I love about you." He closes my door and steps around to his side of the car, leaving me speechless and my mouth dry. That's what he *loves* about—*me*? My lips are totally stuck to my gums. Couldn't move them if my life depended on it.

Once inside the car, he starts the engine and turns the radio on to an easy listening station, allowing romantic songs to filter through the car.

My heart palpitations are at an all-time high here. I'm beginning to wonder if this guy is good for my health. My fingers absently rub across my lips as I relive what just happened, but as soon as I realize what I'm doing, I jerk my hand down.

"I heard you were interested in the Tuckers's property?" Russ says with a glint of amusement.

Though he's talking about the jail episode, for a moment I consider telling him about the commercial thing, but I decide to wait and get his take on it first. "Maybe a little too interested."

He laughs. "They're sure nice folks. I hope they find the right buyer."

We discuss the acreage and property. Treading easily, I say, "Maybe they could get it zoned commercially and get someone out there."

Russ shakes his head. "I don't think so. I think it would break their hearts. Not to mention the county folks would be up in arms. Between you and me, I'd buy the property before I'd let that happen to those sweet folks."

"Well, it's not like it would hurt them. They'd make a lot of money."

He turns to me. "We both know money isn't everything, Char."

A ping of shame stabs my heart. Is that my problem? Have I made money and status too much of a priority in my life? Instead of showing the town how successful I've become, they'd all be mad at me over the deal. Still, if I can convince the Tuckers it's a good thing, then everyone else, including Russ, would be all right with it, wouldn't they?

The hostess seats us at a corner table beside expansive windows that overlook the distant lake beyond a parklike setting of benches, lamp-posts, and a sandy beach.

After praying over our meal, Russ grabs a dinner roll, scoops a pat of butter onto it, and begins spreading it with his knife. I follow suit.

"Look, I'm going to cut to the chase and get right to business." Once his butter is spread, he puts his knife down and looks at me. "I had no right to react the way I did upon seeing you kiss Peter. It's your life, and I have no claim on you. I'm sorry."

I'm not sure what to say, because Russ did overreact, but no more than I did when I saw him and Linda together at the coffee shop. To make matters worse, I'm a little disappointed with his comment, because the truth is, I want him to care that Peter kissed me.

"It's all right. But before we go any further, I think it only fair to warn you, I have a black belt in karate."

His mouth breaks into a wide grin. "So I've been duly warned."

"Exactly."

"Meaning?"

"Meaning, if you get out of line again, I might have to hurt you."

He grabs my hand, holds it next to his cheek, then lightly kisses my fingers, one by one. His eyes never leaving my face, he whispers, "Please don't."

The scent of the filet mignon coming from my plate fails to tempt me. Butterflies in my stomach have chased away my appetite. Another dry-mouth moment.

One final kiss on the back of my hand and Russ clears his throat and releases my hand. He picks up his fork. "So Daniel tells me the syrup process is pretty much over, and he plans the final cleanup for next week."

"Yeah." The comment makes my legs weak.

"Then what?"

I choke down a swallow of salad. "What do you mean?"

"Back to Maine, your job, all that?" Russ holds his fork midair while waiting for my answer. When is the last time a man paused with bated breath for my answer to anything?

"Yeah, I guess." Even as the words leave my lips, I want to snatch them back. Everything has played out exactly as I wanted. I'll have my syrup. Time with the family. Now I go back to Maine. That was the plan. Falling in love was not part of the plan.

"You know, Charley, you may not believe this, but I hadn't intended to get involved with anyone again. My wife—well, I made some mistakes with her. Didn't let her know how much she meant to me nearly as often as I should have."

I'm not sure I want to hear this. My heart is too raw.

He grabs my left hand again, his blue eyes turning my heart to liquid. "I don't want to make that same mistake with you." His thumb gently massages the back of my hand.

Putting my fork down, I give up on the meal. I'm just not into it. The conversation, yes. The meal, no.

"I don't know if you could ever feel that way about me, and I'm not asking you to tell me right now. I just wanted to tell you what was on my mind so I would have no regrets."

I smile, not knowing what to say.

Once more he drops my hand and lifts a weak grin. "I've taken you by surprise. I'm sorry."

With a little too much eagerness, I say, "No, no. I'm, um, glad you told me."

His eyes penetrate mine again. "You are?"

The look on his face and the way he says those two words squeeze around my heart and send a ribbon of warmth through me from head to toe. I smile and nod.

We continue on through our meal, talking over town happenings and his dental business, then make our way to the beach.

"You sure you're warm enough?" Russ asks, adjusting my scarf so it's up farther on my neck. His fingers brush against my skin, causing it to tingle. I've forgotten what it feels like to have someone fuss over me this way. "Your mom tells me they'll be going back to their condo shortly." He pulls on black leather gloves.

"That's good to hear." The tide rushes to the icy shore, dashing the air with a cold mist. Sunlight bathes the lake with a soft glow.

Russ laughs. "Why is that? You ready to get them out of Janni's house?"

"No, I mean, it's good that she said they'd both be going back.

With all that 'he's-trying-to-kill-me' business, I wasn't sure if Mom would go back."

"Oh, that's right. She's been doing a lot better on that, hasn't she?"

"Yeah."

"Why do you think that is?"

"I have no idea. She's still reading her books."

"Odd." He points to the right of us. "There's my property, but I'm not sure we can get up there from here, dressed in our coats and all."

The property is built up and away from the shoreline, which will give him a beautiful view of the lake once he gets his house built.

"It's gorgeous, Russ."

He laughs. "I guess there's not much to see but ground anyway, but it gives you an idea of where I'll be building and what the view will be." He turns back to the lake. "I've always wanted a house out here."

We talk about his house plans, and I can hardly wait to get back to my sketches and see what more I can come up with. The breeze sprays a fine mist toward my face and invigorates me. Surprising both of us, I tuck my arm through his and squeeze.

"I'm so happy for you."

Russ turns to me, the sunlight catching the sparkle of blue in his eyes. With a tenderness that strikes deep into my emotions, he buries his hands in my hair and brushes light kisses against the sides of my face, my cheeks, my nose, and finally my lips. The sound of water rushing to shore echoes in my mind as our lips meet again and again. The slight stubble on his face, the scent of peppermint on his lips makes me heady, causing my mind to spin out of control.

And in this very moment, I know that because of Russ Benson, my life will never be the same.

"*Weren't we just here?" Blake asks with an ornery* glint in his eyes as he and Ethan step through the front door Friday night.

"No, just seems like it," Janni says with a chuckle, pulling her boys into a hug. "We're just getting ready to settle in the kitchen for some hot chocolate. Want some?"

"Sure," Blake and Ethan say.

"Get your things put away, and come join us." Janni makes her way into the kitchen. Daniel is already at the table, clipping coupons from the paper. I'm getting supplies out for Janni to make the chocolate.

"Since everyone else is gone, now seems the perfect time to tell the boys, don't you think, Danny?"

He looks up from the paper and takes a deep breath. "Yeah."

"Listen, I'll go over to the coffee shop for a while, since this is a family affair," I say.

"Yes, and you're family," Janni insists. "Please, Char? I'd like you to be here."

By the time we have the hot chocolate poured into mugs and placed on the table, the boys have joined us. They chatter about what's going on at school, and at the first lull in the conversation, Janni jumps in.

"Listen, boys, I have something I need to tell you." When they look up at her, she tells them everything about Stephanie. Eyes grow wide, mouths drop open, then snap shut. When she's all finished, the silence is deafening.

Janni twists a handkerchief between her fingers, tears streaming down her cheeks. "I'm so sorry I've let you down, and I'm sorry I kept this from you all these years."

Silence.

"We all make mistakes. We're not proud of them. We wish we hadn't made them, but we go on from here. We're a family, and a family stands by each other, come what may," Daniel says.

A knot plugs the breath from my throat as we wait for the boys to respond.

"Please say something," Janni says, staring at her handkerchief.

"Does this mean I can't date her?" Blake asks with a straight face.

"You idiot, of course you can't date her. She's our sister." Ethan gouges his brother in the side, and they both start laughing.

That simple comment and brotherly act sucks all the tension from the room. Both boys go over and hug Janni. "Nothing you could ever do would make us stop loving you, Mom," Ethan says, quoting the very phrase I've heard Janni say to them so often over the years.

"We love you, warts and all, Mom," Blake says, also using her quote and holding her tight.

Just then Stephanie enters the house. "Hi, everyone. Mom went to the store for some popcorn if you all—" One glance at everyone's face, and she stops cold.

Blake walks over and stops in front of her. "Welcome to the family, sis." He pulls her into a bear hug. Chair legs scrape against the floor as everyone surrounds Stephanie, and soon the Ort family is a tangle of arms and tears.

No one notices as I quietly slip away from the room.

"Boy, this week has flown by," I say with a yawn as I come down the stairs the next morning. "Between finishing up the syrup for another year and tying up loose ends for the party, I'm beat."

Janni flops her legs on the recliner footrest. "You got that right."

"Hey, sis, how about I treat you to coffee this morning at Smooth Grounds to celebrate your new family, the end of syrup season, the party, all that?"

Her eyes brighten. Just as I suspected, she's becoming like me, a true coffee connoisseur. "Do we have time? Is everything ready for tonight's party?"

"I'll call the Carpenter Center and make sure everything is in place, see if they have any last-minute questions. Then I'll swing by there this afternoon."

"Well, if you're buying the coffee, I'm going."

We tell the others where we're going and head out the door. By the time we reach the coffeehouse, a group of Tappery coffee drinkers are in line for their morning java.

Coffees in hand, we peel off our jackets and settle in at a table.

I take a drink. "I thought I'd go visit the Tuckers before I go over to the Center. The cake isn't supposed to get there until this afternoon. By the time I get there, things should be pretty much set up."

"I'm just glad we're still having a party. Mom and Dad sure didn't make it easy on us." Janni chuckles.

"That's for sure." Another drink.

"Why are you going to see the Tuckers?"

"There wasn't really time to visit when they bailed us out of jail, so I wanted to go back to their home and properly thank them. They're such nice folks." Never mind that I'm trying to get them to sell their house in a commercial deal so I can get a promotion. I mentally shake myself. What am I saying? Progress is a good thing. There's no need to feel ashamed. After all, it's not as though I'm making them do something they don't want to do. I'm merely presenting another option. "Then I'll come home and get ready."

"Did you hear what you said?"

"What?"

"You called this 'home.'"

That little revelation startles me. "I did, didn't I?"

Janni smiles. "This trip has been good for you, Char."

"It really has. It's changed my view of the past."

"And your outlook for the future?" She's digging for information now.

"Hey, have you been hanging out with Gail?"

Janni cackles, and I hold my breath. The hyena doesn't show. She's getting better at stopping herself short of scaring people.

"The boys took the news of Stephanie well, don't you think?"

Janni smiles. "Yeah, they did. Though Blake's determined to change her health habits."

We both laugh.

"I told Dad last night when he got home too."

"How did he take it?"

"He told me it was about time he got a granddaughter."

"I'm happy for you, sis." I take another sip. "So where do you think your relationship with Stephanie will go from here?"

"We're going to stay in touch, of course. She'll come and visit from time to time. We're planning gifts on birthdays, holidays, all that. She'll be our daughter too, but at arm's length, so we don't intrude on Carol's place."

"You're a good woman, Janni."

"Oh, yeah, real good. I've made a mess of things, but somehow God was able to work through it in spite of it all. It's hard to explain, but Stephanie seems to make our family complete."

"Must be nice to feel complete," I say with a smile.

"You'll get there, Char. I've no doubt. I've seen the way Russ looks at you."

"He's just checking out my teeth."

Janni giggles. "You're awful." She thinks a moment. "You know, you're not rushing around like you did when you first came here."

"How so?"

"Your steps are slower. You seem more relaxed. Not on the phone as much."

For a moment, I figure it's because I've tied up most loose ends at work, but Janni's right, there's more to it than that.

"I guess Mayberry's getting to me."

Janni stops drinking short of choking and laughs. "We've helped more than one city slicker see the error of their ways."

"I'm glad." Taking a sip from my own macchiato, I think about how amazing this visit has been.

"Does this mean you'll come back more often?" There's an ornery flash in her eyes.

I grin. "You can count on it."

While finishing our coffee, we talk a little more about our family and how things have turned out, the last-minute touches for the party tonight.

"Well, I guess I'd better get moving if I'm going to have any time with the Tuckers before tonight." We stand and throw away our cups.

After dropping Janni off at home, I head for Tappery Assisted Living. The warmth of the Tuckers's apartment hits me the moment I walk in the door. Wish I had my fan.

"Charlene Haverford, as I live and breathe," Mrs. Tucker says, extending her thick arms around me and pulling me into a warm hug—and I do mean warm. I can't peel my coat off fast enough. Mrs. Tucker is five foot two and almost as wide as she is tall, but she has an even bigger heart.

"Come sit down, dear." She points toward the sofa. "Earl, Charlene Haverford is here," she calls over her shoulder.

"How about some iced tea with lemon?"

"That would be wonderful," I say, thinking I'll dish out the ice cubes and stuff them down my shirt collar.

We soon settle into our tea and polite conversation.

"I want to thank you both for not prosecuting Janni and me for, well, breaking and entering your home."

Mrs. Tucker laughs. "I got a chuckle out of that one. I could almost imagine the two of you climbing that tree."

"Actually, I'm the only one who climbed the tree. I went downstairs and let Janni in. She didn't want to come in, but I figured we could get a quick look and leave."

"Be sure your sins will find you out, I always say." Earl gives a hearty laugh and winks.

He's been talking to my mother, I can feel it. He walks over to me and gives me a hug. "Great to see you, kiddo."

"You too." We sit down. "So any luck on selling it?" I ask.

"We've had some interest, but no one who fits the place yet," Mrs. Tucker says.

"That's because you don't want to sell it." Mr. Tucker turns to me. "We'll never be able to unload it because she's trying to find someone who will love the house the way she does. Now, how you gonna know that?" He shakes his head and takes a drink from his glass of tea.

"I would feel the same way. I'm a Realtor, and I'm very particular about matching up people with homes that fit their needs. To me the home is the foundation of a family, you know? A place of refuge where we return at the end of the day. I'm on a mission to match families with the right place, I guess. Well—that used to be my mission. I'm dealing more with commercial property these days." My comment is sort of an epiphany for me. Russ has been right all along. My passion is working in residential property, helping families find the right place.

"That's exactly right. You understand why I want just the right family for our home." Mrs. Tucker's eyes light with gratitude, filling me with shame. "We'd be able to sell the house and a couple of acres, then parcel off the rest of the acreage, if we could find the right family. Wish we could find a Realtor like you. You still live out East?"

I nod and explain about Aunt Rose's cottage and how much I love it, but how I'm now a little torn about being away from Mom and Dad, Janni, the homestead. I don't say anything about Russ.

"Family becomes more important the older we get, that's for sure," Mrs. Tucker says, plumping a pillow beneath her feet on the coffee table. "I sure miss our daughter. She's so far away." She looks in the distance as though remembering better days.

"How does Katy like Florida?" I ask.

"Oh, she loves it. Just wish we could see her more."

"How does she feel about you selling the house?"

"Oh, she doesn't care," Mr. Tucker pipes up. "She's too busy with her own life to worry about the house."

"It's a beautiful place. So many wonderful memories from my childhood were played out there."

We talk about the homemade apple pies, working in the orchard, all that.

"Too bad we couldn't get you to move back to Tappery. You'd be a perfect fit for our place." Mrs. Tucker smiles gently, and we move on to the next topic, but her words linger in my mind and heart.

Their home is much more valuable than money can buy. Somehow I know I've kissed that promotion good-bye, and the weird thing is I'm okay with that.

thirty

Though it was hard to keep things secret, Janni and I somehow managed to get Mom into the new cream-colored dress with gold trim we bought for her and Dad into his fine black suit by telling them we were taking them out for a special dinner. Mom seemed a bit distressed that their afternoon had gone by without a party, but she said nothing. That doesn't fool me one bit. We both know if Janni and I hadn't come through for her tonight, we'd need twenty-four-hour police protection by morning.

I spared no expense for this affair, and one look at our parents' faces when Janni and Daniel usher them into the room tells me it was worth every penny. Cameras snap and bulbs flash the moment their heels click onto the shiny hardwood floor. Crystal chandeliers sparkle overhead, while music from the grand piano and string quartet filters around the room, joining tinkling silver against china and ice cubes against crystal. The tables and chairs are laden with ivory linens. Greenery and tapered, gold candles flank the table centers while candles, greenery, and a bouquet of white roses decorate the honored couple's table. Smiling faces of old and new friends fill the room.

Mom cries and my heart warms to family in a deeper way than ever before. What started out as a plan to impress the town with the "new me" somewhere along the line changed to making this the most memorable night in Mom and Dad's lives. By the look on their faces, I'd say it's happening.

I grab each parent's hand and walk them over to the microphone in front of the tables. "Ladies and gentlemen, our guests of honor, Milton and Lavina Haverford."

The room erupts with uproarious applause as people stand to their feet, causing Mom to cry some more. This time Dad joins her. The only time I've ever seen my dad cry was when he prayed. A lump forms in my throat, and I dab at the tears in my own eyes.

After Mom and Dad take a moment to welcome everyone, beautiful stringed music begins to play, while waiters serve each table. A movement at the edge of the entrance catches my attention. Gertie Becker. Just then Dad gets up from the head table where the family is sitting and heads toward Gertie. Janni is sitting beside me, so I nudge her with my leg. When I catch her attention, I nod toward Dad and Gertie. Suddenly, Mom notices them, frowns, and gets up from the table. Janni and I exchange a worried glance and follow after Mom.

Dad and Gertie disappear around the corner into the entryway. Mom's steps quicken, and we pick up our pace to a trot. Silverware clangs on china, the smell of gourmet food perfumes the air, and the quiet murmur of happy people follows us out of the room, but there's a feeling of doom that haunts my every step.

Upon nearing our parents, we hear Mom shouting something about Gertie and Dad in cahoots. We step around the corner just as Mom turns on her heel to leave.

Somehow I imagined the memorable night a little different than this.

"Oh no, you don't," Dad says, grabbing our shocked mother by the arm. "You will hear me out this time, Viney Haverford."

Mom turns to Dad, and we all stand frozen in time.

"She saw me hugging Gertie, and she's all in a snit," Dad says to us by way of explanation. "What she doesn't know is that Gertie helped me a lot in a certain matter, and I gave her a friendly hug in appreciation for her kindness."

"I don't want to hear another word. You let me go right this instant, Milton, do you hear me?" Mom's arms are in full motion, and I'm thinking once her legs kick into gear, look out.

"We're going back in there, and you're going to hear what this is all about," he says.

Janni and I step aside as Dad holds Mom's arm and ushers her back into the room with all the guests. With one look at a confused Gertie, I offer a weak smile, and we step back into the banquet room.

"The next five minutes could make or break this party," Janni says.

I nod. "We should have thrown the party last year."

"People don't throw big bashes for forty-nine years, Char."

Mom's holding her tongue, but I'm sure it's only because she has an audience. Dad grabs a chair for her, and she reluctantly sits down. He then lifts the microphone from the stand, walks over to where Mom is seated, and faces the crowd.

"As I'm sure all of you know, I retired from the church several months ago. It's hard to give up what I've done for so many years, but you've graciously loved us through it." He turns aside to cough, says "Excuse me," then looks at the people again. "Our daughter Char came back to help us with the syrup and to no doubt help out with this big surprise party, but I'm sure she and Janni, our other daughter, don't realize they've done so much more."

Tears spring to my eyes, though I have no idea where Dad is going with this.

"I've had trouble with the idea of retirement. After being busy and involved in people's lives, it's hard to sit in a recliner and watch TV."

Chuckles and nods ripple around the room.

"Some pastors move from church to church, but as you know, we plunked ourselves down in this town forty-two years ago, and you've been hard-pressed to get rid of us."

More chuckles and shaking of heads.

"I had gallbladder surgery recently, and I wondered if this is all I have to look forward to, sickness and boredom." He turns to Janni and me and extends his arm so we'll join them up front. "But I've watched our girls weather some recent storms and changes. They've made me proud and ashamed all at the same time. Proud of them for trusting God to see them through. Ashamed that I've not been as trusting. They've moved beyond the past, and they're making a future for themselves." He squeezes my hand when I reach him, and Janni stands on the other side of me, both of us with tears streaming down our faces. "That's what I want to do with the years I have left, make a future with my bride of fifty years, and continue to serve you folks—as your friend, not your pastor."

Now Dad turns to Mom. "When Viney and I married fifty years ago, we had little money in our pockets. I was only two years into pastoring my first church, where I met her. Needless to say, we had very little money to live on, but we had our love." He looks at Mom and winks. She makes an attempt to smile, but it comes out as more of a smirk. I shove the memory of Victoria's Secret away as quickly as I can.

"I gave her a cheap wedding band as a symbol of our love, and she never complained. Through the years, we've counseled many young couples at our church, congratulating them on their engagements, and each time I saw a flashing diamond, I wished I could give Viney one. Oh, I know she doesn't care about such things, but it was something I wanted to do for her."

He has Mom's full attention now. In fact, the whole room seems to take a collective breath as Dad bends down on one knee. I'm wondering if we'll have to get him up when this is all over.

Reaching into his pocket, he pulls something out. He then lifts Mom's hand and says, "You've deserved so much more, Viney, but as we begin this new adventure into retirement and a new phase of our lives, may this symbol represent my undying devotion to you now and for always."

Dad slips the new wedding set on Mom's finger, and there's not a dry eye in the house. Mom helps Dad get back up, and they embrace while the room breaks into booming applause once again for the deserving couple I'm proud to call my parents.

After everything dies down, Dad lifts the microphone once more and says, "I want to thank Gertie Becker and her son, Paul, who is a jeweler, for helping to make this moment possible. Thank you."

More applause, then the music begins again. Congratulations abound as Mom and Dad make their way back to the table. The first place Mom stops is at Gertie's table. Through tears, they exchange some words and embrace in a long, friendly hug.

"Well, I didn't see that one coming," I say to Janni as we head for our table.

"Me neither."

During dinner, friends approach the microphone and share their stories of the honored couple, as we laugh and cry our way through the meal. Afterwards, people amble around, browse through the scrapbook Janni made, the display of photos on the table, and they catch up with one another's family lives.

Spotting Gail Campbell, I walk over to her. "Listen, Gail, about that night in the coffee shop, I shouldn't have—"

Gail holds up her hand. "Yes, you should have. Linda and I both deserved it. I don't know why I have such a problem keeping my mouth shut." She looks genuinely sorry.

"Well, obviously, we both have the same problem."

We laugh together. Gail Campbell and I. Together. "Friends?" she asks. Something in her expression almost makes me sorry for the years missed. Almost.

"Friends." Not best of friends, mind you, but I think I can at least be social when I see her now. We talk a little longer and finally part ways, vowing to stay in touch as old friends often do.

I join Russ, Janni, and Daniel at a table. "Well, it seems to be a success."

"Yeah, it does. This was far more beautiful than I could have imagined, Char. I'm glad you did most of the planning. They'll never forget this," Janni says, watching our parents as they interact with friends.

"Thank you for understanding that I needed to do this, Janni. It was my way of apologizing for—well, everything."

"I understand." She pats my hand. "I can hardly believe this is it. All the months of work and planning for the party and the syrup, and now we're done. What will we do with ourselves?" Janni chuckles.

"Hey, if Dad can do it, we can do it." We laugh. "I figure I'll stay for church tomorrow and leave on Monday, if that works for you." Sadness clogs my throat. I can't say any more.

Russ squeezes my hand. "I'm trying to get her to stay and help me with my house but can't seem to talk her into it."

"I wish you could stay longer, Char. Just stay and have fun with me for a while," Janni says.

"There's a house waiting on me back in Maine, you know."

Janni stares at her fingers glumly. "Yeah, we know."

"Do you guys have any plans now that everything is finished?" I ask.

"Back to the same old grind, I reckon," Daniel says. Disappointment flickers on Janni's face. I glance at the boys at the end of the table. Things will be hard for her once everyone leaves. The boys, Stephanie, and Carol are all leaving tomorrow.

"Hey, I've got an idea." Everyone turns my way. "Why don't you and Danny go up to my place for a little vacation?"

Janni's eyes widen. "We couldn't do that."

"Why not?"

"Who will take care of the chores around here? The animals, all that?"

"I will." Everybody is staring at me now. "I'll stay here while you're at my place. That way I can rest a little before having to go back to work, you can enjoy a vacation, and everybody is happy."

Excitement sparks in Janni's eyes, and she turns to Daniel. "Could you get away from the store?"

"Sure," he says with enthusiasm. "Things are slow, what with that new store just opened, and my crew would be fine with it."

Janni gives him a worried look.

"It will give us time to think through what we want to do in the days ahead, come up with some new marketing strategies maybe for the store." He squeezes her. "We have enough money to get us through. Hey, the sky is the limit."

His comment chases the doubt from her face, and she laughs. I'm going to talk to him later about that money thing. It's time they do a little remodeling around the house.

Janni turns back to me. "What about your job, Char? Can you afford to miss any more work?"

"No problem," I say as though I'm absolutely certain, which of course, I'm not. But that's okay. I'm not worried about it. I've made enough money for the company in the last six months, Peter will give me the time I need—at least I think he will. If not, with my sales record, I'm pretty sure I could land another job in town.

"Well, what do you think, babe? Want to go hang out in an ocean paradise?" Daniel gives Janni another hug while she beams from ear to ear.

Daniel and Janni are soon lost in their vacation plans. Russ presses my hand against his cheek and closes his eyes as though he wants to remember this moment forever.

"You know what this means?" he whispers against my hair.

Shivers run through me, and I try not to tremble. "What?"

"I'll get to have you with me for a little while longer," Russ says.

I smile and act surprised. Silly man. Like I hadn't thought of that.

When most of the well-wishers have gone, Mom and Dad walk over to our table and sit down. They look completely exhausted but also very content.

"Girls, I have to say"—Mom pulls her hankie from her purse again—"this night has been—well, it's been magical, that's all." She wipes her nose. "It's as though I've stepped into Cinderella's glass slippers." We all admire her sparkling diamond.

Daddy squeezes Mom's hand and gives her a peck on the cheek. This time I let my own tears roll. How could I have stayed away? No matter our differences, my family means the world to me. I get up and hug them both.

After our hug, Mom turns to Dad. "Milton, I guess I owe you an apology. I should have known you wouldn't try to kill me."

"I wouldn't have the strength, Viney. You know that." Dad chuckles.

"Well, I'm sorry." She pauses. "Still, if it's all the same to you, I'm getting rid of the rat poison."

We all laugh.

"Oh, I almost forgot. There's one more thing Janni and I wanted to give you," I say, reaching into my purse. Janni gives me a questioning look. She doesn't know what's coming, and I hope she doesn't mind.

"You've done more than enough with this whole party, girls," Mom says, no doubt already worrying about our finances.

Pulling out the envelope, I extend it to Dad. "These are your plane tickets for Prince Edward Island. There you will stay at a bed-and-breakfast owned by one of my clients."

Mom's hand flies to her chest. "Prince Edward Island!" She throws her arms around me and then Janni. "Milton, Prince Edward Island!"

Dad laughs. "I know, Viney. Won't it be grand?"

Carol and Stephanie join us with the boys, and we talk about the island, what to see and how to make the most of their time there. Finally, we call it a night and head back to Janni's house.

"How much do I owe you for the plane tickets, Char?" Janni asks.

"Nothing. I've saved a hunk of money by staying at your house, and I know it's no small thing to feed me, so let's call it even."

"I'm happy to help."

"I know. You helped enough with the party itself."

"Why didn't you give Mom and Dad their gift in front of the crowd so they could have talked about it with their friends?"

"Maybe I should have done that, but honestly, I wanted this to be private. Guess I don't need to prove myself anymore."

"You've come a long way, Char."

"We both have," I say, squeezing her hand. "We both have."

After church and lunch the next day, we gather at the front door of Janni's house to say our good-byes to the boys, Carol, and Stephanie.

Janni and Daniel stand side to side, arms around each other's waists. "Thank you so much for your help with the syrup. We couldn't have done it all without the help of family and friends," Daniel says. "By the way, Carol, you don't want to forget to take your share." He starts to run for the pantry, but Carol holds up her hand.

"As much as I'd love to have some, I can't eat it. It doesn't set well with me. I think I might be allergic to it or something."

Sharp intake of breath as we all turn and look at her as though she has leprosy.

"What an awful way to live," I say with utmost sympathy.

"I have a friend who is allergic to milk. When she drinks it, she starts acting a little crazy. Paranoid and all that. It's strange what food allergies can do." Carol laughs.

What she says makes me wonder about Mom's recent paranoia—though not completely without foundation, she did overreact a tad. "Say, Mom, do you think you could have a food allergy of some sort?"

Mom blinks. "What are you saying, that I'm paranoid?" We all seem to hold our breath, bracing for what may come.

"Not paranoid as in weird, just not your normal self," I say.

Mom shrugs, and we all sigh with relief. "Could be. I might have it checked out."

Maybe there is hope on the horizon. We'll do whatever it takes to keep Mom at peace. 'Cause when Mama ain't happy, ain't nobody happy.

We pause at the door while Dad leads us in prayer. Afterwards, everyone grows quiet as Janni turns to Stephanie. "I love you, Stephanie. I've loved you from the day I gave you birth, held you in my arms, and said good-bye." Tears make wet tracks down her cheeks. She turns to Carol. "I've prayed for you daily as you raised 'our daughter,' and I can't thank you enough for giving yourself to her in a way I never could." Janni pulls both of them into a hug. "In no way do I ever want to come between you two. What I do want is for both of you to be an extension of our family. So I hereby invite you to all holidays with us. You told me yourself, Carol, that your parents are gone, and Stephanie is all you have. We'd love to 'adopt' you as part of our family. Think it over."

Everyone joins in with hugs, laughter, and tears. After all the good-byes, we wave after Carol, Stephanie, and the boys as they each make their way to the cars. Once the door is closed behind them, Russ, Daniel, Mom, and Dad head for the family room to watch a movie, while I go up to Janni's room with her to help her pack for their trip in the morning. We talk awhile about the party, Stephanie and Carol, and Janni's upcoming vacation. My mood is considerably better knowing that Russ and I can put off our "good-byes" for a while longer, and Janni and Daniel can have their much-deserved time alone at my house.

"Oh, in all the excitement, I haven't had time to tell you about my trip to the Tuckers," I say, folding a blouse and laying it in the suitcase.

We discuss my visit there and what they said to me about their house.

"Would you truly consider buying the Tuckers's home?" Janni stops packing the clothes in her suitcase and stares at me. A slow incredulous smile creeps onto her face.

"Oh, I don't know. It's a long shot. But it's kind of fun to think about."

"And the fact that Russ Benson lives in town is certainly a draw," Janni teases. "But what about your job back in Maine? And your house? You can't sell your house."

"I've been thinking a lot about all that. Russ might be right. I've been working on commercial real estate when my heart is in designing and building homes. I've decided I don't want that promotion after all."

"What promotion?"

"It doesn't matter. There's a lot to consider. I would never sell the cottage in Maine. I would keep it as a summer house or something. A vacation home for all of us."

"Wow." Janni flops onto the bed. "I would never have thought it possible."

"I'm not saying I'm doing it. I'm just saying it's not completely out of the question. Still, it might be hard to give up my ocean view. Are you all packed?"

Janni makes a face. "Do you think I have enough clothes?"

"You'll be on vacation, you don't need many clothes. Sweats, jeans, one nice outfit for going out."

"Hey, Janni, can I get you to come outside for a minute?" Daniel asks, walking into the room.

A puzzled expression covers Janni's face, and Daniel grabs her hand. "It won't take long." With a discreet wink my way, he ushers Janni out of the room, and I follow. It seems I have more in common with Gail Campbell than I realized.

"Danny Ort, what are you doing?" Janni makes an attempt to protest, but she's giggling the whole way.

"Now put your hands over your eyes and close them tight."

More giggling.

Mom, Dad, and I rush out to see what all the excitement is about, though I'm pretty sure I know.

"Okay, now you can open your eyes."

Janni drops her hands and looks straight ahead at the Harley she'd been keeping in their barn. There's a pink bow on the seat. She turns to Daniel. "What's this about, Danny?"

"This is my gift to you. I bought it from Gertie's son. They just got home. Gertie mentioned he was going to sell the Harley, and I let him know I'd like to buy it from him—if you decide you want it." Daniel hesitates, worry lining his face. "Do you want it?"

"It's perfect." Janni throws her arms around her husband. He lifts her off the ground and swirls her around until I get dizzy watching them.

Once the hubbub over the new gift dies down, Janni turns to Daniel. "We're not taking this to Char's house, are we?" Her eyes are wide and she's so excited, I'm thinking she could whip up a Thanksgiving meal single-handedly in two hours flat.

He throws back his head and laughs. "I'm adventurous, but not stupid. It's too cold for that. Not to mention, we're out of practice and wouldn't be able to peel ourselves off of the bike after a trip cross-country."

Janni looks disappointed.

"But I thought we could take a ride around town today. You okay with taking a little spin?"

"I'm okay with that." They share a kiss while Mom, Dad, and I head back to the house. All the while I'm hoping they hurry up and get a license before Toby finds out.

"You're sure Peter was okay with this when you told him of your plans, Char?" Janni asks once we're all back in the house.

"He was fine with it. He's just hired a couple of new sales associates, so there are plenty of people around."

"Well, I must say he's something to give you time off after you dumped him," Mom says with her usual tact.

"Oh, no problem. He's already moved on. He's in another dating relationship."

Janni gasps. "You okay with that?"

"I'm fine," I assure her.

"Who wouldn't be fine with a man like Russ Benson waiting in the shadows?" Mom says candidly.

After coffee and dessert, Mom and Dad head back to their condo with a promise to come over in the morning to see Janni and Daniel off. Russ and I decide to visit the beach and his property, while Janni and Daniel take a spin on their new wheels.

With everyone leaving tomorrow, it will be a quiet day. For the next couple of weeks it will just be me and the farm animals. Well, and maybe Russ.

I sure hope I'm doing the right thing.

thirty-one

"Hey, where you going?" Russ calls after me from the porch. Dressed in layered shirts with a smart cream-colored button-down on the outside, the rugged look of Levis covering his long legs, and brown casual lace-up oxfords completing the look, he causes my heart to flip with one glance.

"Taking a walk in the woods," I call back to him. With a pure blue sky and bright sun shining overhead, the hint of warmth in the air, I couldn't stay cooped up in the house any longer.

"All right if I join you?"

I grin at him over my shoulder. "If you can catch me."

His grin matches mine, and we both take off at full speed. Though I'm a ways ahead of him, he catches up to me in no time. Breathless and spent, we fall against the first maple we come to.

"Boy, I had no idea those pancakes would lodge right here," Russ says, pointing to his midsection.

Wish pancakes looked that good on me.

I laugh. "Sure was sweet of Janni to make pancakes for everyone this morning. I think she's excited about her trip."

"Yeah, I think you're right." Russ turns a teasing glance my way. "You know, if you keep eating pancakes, you're going to need a good dentist."

To say nothing of a good weight-loss program and a new wardrobe. "You think?"

"I think." The twinkle in his eyes melts me with one glance. Bending his arm against the tree bark, he comes toward me, licking his lips as he leans closer, until his lips touch mine. Something about the tenderness of the moment, the smell of the woods—my refuge from the harsh realities of life—having Russ near me this way, all have a profound effect on me.

Though our lips part, he keeps his head bent and his eyes fixed on me. "I'm so glad you're staying awhile." His voice is husky and low as he plants soft kisses by my temple and nuzzles into my hair.

"Me too."

He pulls me closer to him and kisses me again, long and hard, our hearts pounding against one another.

He finally pulls away as though he's forcing himself. "We have something between us, you know. Something real." His words are thick with emotion.

"I know."

"What are we going to do about it?"

"I don't know."

"Well, I think we should spend the next several weeks deciding, don't you?"

I look up into his smiling eyes. "Yeah." I dare not tell him about my consideration of the Tucker home. He might pressure me, and I need to sort things out. My heart is pressuring me enough as it is.

We hear a commotion up at the house.

"Sounds like people are leaving," Russ says. "Want to go back?"

"Yeah."

His sturdy, warm hand engulfs my own as we trudge our way back to the house, where Mom and Dad are headed toward their car.

"You sure you don't need us to take anything to your condo for you?" Russ asks Dad.

"No, thanks. We've been taking things over little by little, so we're in good shape."

"If you need anything at all, let me know," I say, hugging Mom and Dad good-bye.

"Same to you, honey." Mom's having a sappy moment. I'd blame it on the syrup, but she seems different lately—or maybe I'm the one who's changing. "We'll never forget our anniversary celebration, girls. Thank you so much for your trouble and the expense you went to for us."

"It's the least we could do," I say.

"Zip, watching you come to terms with your past has made me think about how I struggle with letting go of things. As I said at the party, you're paving the way for a new future, and I'm going to try to step out of the glory days and make some new memories while I still can." Dad gives me a squeeze, causing tears to sting my eyes.

"I love you, Daddy."

"I love you, baby girl." He turns away, then swivels back around. "'Course, that doesn't mean I won't remember the good old days every now and then. It's what old people do, you know." He grins.

"I know." We wave and watch them drive off.

"Well, I guess it's our turn," Janni says, her eyes sparkling with adventure. She leans in to give me a hug. "You behave yourself, and don't get engaged until I get back."

Her words cause my breath to stick in my throat, and my heart gives a leap.

With one glance at the look on my face, Janni whispers, "Fairy tales can come true, you know. Just promise me you'll give it a chance."

Happiness has been so elusive that I can't imagine life changing for me, but it's also hard to imagine that I've come this far—to the point where I'm open to another relationship—a real one—not just a comfortable one or one for status' sake. I breathe a prayer of thankfulness, then look to Janni with a nod and a smile.

"I can't thank you enough, sis. You have no idea how much I need this getaway."

"Oh, I think I do." I smile at her. "Help yourself to anything at my house—except the cookies—and just have a good time."

She laughs. "Remember, if you need help with the animals, you can ask the neighbor boy. He doesn't mind getting up early and tending to them before school for a few extra bucks."

Daniel gives Russ a hearty handshake and hugs me good-bye. "Thanks for everything, sis. We owe you."

"You can pay me off in syrup."

He throws out a gut laugh. I give him a deadpan stare, and he stops. "You're serious."

"I'm serious."

Palms up, he backs away slowly. "You'll get your maple syrup."

"Smart man."

Together, Janni and Daniel climb into their SUV.

"Be careful if you ride the cycle," Janni calls out.

"You worried about me or the cycle?"

A wide grin splits on Janni's face. "Both."

"No worries. I'm not into cycles. I don't wear leather well." Russ comes over to my side and slips his arm around my waist.

"You kids behave yourselves," Daniel says with a smile and a wink.

"Okay, big brother." Russ laughs.

"Have a great time." I wave at them.

Daniel starts the car engine. We watch them edge out of the driveway and wave to the happy couple as they take off into the distant horizon.

"Looks like it's just you and me, kid," Russ finally says when we're left in the silence.

"Guess so."

"Unfortunately, Dad covered for me this morning, so I have to get back to work."

I nod. "Hey, don't forget your syrup." I point to his crate of bottled syrup on the porch.

"How about I come back and get it tonight when I take you out for dinner?"

I look up to him and smile. "Sounds good to me."

"I have to admit that syrup was worth the work."

"Uh-oh, looks like I'm going to have some competition on my future stash of syrup." I laugh.

"Either that or we can combine our stash." His eyes search my face, and words escape me. "Look Charley, I'm not trying to scare you, but I lost you once. I don't want to lose you again. I felt something drawing me back here, beyond the dental practice to help my dad. I didn't know what it was, but now I know. It was you." He kisses my hair and holds me close.

Tears sting my eyes as I linger in the strength of his arms. I glance at the syrup, think of my time spent here over the past few weeks, the struggles, the fun, the revelation, and it hits me. Though I've had hard knocks in life, I've survived. Just like the trees. The storms may break us down for a season, but faith and family will get us through.

"I don't know what the future holds, Charley," Russ whispers into my ear, causing a pleasurable shiver, "but I'd sure like to give it a chance to see where it takes us."

He squeezes me once more, then pulls away to look at me. One glance in his eyes, and I realize for the first time in many years, I'm ready to risk my heart and give love a chance once more.

"Walk with me to my car?"

I nod. He puts his arm around my waist as we walk across the pebbles together, the spring sun warming us along the way.

"I could get into this, you know."

I give Russ a puzzled look.

"You, me, around here." His arm takes in the homestead.

"Me too."

He stops and looks at me. "Really?"

"Really."

His gaze holds mine, then he kisses me gently once more. Afterward, with our arms nestled at each other's waists, we start walking toward his car again. With one glance at the DKNY sneakers on my feet, I smile and snuggle deeper into the chest of the man I love. Dorothy can keep her slippers.

I've already found my way home.

acknowledgments

It took a lot of wonderful people, dozens of pancakes, and several gallons of maple syrup to get me through this book.

First and foremost I want to thank my incredible husband, Jim, for his constant support and encouragement. I couldn't do it without you, babe!

To my daughter, Amber, for believing in me when my spirit wanes and the chocolate supply is low, and who offers complete understanding when I have to go "out of state." Well, most of the time.

To my son-in-law, Kyle, who's always trying to come up with new marketing strategies for me. Thank you!

To my son, Aaron, a high school English teacher who tolerates my dangling participles and even admits to being blood-related. I owe you.

To my daughter-in-law, Megan, who shares my love for books.

To Garry and Nancy Sink for sharing their valuable time with me and explaining the sugaring process. The syrup was delicious!! Thank you!

To my brainstorming buddies: Kristin Billerbeck, Colleen Coble, and Denise Hunter, whose writing inspires me to greater heights.

To my fantastic agent and friend, Karen Solem. Thank you for believing in me and pushing me to keep learning and growing in the craft.

To my genius editor, Ami McConnell, who sees things in story like no one else can, and Natalie Gillespie for her support and expertise!

To the creative Thomas Nelson team who brings story to life: Allen Arnold, Lisa Young, Jennifer Deshler, Natalie Hanemann, Carrie Wagner, Mark Ross, the copyeditors, and the sales reps. We did this together! Thank you!

And finally, to those of you who curl up on the sofa with a cup of coffee, a box of chocolates (you know who you are) and my book—thank you for allowing me to share my story with you.

Until next time, God bless you all!

reading group guide

If your book club has ten or more members and you choose to read one of my books, I would be happy to "visit" your group (free of charge) by telephone and discuss the book. If you're interested, drop me a line at diann@diannhunt.com to schedule a date! I will also send you free autographed bookmarks!

1. Charlene thought she had her life all together, but once she arrived at her childhood home, she realized she had merely moved away from the problems. Have you ever felt as though you had worked through something only to have it crop up later when you least expected it?

2. When Charlene saw people from her past, it brought back bitter memories. She had to move beyond her past and forgive those who hurt her. Is there someone in your life who has hurt you that you need to forgive? If you haven't forgiven them, what is holding you back?

3. Charlene has issues with her mother, and yet she still wants her approval. No matter how old we are, we never outgrow the need for our parents' approval. Have you experienced that? How do you handle it when you feel you don't measure up to their expectations?

4. Charlene and Janni were as different as night and day, as are many sisters. Charlene always saw Janni as the saintly one, and when she discovered Janni's crown was a tad off-kilter, Charlene was shocked to the core. Have you ever put anyone on a pedestal only to have them fail you with their human weaknesses? Did that help you grow stronger in your own determination to do what's right, or did you want to give up? Could someone be watching you?

5. Charlene's mom struggled with a few insecurities of her own. She misjudged her husband's behavior and things got a little crazy. Have you ever misjudged someone and said things you wish you hadn't? Do you make it a rule to always apologize?

6. Has anyone ever misjudged you? How did it make you feel? Did you confront them with the truth or let it go? Did it help you be more compassionate toward others whose situation you don't understand?

7. Gail Campbell was the town gossip. As we know, the Bible warns against gossip, and for a good reason. It can divide the closest of friends. Has your life ever been affected by gossip? What did you do? If you know someone who gossips, would you consider telling them that what they're doing can hurt people and break up relationships?

8. Charlene seemed to have it all—a seaside cottage, a lucrative career, and all the amenities that they bring. Still, she longed for something more. Being with family made her realize just how much she had missed by being away. Do you struggle with trying to balance what's

important in life? Are there some steps you can take to remedy that problem?

9. Charlene not only had to deal with her husband's betrayal, but also her one chance to have a child was forever gone while the "other woman" bore Charlene's husband's child. Sometimes there's just no way around it, life can be unfair. Have you had situations in your life where you've said, "Life is hard, but God is good"? Explain.

10. Ultimately, Charlene realized she didn't always "feel" sweet, but as she learned to let go of her past and trust God with her future, then she could experience the true joy and peace that Jesus gives. Have you gone through a similar experience that eventually brought you to this same place?